Her Guardian Angel

Felicity Heaton

First printed July 2011

First Edition

Layout and design by Felicity Heaton

CHAPTER 1

Marcus stretched his left arm out above his head on the pillows of his double bed, buried the fingers of his right hand into his overlong black hair and stared into the inky dark of his bedroom. The open window to his left allowed pale light to filter in from the street far below but it barely cut through the gloom and it wasn't the reason he had lifted the sash around midnight. The stifling summer's day had given way to a humid night that showed no sign of cooling down before dawn broke and heralded the next unbearably hot day. A light breeze washed in through the open window, refreshing him as it caressed the left side of his bare body. The heat wasn't the only thing robbing him of sleep.

The banging came again, more persistent this time, and Marcus clenched his teeth to contain his growing irritation, his focus wholly on the hall outside his apartment. The man had been attacking the door of his neighbour for almost twenty minutes now, rousing Marcus from sleep and throwing him straight into a bad mood that had gradually deteriorated into a desire to beat some sense into the mortal.

He drew in a long breath, held it a moment in a vain attempt to regain control of his temper, and then exhaled slowly. The man hurled another string of impotent threats at his neighbour's door and Marcus's anger spiked right back up. His silver-blue eyes slid towards the digital clock on his bedside table. The display mocked him with the ungodly hour this man had chosen to air his bitter disappointment to not only the female but the entire apartment block. Three in the morning.

Because of the humidity that showed no sign of abating and had made it impossible to get comfortable, Marcus had only been asleep for a scant few hours. He hated waking early, especially when he was stuck in the hell known as the mortal realm.

The man banged again, rattling the wall with a tremor that reached Marcus. He was no threat to the woman because she wasn't foolish enough to answer her door, but it grated on Marcus's nerves nonetheless.

His temper frayed when the man shouted foul accusations at her.

All of them false.

Marcus had known Amelia all of her life, although she had only known him this past month. He had watched over her and she was a pure soul with terrible luck when it came to men, and the man knocking down her door didn't deserve her.

Unable to bear another second and sensing Amelia's increasing fear through the wall that joined their apartments, Marcus rose from the bed and slung on a pair of dark grey jogging bottoms. He walked through his unlit apartment with ease, not bothering with the lights as he could easily map a safe path around the furniture without seeing it, and unlocked his front door. He yanked it open and stepped out into the dull cream hallway on the other side, his gaze immediately fixing on the mortal that was daring to break his sleep and threaten Amelia.

The dark haired man looked at him.

Marcus coolly stared back.

"What's your problem, mate?" The man's fingers curled into fists at his sides. Marcus noted everything about him in under a second.

He was drunk. He was itching for a fight. And he was a fool who thought this sort of abuse would win Amelia back. On the surface, the man wanted to upset her and hurt her, but Marcus could see beyond the façade to the pale hope in this man's heart that Amelia would be his again.

That was something Marcus would never allow.

"You." Marcus pinched the bridge of his nose, rubbed sleep from his eyes, and then leaned back against the doorjamb, folding his arms across his bare chest and crossing his legs at his ankles.

The man regarded him for a moment and then turned back to Amelia's door.

"I think you should leave now." Marcus stepped forwards, bringing the man's attention back to him so he wouldn't bang on the door again and cause Amelia's fear to increase. "Before things get out of hand."

The man smiled, amusement touching his dark brown eyes. "What you gonna do about it? She's my girlfriend… not yours. Piss off back inside and get your nose out of my bloody business before I break it."

Marcus sighed. He had warned the man. He had done everything by the book. His patience wearing thin, he looked the man over again, taking in his dark jeans and the loose t-shirt that covered a physique half his own and the way his fists shook as he shouted at Amelia's door. Without resorting to violence, Marcus wasn't sure how to convince the man to leave. He could compel him, but using his powers on such a base creature was beneath him and would do nothing to teach the man a lesson in manners towards women.

The man banged on the door again before Marcus could stop him, hard enough this time that the white painted wood creaked under the attack, and he heard Amelia gasp.

"That is it." Marcus took another step forwards and the man swung at him. Marcus dodged his fist, clamped his left hand down on the man's wrist, and twisted his arm behind his back. The man bent forwards to stop his shoulder from popping out of its socket, facing away from Marcus, and grunted in pain. Marcus glared at the back of his head. "I said to leave."

The man struggled in his grip but stilled when Amelia's apartment door eased open a few inches and she peered around it. Marcus stared at her, frowning at the tears that streaked her flushed cheeks and the fear in her grey eyes, and tightened his grip on the man's arm until he let out another deeply satisfying grunt.

"What do you want?" she whispered, voice hoarse and trembling.

It wasn't like Amelia to look afraid of anything. Marcus had seen her fight it out face-to-face with her exes without showing a trace of fear but this one had rattled her. Weariness shone in her grey eyes, lending them a cold edge he hadn't seen before. Her gaze tracked up Marcus's arm, lingering a moment on his bare torso, and then reached his face.

"I'm sorry if he woke you." Her gentle tone dissolved some of his anger.

Marcus loosened his grip on the man's wrist but held on to him. "It's not a problem. I couldn't stand by and do nothing."

The man twisted enough to look back at Marcus over his shoulder and then turned his head towards Amelia.

"Oh, I see how it is. Dump me and then move on to the next bloke, right? You've probably been fucking him from the moment he moved in. Well, I'm sure Mr Muscle is a great catch…" The man wrenched free of Marcus's grip and stumbled forwards a few steps before righting himself. "But I'm gonna have to fuck up that pretty face of his."

Marcus reacted on instinct and launched his left fist at the man to counter his attack. The moment he did, he felt the strength drain from his arm and pushed harder. He had been holding back to avoid seriously injuring the mortal but now that Heaven had stripped him of his immortal strength he needed to do the opposite and give it everything he had.

He leaned back to avoid the man's punch while still pushing forwards with his own and slammed his fist hard into the man's jaw, cracking his head to one side and sending him crashing into the cream wall. The man bounced off it, hit the dark banister opposite and then collapsed into an ungainly heap on the wooden floor of the hallway.

"Shit." Pain shot along every bone in Marcus's hand and up his arm to his elbow. It had actually hurt.

The man groaned and dragged himself to his feet and Amelia hesitated in the doorway of her apartment, looking as though she couldn't decide whether to assist him or keep back. Marcus shook his hand and waited for something to happen. Instead of the instant punishment he had expected, there was only silence as the man stared hard at both him and Amelia, and then stumbled down the stairs to the next floor.

Marcus still waited.

Part of him couldn't believe that he had struck a mortal and the rest couldn't believe that he wasn't being punished.

Heaven had limited his power the moment he had subconsciously decided to hit the man, leaving him with only the strength of a mortal and therefore open to attack himself. The punch had hurt him. Perhaps that was punishment enough. Perhaps all of this was punishment for his misdeeds.

Marcus sagged against the wall and blew out a sigh, clutching his injured hand to his chest, convinced that Heaven would call him in to reprimand him soon enough. He had committed an act of violence against what could be considered an innocent human. Marcus couldn't think of the man that way. He was vile and cruel, seeking to scare Amelia and hurt her. Marcus had only done his duty by protecting her.

He opened his eyes and looked across at her where she stood at the banister peering down into the stairwell, her hands clutching the wooden railing.

His gaze drifted down over her shoulder-length straight dark hair to the plum-coloured slip that only emphasised her sensual curves, to the lean lengths of her legs. She was so soft and pure. Delicate yet strong of heart. Her fear was gone now, leaving behind the confident woman he was used to seeing in her.

She looked across at him and his eyes dropped to her bare feet. He frowned at the tattoo on her left ankle. A cherub? The plump winged babe sat just above her ankle bone, staring back at him. He smiled. Is that what she thought his kind looked like? The image humans had of angels couldn't have been more wrong. It amused him, stealing away his pain and pushing it to the back of his mind.

His strength returned and the pain dulled further, leaving only a gentle throbbing and bruised knuckles behind as a reminder of what he had done.

"I really am sorry about that." Amelia's soft voice stole into his thoughts and he glanced up at her. She crossed the hall to him and peered at his left hand. "You should put some ice on that."

Marcus studied his red knuckles. Is that what humans did in this sort of situation? In his world, they had angels with the ability to heal others. Such an angel could easily fix this issue for him. Even if he couldn't find one, the red marks would be gone in less than a day, his body's superior healing ability quickly erasing them.

"Would you like to come in for some coffee or a drink? It's the least I can do as payment for being my hero."

Marcus stared at her. Coffee was payment for being a hero? He hadn't indulged in such drugs in a long time and while he knew about the sexually stimulating effects that caffeine had on his kind, he had no interest in drinking coffee with Amelia. If he did that, he wasn't sure what would happen between them, but it would certainly be embarrassing for him.

"No, thank you," he said and when she looked as though she needed a reason for his refusal, he added, "It will keep me awake."

She still didn't seem satisfied. She shifted foot to foot, her gaze darting down to her hands in front of her, and then looked right into his eyes again.

"How about I ice those knuckles instead then?"

Marcus glanced into her low-lit apartment and then back at her, and caught the fear in her eyes as she looked down at the stairwell. She was afraid that the man would return and begin harassing her again. He would accept her offer but not because he needed her to assist him with his healing. He would go with her because he could see that the man had won and had shaken her up, and that she was asking him to stay with her a while because she was scared.

It was his duty to protect her. Tonight, that duty could extend to guarding her a little more closely than usual. Once she had settled and was comfortable with the idea of being alone again, he would take his leave.

He nodded when her attention returned to him.

Amelia led the way into the apartment, leaving him to muse what he had done tonight and his duty.

She deserved better.

A better life.

That was the reason he was here—to keep her safe and watch over her. To protect her from the creeps and from something else.

To give her that better life.

He was sure of it.

Marcus followed her towards the kitchen, noting that the layout of her apartment differed slightly to his as he passed through the pale square lounge. There were no windows in it, just like his one, because the bedroom and bathroom lined the exterior wall opposite him. Their positions in the apartment were reversed in his. He stared through the open door of the room to the right. Her bedroom was next to his and the head of her bed rested against his wall. She slept so close to him, yet he couldn't feel her when he was in bed, couldn't sense her on the other side. At such proximity, he should have been able to even when her signature was dulled by her sleeping. His gaze fell to rest on the long cream couch angled towards the television set to his right in the corner of the lounge. A pillow occupied one arm of the sofa and a scrunched up dark blue blanket sat at the other end.

Did she sleep on the couch?

He looked through into the bedroom again, frowning at the smooth covers on the double bed.

Was that why he couldn't feel her when he was in his bedroom?

Back when he had been watching over her from Heaven, she had always slept in her bed. Had something happened recently to change that? If it had, it must have occurred in the past month when he had been in the mortal realm. When he was here, he couldn't watch over her as he had in Heaven, able to view her through buildings using the power granted to the angels of his division. He had to physically see her.

Amelia came back out of the room to his left. He dragged his gaze away from the bedroom and the bathroom next to it, and finished crossing the room to the open double doors that led into the kitchen. Her small kitchen was brighter than his, the cupboards a pale type of wood, with stainless steel appliances.

Some former owner of his apartment had deemed it stylish to have a dark kitchen. Marcus deemed it impractical. It was a nightmare to keep clean so he had given up feeding himself shortly after moving in and had resorted to eating take away food, instant meals or eating out.

Marcus leaned against the kitchen counter, his hand throbbing. It had been a while since he had felt physical pain. He couldn't remember the last time it had hurt to punch something.

He couldn't remember the last time he had fought someone.

Amelia placed a red and white chequered tea-towel down on the side and emptied out several trays of ice cubes into it. She gathered the ends and twisted the bulk of the cloth around to keep the ice in, and then came over to him. He started when she took hold of his hand, gently slipping her fingers under it so they brushed his palm, and raised it. Heat travelled up his arm and it had nothing to do with pain this time.

She rested the ice pack on his knuckles and he didn't feel the cold at all. He stared at their joined hands, urgently trying to decipher how she had warmed him with only a light touch and alarmed by the hard beat of his heart against his chest. She looked up into his eyes, her grey ones full of warmth again, softening her delicate features and holding his attention.

"Thank you." She glanced away again, her gaze briefly dropping to their hands and the ice pack, and then met his eyes. His pain faded in an instant, driven away by the heat of her touch and her concerned expression, and he marvelled at the effect she had on him. It wasn't real. It couldn't be. She was his duty and that was all she could ever be. Once he had fulfilled his mission, he would finally request his transfer and would never see her again. Her thumb brushed his and fire shimmered over his skin. "I really am sorry that he woke you and that you had to hit him."

"I said it was nothing." Marcus hadn't needed to hit the man. He could have compelled him to stop but he had reacted on instinct, and for some reason that instinct had been to punch him. He could think of a million situations with mortals when he had been in danger and had compelled them. Why not this time?

Had Amelia's presence as a witness deterred him?

Or was she the reason he had struck the man?

He had been consumed by anger, enraged by what the man had said about himself and Amelia, driven to violence by a handful of words.

He was Amelia's protector. Her guardian.

He was not her lover.

Her fingertips grazed his palm as she removed the ice pack and inspected his left hand. A shiver tripped up his arm and down his spine, and his shoulder blades itched. He took his hand away from her and rolled his shoulders, trying to relieve the tension building there.

His wings wanted out.

"How are they feeling?"

Marcus's head snapped up, his eyes immediately locking on Amelia. His wings? She nodded towards his knuckles and relief swept through him.

"Fine," he said absently and breathed slowly to steady his racing heart.

There was no way she could know about his wings but, for a moment, it had felt as though she had been reading his mind. It had been a while since his wings had wanted to come out. After five centuries of living with them sealed away, he had grown used to them not being there. It had been strange becoming accustomed to them again when the binding curse had started to lose effect over thirty years ago. Most of the time, he was content to physically put them away as he was now. It took concentration to maintain their disappearance but it used less energy than hiding them from human eyes with a glamour, and it was far easier to move around in the mortal realm without worrying about accidentally knocking things over with them.

"Are you alright?" Amelia ducked towards him, interrupting his view of his knuckles and replacing it with an altogether more pleasant one of her face and her cleavage.

Marcus stared at her plump full breasts, his pulse picking up again, and then averted his eyes. Women had no shame. It was little wonder his master had decided that they should not serve him. They were wily, manipulative, a distraction, and considered by most as the source of all sin.

"Fine," Marcus repeated and took the ice pack from her, ramming it onto the back of his hand when all he wanted to do was stick it down his jogging bottoms to bring his libido under control.

His fellow warriors had warned him about women, especially ones as beautiful as Amelia, and he wholeheartedly believed every word that they said. Women were dangerous. He would not falter though. Amelia was his mission and his allegiance was to his master, his loyalty to his duty, and nothing would change that.

Once this irksome mission had ended, he would return to Heaven and request his transferral as originally planned, and would join the ranks of the soldiers who protected the realm of Heaven from intruders and wars. He would defend that which he believed in. Not this mortal world, but his world.

He had never physically guarded a human before but was certain that his assignment to act as her next door neighbour was a sign that his mission was progressing and soon he would be free of it.

He couldn't wait to return home.

"How are you feeling?" Marcus took the ice pack away from his hand and set it down in the stainless steel sink beside him.

Amelia shrugged. "Better, I guess."

She didn't look better. The weary edge was back in her eyes, draining them of warmth, and he found himself desiring to comfort her.

"He won't come back." His words had the desired effect and she brightened for a brief moment and then it faded again.

"You don't know that." She closed her eyes and shook her head. "I do pick them."

Marcus turned and ran his hand under the cold water, letting it wash away the trace of blood on his knuckles. When he reached for the tap to shut it off again, he felt Amelia's eyes on his bare back, boring into his shoulders, and lingered a moment. Would she mention the marks he had revealed by carelessly turning his back on her?

"It won't be long before I drive you away too."

Those words, softly spoken, caused him to look over his shoulder at her, a frown drawing his dark eyebrows tightly together. She dropped her gaze and then met his with resolution that didn't surprise him. This was the Amelia he had come to know these past three decades. Strong, able to face anything head on, unflinching.

"What makes you say that?" Marcus turned back to face her, aware now that he was bare from the waist up and was probably only encouraging any attraction she might feel towards him. He should have put on a t-shirt before leaving his apartment but he'd had one thing on his mind—getting the irritating bastard in the hallway to shut up so he could sleep.

Or was it purely so he could sleep?

He stared at Amelia, taking in the way her cheeks coloured as he did so and how she couldn't hold his gaze.

He had thought only of protecting her.

Defending her.

"The last bloke who lived alone next door to me left only a couple of months after moving in."

Marcus knew for a fact that the man had been forcibly evicted due to a minor error in payments caused by Heaven's intervention but had later won money on the lottery that had allowed him to place a down payment on the house of his dreams. The young man had been the easiest target to remove in order to place Marcus close to Amelia. The old lady who lived in the apartment on the other side of Amelia was frail and had lived in the building for over twenty years and relied on those around her to assist her. She also slept heavily, meaning that Amelia's ex-boyfriends didn't wake her when they came to knock down her door. Marcus would have had a contender in the guardian stakes if the young man had remained living next to her and they had moved the old lady.

"You do live alone, don't you?" There was a tremble to that question.

Marcus nodded without thinking and then considered the implications of his answer when Amelia's grey eyes warmed again. A loaded question. She had cleverly used it to discern his availability.

He briefly considered making up a girlfriend in order to obliterate any attraction she might feel towards him so he could continue his mission in peace but couldn't get the words out when he looked into her eyes again.

The space between them shrank until it felt as though she was barely inches from him. Her soft breathing filled his ears, drawing his attention down to the sensual bow of her dusky pink lips. The tip of her tongue swept across them, leaving moisture in its wake, luring him in.

How long had it been since he had kissed a woman?

Not in this lifetime, that was for sure.

Marcus dragged his eyes away from her, shutting down his emotions at the same time. Amelia was a mission. He couldn't allow things to become complicated. Not when he wasn't even sure why he had to protect her.

He couldn't get involved with her.

He had to maintain his distance.

No matter how impossible that seemed now.

No matter how much he wanted her.

CHAPTER 2

The moment Marcus set foot back in his apartment and closed the door, a bright shaft of light encased him. His wings swiftly emerged, silver-blue feathers warming as the light touched them, and his sweat pants disappeared, replaced by his dark blue loincloth. His armour appeared next. Dark leather boots slowly materialised on his feet, followed by rich blue metal vambraces that covered his forearms and greaves that encased his lower legs. His blue back plate and breastplate melted into existence, protecting his upper torso, moulded into muscles to mimic his body. The raised silver edging on his armour shone brilliantly, reflecting the blinding white light.

When the light faded, an equally bright room surrounded him. Marcus straightened, flapped his wings to bring his feathers into line and then furled them against his back. He noted with annoyance that neither of his weapons had appeared at his hips. It seemed Heaven didn't want him armed for this meeting.

He walked forwards and the brightness dimmed, revealing what most mortals would consider a waiting room. The pale furniture melted into the white walls and floors, making it difficult to distinguish them, and for once the room was empty. He couldn't remember the last time he had reported to Heaven's Court and it had been like this. Normally his fellow guardians were here on some business or another, escorting detainees or sinners, or reporting on missions themselves.

Putting it down to the late hour, he strode towards the white double doors at the opposite end of the room, passing the empty reception desk and armchairs.

He pushed the heavy doors open, revealing the equally white room beyond.

It appeared much like a human court, only everything was white. The benches where those awaiting their hearing would sit, the barrier between them and the area where the judges and jurors sat, and the dock were all so bright that they blended together and made him wonder for what must have been at least the six hundredth time why everything was so irritatingly pale in Heaven.

He looked down at his blue armour.

At least that had colour to it.

The weight of it felt good against him and he ached to beat his wings and feel the wind cut through his feathers. He was so focused on himself that he failed to notice that he wasn't alone until someone spoke.

"Report, Marcus."

Marcus jerked his head up, eyes fixing on his superior, a man with short sandy locks and dark eyes that rarely held any trace of emotion. They were cold now, devoid of feeling as he stared at Marcus with a critical air about him. Marcus calmly walked towards him, opened the white gate, and stepped into the dock directly on the other side.

There were no lawyers in Heaven. Each sinner, detainee or reporter had to stand for themselves. It was even rare to have a jury. Ninety percent of cases were decided by three judges.

His sat before him on a raised platform encased by an elaborate curved white wall that bore a beautiful carving of angels in battle and hid their bodies from their chests downwards.

The two men nearer the back, flanking his superior, were there to oversee his report and to ensure that everything followed the rules of their kind. They were angels from a different division to Marcus and his superior. The dark haired man to his superior's left wore white armour edged with gold and had pure white wings, the sign of a mediator and intervention specialist, and the white-blond haired man to his right wore black armour edged with gold and had raven-black wings, the sign of those affiliated with death. Marcus's own armour and wing colour signified him as a guardian, one of the angels who were responsible for shepherding souls through Heaven for judgement and then leading them to their respective resting place in Heaven or escorting them to Hell. There were watchers who wore armour like his too, and even a faction of the army. He bit his tongue as desire to mention his request to join that army welled up inside him and saluted his superior instead, bowing his head in greeting.

"Am I to be punished?" Marcus said without a trace of fear in his voice.

He wasn't sure what punishment for striking an innocent would entail, but it couldn't be any worse than what he had already suffered because of his sins.

"That is yet to be determined. We are gathered here to review your actions tonight. We withheld punishment in order to see if your actions engendered a positive emotional response that may forge a stronger connection between yourself and the mortal."

Marcus frowned. "And why is there need for a connection?"

His superior didn't hesitate. "So that she might trust you."

Marcus leaned forwards, looking right into his superior's dark eyes, eager to spot some truth in them, some answers to the thousand questions he had asked in the past and they had refused to answer.

"And why must she trust me?" Marcus knew he had pushed too far when a dark look crossed all three men's faces.

"Enough questions, Marcus. Report."

He ground his teeth. Always the same response whenever he pushed them to elaborate on his mission. He hated being left in the dark about everything almost as much as he despised having to live in the mortal realm.

"There was a problem with an ex-lover of the female's. He was causing her fear and emotional harm. He was also causing me to lose sleep. I took it upon myself to forcibly remove him from the premises and deter him from attempting a repeat performance."

"So you might gain more sleep?" His superior didn't look impressed and neither did the two angels flanking him.

"No, so that the female may not come to physical harm."

"You had reason to believe that this male might act in violence towards her?"

"She was afraid. I have watched her for thirty one years. Never once have I witnessed her this afraid. Seeing that the man was bent on violence, I took it upon myself to ensure that he would leave her alone."

"Did the man say anything in his defence?"

Marcus frowned. Had he? He had accused Amelia of a lot of things, all of them false. Nothing the man had said had held any credit.

"No. He was intent on harming her and laying false accusations at her door."

"So you struck him?"

"No!" Marcus leaned forwards. "It didn't happen like that. He turned his foul derision in my direction and attempted to hit me."

"Why did he do such a thing?"

His superior and these two angels were already aware of what had occurred tonight so why were they trying to draw it out of him? Were they hoping to embarrass him or cause him to reveal something? If they believed him attracted to her, then he would have to disappoint them.

"I was accused of being her lover. The man decided to… damage my face… in order to teach both myself and the female a lesson. I believe he sought to render me less attractive to her."

"So you struck him?"

"I acted to defend myself and the female, as per my orders. I eliminated a threat to her."

"And do you concur that the female is attracted to you, as this man believed?"

Marcus stared blankly at the three angels, mind working furiously back over tonight's events as he tried to compute an answer to the question. Did he? Was she?

Amelia had certainly looked upon him with desire darkening her grey eyes and those eyes had lingered on his bare torso more than once. She had been gentle with his hand and had blushed several times during their talk in the aftermath of the event. He had little experience of females and couldn't easily conclude what her reaction had meant, but it had seemed positive.

"I am not sure." Marcus pushed the words out, his mouth and throat dry as he contemplated the answer he had wanted to say. Yes. Yes, the mortal did desire him. He wasn't certain why, but the telltale signs had been there.

"Then we shall not punish you."

Marcus frowned again. "Why not?"

"Because we require that 'pretty face' of yours to remain attractive to the female in order to form a stronger bond between you." There was a definite smirk in his superior's tone although it didn't touch his stony face. "You will return to Earth and continue with your mission as planned."

"When will my mission end?" Marcus wasn't going to give up this time. Things were becoming critical on Earth and his desire to complete his duty there had increased a hundredfold tonight when he had been with Amelia, and a thousandfold just now when his superior had implied that Amelia was attracted to him and they would use that as a means of bringing them closer together. He needed to end this and return to Heaven. It was his heart's desire.

His heart denied that and an image of Amelia flickered across his mind, wearing a plum-coloured shimmering slip that inflamed his desire.

He shoved the vision away and stared at his superior.

"When will it end?" Marcus spat out and the sandy-haired man leaned back in his seat and regarded him with flinty eyes.

"When you have completed it."

"What must I do to achieve that?"

"Be patient. All will be revealed in time."

"Time," Marcus snapped and gripped the white wooden railing that ran around the dock, digging his fingers into it so hard that his bruised knuckles burned fiercely. "It is always the same. I tire of this mission. I demand to know when it will end!"

His superior shot to his feet and the air in the room grew heavy, draining the light from it and leaving it grey.

"It will end when you have completed it! This is your duty, Marcus, and you *will* obey my orders."

Marcus clenched his teeth and lowered his gaze, staring at his hands where they trembled against the railing, a visible sign of the pressure bearing down on his body. The hot thick air in the room stuck in his throat and stole the breath from his lungs, leaving him wheezing. His mind turned foggy, thoughts swimming in and out of focus, and he blinked several times, fighting for consciousness. His heavy limbs shook, bones aching as darkness descended on him, the power of his superior too intense to withstand.

A moment later it lifted, the room brightening as it faded away, and Marcus sucked in much needed air as the strain on him eased. His body continued to tremble and he clung fiercely to the railing to remain standing as his legs threatened to give out.

Marcus cursed under his breath. He shouldn't have lost his calm. He had never snapped like this before but the pressure of living in the mortal realm, of having to endure being so close to Amelia, was getting to him. He had been waiting over thirty years for this mission to end and they had always given him the same answer to his questions. It was his duty. He had to obey.

His loyalty was to Heaven, born of faith and his belief that they knew what the future held and what each of his master's servants were destined to do, but when they withheld information from him, when they shut him in the dark and expected him to blindly obey their orders without question, he found his faith wavering. He only wanted answers.

He had tried countless times and in countless different ways but each time they told him the same thing. His duty was to watch over Amelia until a certain point in time. They had never expanded on the nature of his mission or given him any other details. Each time they brought him back to Heaven, they asked the same questions and gave him the same answers.

It wasn't necessary for him to know such information.

It was only necessary for him to obey their orders.

So he obeyed, and every time he left them, he hated his mission a little more.

His shoulder blades tingled where his wings joined them. Amelia had seen the marks there. He hated them too. If it wasn't for them, he wouldn't be in this situation. He would have asked for a transfer and would have been a soldier. It was his fault though and he accepted this mission as punishment for committing sin.

"Have you experienced any difficulties with your wings since living in the mortal realm?"

That softly spoken question came not from his superior but the dark haired man to his left. A mediator. Marcus didn't know him or the other angel, but he could see from the embellishment on their armour that they were high ranking, and clearly they knew of his problem.

"There was one incident and that is all." Marcus couldn't meet the man's eye. He hated talking about this with anyone, even his superior and the medical staff who had assisted him throughout the centuries since the marks had appeared on his back. It made him feel vulnerable and weak, and disgraced.

"Can you recall what you felt in that situation or anything that may have caused the curse to trigger again?" His superior this time.

Marcus risked a glance at him. The concern in his dark eyes surprised him and buoyed his spirits, and Marcus thought about what had happened the last time his wings had failed to appear. Thankfully he had been on the ground and had only attempted to take off but it was always there at the back of his mind whenever he flew. His wings were unpredictable. There was nothing stopping the curse from triggering mid-flight and sending him plummeting to Earth. He had no desire to hit the ground from a great height. While the fall wouldn't kill him, it would certainly render him unconscious and vulnerable to attack, and it would definitely hurt.

"Nothing particular. I had merely wanted to stretch my wings and fly somewhere new for a change of scenery."

"Report back to us if anything happens. It should not be long now, Marcus. Your destiny awaits."

Before Marcus could ask exactly what that destiny entailed, the light engulfed him again. When it receded, it revealed the low-lit lounge of his apartment.

He looked at the clock on the DVD player in the entertainment centre to his right and frowned at the time. Almost six. He rubbed his eyes and locked the front door, and then trudged wearily across the living room, stifling a yawn as he did so. When he reached his bedroom door, he beat his wings, glad to feel them and sense that they were stable, and then focused so they would disappear. They gradually shrank into his back and when the last feathers were gone, the marks there flushed with heat and then settled again.

Marcus didn't bother to remove his armour. He flopped down on his back on his double bed, enjoying the cool of the covers against his bare skin between his back plate and loincloth and on his arms and thighs. A gentle breeze drifted in through the open window, washing over his head and shoulders, bringing with it the scent of dawn and carrying some of his irritation away. He stared at the ceiling, watching the room brighten with the rising of the sun, his mind racing but not with questions about his mission. He focused on his shoulder blades and the marks there.

When they had appeared five centuries ago, he had thought it was castigation for sinning. He had broken the law that night and had indulged in mead, a heady drink that at the time had been a banned substance for angels due to its alcoholic nature. When he had come around with his head on the verge of exploding and his stomach rebelling, his shoulder blades had been ablaze, burning so fiercely that he had felt as though someone had branded him. He had tried to bring his wings out but they had failed to appear.

When Heaven had called him back to them, Marcus had discovered that it wasn't punishment at all but rather a curse. It took weeks for the medical staff to discover what it meant, and months for it to sink in that it was inerasable. The marks sealed his wings for five hundred years, leaving him stranded in Heaven, only able to do the duty of a watcher.

In the same week that Heaven had assigned him to watch over Amelia, his wings had finally escaped their prison. The medical staff had declared that the bond of the curse was weakening with time but that he might still encounter difficulties. He had been too intoxicated by the thought of flying again to care that there might be future incidents where his wings would refuse to appear.

There were many at first but as time continued to flow, so the curse continued to weaken, and the space between the incidents grew. During his last assessment, the medical team had announced that his problem was no longer the curse but psychological barriers he had constructed. Something about it being his mind causing his wings not to appear. Marcus had found it difficult to believe since he had no desire to drop from the sky and hit the pavement, but when they had explained it in layman's terms, he had understood their point a little better. If he feared that his wings would disappear, or not appear when he needed them, then he could actually cause such a thing to happen. The power of the mind was frightening.

Since then, he had spent every moment when flying thinking about how wonderful his wings were and that he was glad to have them, and he really didn't want them to go away, and that his curse wasn't in effect anymore.

It seemed to have worked well so far.

There had only been that one incident since coming to the mortal realm, and the incident before that had been almost thirteen years ago when he had come to Earth to oversee Amelia as she moved out of her family's house in the countryside and into her own apartment in London at the age of eighteen. He wasn't sure what had happened then either.

His mind drifted over the past incidents and how his superior had conveniently used each one to deflect his questions and get him off the subject of Amelia's destiny. Skilful old bastard. His superior was ancient in angel terms, reborn almost six thousand years ago, although he appeared no older than Marcus. Marcus had been reborn in a time of peace two thousand years ago and could only remember that his previous position had been that of a guardian too. Most angels changed roles on their rebirth, with the exception of a few who bore destinies that kept them harnessed into a specific role, but all forgot their past lives. It was common for some to recall main points about themselves and all retained their former appearance, although wing colour changed from role to role.

Marcus couldn't recall ever being something other than a guardian.

He knew angels who had changed roles, dying one day as a guardian and waking the next as a mediator or assistant of death or a hunter.

Death himself, Apollyon by name, had been reborn countless times into the same role, forever a black-winged messenger of destruction, and was a singularity in that he could remember important historical events in which he had been involved. Namely horrific times of devastation such as the flood, and the fall of civilisations, and the punishment inflicted upon Sodom and Gomorrah.

Perhaps Marcus was eternally reborn as a guardian because he had a destiny.

He just wasn't sure what that destiny was.

But he knew it had something to do with Amelia and the event that would occur in the future. His reason for keeping her safe. Once the event occurred, his mission would end. What was her destiny? Whatever it was, it was important enough that Heaven had assigned him to watch over her as she walked the path towards her fate. Not many mortals had personal watchers. Most angels in the Higher Order of Watchers were assigned to thousands of people at once.

Amelia had her own guardian angel.

Himself.

Why?

Marcus threw his left arm across his face and grimaced when the hard cold vambrace protecting his forearm struck his nose, sending dull pain splintering across his skull. He sighed and focused, using his power to remove his armour, and lay naked on the bed, contemplating what the future held for him and for Amelia.

Heaven hadn't punished him.

His actions tonight had engendered a positive emotional response in Amelia.

He didn't like the sound of that or what his superior had implied.

He tilted his head to his right and stared at the wall that separated his apartment from Amelia's. He couldn't feel her in the bedroom, which meant she was sleeping on the couch, too far away for him to easily sense.

Was she attracted to him?

If she was, could he bring himself to use that against her and forge the connection between them that his superior had mentioned?

He wanted his mission to end.

But he wasn't sure he was willing to pay the price his superior had placed on it.

Marcus had always obeyed his orders and did all in his power to remain a faithful and loyal servant of his master, but he was also a man of principles who followed a code of honour, and using Amelia's feelings against her was wrong. As little as he cared about mortals, he couldn't ensnare her in such a way or gain her trust through manipulation.

He would gain her trust and connect with her, but not as his superior had ordered.

He would do so in a mortal way.

He just had to figure out what that entailed.

This was going to take some research.

CHAPTER 3

Marcus was still pondering how to gain Amelia's trust the next evening as he walked back towards his apartment building near the centre of London. The street wasn't affluent or run-down. It sat somewhere in the middle, and was far nicer than the first area Amelia had lived in when she had moved out of her parents house. This was a safe neighbourhood, full of mortals who worked in Central London and were paid well enough to live only a few Tube stops from the office. Cafés, restaurants and shops lined the busy street, mortals coming and going as they went about their business. It was Saturday and, since waking around noon because of the heat, he had passed the entire day wandering the city, watching mortals as they interacted with each other. The local park had produced the most interesting results. The bright sunny summer's day had drawn many couples, both long-term and aspiring, into the lush green park, where they had sat on blankets and talked, amongst more carnal things.

Marcus had sat in a large oak tree, invisible to mortal eyes and shaded from the heat by the thick leafy canopy, surveying them with interest. Given the number of couples that were kissing or looking as though they were going to kiss given an opportune moment and the correct signal from their chosen partner, a picnic seemed too intimate for his requirement but it had given him some ideas about how to gain Amelia's trust, although he wasn't sure if it was necessary for his mission at all. Amelia had allowed him into her home last night. Based on that, he concluded that she already trusted him on some level, and since he had protected her from her ex-lover, proving his ability and strength, when the time came, she might do whatever he had to ask of her.

He only wished he knew what he was going to face during the event they were heading towards. If he knew that, if his superiors would give him more information about what they had seen, then perhaps he would be better prepared to deal with it and complete his mission. There had to be a reason they weren't telling him though, and it was his duty to obey his orders without question. A good soldier did what was asked of him, regardless of what it was.

Marcus blew out a sigh. He could do that because the mission would end if he did and he would be free of Earth and the mortals.

"Hi."

Marcus raised his head and looked at his surroundings, surprised to see that he was back at the old redbrick apartment building.

Amelia stood before him, her hand still raised in greeting, a smile on her face.

"You spacing out?" She bit her lip. "Don't tell me it's lack of sleep. I still feel terrible about last night."

Marcus shook his head and scrubbed a hand down his face.

"Shoot, it is lack of sleep, isn't it? I'm sorry." She nibbled her lower lip again, entrancing him.

It wasn't just her soft mouth that held his attention today. The evening sun shone down on her, highlighting her shoulder-length dark hair with ribbons of gold and warming her skin almost as much as her blush. She was radiant and the trace of shyness in her eyes as she glanced at anywhere but him only added to her allure.

She had always been so confident in the past when he had been watching her. What had her acting so feminine and shy now?

Her grey eyes briefly touched on his and then dropped to the black leather purse she clutched over her shoulder.

Marcus resisted the desire to follow the strap down over her slender bare shoulder and take in her body. The thin cream ribbon of material that sat close to her bag strap hinted at another flimsy dress. It had been hard enough to cope with the feelings her slip had produced in him last night. He wasn't sure how he would react to the sight of her in another revealing item of clothing.

She cleared her throat and his silver-blue gaze drifted back to her face. Her cheeks darkened and she covered her mouth with her hand and then let it fall away and raised her head, locking eyes with him.

"I'm going to buy you a coffee."

Marcus raised a single dark eyebrow at the force in her tone and the command in her words. That was more like the Amelia he knew so well, yet the quaver in her voice gave away her underlying nerves as much as her rapid heartbeat pounding in his skull. Perhaps his superiors were correct in their assumption. Amelia liked him.

Could he use that against her in some attempt to gain her trust?

It felt wrong to do so and nothing at all like the correct behaviour for an angel.

He followed her gaze over his shoulder to the small café a few doors down from their building. There were some couples sitting outside at the tables that lined the pavement close to the wide glass windows, shaded by large pale sun umbrellas.

Marcus considered declining her order but found himself nodding before he could put voice to his refusal.

A bright smile curved her lips and lit her eyes, and his heart thudded hard against his chest.

Amelia breezed past him and his eyes followed her, slowly dropping to the cream summer dress she wore. It hugged her slender figure even more than the slip had, revealing the tempting luscious curve of her waist and flaring out over her full hips. Marcus stared at her backside, riveted by how the pale-pink-flower-spotted material swayed with each step.

An angel.

Or perhaps a demon for tempting him so easily.

He cocked his head to one side and followed her, unable to resist her silent siren's call. She looked back at him as she reached the glass door, the evening light adding to her radiance, and it struck him that she had never looked as beautiful as she did today. The usual warmth in her look had increased until she shone with what he could only conclude was happiness. She radiated it in waves that reached through him, warming him too and bringing a smile to his face. He had never seen her like this. She had been through a lot in life, especially since deciding to leave home at eighteen. A string of bad relationships had followed that, and poor luck with employment and also with her family. She had lost her mother three years ago and even though he hadn't realised it at the time, he had felt for her as he had watched her grieve, had desired to go to her and offer her the comfort she clearly needed. Her family had neglected to give it to her, or perhaps they hadn't seen what he had. Around them, she had put on a brave face, playing the role of the strong daughter and giving comfort to others, taking none for herself.

She deserved so much better than this life that fate had given to her.

If her smile was because of him, if he was the cause of her happiness, then he was glad.

He had never cared much for mortals.

But he was starting to think he cared for her.

He wasn't sure where that would lead though. Their worlds were separate and he had always maintained his belief that they should forever remain that way. Other angels he knew had fallen for mortals and forsaken their position to be with them, but that wasn't something that he could do. His duty was his reason for living. He had been given this existence in order to serve his master, not so he could callously turn his back on his creator and the gift given to him.

Marcus surmised that it was his duty to watch over Amelia and protect her. It was natural that he cared for her because of it. That was all this feeling was. Compassion born of duty.

He cared about her because he cared about his mission.

She crooked her finger and Marcus obeyed, following her into the colourful interior of the café. The scent of coffee filled his nostrils, swirling in his senses, and stirred a curious hunger to taste the liquid that went with it.

He couldn't.

He wouldn't dabble in such substances.

Not again.

"What can I get you?" Amelia said when he reached her at the glass cabinets full of delicious looking pastries beside the counter and he stared at the black boards on the wall, unsure of what any of it meant.

He had studied the mortal realm and knew more than most angels about living on Earth and what things were. Most angels only knew mortal inventions from the regular reports they received. Those fortunate enough to watch over Earth in the pools in Heaven that recorded the history of mortals had learned more about it than others, including languages throughout the ages, and about food too. He had been studying Amelia for her whole life and had come to know her favourite foods, drinks, and all about the technology she regularly used. In his month on Earth, he had learned how to use such modern items too, and had indulged in tasting a lot of human foodstuffs and drinks. Food was a necessity. Angels used vast amounts of energy in the mortal realm, mostly expended on maintaining their glamour, which is why he often opted for the less energy consuming path of putting his wings away and donning mortal clothing.

The couple in front of them at the counter ordered. The female opted for a latte and the male for a cappuccino. He searched for those on the board behind the people serving the coffees and taking orders. Latte and cappuccino fell under the coffee heading. He raised an eyebrow again when a small footnote on the board declared that coffee was also available decaffeinated. Marcus presumed that meant they had removed the stimulant. He turned to Amelia.

"I am not really a coffee drinker. It's the caffeine… it keeps me awake."

Her grey eyes widened and her lips parted. "There's herbal tea."

Tea didn't seem a very manly drink. He frowned.

"Decaffeinated means without caffeine?" It wasn't exactly how he had wanted to find out. Asking her what something meant was bound to make him appear less appealing to her. He didn't know something so basic. How had he missed such things?

He realised that Amelia always drank straight coffee. She had never opted for anything foreign sounding or decaffeinated in all the times he had watched over her. These past thirty years, he had been so focused on her that he had only learned about the things that she liked. Chinese food, Italian cooking, Spanish tapas, and straight coffee. Sometimes a fruity shake, a smoothie they called it, or some frozen coffee drink. Occasionally a glass of wine with friends. Never beer or mead. He grimaced, stomach turning at the memory of what too much mead could do to an angel.

"It's not quite without caffeine. I think they sort of extract it or something. It leaves a hint of it behind." Amelia didn't look sure.

Marcus nodded. "Decaffeinated cappuccino then."

It sounded manly enough and he could handle any effect it might have on him. He hadn't tucked in his white linen shirt today because he had wanted to feel the slight breeze, needing it to cool down in the hot summer sun. The tail hung loose, covering his dark jeans to the apex of his thighs. If the coffee produced any sort of negative effect on him, he would be able to conceal it.

Amelia ordered the drinks for him and even paid. He hadn't noticed in time to stop her, dropping more points in the manly stakes. He had wanted to insist on paying so her trust in him would increase. It seemed to work for the other men in the queue, gaining them smiles from their females.

Chivalry, he supposed. A code of honour he was familiar with. Did it only take chivalry to gain a female's favour?

He caught Amelia looking around the coffee shop. There were a few tables free on the buzzing inside, but some outside too.

"Why don't we sit in the sun?" he said before she could make a decision and then added, "I will pick up the coffees while you find us a table."

She nodded and smiled at him, a brilliant one that drew another hard thump from his heart. At this rate, he wouldn't need even a trace of caffeine to embarrass himself. Whenever Amelia smiled at him, her grey eyes warm with it, he wanted to reach out and brush the straight lengths of her hair from her face so he could take it all in. The feel of her skin beneath his fingers would definitely be too much. When she had touched his hand last night, he had felt the warmth of her caress for minutes after she had released him. In fact, he could still feel it now if he focused hard enough on remembering that moment, as though a ghost of her touch remained.

The man making the coffees pushed two white mugs towards him and said something about decaffeinated. One looked frothy with a sprinkling of chocolate on top and the other was straight white coffee. Definitely their drinks. He took the two mugs and wove through the patrons in the café, heading for Amelia where she waited for him at a table in the sun.

The evening was drawing on but the light was still warm on her face, highlighting her soft features and shattering the momentary control he had gained over his emotions. How was it that she could distract him so easily?

He placed the coffees down on the round dark metal table and took the seat opposite her, studying her face and trying to keep his attention on the conversation and what she was saying. It was impossible as he looked at her, his knuckles throbbing with the memory of how she had iced them for him, and how gently she had held his hand.

Being around her today was different. Was it because of last night? They had never touched before. They had barely spoken a word to each other beyond pleasantries on meeting in the hallway outside their flats. She had rarely looked at him in the past.

But now she was looking right at him, her gaze boring into his with such intensity but such shyness that he couldn't look away. Transfixed. Mesmerised. Bewitched. Three words that sounded so innocent yet felt so dangerous to him.

He couldn't allow things to head in this direction, but he felt powerless to stop them.

Marcus sipped his drink, making appropriate responses whenever he caught what she was talking to him about and enjoying the slight buzz the remaining trace of caffeine gave him. Not enough to cause adverse effects on his body but enough that it created a tingle in all the good places.

Amelia was animated now but the shyness still lingered beneath her layers of confidence, betraying that inside her tough exterior beat the heart of a female, a woman that he was affecting by only sitting and drinking coffee with her. Was this enough to gain her trust? Would it satisfy his superiors or would they demand he took things further?

He wasn't sure how he would respond to such an order. Drinking coffee with her seemed innocent enough. He wasn't seducing her or using her feelings against her. He was merely being friendly and it was forging a stronger connection between them. Every minute that passed, each sip of coffee she took and smile she flashed, she was growing more confident and more at ease around him.

The sun bounced off the shop windows on the opposite side of the street and played on her face and her body, stuttering as cars and red double-decker buses broke the beams of warm light. Amelia didn't seem to notice. She continued to talk about small things such as their neighbours, work and the weather. Idle conversation. He'd had practice in that during previous missions on Earth and also from his time in Heaven when he'd had to speak with angels he wasn't overly familiar with.

Her eyes sparkled as she smiled again, overflowing with warmth and life, gloriously radiant.

Marcus forgot his coffee and just watched her, stealing this moment with her, unable to believe that after all this time he was actually speaking with her directly, talking to her like a mere mortal and not her protector. It was a strange experience. He had never truly spoken to a mortal before and the workings of her mind were fascinating. She bounced around subjects so quickly that he couldn't keep up with the flow of conversation, and whenever he fell behind, she smiled brightly and apologised.

Another thing he had never noticed about her before last night.

He had never seen her apologise so profusely to anyone.

She paused in the middle of her conversation about a news programme she had watched about the upcoming planetary alignment.

"Are you sure last night didn't wreck your sleep?" she said, concern in her eyes as she leaned across the table, affording him a view down her cream dress that he refused to take advantage of.

Marcus held her gaze instead and smiled faintly. "Maybe a little. Have I been… spacing out again?"

That was what she had called it. Spacing out. He presumed that meant he was currently occupying another galaxy. It seemed apt for his behaviour over the past half an hour with her.

"I'm sorry." Amelia reached across the table and took hold of his left hand, her touch jolting him. His gaze leapt down to her fingers. Her thumb softly caressed his knuckles and her fingertips brushed his palm, bringing everything he had felt last night back to a rolling boil inside him. His pulse raced and his breathing quickened.

Desire?

Couldn't be.

But even as he stared at their joined hands he couldn't form a denial.

He inhaled sharply, trying to catch his breath and instead catching her sweet fragrance on the dusty warm air. Blood pounded in his temples and he could only watch the gentle sweep of her thumb across his fingers in abject fascination.

Images of her flashed across his wide eyes, dressed in her satin slip or in the tight summer dress she wore now, twirling and spinning towards him until her hands pressed against his chest and she was smiling right up into his eyes, her lips parting in invitation.

No.

He had never cared about anyone.

Had never desired a female.

He couldn't start now.

CHAPTER 4

Amelia sat back in her seat when Marcus took his hand away from hers and leaned back in his chair. She toyed with her slim black mobile phone for a moment to distract herself from the disturbed look on Marcus's face. When he didn't stop glaring at her, she put her phone down on the round dark metal table and nursed her drink, feeling incredibly foolish for taking hold of his hand. She sipped her coffee, grimacing internally as the cold liquid touched her tongue. Nothing was going right for her today. No, some things had been going right. She hadn't been imagining the way Marcus's eyes had lingered on her body, or how quick he was to smile at her whenever she smiled at him. Those smiles had reached his beautiful silver-blue eyes too, lighting them in a way that wasn't fake and that told her they were real this time, not the usual polite ones he forced whenever someone spoke to him.

He had been different since last night.

She wasn't usually in the habit of relying on men to fight her battles for her but she had appreciated his intervention. It was the first time that a man had come to her rescue and when he had punched Mike, her heart had fluttered and she had looked at Marcus with new eyes. She had noticed him the moment he had moved in next door to her, had registered him as handsome, but she had never really taken the time to look at him. The man had a body that could put models to shame and she hadn't stopped wondering what he did for a profession since setting eyes on it. Was he a model? She hoped to God he wasn't a hand model because her own stupid choice of men had gone and wrecked one of his lovely strong hands.

Amelia stared at his injured one, her heart beating hard in her throat. He had large hands, made for cupping and holding, or made for fighting. He had landed a hefty punch on Mike, sending him down with one blow, and for a brief moment she had feared he wasn't going to get back up. She had almost gone to him but then instinct had kicked in and reminded her that Mike had been intent on fighting Marcus. He must have been drunk. Only an idiot would pick a fight with Marcus if they were sober, and Mike wasn't that stupid. He should have known he didn't stand a chance.

Marcus had a seriously cut physique, lithe muscles that radiated strength and raw masculinity.

Once she had noticed that he was topless, it had been difficult not to stare. The few times that she had managed to peel her eyes off his body and found the courage to meet his, he had been looking at her with wide pupils darkening his amazing eyes, a sure sign of desire.

So why had he been so quick to snatch his hand away from hers?

Amelia almost laughed at herself. Since when had she given a damn about what men thought of her? Men were trouble. Mike had hammered that nail so firmly into her head that she had got the message this time. Men were something she could live without and that life would certainly be a lot easier and less painful than hers had been up to this point.

Her eyes betrayed her and snuck back to Marcus. He sat opposite her with his head tilted back and eyes on the sky. The lines of his defined jaw led her gaze up to his square chin and sensual mouth and her pulse picked up, jittery in its beat, when she licked her lips and contemplated what kissing him would be like. He lowered his head, their eyes met and then he looked away, an air of irritation about him.

Her fault?

She had taken his hand last night when icing his knuckles and he hadn't reacted so coldly then. If anything, the desire in his eyes had increased. What had happened between then and today? Had she said or done something wrong? She could have sworn that she had read the signals right and that Marcus liked her. Now she felt as though a vast frigid ocean had opened between them and that she would drown if she tried to traverse it to reach him.

She wanted to.

Last night had opened her eyes to the fact that there was a fantastic man living next door to her and since then she had felt tied up in knots, twisted inside out and back to front. She had never been backwards about being forward before but something about Marcus made her hesitate. It wasn't just because he would think she was rebounding. It was because he seemed like a nice guy, a cut above gorgeous in looks and personality, and she didn't want to screw things up. He had been on her mind all day and she had tried to think of a way to bump into him again so she could strike up a conversation and get to know him better. When she had spotted him outside their building, it had felt as though fate had brought them together, but her nerve had failed at the sight of him standing staring at the floor as though it was the most fascinating thing in the world. He hadn't heard her at first. It had taken her three attempts before he had lifted his head and noticed her, and by then her confidence had been shattered. Had he been thinking too?

About her?

Amelia rolled her eyes at her thoughts. As if. The poor man was sleep-deprived thanks to her terrible choice in men. He had probably been spacing out just as she had said he was, unable to function with only a few hours sleep. When he had gone back to his own apartment half an hour after she had iced his left hand, she hadn't heard a peep out of him until gone six in the morning when there had been some movement next door. She hadn't been able to sleep herself. Fear had kept her awake and she had watched one movie after another in an attempt to push it to the back of her mind. She was running on empty today, half asleep and feeling as though what had been a dream was turning into a nightmare.

Amelia leaned one elbow on the metal table and stared at Marcus, studying the nuances that crossed his handsome face as he watched the people passing them by on the pavement. For all she knew, Marcus was Mr Right for someone already. It wouldn't surprise her. He had looks, a fabulous body, was quick to defend women, and had proven himself intelligent in the brief conversations they had shared. Her younger sister would have taken one look at him, with his dark tousled hair that caressed the nape of his neck and sometimes fell down to brush his forehead, causing him to sweep his fingers through it to groom it back, incredible pale blue eyes, and scorching hot body, and declared him 'smexy'. Smart and sexy apparently. Her mother would have taken one look at him and told her that he was a keeper and not to give up on him.

Someone else was probably already keeping him.

Maybe that was why he had taken his hand back so quickly.

Marcus looked across the table at her and Amelia felt cold inside from the emptiness in his eyes. Where had the nice Marcus gone? Had she chased him away? A sense of impatience surrounded him, as though he didn't want to sit with her anymore, and he couldn't hold her gaze for more than a few seconds.

Amelia mused that he was always detached from everyone and distant. She shouldn't be so surprised that he had withdrawn from her.

"I wouldn't be any good for you," he said, his deep voice as devoid of emotion as his face, and Amelia held her hands up, desperate to shift the course of conversation away from her feelings. "You are better off keeping away from me."

"I didn't mean it like that." She had but he didn't need to know that. Her heart ached as he crushed it in her chest with just a glance and a handful of words. She blushed, her face on fire, and stuttered, trying to get an excuse into order.

She couldn't find the words as he stared at her, his expression gradually turning from awkwardness towards anger, and she knew in her heart that she couldn't have been more wrong about him.

His appearance now was a harsh contrast to how he had looked just a few minutes ago and last night. The heat that had touched his handsome features then, warming them and giving her the impression that she stood a chance with him, and the undeniable spark of desire that had lit his eyes, made her feel as though she had met a different person in that moment and not the real Marcus.

Perhaps all her thoughts about him were wrong, even last night, and he was right. She really didn't know anything about him. Her white knight might just be another black one in disguise and she really didn't need that on top of everything else. What would she do if Marcus turned out to be another wrong choice when he looked so much like a good man? It would certainly compound the growing notion inside her that she was doomed to spend her life with a string of Mr Wrongs in an impossible search for one Mr Right.

"Did I thank you for last night?" Desperate times called for desperate measures. All she could do now was try to deflect his attention away from what she had done in some dire hope of easing the tension mounting between them.

He nodded. Silent treatment was it? He was the first man to do that to her, but it wasn't going to deter her. Once they were back on steady ground, she would make her excuses and leave, and hopefully things wouldn't be too awkward between them whenever they met in the hallways of their apartment building.

"Was your coffee good?" Amelia looked at the white mug. He had barely touched it. In fact, he hadn't done or said much since sitting down with her. He really didn't want to be here. Had he only agreed to coffee out of politeness?

Marcus lifted his broad shoulders in a shrug. He had looked so good in only his deep grey sweat pants, his bare upper body on display as a midnight feast for her eyes. She tried to keep her focus on the more pressing matters of her present situation and failed, ending up picturing him as he had appeared last night instead. He had an athletic physique, toned and powerful but not overly built. The sort of body she would love to run her fingers over and had fantasised about. The sweat pants had barely hidden the muscular shape of his thighs and had rode low on his hips, revealing a V line that had stirred all manner of wicked thoughts in her head, as well as a treasure trail of dark hair that her lips and fingers ached to follow. When he had punched Mike, his entire body had come alive with movement, fascinating her. The way his muscles shifted and moved with him, tensing or stretching beneath his pale skin, had been mesmerising. It had taken her a moment to realise that Mike was flat on his backside and that she should react to it in some way other than gawping at Marcus.

When she had taken him into her apartment and iced his knuckles, she had put his body to memory, including the beautiful tattoo of angel wings he had on his back. She hadn't figured him as a tattoo type so the swirling blue-grey elaborate wings that decorated his shoulder blades had surprised her. She had wanted to ask him about them but hadn't been able to find her voice at the time, and asking him about them now certainly wouldn't help her cause, not when she wanted to ask him why such an elementally masculine man had such beautifully delicate tattoos. They seemed like a strange choice.

Unless he was gay.

Was that a possibility?

Amelia's gaze darted to his face and her eyes widened when she caught him staring at her chest. He quickly looked away, turning his right cheek to her and taking in the people walking along the street, lending her a view of his noble profile. Bi? He was gorgeous, clearly looked after himself, and also kept to himself. Was that a bad sign? Amelia frowned at her thoughts. She was overanalysing things. Just because he was good looking and not interested in her didn't mean he was gay or involved in a relationship, or any of those things that she wanted him to be so she would feel better about his rejection.

He just didn't find her attractive.

He had said it straight. Stay away.

Maybe she would do just that.

Amelia went to pick up her black leather handbag and then hesitated. Flushed with bravery and unwilling to give up so easily, she fixed Marcus with a hard look and was surprised when he turned his head and looked at her, as though he had felt her staring.

"Is something wrong?" Not a trace of a tremble in her voice. Her heart pounded, adrenaline thundering in her veins, but she held her ground. It was a horribly personal question to ask him but she had to find out whether his reaction to her touch was because he didn't want her or because he did but felt he wasn't good for her, as he had said.

Marcus stared at her for almost a full minute, the fading evening light reflecting off the windows and his white shirt, illuminating his face and chasing the shadows away. The edge of darkness his expression had gained lifted to reveal something that wasn't quite warmth, but wasn't icy cold either.

"Why?" A slight frown pinched his black eyebrows together.

"You… it's just you seem more out of spirits than normal."

He gave her an odd look. It was the truth. He never seemed very happy and now she couldn't help wondering why. His warning to keep away from him had brought back all the previous times she had seen him and the distance he maintained between him and everyone in their building, and now she wanted to know whether the man sitting opposite her was more similar to her than she had thought possible.

Did he go from one bad experience to the next too?

He had to have a reason for wanting to keep his distance from everyone and not letting anyone in. Was he afraid of being hurt or feeling something for someone? She feared that too, entered into relationships believing that eventually they would end and she would be hurt, but as much as she tried to live alone and be the independent woman she wanted to be, she couldn't help feeling lonely and wanting to share her life with someone.

For a brief moment, Marcus had seemed like someone she could do that with, and this time she had felt it wouldn't end in tears.

He could have been her Mr Right, but such a man wouldn't have told her to keep away from him. That hadn't been in her dream of what would happen today when she bumped into him. She hadn't anticipated that response at all. She couldn't blame him though. Chatty old Mrs McCartney next door had probably told him all about her poor choice in men and he was telling her to keep away because he didn't want to get sucked into her miserable life.

Amelia jumped when her mobile phone rang, the jaunty tune breaking the heavy silence as it buzzed on the table. Marcus frowned, his blue eyes darting to it. She wanted to ignore it, knowing that it would be Mike calling to chew her ear off about last night and make her feel wretched for the rest of the weekend, but the ring was so loud that people around her were staring.

Instead of answering, she picked it up, put her handbag on the table, and dumped the phone into it, muffling the annoying ringtone.

"Why didn't you answer it?" Marcus stared at her bag. Amelia tapped the table, cringing inside and wishing the phone would stop ringing.

"It's my ex." Ignoring him was preferable to speaking with him.

Marcus surprised her by reaching across the table, fishing the phone out of her handbag, and flicking it open. Amelia could only stare as he brought the phone to his ear, his face set in grim dark lines, and glared at the table as though he wanted to kill it.

"I thought I told you to leave Amelia alone?" He paused, his expression darkening further and the muscle in his jaw tensing. Amelia's heart pounded hard and she wished she could hear what Mike was saying to Marcus, because he looked close to going ahead and breaking something. Anger radiated from him in strong waves and everyone stared as he barked into the phone, "Stay away from her because the next time you dare to go near her, I'm not going to be so kind as to let you walk away."

Amelia's hands shook, her limbs trembling with them, and she joined everyone in staring at Marcus as he clicked the phone shut and dropped it back into her purse. What had just happened?

He had defended her again when she had been convinced that he wanted nothing to do with her.

His eyes met hers across the table and the trace of compassion in them only confused her further. He blinked slowly, dark lashes shuttering his pale blue irises, stealing them from view before lifting again to reveal the full extent of their beauty. Warmth shone in them, a softness that reached out and curled around her, filling her with a sense of safety even as her whole body quaked with the fear that Mike wouldn't heed Marcus's warning and would come after her again.

"I won't let him near you, Amelia. You don't have to worry about him. I will keep you safe." Those words, so softly spoken in his deep voice, weren't a lie. There was truth in his eyes and his open expression, and she believed him.

She just wasn't sure what to make of him.

What sort of man told a woman to stay away from him and then promised to keep her safe?

Marcus was an enigma and something inside her was telling her to take his advice and keep away from him, because if he turned out to be another black knight and broke her heart, she didn't think she would recover from it.

She gathered her things, rose from her seat and hesitated only long enough to catch the confusion surfacing in his eyes before making a swift exit.

CHAPTER 5

There was no doubt about it.

Marcus had put his foot in it.

Everything had been going well yesterday until Amelia had taken hold of his hand and he had quickly withdrawn his, and rather than making an excuse as planned, he had warned her away.

Instinct had pushed those words from his lips.

He had no desire to get any closer to her than was necessary.

Marcus raked his fingers through his overlong black hair, combing it away from his forehead, and stared into the distance across the rooftops of London.

Who was he fooling?

Not himself, that was certain.

The spark of desire her touch had reignited in him, bringing his hunger to caress her in return back to boiling point, and the warmth that travelled through his flesh, spreading outwards from the point where her fingers rested against his skin was unmistakably a sign of him harbouring an attraction towards her.

He paced the black tarred roof of his apartment building, scouring the horizon for an answer to his troubles. The problem of gaining Amelia's trust had been all but solved until he had foolishly told her to keep away from him.

He had always been aware that his instinct to protect her ran deep in his veins but had never suspected that it had corrupted his heart too and that he would even deem it necessary to protect her from himself. She'd had her share of pain and suffering, more than such a pure kind soul deserved, and he couldn't bring himself to add to it. When his mission was over, he was leaving Earth and Amelia behind him for good. If he used her desire against her, her heart would break when that happened. She would never understand. She would blame herself, just as she did whenever one of the vile men she involved herself with decided to leave her or did something that forced her to leave them.

He couldn't be like them.

Amelia deserved better.

Far better than him, that was for sure.

One day, she would meet the man who would become her world and who would treat her right and make her happy.

A flash of her smiling at him yesterday cut into his thoughts and deep into his chest.

He had made her smile.

Truly smile with happiness and warmth.

And then she had looked wounded, leaving him at the café alone to ponder what had possessed him to say such things to her and why he had decided to once again intervene in her destructive relationship with her ex-lover.

Duty.

In part it was a lie to say he did these things out of his sense of duty, but it was also his shield and he would not cast it aside.

The dying rays of the sun warmed his skin, the lingering heat of the day cocooning him in a soft breeze that stirred his soul as he watched the sun set over London. It was growing late. Time had passed quickly while he had been lost in his thoughts, hidden away from the hustle and bustle of the mortal realm far below him, and he still hadn't found the answers to the questions that plagued him. Questions about his mission had been joined by ones about Amelia and her feelings for him.

Why would a beautiful mortal female look upon him with such desire?

Marcus looked down at his hands and turned them palm up. These hands had killed many in the line of duty, harvesting souls of sinners and detaining them for judgement. In times past, when wars had been frequent, he had reaped battlefields and cities alike in the name of Heaven, following orders to the letter to assist the angels of death in their mission, never once feeling remorse over his actions.

Until now.

He had told her to keep away from him.

She deserved better than a man who had killed so many of her kind without flinching.

A role he would gladly resume once his current mission had come to an end.

He was no better than those men who had hurt her.

If anything, he was worse.

For all their noise and disgraceful behaviour, none of them had ever taken the life of another mortal. Amelia believed him good and kind, thought that he was different to the men she had previously been intimate with, but she would never see him that way if she knew the things he had done in his past, in the time before he had lost his wings.

Since being cursed, he had led a different life. Wars had become less frequent and the angels of death had no longer required outside assistance from the other branches of angels in Heaven. His kind, the guardians, had returned to their normal duties, shepherding souls and protecting Heaven, or watching over the mortals, both in the present and in the future.

He had never seen the single pool which held the future. Only a few angels were allowed entry to the room containing it in the grand palatial house of Heaven, and those angels were sworn to silence, allowed only to speak to their superior, who in turn relayed necessary information on critical events to other high ranking angels.

His superior included.

Which led Marcus to believe that he was aware of what fate awaited Amelia.

Marcus curled his fingers into fists and frowned at the vambraces protecting his forearms, watching the way the sunlight danced across the blue armour and reflected off the silver raised edges and the silver buckles on the leather straps against his underarms.

There was something freeing about changing out of his mortal appearance and donning his armour. He felt closer to home again and distant from the goings on of the mortal world around him. He shrugged his shoulders, raising the blue breastplate of his armour and exposing his bare stomach, and then stretched his arms out at his sides and closed his eyes as he unfurled his wings.

Warm summer air tickled his silvery-blue feathers, teasing his senses, and he basked in the sunlight, absorbing the heat and allowing it to relax him and chase away his troubled thoughts.

He was a soldier.

Soldiers followed their orders.

He didn't have to think. He just had to follow orders and his mission would be over.

Marcus opened his eyes and looked at the infinite sky. The pale blue dome turned to green and then hues of orange near the horizon, scattered with ribbons of cloud that caught the fading sunlight and burned gold and pink. It was beautiful and this evening it would be his playground again, his world in which he would immerse himself to escape the mortal realm and find peace for a few brief hours. He would fly until he ached from the exertion, until he couldn't beat his wings one last time, and then he would return to his apartment and sleep until morning finally came.

Free of this world.

Five centuries without wings and every day had been torture.

He beat his wings and lifted off the tarred roof only to be struck by a shaft of brilliant white light.

Marcus closed his eyes and waited for the tingling sensation caused by the light to pass before opening them again.

He sighed at the sight of the white double doors ahead and the reception room surrounding him.

All he had wanted was to fly for a while. Couldn't they have waited? By the time they returned him, it would be deep night. These things never moved swiftly and while they could return him to the same moment they had taken him, they never did.

Marcus pushed the double doors open and marched straight to the dock, facing the same three angels who had questioned him the last time they had brought him here.

"There has been a development." His superior sat at the head of the triangle closest to Marcus, his sandy hair as neat as his blue armour and the large silver-blue wings tucked against his back.

The dark haired mediator and white-blond haired angel of death murmured in agreement.

"May I ask what this development is?" Marcus hid none of his displeasure at having his plans for the evening ruined. They had brought him here and he would make the most of it. While they hadn't answered direct questions about his mission, perhaps they would answer one about the date of the event if he asked it in such a way that linked it to this development. "Does it mean my mission will end soon?"

All three angels nodded.

"Your final task approaches." There was no lie in his superior's expression, or that of the other two angels. "Soon your mission will end, Marcus."

"You have been patient in your duty and we appreciate everything you have done for us. Once this final task has been completed, you will be free to return to Heaven." The mediator to his superior's left smiled at him and then looked across at the angel of death.

"You must be relieved to know that your final task will be over soon and you can return home," the white-blond haired man said.

Marcus nodded and his shoulders relaxed with the relief that swept through him but he didn't quite feel as he had expected to on hearing such good news. There was something about the appearances of all three angels, and the soft way they spoke to him, that set him on edge and filled his head with more questions than ever before.

"What is my final task?" All three angels had mentioned it so all three knew what it was, but the moment the question left his lips, their expressions turned stony and closed.

"You will find out soon enough." His superior leaned back in his chair on the raised platform. The other two angels seated slightly behind him looked at each other and then at his superior, and then at Marcus.

"In the meantime, you must continue to protect her from the world." Those words leaving the mediator's lips startled Marcus into looking straight at him.

It was more than he had been told before.

"Am I to believe that there is someone who seeks to harm her?" It had always been there at the back of his mind. Why would a mortal need an angel to watch over them until a certain point in time? Why would they need a protector unless someone intended to hurt them? He had never been told to guide her on her path. His mission had always been phrased in a way that made him believe it was physical protection that she had needed in order to achieve her destiny.

"You must not allow demons to interfere with her existence."

Marcus's gaze snapped back to his superior and he stared wide-eyed at him. "Demons?"

The sandy-haired man nodded. "You must keep the female safe until the event that we have witnessed comes to pass."

"And what is this event?" Marcus knew he had pushed too far again when darkness crossed his superior's face.

"It is not necessary for you to know that right now, Marcus. We need you to focus on your mission. It has become critical that you gain her trust. Your attempt failed. Your mission was clear. You will get closer to her by any means. Do you understand?"

Marcus wasn't sure that he wanted to understand.

"What are you implying exactly?" He frowned at his superior, wanting him to say the words so he knew exactly what they were ordering him to do. So everyone here knew and acknowledged the order they were giving him.

"The female is enamoured with you. You are to use that to gain her trust."

Marcus's heart raced, anger curling through his body as he looked at all three men seated before him and searched each of their faces for a sign that this was some sort of sick joke. Their expressions remained cold and fixed, hard as they stared back at him. He reined in his outrage and stifled it, unwilling to allow it to control him and give away how much he despised the thought of what they were asking of him let alone the reality of it.

He had no desire to be false with Amelia or hurt her, and they were ordering him to do just that.

"Why is having her trust so important?" he bit out the words and then clamped his jaw shut before he could add that it was despicable of them to do such a thing to a mortal. He had no love for the mortals himself but he had principles. He was an angel, born into a race created to protect humans, not deceive them and lead them into sinning. That was the job of those in the service of the Devil.

"Silence, Marcus."

He glared at his superior, barely restraining his fury and desire to argue. Using Amelia's feelings in such a way went against everything he stood for, all of his principles and his honour, and was callous and cruel. He had no desire to hurt her.

"Follow your orders."

Marcus went to speak but the light engulfed him again. When it faded, he was standing outside the café where he had shared coffee with Amelia.

He tilted his head back and frowned at the colourful evening sky. They had returned him to the exact moment in time that they had taken him. Why? It wasn't like them.

He looked down at himself and noted that he was dressed now, wearing a dark blue shirt and dark jeans with his boots. It was a little smarter than his usual attire and it was his true appearance, not a glamour they had cast upon him. They had even neatened his hair for him, combing the unruly black lengths back out of his face. Why? They had to be up to something.

The answer became apparent when Amelia walked past him, heavy white plastic grocery bags hanging from her arms.

They certainly weren't wasting any time. They had dressed him up and sent him back to the moment they had taken him so he could seduce Amelia tonight.

Marcus shook his head. He couldn't do such a thing and he doubted she would go for it even if he tried. His actions the other day had driven her away and she hadn't even looked at him the two times they had passed each other today.

Although, he suspected that her reason for ignoring him just now was because she literally hadn't seen him.

He waved at another passerby, his hand close to their face, and they didn't even flinch.

When the person had passed him and there were no others in sight, he lifted the glamour that made him invisible to mortal eyes and hurried towards the entrance to his apartment building, determined to reach it before Amelia stepped into the lift. The dull silver lift doors were closing just as he stepped into the foyer and he raced for them.

"Hold it," he hollered and was surprised when the doors opened again and he stepped inside to find that Amelia was alone.

Had she known it was him and that was why she had held the doors, or hadn't she realised? He pinched the bridge of his nose. A man could go crazy trying to figure out the inner workings of the female mind. It was little wonder he had never bothered to try before now.

The journey up to their floor passed in uncomfortable silence and it was only when they were stepping out of the lift that inspiration struck Marcus.

He couldn't disobey his orders to gain her trust but that didn't mean he had to play the cad and seduce her. He would try the friendship thing again and hopefully this time he wouldn't mess it up. Rather than using her attraction towards him, he would do something he had never done. He would lower his guard and let her in instead, and gain her trust that way, as a man would, not a devil. No deception.

Marcus reminded himself that he was already deceiving her. She had no idea what he really was and why he had been living next door to her for a month now.

"Amelia," he said and she stopped at her door and turned to face him. Her beauty arrested his steps and his breath, chasing away some of his anger. He hesitated and then walked over to her, broadcasting as much confidence as he could manage given the unfamiliar situation. "I apologise about yesterday. Can I make it up to you somehow?"

She smiled. "Dinner would be good."

Like a date? That didn't sound good at all. That sounded like what his superior had ordered him to do. Marcus squirmed for a few seconds, battling the part of him that said it wouldn't be so bad to seduce her. She was beautiful and he was finding it increasingly difficult to get dancing Amelia out of his head and his dreams.

"How about dinner at my place?" he said without thinking and the way her face lit up was all the answer he needed. It had been impulsive but it had avoided taking her out to dinner and therefore any sense that this was more than platonic.

He frowned.

Or had he only made it sound more like an offer of sex?

Dinner in his apartment could easily be classified as more intimate than dinner in a restaurant.

"Great. I'll be over in half an hour." With that, she opened the door to her apartment and closed it behind her, leaving him standing in the cream hallway trying to figure out what he had offered her.

Perhaps he should call for assistance. He knew one angel in London. Einar was fallen thanks to his forbidden relationship with a female half-demon but that very fact only meant that he was qualified to answer Marcus's questions.

Marcus opened the door to his own apartment with the intent of calling Einar and interrogating him about women and whether he had just offered something a touch more intimate than anticipated but halted halfway to the telephone. The apartment was a mess.

He had never really paid much attention to his living quarters but it certainly didn't look like the sort of place a man should invite a woman into. He swapped calling Einar for a quick sweep of his apartment, using his supernatural speed to toss all dirty clothes into the laundry basket in his bathroom, straighten furniture, and clear the dust away before Amelia knocked on his door. If there was any time left on the clock, he would phone his friend for advice, but it wasn't looking promising. The bathroom was a mess too and so was the kitchen, and she was likely to visit both of those places.

Dinner in a restaurant suddenly looked more appealing.

Marcus stopped dead in the middle of the kitchen, turned on his heel, and gingerly opened the white refrigerator. The only thing in it was some old cheese he hadn't particularly enjoyed the taste of and a half eaten melon that had seen better days. There was no need to inspect the dark wooden cupboards. He could definitely recall eating the remaining half a box of cereal this morning whilst thinking and the carton was still on his bedside table to prove it.

Someone knocked on the door.

Marcus spun to face the kitchen doorway and looked through it to the entertainment centre in the living room. He glared at the clock on his DVD player. Amelia was ten minutes early. He cursed. No time to correct the food problem or call Einar. He scanned the pale apartment en route to the door and, satisfied that it now appeared far less like the bachelor pad it was, opened it.

His greeting fled his lips the moment he set eyes on her.

She had changed out of the short jacket, t-shirt and jeans she had been wearing in the lift and into a rather alluring little dark red dress that had him clearing his throat and searching for a compliment.

"You look…" What would she like to hear? The expectant shine to her eyes and the tentative smile curving the corners of her glossy cherry lips said that she was hoping to hear beautiful or similar, and he would be a liar if he said anything less. "Stunning."

Stunning was apt. He certainly felt as though she had clobbered him.

"You don't look half bad yourself." She smiled and he went to follow suit but then she held up a bottle in front of her and he froze. "I only had rosé. I know it's a bit girly but it would've been rude to bring nothing."

He hadn't really taken in anything she had said whilst he had been staring at his nemesis.

Alcohol.

Of course she would bring alcohol. It was the right response to the situation, wasn't it? A man invited her to dinner in his apartment. She brought something to make the evening go without a hitch.

He forced a smile and reached out to take it, but she drew it back to her chest, clutching it there and eyeing him closely.

"That's not a good smile. I've seen that smile before," she said with a small frown and looked down at the bottle. "It's really all I had but then I guess you're probably a beer drinker."

"No." He snatched the bottle from her, accidentally brushing her cleavage at the same time. Could someone in Heaven reverse the past thirty minutes for him and give him a second chance in which not to make a complete idiot of himself?

The blush on Amelia's cheeks and the way she was staring at her breasts said it all. He had practically groped her. Considering he had wanted this evening to be little more than just opening up to her and gaining her trust through friendship, he was certainly sending out the wrong sort of signals. Were his superiors in Heaven tampering with him or something? He didn't feel at all like himself and he was currently on course for gaining her trust the way they wanted.

Still, the feel of her soft breasts beneath his fingers in that flash of a caress had his heart racing and palms sweating. He was a stranger to physical intimacy but had witnessed enough carnal matters as a watcher to know the sordid things humans did. It hadn't interested him much in the past, but the more he focused on his hand and the area that had brushed her chest and on how beautiful Amelia looked tonight, the more appealing interacting with her physically became.

Cad.

The object of tonight's mission wasn't seduction. It was forming the foundations of friendship.

She stared at him, making him heavily aware that he should have said something to explain his reaction rather than drifting off into a fantasy world.

"The wine you have brought is not the problem... and it is most appreciated... but... I just don't really drink." He shrugged and hoped she would let it go and not pursue the subject. He wasn't sure what he would say if she asked him why he didn't drink. Could he play the role of recovering alcoholic? Would that dampen Amelia's desire for him?

Marcus wasn't sure whether that would be a good thing or a bad thing.

"Oh." Her eyebrows rose, bringing her head up with them, and he wished she would stop looking at him in a way that left him feeling emasculated. She nodded a few times and then said, "So you don't drink coffee and you avoid alcohol. Are you one of those vegan types too?"

"Hell no." He stepped back, horrified at the suggestion. He could eat a whole cow in one sitting when on Earth. In Heaven, he didn't have to eat at all, but that certainly didn't place him in the vegan category. There was nothing wrong with abstaining from certain substances that didn't agree with your lifestyle choice, but this wasn't one of those times and he would be happy to prove it to her.

Amelia closed the door behind her and walked into his apartment, casting her gaze over everything and then him, and he felt the challenge in her look. She was trying to figure him out and he didn't particularly like the tone of her expression.

In a fit of desire to prove himself a man, he strode into the kitchen, unscrewed the cap on the wine and set it down on the counter. Another flaw in his plan produced itself as he searched the dark wooden cupboards for wine glasses but he overcame it by using two short tumblers instead. If anything, rosé wine could only look more manly in such a glass, surely?

He poured two healthy glasses of wine as Amelia approached the open double doors and then held one out to her. She took it without questioning his choice of glass and then raised it towards him.

"Cheers," she said in a low sexy voice that had his gaze drifting towards her lips so he could watch her drink and then added, "Cheers?"

Marcus realised he was supposed to respond in kind, so raised his glass too. "Cheers."

"Or bottoms up." Amelia giggled, turned and walked back into the living room.

Bottoms up.

Marcus's eyes dropped to her backside. The deep red material of her dress clung to it, emphasising the shape of her bottom in a way that had his blood pounding through his temples again. He took a deep breath and joined her in the living room. Amelia sipped her drink. Marcus stared at his.

Alcohol hadn't passed his lips in five centuries, not since the one and only time he had dared to drink it and had awoken with a demonic curse scrawled on his back. Back then, it had been a forbidden item. Now, any angel could drink it without castigation.

Marcus had no desire to do such a thing.

He took another deep breath and blew it out, trying to psych himself up. He could feel Amelia's gaze on him and he hoped she didn't think he was spacing out again or had noticed his fear of what might happened when he finally took a sip of the wine. Blood whooshed through his ears, drowning out all sound as he stared at the innocent looking pink liquid in the glass. Alcohol released inhibitions. It would be a good way of lowering his guard so he could grow closer to Amelia and gain her trust.

Marcus lifted it to his lips and breathed in, catching the fiery hint of alcohol in its scent, and then continued. The moment it passed his lips, a shiver raced down his spine and along his arms, and heat followed it down his throat.

The effect was instantaneous. He had spent the whole day thinking over his mission and had ignored his body's cries for nourishment, leaving him ravenous and his stomach empty. The wine rocketed straight to his head, sending it spinning, and a second sip only made the situation worse, lessening his control over his body.

His eyes widened in alarm when his wings pushed for freedom and he concentrated hard in an attempt to contain them and stop them from tearing through his navy shirt.

"I'll be just a minute." He rushed into the bathroom, slammed the door, and turned to face the white vanity unit and the large rectangular mirror above it on the wall.

Marcus set his glass down and fumbled with it, almost knocking his wine down the sink, and then turned the cold tap on so fast that he had to dash to his right to avoid the spray of water that bounced off the porcelain, threatening to douse his crotch. With a grimace, he turned the tap down to a steady flow and splashed the water on his face. His wings pushed again and he ached with the desire to strip off his shirt and unleash them for a moment, to surrender to his desire to beat them and shed his mortal appearance.

He couldn't.

Not only could Amelia end up seeing them, ruining any chance of gaining her trust, but he might not want to put them away again. He couldn't spend the whole evening in the bathroom.

His stomach growled and he pressed his damp hand against it.

If tonight was going to be anything near to a success, he needed to eat and soon, but there was nothing in his apartment. He had promised Amelia dinner. Even if she was kind enough to offer her own groceries, he wouldn't know how to cook her anything. He had never used a stove for anything other than warming basic foodstuffs, such as soup and other items that came in neat little cans with clear instructions on the labels.

This whole plan was ridiculously flawed.

His head turned again and he reached for his wine, taking a greedy gulp of it in the hope that it would dull his senses enough that his wings would relent and he would forget his desire to fly off somewhere.

With Amelia.

That was a thought.

He looked into the mirror at the reflection of the white door behind him. Water dripped from the tip of his nose and rolled off his jaw. His heavy breathing filled the silence.

How would a human react to the sight of his wings and the knowledge that angels existed? If she knew what he was, he wouldn't be deceiving her and there was a chance that he could convince her that his reason for being here was to protect her. Would that gain her trust?

He laughed at himself.

Any sane mortal would run a mile if they saw an angel.

She would never trust him.

"Are you feeling alright?" The sound of her voice, soft through the door, roused a different sort of hunger in him. He stared at the door, picturing her on the other side, how concerned she would look and how that caring edge to her expression would only add to her beauty.

If forced, could he seduce her?

Could it be called deception if he wanted her too?

It wasn't going to happen.

Marcus dried his face on a hand towel, opened the door and smiled at her. "Never better."

She gave him a hesitant and unconvinced smile in return, and looked past him at the bathroom, her eyebrows raised high. What was she looking for? It dawned on him that she thought the wine had made him sick. He could laugh at that. The one time he had turned to drink, it had taken close to a barrel of mead to render him unconscious, and even then he hadn't thrown up.

He picked up his glass of wine, sipped it again to prove that he could handle it, and then smiled at her. Crimson spread across her cheeks, a delightful rosy tint that his smile had caused, and she held her own glass up, revealing that it was already empty.

Marcus took it from her and went into the kitchen to top it up. He took another swig from his own glass to give himself a little Dutch courage and then filled it too. When he walked back into the living room, Amelia was perched on the arm of his pale couch, her slender legs crossed at the knee, smiling at him. A different urge struck him, one that would definitely give her the impression that he was out to seduce her should she notice the effect it had on him.

He handed her the glass and stood in a way that wouldn't reveal the growing bulge in his jeans, waiting for it to pass.

Amelia toyed with the glass, delicately running her right index finger around the rim, mesmerising him and filling his head with images of her stroking him in such a fashion. She looked up at him. "So what are we eating?"

Marcus grinned. "About that… you see… I don't actually have any food that is edible and even if I did, I am not a good cook."

The expression that settled on her face looked decidedly like relief.

"Something I said?"

A smile teased her lips. "I half expected you to be this incredible cook and to show me up. I'm atrocious."

Marcus felt her relief sweep through him too and remembered how often she ate take away food. His gaze dropped to the bare slip of a dress she wore. Take out didn't look bad on her. She had to work out more often than he knew. He had watched her jogging around Hyde Park before and had even jogged there once or twice himself before giving up the pretence and flying above her instead, invisible to mortal eyes.

"How does Chinese food suit you?" She took another sip of her wine before picking up the black cordless phone from the coffee table. "I know a great place that delivers."

Marcus nodded in approval and then listened as she recited what sounded like the entire menu. He didn't care what he ate as long as it got here fast and gave him some defence against the wine so he let her order some of her favourite dishes for them to share.

He paid for the food when it arrived twenty minutes later and Amelia helped him arrange the dishes on the long wooden coffee table between the sofa and the entertainment centre in the corner of the room. While he went to top up their drinks and get some plates and cutlery, she found a movie in the small collection of DVDs he had acquired in his short time on Earth, and put it into the player.

It felt far too much like a date as he sat beside her on the couch. He wasn't sure what a date felt like, but in all the movies he had watched on Earth and couples he had observed during his time in Heaven, this sort of thing was frequently classified as one. Dinner. Movie. Wine. Man and a woman. Date.

Marcus finished off the remains of his food and leaned back into the corner of the couch, bringing his wine with him. He crossed his legs and stretched his right arm out along the back of the sofa, settling his hand close to Amelia, and rested the bottom of his glass on his knee. He paid little attention to the movie playing on the large flat screen television. Amelia held it too firmly, keeping his eyes locked on her face as she laughed, oblivious to his watching her. She was beautiful, and it wasn't the wine talking.

A pure soul, full of kindness and warmth. Her internal beauty shone through, enhancing her external looks and leading him to wonder how such a pretty woman could fall for such disgusting men. She couldn't see the damage to their souls, so it was understandable that she would occasionally fall for males who were beneath her, but to always find the bad seed amongst the many decent men in the world? He had at least expected her to get rid of them the moment she realised they were no good for her, but she persevered, attempting to change their ways, as though she hoped that she could make them into a good man if she tried hard enough.

Impossible.

Men were resistant to change.

As were angels.

Amelia looked at him over her shoulder, her laughter dying away when she caught his gaze and her expression turning serious.

"Do I have something on my face?" she said with a hint of a smile and a blush.

Marcus wanted to say that she did and use the excuse to reach across and sweep the backs of his fingers across her cheek. He wanted to see if his touch could affect her with the same intensity that hers affected him. He shook his head instead, expecting her to go back to watching the movie. She didn't.

She turned and leaned over him, kneeling on the couch seat, and pressed her hand against his chest.

Marcus stared at her mouth, everything good in him screaming to break away and stop her. He didn't. He stayed stock still and let it happen.

His first kiss in this lifetime was a tentative sweep of soft lips over his followed by the press of her body into his. The feel of her against him sent a flood of feelings surging through him, setting his blood aflame with desire and the need to clutch her to him and possess her. It overwhelmed him and his restraint, crushing the good part that was still struggling to resist, and while he stopped himself from sliding his arm around her back and pulling the full length of her body flush against his, he couldn't stop himself from kissing her.

She moaned softly when he responded, grazing his lips against hers in a gentle caress that fanned the flames within him until he burned for her and for more. Her tongue brushed along the seam of his mouth and he brought his to meet it, tangling softly and luring it into his mouth where they danced. He couldn't remember kissing in his past lifetime but he certainly would have if it had felt like this. Warmth suffused him right down to his bones and every breathy little moan he elicited from Amelia turned the heat up another notch, until he was close to grabbing the nape of her neck and holding her mouth against his.

He breathed hard when she broke away to kneel on the sofa in front of him, her grey eyes wide and hand coming up to cover her mouth. She touched her lips, drawing his hungry gaze there, and he was ravenous all over again, starving for the sweet taste of her on his tongue.

"Shit… I'm sorry," she said, instantly deflating his desire, and scrambled from the couch.

She was leaving?

Not good.

Marcus was off the sofa and had his hand locked around her wrist before she could reach the door.

"Wait," he said and wasn't sure what to do when she looked back at him so he pulled her into his arms and kissed her again.

And damn she tasted just as good as she had the first time.

And damn he needed more.

She moaned when he backed her into the wall beside the door, pressing the hard length of his body against hers, and grabbed his shoulders. For a moment, he thought she would push him away, and then she dragged him closer still and wrapped her arms around his neck, burying her fingers into his hair.

Part of him was vaguely aware that alcohol was responsible for his current situation and that he was going to regret it come the morning but the rest of him didn't care. He had wanted to release his inhibitions and he had. He just hadn't expected that this would be the result, and right now he didn't care that he was on the verge of doing exactly as his superior had ordered.

All he cared about was satisfying his hunger to taste Amelia.

The part of him that was chanting about deception wouldn't shut up and the more he listened to it, the more he felt like a demon.

Marcus stepped back, leaving Amelia sagged against the wall, panting so hard that her breasts rose and fell with each breath, presenting him with a glorious view that had him reconsidering what he was about to say.

She slowly opened her grey eyes and smiled shyly before raking her gaze over him. It lingered on his groin and her eyes widened, pupils dilating until her irises turned dark with desire. There was a wicked edge to her eyes when they met his again and she inclined her head, her pouty come hither look almost luring him in. Desire wasn't the only thing written plainly across her face. There was expectation there too, and that alone pushed him into saying what he needed to.

"I think this is a bad idea."

Her sultry temptress look immediately dissipated, leaving the Amelia he was familiar with standing before him.

"You really don't like me," she whispered and the hurt in her heart beat within his.

He wasn't saying anything of the sort. But what could he tell her? He was halfway to drunk and not only did he need to get his head on straight so he was certain that he wasn't doing this because he was subconsciously following orders but he was hardly going to produce the stellar performance she expected of him.

He had been celibate this entire lifetime.

And he was damned if his first time was going to be under orders.

If something was going to happen between them, it was going to happen naturally. He wasn't going to seduce her and use her feelings against her.

"I do… but… I think the wine has gone to my head and I think it might have gone to yours too."

"And that's a bad thing?" She glanced at the empty bottle and his half-full glass on the table.

"It is." Marcus ventured a step towards her and brushed the backs of his fingers against her cheek, sweeping her straight dark hair from her face. Her skin was as smooth as he had imagined it would be and the way she closed her eyes, slowly inhaling at the same time, empowered him. He opened his hand and cupped her face, resting his fingers along her jaw and bringing his thumb close to her mouth. Such soft lips. He wanted to dip his head and kiss her again but he wasn't sure he would be able to stop at just kissing if he did. "It is all a little quick and I don't want you waking tomorrow feeling like crap because of what we did tonight."

"I doubt I would feel crappy." There it was again. Blatant expectation. Why? Because he was handsome to her? That instantly made him Casanova?

No pressure then.

"Amelia… how about we take it slow and steady?"

Her eyes lit up and he realised there could be another meaning in his words but he didn't bother to correct her because he wasn't about to let things get that far. His final task was coming. Everything that had happened tonight would satisfy his superior and his orders to gain her trust. He would date her a few times, keeping a suitable distance, and once his mission was over he would leave.

She nodded, tiptoed and kissed him.

Resisting was impossible.

He swept his lips over hers, tasting her again and savouring this brief contact between them. When she broke away this time, he led her back to the couch and settled there with her, his thoughts weighing him down. He watched her again, fascinated by the amusement she got from the movie and how she curled up next to him, her bare knees brushing his thigh. A deep ache to slide his arm around her shoulders and draw her closer still beat in his bones but he resisted.

He couldn't use her feelings against her.

Not when he was starting to feel something for her too.

CHAPTER 6

Amelia ambled along the hot pavement, her head already home in her flat or, more precisely, next door to it with Marcus. He had been a gentleman last night when she had wanted to take things further, and while it had irritated her at the time and made her doubt his attraction towards her again, it had taken on a certain appeal as her day had progressed. In the morning when she had gone jogging, she had done so out of frustration at how the night had ended on what could only be described as a very chaste kiss. By the time she had made it to lunch with her friends, she had been replaying their more passionate kisses in her head, so much so that her friends had commented on her unusual silence. She had made her excuses and not mentioned Marcus. Her friends would think she was rebounding.

Did Marcus think that?

She didn't want him to see himself as just a rebound guy. He was more than that. She couldn't put her finger on it but there was something different about him. Something that set him apart from the average man.

Amelia had never had a man treat her in such a gentlemanly fashion and wasn't sure what to make of it. All of her previous boyfriends had been as passionate as she was and at times she wondered if that was part of their appeal. Because of her attraction to Marcus, she had expected him to be similar to the previous men in her life in that respect. That expectation couldn't have been more wrong.

The moment he had said that he wanted to take things slowly, she had realised that Marcus really was nothing like her exes, and was everything like the man she had always hoped to meet.

Maybe he was right and they should take their time, if only so she could prove to Marcus that he was more than a rebound to her. She really did like him. Her mind had been stuck on him since the night she had paused to take a good look at him and even now she was itching to see him again. She wasn't good at going slow. Once something seized hold of her, she generally forgot everything else in a passionate pursuit of what she wanted.

In this case, Marcus naked and pressed against her.

He had been hesitant and strangely polite to her after their kiss, and his sweet goodnight played on her mind, filling her head with doubts.

He had kissed her though.

And it had felt good.

Really good.

She could do the softly-softly thing with him any day of the week. She wouldn't care how slow things went between them if he just kept kissing her like that.

Amelia was so lost in her thoughts that she didn't realise that she had gone the wrong way until she heard three men addressing her. She quickly scanned her surroundings, eyes darting around for an avenue of escape in case things took a turn for the worse.

"Lost?" The innocent expression on the face of the man in the middle didn't fool Amelia.

It wasn't dark yet but the sun had already set and she had wandered into the quiet side streets behind the apartment buildings. She looked around again, hoping to spot someone other than the three men, but she was alone.

"Not really." Amelia turned to walk the other way but another man was there.

No, not another man.

The same man. His dark hair hung in messy threads across his eyes, obscuring his face enough that she wouldn't be able to describe him well to the police if it came down to that. God, she hoped it didn't. She hurried to get a good look at the other two men. Both around the same height as the first, tall and with slim figures, and both sporting dark jeans and jackets, clothing that seemed far too warm for such a hot summer evening. She was sweltering in her small pale blue dress.

"I don't want any trouble." She clutched her leather handbag closer to her, holding it in front of her stomach. Could she use it as a weapon? She kept so much junk in it that it was probably heavy enough to knock someone out if she swung it hard at their head.

Her heart accelerated at the thought of actually trying to fend off these three men. They didn't look strong, but they had the advantage of numbers and she couldn't tell from their clothing just how built they were. For all she knew, they could be like Marcus. His build didn't show when he wore loose clothing like these men were.

She did have one weapon she could use without too much fear and it might be enough to deter them.

Amelia shoved her hand into her black bag, pulled out her mobile phone and flashed it around so all three men got a good look at it.

"I'll call the police." Not a tremble touched her voice. Brave Amelia. She held the phone out, standing her ground, unwilling to let these men get the better of her and see her scared.

The two lighter haired men smiled at her, as though her words were more amusing than threatening.

She flipped the slim black phone open and quickly punched 999 but before she could bring the phone up to her ear, she dropped it.

No. Not dropped. It had shot out of her hand and clattered along the ground to the first man, the one she presumed was the gang's leader.

What the hell?

The dark haired man casually bent down and picked it up. He brought it to his ear, raised an eyebrow, and then snapped the phone in two as though it was made of tinder wood.

Double what the hell?

Amelia spun on the spot when one of the men behind her grabbed her bag. She swung her fist on instinct, smashing it hard into his temple, but he didn't let go. He didn't even flinch. Shit. This wasn't going to go well. She opened her mouth to scream but the sound died when the man who had grabbed her suddenly levitated before her wide eyes.

Not levitating, she realised as she saw the fingers tightly grasping the man's neck with such bruising force that they dug hard into his flesh. Her heart missed a beat when the man's attacker threw him to one side.

Marcus stood before her, fury darkening his handsome face and rage burning in his blue eyes.

The man hit the wall with a startling bang and Marcus grabbed her hand and ran. She only had a moment to look back, but it was all she needed in order to see that the two remaining men were coming after them, and that the third lay on the tarmac just below a crater in the bricks of the building at his back.

Amelia stumbled and Marcus dragged her up, bringing her attention back to him and his fierce grip on her. How strong was Marcus? Could a human throw a man into a wall and create a dent like that? Was it the anger she had seen in his eyes that had given him the strength to do such a thing? She was being ridiculous. The buildings were old around here. Maybe it was just weak brickwork.

Or maybe there really was something different about Marcus.

"Focus," he snapped and her mind instantly cleared, her attention shooting to her feet and to running as fast as she could.

The men were still in pursuit and she didn't want to be responsible for Marcus having to take both of them on.

Everything else drifted to the back of her mind as she ran, her breathing loud in her ears, following Marcus as he wove through the back streets. She didn't dare look over her shoulder to see if the men were still coming after them. Marcus kept glancing back, his silver-blue eyes either lighting on her or the path behind them. She presumed the men were still there since he kept running. Her legs were beginning to tire and her feet were aching. How much further did they have to go? Why hadn't Marcus made a break for the busy main street where they would be safe rather than pounding through the alleys and side roads?

Amelia frowned. She had left her bag back in the alley. It had come off her shoulder when Marcus had torn the man away from her. She could remember seeing it next to him where he lay crumpled on the floor. Dead? She hoped not. She didn't want to be linked to the man and if he were dead that would make Marcus a murderer. She glanced up at his profile. It wobbled in her vision as they ran but she didn't miss the steely look of determination etched on his profile.

"We should go right," she said, out of breath and desperate to reach the main roads and growing afraid that the men would catch up and Marcus would be forced to fight again.

"No," he said without sounding at all tired or strained and looked up. "This way."

Amelia couldn't believe it when he kicked in a fire exit door with a single blow of his booted foot and started leading her up the back stairs of an old building. Was he insane?

"Where the hell do you think you're going?" she ground the words out between breaths, trying to keep up with him as her legs began to flag. Running on the flat had been tiring enough. She wasn't going to make it more than a few flights of steps without collapsing.

"The roof."

Insane.

"Dead end," she squeezed out. "We'll be trapped."

Panic sent her heart rocketing and she looked back down the dark stairwell, afraid that the men would be following them and would be faster than she was. Adrenaline kept her legs moving but each step was becoming increasingly difficult. At this rate, the men would catch her. She jogged her backside off most weekends and some weekday mornings in order to remain fit and healthy, but she had never been good at flat out running.

When she turned back to Marcus, he was looking at her, his eyes unusually bright in the low light.

"Trust me on this." He paused on the next floor, not at all out of breath.

Amelia panted like a dog, her throat burning as she dragged in each breath, her breathing so loud that she couldn't hear anything else. Were the men coming? She stared down the stairs and then looked across at Marcus. His eyes had to be a trick of the light but they were so vivid and bright, bluer than she had ever seen them.

"I need to get to the roof and then I can deal with the men."

"As in, fight them?" Her expression turned to horror but Marcus just nodded.

"I said I would protect you, Amelia. I meant that."

"You think they're coming after me? Why? I dropped my bag. They've got what they're after."

The look in Marcus's eyes said different. He knew they were coming. She didn't want to know how he knew or why they were after her, but she did know that going with Marcus was her only option. She couldn't fight the men alone. Perhaps when they reached the roof, they would find that the men hadn't come after her at all and could escape another way.

Marcus grabbed her hand again and started running, his footsteps heavy on the staircase. Amelia stumbled after him, keeping up as best she could, her legs cramping and threatening to give out. A warm rush of air burst against her when he kicked the door to the roof open and the brightness of the light blinded her for a moment. She kept running with him, one hand clutched in his and the other trying to pin the skirt of her dress down.

Marcus stopped.

Her eyes adjusted.

The two men were standing a few metres in front of them, near the edge of the black tarred flat roof.

Impossible.

Amelia looked back at the door she had come out of with Marcus and then around her at the roof, her heart pounding and sweat trickling down her back, sticking her blue dress to her skin.

There weren't any other routes onto the roof. No ladder or adjoining building. How had the men reached the roof before them?

"Marcus," she said but the rest of her sentence died when she saw him.

He stood with his back to her, the warm breeze tousling his black hair, his broad shoulders relaxed as though he wasn't facing two dangerous men.

But what stole her breath, what made her heart flutter in her throat, was his clothing.

Gone were his jeans and shirt and boots.

In their place was something she could only describe as armour but it seemed ridiculous that he would be wearing such a thing. The deep blue back plate shone like mother of pearl in the fading light of evening, reaching only mid-way down his back, and had two long slits over each shoulder blade. She could see his tattoos through them. Strips of armour in a similar material covered his backside like a short skirt but revealed the dark material beneath. His muscular thighs were bare and taut, exuding strength as he stood firm with one hand at his side and the other still clutching hers. The armour encased his bare forearms too, brilliant blue and edged with shining silver and decorated with rearing silver unicorns.

Amelia stared at him, head light and fuzzy, confused and unable to comprehend what she was seeing.

Marcus was wearing armour.

She looked around for his clothes, convinced it was a trick of some sort and he had somehow been wearing this incredible costume beneath his clothes, but she couldn't see them and he hadn't once let go of her hand.

His other hand moved at his side and her eyes widened as they fell on the short sword strapped there. He removed it from the sheath, the curved steel blade around the length of his forearm and hand combined, and held it down at his side.

"Leave," he said and she wondered if he was speaking to her until she leaned to one side and looked past him.

Her eyes popped wide.

The two men had changed appearance too and this time she decided that she was hallucinating. The fear had gone to her head or perhaps she had passed out, because rather than two humans, she was looking at two human-shaped things with pitch-black skin and glowing red eyes. They were huge, at least three feet taller than before, and built like brick shit houses and both were staring intently at Marcus, lips peeled back in a sneer that revealed sharp red teeth.

Amelia felt faint but held it together. She couldn't pass out in her own nightmare.

Or was it a dream?

Her gaze slid back to Marcus. He turned at the waist and looked over his shoulder at her, his face a mask of calm confidence, and released her wrist. He certainly looked like something out of a dream. A warrior. Otherworldly. Elementally masculine. She resisted her temptation to look at his body again and see the way his muscles twisted with him, full of strength and power. He would look beautiful if she stepped back and took him all in. Sexy as hell.

A chill settled on her skin.

Dangerous.

Amelia stepped back on instinct, distancing herself from him without thinking, and pain flashed in his vivid silver-blue eyes before he turned away.

Had she caused it by placing more distance between them? Her heart had made her feet move, afraid of what she was looking at and the knowledge that Marcus was dangerous. He had possibly killed a man in the street and looked as though he was going to kill these two men, or whatever they were. What insane world had she fallen into? Marcus had said to trust her. He had promised to protect her.

And she believed him.

She just couldn't bring herself to believe what she was seeing.

Amelia flinched when Marcus flicked his left hand out at his side and the handle of the blade extended into a long staff that rivalled his six foot plus frame. The silver engraving that covered it reflected the dying sunlight.

She blinked and Marcus was gone. A boom shook the ground and a hot wave of air knocked her onto her backside. She sat there with her hands pressed into the tacky tar roof on either side of her thighs, staring, unable to take her eyes off the battle happening right before her.

Marcus was fighting.

For her.

The two black creatures snarled and evaded Marcus as he swept around them, his spear gleaming brightly as it cut through the air bare inches from his enemies. The creatures gained ground and then reached out at their sides. Dark swords materialised in their hands. She was going crazy. She had never dreamed of battles before but this couldn't be real. It just couldn't be.

Her heart leapt in her chest when one of the creatures slashed at Marcus, forcing him back into the other one. He turned in time to block its attack with his spear but it caught him hard across the jaw with its bare fist, sending him tumbling across the roof. He shot to his feet, launched himself through the air at the beast, and brought his spear down in a swift arc that cut straight through its arm, tearing an ungodly shriek from the creature. The wound poured with blood, creating a slick river down the creature's bare black leg, but it didn't stop the fight. The other monster attacked Marcus and he leapt backwards, high in the air, and then drew another blade from his waist. It was the same as the spear had been at first, a short handle with a long gleaming curved blade, but he didn't extend this one. He slashed at the creatures with it, driving them backwards.

Amelia struggled to her feet, pulse pounding and stomach turning whenever the monsters managed to get close to Marcus. He was incredible as he fought, both violent and graceful, his movements swift and fierce, and aim true. He sliced down the back of one of the beasts and then turned and brought the spear up again, twisting it at the same time so he could cut through the second beast's chest. It snarled and then roared, and the sound deafened her. She covered her ears and then shook her head when the beast with the cut arm and back turned her way.

It thundered towards her, heavy footfalls shaking the roof, and her heart felt as though it was going to explode or stop.

Before it could reach her, Marcus was in front of her, his right hand pressed against her stomach, forcing her backwards. He yelled and pushed forwards with the spear, and everything slowed down as it sliced straight into the monster's stomach. Marcus didn't stop. He pressed on, his hand leaving her and revealing a hot patch where it had touched, and she could only stare as the staff of his spear shortened again and he tugged it free of the creature's body, twirled and hacked its head off.

"Keep back," Marcus said in a thick growling voice and launched himself forwards.

He shot towards the other black creature at the opposite end of the roof, his spear extending again.

Amelia didn't take her eyes off the monster in front of her. It dropped slowly to its knees, one scaly clawed hand still pressed against the wound in its stomach, and hit the tar roof and collapsed forwards. A pool of blood spread outwards from the neck and she looked down, following it, the world silent as her gaze tracked its slow progression towards her feet. She couldn't move. She wanted to step back, out of the path of the blood, but her legs wouldn't cooperate. The slick liquid touched the toes of her cream summer shoes and edged around it, engulfing them. Bile burned up her throat and she swallowed it down, unwilling to be sick even at the sight of such horror.

Marcus yelled and her attention shot back to him. He was fighting the remaining creature, doing all he could to protect her just as he had promised. Blood marred his pale skin and his armour, and his movements were slowing, clumsy now and scaring her. Fear for her own safety became fear for Marcus's as she watched the fight, unable to tear her eyes away from him, her blood rushing through her head and heart quaking in her chest.

It leapt to her throat when the black beast turned, bringing its sword swiftly upwards and cutting across Marcus's thigh. His knee hit the roof and he blocked the next slash of the creature's sword with the armour around his forearm. The sharp metallic ring shot through her, turning her insides, pushing her fear to the limit. Marcus yelled and thrust upwards with his forearm, forcing the beast backwards and gaining more room but Amelia feared that it wouldn't be enough. He was tiring and the creature showed no sign of stopping.

Marcus dragged the blade of his spear across the roof, scarring the black tar, and lashed out with it. The attack missed but forced the creature away. Marcus breathed hard, held his right hand out towards the creature, and vivid white light shot down from the sky, engulfing it. The beast roared and snarled, clawed at the beam as though it was a tangible thing that it could attack, and then rose into the air and disappeared.

Amelia stared up at the sky, breathing fast and shallow, on the verge of collapse. Heavy footsteps echoed in her ears and the sounds of the world started to return. She brought her gaze downwards.

Marcus slowly walked towards her across the roof, blood sprayed across his blue chest armour and face, smeared on his bare shoulders and thighs. She told herself not to go to him, that he was as dangerous as the monsters that had attacked her, but the weariness in his expression and in his eyes forced her to move. She stepped past the body of the fallen creature and hurried towards him. The warmth that filled his eyes when they fell on her heated her through and chased away her fear. She wanted to throw her arms around his shoulders and cry with relief that it was over and he was safe. She stopped short of him instead, afraid for once of doing what she wanted. Whatever had just happened, it had been real.

Marcus had saved her from men that had been monsters.

He sheathed the two blades at his waist, closed his eyes and hung his head as he drew a deep breath. The weariness written across every inch of him called to her, told her to go to him and soothe his pain, to give him respite and comfort. She looked at his thigh and the long gash there, and the ribbons of blood that trailed down from it towards the armour that protected his shin. The sight of the wound made her take a step forwards but she still hesitated, fearing that she was making a terrible mistake and that she had been right about Marcus. He was another black knight. A man more dangerous than any before him.

And she was afraid of losing her heart to him.

He wiped the back of his hand across his forehead, clearing away the beads of sweat gathered there and pushing his black hair out of his face, and then looked at her.

"Are you alright?" he said.

How could he ask her such a thing when he was hurt because of her, when he'd had to fight those foul things to protect her? Why? Tears welled up but she sniffed them back. She was stronger than this, made of sterner stuff that could withstand whatever life threw at her.

Even this.

Marcus reached out and she didn't flinch as he smoothed his fingers across her cheek as though wiping something away. She leaned into his touch and the hurt in his eyes lifted again, until he looked almost as he had done last night when they had kissed. Happy? She had felt happy in that moment too and she wanted to feel that again.

She didn't want to feel scared, not of those things that had tried to hurt her or of Marcus.

He had protected her, had fought for her, but she couldn't look at him without feeling a lingering trace of fear.

She would overcome it. Marcus had done nothing to deserve her fear. He had done everything to deserve her trust. She was stronger than this. She was.

Her legs betrayed her and her knees gave out. She didn't hit the floor. Marcus's arm was around her in an instant, strong and steady against her back, supporting her and holding her pressed against his body. She felt the wet slide of blood on her leg where his touched it, and felt the granite hardness of his armour against her chest, and the warmth of his skin on her side where his arm curled protectively around her.

Amelia stared up into his silver-blue eyes, amazed and transfixed as the darker flecks of blue in them moved and his irises brightened again.

"Amelia?" he said thickly and she melted into him, her strength leaving her, and couldn't stop the tears from escaping. A pained look crossed his face as his gaze tracked them over her cheeks and then it softened as he gently wiped them away. "Are you alright?"

She nodded mutely even though she wasn't sure if she was alright. She was alive, and so was he, and right now that was all that mattered to her. He wasn't something to fear. He had saved her and she was safe with him.

"We have to leave… I know this is a lot for you to take in, but we are not safe here." His words brought with them a flash of the man they had left in the alley.

Wasn't he dead?

She didn't want Marcus to fight another one of those things.

Amelia nodded again. He was right. They had to leave. But how?

She looked at the roof exit. The man would come that way, wouldn't he? The others hadn't. They had been here waiting for her and Marcus. How?

Marcus shocked her back to reality when he bent, slid his other arm under the crook of her knees, and lifted her. Her arms instantly looped around his neck, fear of falling chasing away the madness of everything that had happened for a sweet brief moment before it came crashing back again. She stared at Marcus, trying to force herself to see him as he was. A man wearing armour, bloodied from his battle against two monsters. A warrior who had protected her.

"Trust me, Amelia," he whispered so close to her face that his warm breath fanned her neck and she looked at him, deep into his eyes, seeing only hope in them.

"I do," she said in a low voice and then wasn't sure it had been the right thing to say when he ran towards the edge of the roof and leapt off.

Amelia's eyes slowly widened as they hurtled towards the roof of the next building over fifty feet below them and she dug her fingers into Marcus's hair, holding on for dear life. She opened her mouth to let out a scream and curled up, bracing for impact. Was this how her short life was going to end?

She turned to face Marcus and his gaze met hers, expression awkward and bordering on irritated. Not the sort of face she had expected from a man about to die.

They hit the roof.

Rather than the collision she had braced for, it felt more like Marcus had jumped barely a few feet. He landed in a crouch with her tucked as close to his chest as his blue armour allowed, and then stood. Her heart slowly came unstuck from the back of her throat and dropped into her chest, and she stared back up at the roof of the building he had leapt from, unable to believe they had fallen so far without injury.

Something in Marcus's eyes said that he hadn't expected that to happen either. He looked over his shoulder at the back of his armour, frowned, and turned to her. There was worry in his eyes that hadn't been there during the battle on the roof or their escape from the alley.

"Is something wrong?" she said and his silence and the confusion mixing with the fear in his eyes told her there was.

Amelia looked at his shoulders, remembering the two long slits in the back of his armour.

He hadn't expected to fall.

Just what had he expected to happen?

CHAPTER 7

Amelia walked through the dark London streets in a dream, distant from the world around her, her focus split. One half was turned inwards as she struggled to comprehend everything that had happened and make sense of it. The other half was fixed on Marcus where he walked close beside her, his hand firmly gripping hers, steady and strong. She followed him without question, relying on him to help her understand the things she had seen and what was happening to her.

She hadn't lied when she had said that she trusted him. He had fought for her and she hoped that meant he was on her side. She held on to that belief, using it to keep her niggling fear of Marcus at bay. He wouldn't hurt her. He had promised to protect her and he had done just that, and she was safe with him.

People passed them in the busy street, coming and going between the late night stores and places unknown to her. None of them even glanced at Marcus, which led her to wonder if they could see what she could.

Did they see a beautiful man wearing blue armour that was moulded like muscles, a warrior splattered with blood and grim in appearance?

Or did they see whatever she saw whenever she happened to catch their reflection in a window?

The normal Marcus.

The one she had been foolishly falling for.

In his reflection, he appeared to be wearing a pale shirt and dark jeans, dressed as though he was going out for the evening to somewhere casual, like a pub or a relaxed dinner in a restaurant.

Was it some kind of magic? She had never believed in such things before, but she was finding it difficult to deny the possibility of anything anymore. Those creatures Marcus had killed had been like demons from fairytales, a bright white light had caused one to disappear, and Marcus had donned armour in the blink of an eye. Anything seemed possible at the moment, even if she couldn't quite bring herself to believe it was real.

She slowly brought her gaze back to him.

If it was magic and the people passing them by saw the Marcus she did when she looked in the windows, why wasn't she seeing that when she looked at him?

When she looked at him directly, the armour was there, barely covering his muscular body, and two deadly curved silver blades hung from his waist, shifting with him as he walked, his strides purposeful and intent.

Amelia hadn't asked where they were going.

Since leaving the rooftop of the second building, Marcus had been silent and pensive, his grip on her hand unrelenting. She was glad of that. It was her anchor in the storm of her confusion and the whirlwind of emotions inside her. She clung to it, afraid to surrender it in case everything turned crazy again. As long as she was holding his hand, his long slender fingers locked tightly between hers, then she was safe.

Marcus would protect her.

His eyes briefly met hers and then he blinked and they were fixed ahead again, focused on the distance. The worry that had been in them after his leap from the roof with her was still there, and the question still burned on her tongue, desiring to be said.

What had he expected to happen?

There were so many other things that she wanted to ask him too. Was he a good man? Was he going to hurt her? His warning came back to her and she couldn't ignore it. He had told her to stay away from him and that he wasn't good for her. Was this why?

What was he?

"This way," he whispered, so quiet that she barely heard him, and then turned with her down a beautiful tree-lined avenue. The pale streetlights shone down on the path, highlighting expensive cars and the narrow front gardens of the townhouses. They had walked a long way from their own neighbourhood and her feet had started to blister over an hour ago but she hadn't said anything because she hadn't wanted to draw Marcus's attention or her own to her bloodstained shoes, but now she had to stop. She couldn't take another step.

Marcus stopped with her and she could feel his eyes on her as she lifted one foot and rubbed her toes through the thin pale material of her shoes. He released her hand and she made a reach for his, not wanting to let go of him, but he evaded her and crouched before her, one knee against the pavement and the other raised, as though he was proposing. He carefully took hold of her ankle, removed her shoe, and rested her bare foot on his hard thigh. His warmth seeped into her and she stared at the long cut across his muscles just millimetres from her toes, feeling guilty inside that she was making a fuss over a few blisters and sore spots when he was injured.

The gash on his thigh was deep, a thick valley that looked black in the streetlights. The blood around it had dried but there were damp spots that sparkled, marking places where the wound had reopened.

Tearing her gaze away, she watched Marcus as he touched the toe of her shoe that he held and then looked down at her other one.

"What happened?" He looked up at her, and for a moment she felt like Cinderella as he held her slipper out to her. "There is blood on your shoes."

"That thing… when you…" What did she say? She wanted to phrase it delicately in case she had just imagined it. Her eyes darted to his chest armour and she drew a deep breath. She wasn't insane. "Chopped its head off… I… I think I was in shock."

"I didn't mean for this—" He cut himself off and she nodded, seeing the rest of his words in his eyes and feeling them in her heart. He had wanted to protect her and not let anything happen to her, not even something as minor as a bloodied pair of shoes. She smiled to reassure him and took her foot down from his thigh, and then eased down to kneel before him and tentatively reached out. He stilled right down to his breathing when she touched his thigh near the wound. For some reason, touching him, laying her fingers on his bloodstained flesh, made it all seem real.

Marcus was hurt, and it was all her fault.

"We should get this seen to," she said absently and then her vision blurred and she frowned. It cleared when she blinked, sending hot tears running down her cheeks. Her fingers trembled against him and her strength faded again, leaving her weak and afraid. Raising her head, she looked right into his eyes, silently asking him for something. She wasn't sure what she needed. Reassurance. Comfort. His strength? "Marcus…"

She was in his arms before another heartbeat had passed, her forehead pressed against his neck, her cheek resting on the cold hard edge of his armour. The buckles of the leather straps over his shoulders that held his breastplate and back plate together jabbed into her face but she didn't care. She broke down, surrendering to the pressing wave of emotions inside her and the weight of everything that had happened. She had always been strong, capable, the dependable one who everyone looked to in times of sorrow, but here in his arms she couldn't be that woman. With a soft caress and a promise to keep her safe murmured against her cheek, he stripped away her strength right down to her heart and left her quaking in his arms, afraid to come out in case the beasts had returned and she was in danger again.

He held her close, his hands rubbing her back, easing away her sobs as she pieced herself back together and slowly found her strength and her resolve to face whatever madness had descended on her world.

"Shh, Amelia. We will be somewhere safe soon enough. It is not far now." His words were pure comfort to her soul, chasing away the darkness, and she wrapped her arms around him, nestled with her back against his inner thigh, and hooked her fingers into the slots on the back plate of his armour. His arms tightened around her, drawing her deliciously closer to him, and she breathed him in. He smelt of the tinny odour of blood and dirt but underneath it all she could still smell the aftershave he wore and it transported her back to their moment in his apartment, filling her with warmth and happiness until she was no longer afraid. "I will keep you safe. I promise."

He had said that so many times now and she believed him with all of her heart. Here in his arms was the only place she felt safe.

Marcus helped her to her feet and she cleared her throat, sniffing back her tears. Her eyes widened when he slipped her shoe back on, his actions gentle and careful, and then rose to his feet. He smiled and she was glad that it was a real one this time, and then waved his hand a produced a handkerchief out of thin air.

Magic.

He held it out to her and she took it, using it to clear her tears away and dry her nose so she didn't look like a complete mess. Her stomach flipped when it came away bloodied and she touched her nose, fearing it was bleeding.

Marcus took the cloth from her and wiped her cheek and around her nose. "I am sorry. I will do a better job next time."

Next time? She had hoped this was a one time deal but Marcus made it sound as though it wasn't over yet. Would the man from the alley come after her? Would Marcus protect her if he did?

She touched her cheek.

Marcus had brushed her face back on the rooftop too. Had some of the blood sprayed onto her during the battle? Her stomach twisted and her hands shook as she looked down at her chest, afraid that she would see streaks of blood marking her as they marked him. Nothing.

"We should keep moving. Are you able to walk?"

Amelia wriggled her feet. They did feel a little better for their rest but she wasn't sure she would be able to walk far before they started to hurt again. She slipped her shoes off and held them in her left hand. The pavement carried the heat of the day and looked clean enough, and it was better than hobbling to their destination.

She nodded.

Marcus took hold of her hand again, slipping his fingers between hers, the straps of his forearm guard brushing her skin, and started walking with her past the elegant Georgian townhouses.

He hadn't been lying about the distance. They had barely walked a hundred metres before he stopped in front of one of the beautiful four storey stone buildings and looked up the height of it. He opened the black metal gate for her and led the way up the path to the stone steps and the porch.

He knocked three times on the wide black door and then moved into line with her.

No one answered.

Amelia cast a glance around the street and told herself that the monsters weren't coming when her nerves spiked. They were safe. Marcus knocked again. After a minute had passed and she had come close to knocking too, a shadow appeared on the etched glass beside the door. The black door opened to reveal a handsome tawny haired man on the other side. His broad build almost filled the doorway as he stepped forwards and looked both ways up the street before his rich brown eyes settled on Marcus.

"I received your message." He stepped back into the bright marble foyer of the house, his boots heavy on the chequered black and white floor. "Come in."

Marcus nodded and entered, bringing her with him, and stepped to one side to allow the man to close the door behind them. Amelia remained tucked behind Marcus, unsure of the newcomer. He looked stronger than Marcus and she wasn't going to let the normalness of his appearance fool her into relaxing. Marcus had looked normal once too.

The man's faded black t-shirt hugged his bulky muscles, drawn tight across his thick arms, and his deep blue jeans were taut over his muscular thighs. If he was different, like Marcus, could Marcus protect her from this man if he needed to?

"Is this the female?" The man peered around Marcus to catch a glimpse of her.

Amelia backed behind Marcus, evading him. When had Marcus told him that they were coming? He hadn't called anyone since the attack. Had he known this would happen and had warned this man in advance?

She wanted to see his face so she could read it and know whether he had, but that meant moving out into the open. If she did that, the other man would stare at her, and she wasn't in the mood to be stared at.

"Timid creature, isn't she?" the man said and defiance curled through her.

Amelia stepped out of Marcus's shadow and glared at the man. Marcus put his hand on her shoulder, steering her into his embrace and then sliding his arm around her waist. The feel of it around her bolstered her courage.

"She has been through a lot, Einar. Leave her be. I know I am asking much of you, and it had not been my intention to bring her here after the attack. I had no other choice."

"It happened again?" the man named Einar said with a quick glance over him.

Marcus nodded.

Amelia frowned. What had happened again? The attack or something else? She looked to Marcus for an explanation but he looked away from her, focusing on the other man.

"Come upstairs and we can have Taylor have a look." Einar's deep voice echoed around the hall.

Marcus followed him towards the elegant wooden staircase opposite the door in the foyer. Amelia trailed behind them, her focus on her bare feet and the treads as she followed them around the tight rectangular turns of the staircase. Taylor? Did the man have a male partner? There had been warmth in his eyes when he had said that name, deep affection that he hadn't tried to hide. She stared at his back as she trudged up the stairs. Strands of his mousy hair had fallen out of the short ponytail at the nape of his neck, curling around his ears. Marcus's black unruly hair grazed the nape of his neck too, not long enough to tie back into a ponytail, but she could imagine it longer and worn that way, and she liked it. It took her mind off the situation and the strange new environment around her.

Her moment of peace shattered when they entered a large elegant drawing room on the second floor. The dark antique furniture and the oil paintings that adorned the deep red walls didn't suit the man who had led them up to this room, but the masses of weaponry that occupied the sofas, chairs and even a large oak table certainly did. Everywhere she looked there were guns, swords, bows and knives.

What sort of help did Marcus want from this man and the one he had called Taylor?

Marcus moved to one side.

Amelia stopped dead.

Taylor wasn't a man after all.

A beautiful lithe woman dressed head to toe in tight fitting black clothes similar to Einar's strode towards them, her knee-high heeled boots heavy on the polished wooden floor. Long glossy dark hair curled around her face, lending her skin a milky look and brightening her blue eyes.

Amelia set her jaw and straightened in the face of the challenge.

"What's up?" Taylor said and pecked Einar's cheek before draping her arm over his shoulder and looking Marcus's way. "Romeo said there was trouble. I was getting ready to gear up."

Romeo? The unimpressed look on Einar's face suggested that it was a nickname for him that he didn't particularly like.

Amelia didn't particularly like a few things about Taylor herself. Namely the fact that she had now left Einar's side and was stalking across the room towards Marcus, her sultry smile directed straight at him.

"I need to know about any demon activity in the city. Especially about any black skinned demons that can materialise weapons," Marcus said and Taylor's pretty face turned thoughtful. Amelia looked across the room at Marcus. Had he gone crazy at the same time as she had? Demons? She took in all the weapons again and then Marcus and decided that demons were actually looking like a reasonable explanation for what had happened tonight.

She had always been sceptical about the supernatural, but Marcus had killed two black creatures with flame red eyes and sharp teeth right in front of her. Demons were real. These people clearly knew about them and Marcus had come to get more information on their enemy. Which was insane.

Taylor looked cagey and fiddled with one of the knives strapped to her sides below her arms. Each knife had a ring on the end that Amelia supposed was so the beautiful woman could quickly unleash them.

"Taylor?" Einar said and she closed her eyes.

"I know them," she whispered and a nervous edge entered her blue eyes when she fixed them on Marcus. "Angels."

Marcus and Einar both stepped towards her.

"Hell's angels? I thought they had a human appearance?" Marcus said and Taylor nodded.

"They do normally… but that isn't their true appearance. In reality, they're black skinned, with red eyes and sharp teeth, larger than human, and can materialise objects in much the same way as you boys. I guess that part is left over from being an angel."

Amelia found it difficult to keep up with the conversation. Angels. Hell's angels, but she suspected they weren't the sort who rode motorbikes. Materialising things like Marcus and Einar could.

Marcus had made a tissue appear in the street, and had changed the handle of the blade at his waist into a staff, creating a spear. Supernatural powers. What had she gotten herself into?

"They came after Amelia. I need to stay here a while, not for long. Just until I know it is safe and we can move again. I need to know that she is safe." Marcus's words warmed her heart and she wanted him to see how much they had affected her.

She stepped forwards and all eyes were on her.

Taylor raked a quick assessing gaze over her and then looked back at Einar. "You didn't mention mortal female in the Marcus-has-a-problem report."

"You could consider her the source of the problem." Einar picked up a crossbow.

Amelia's eyes shot wide, locked on the weapon, and her pulse rocketed. "Now wait a minute."

She held her hands up and Marcus stepped forwards, towards Taylor and Einar, placing himself between her and them.

"No one here will hurt you, Amelia," he said without looking at her and Einar eyed the crossbow, an apologetic look entering his dark brown eyes as he lowered it.

"I wasn't meaning to shoot you. I was just checking it over before patrol tonight."

She wasn't sure whether to feel relieved or not. The flood of adrenaline caused by the thought of coming under attack again swept her along.

"What the hell is going on?" Amelia moved further into the room, defiant of her fear and resolved to face whatever insane suggestions they spouted.

It was Marcus who spoke.

"You are in danger." The soft tone of his voice would have soothed her if she hadn't been hanging on every word.

"Danger?" She turned towards him. The warmth in his icy blue eyes calmed her a little but not enough that the tremble running through her body stopped. The thought that she was still in danger brought everything back and she wasn't sure that she was strong enough to face more of the creatures that Marcus had fought let alone anything worse. Would other demons be coming after her? Why? What had she done to deserve this? Her life was bad enough already.

Marcus moved closer and took hold of her hand again, his fingers pressing into her palm and his thumb resting gently across her knuckles, and nodded.

"It is my mission to protect you, Amelia, and has been from the moment you were born…" His hesitation sent her blood thundering and breath stuttering.

She wasn't sure what she had expected him to say but the words that left his sensual lips dropped on her like a tonne of bricks and the shockwave carried away her fear, leaving her empty inside.

"I am an angel."

Amelia stared at him for a few seconds, waiting for him to tell her that it was a joke, and that none of this was real, and perhaps even that it was just a horrible dream brought about by a fainting fit when she had been mugged, but none of it happened.

So she laughed.

His expression remained deadly serious.

This wasn't happening. The quiet voice inside her said that it was and it was real, and she had better start accepting it or she wasn't going to survive whatever was after her. Marcus was an angel, sent to watch over her and protect her, to keep her safe from the monsters that were out to get her.

It felt so impossible though.

She looked to Einar and Taylor, hoping to catch a glimpse of humour in their faces so Marcus would give up and tell her that he was kidding, but both of their expressions remained stony.

An angel.

"If you're an angel, where are the wings—" Her face fell as it hit her and their plunge from the roof came back in glorious Technicolor. It all made a hideous sort of sense that she didn't like because it meant she could no longer deny what he was telling her and had to admit that this whole crazy scenario was real. "That's what you looked worried about."

Marcus turned his head away from her.

He had expected to fly when he had leapt off the roof and it hadn't happened.

"I had thought you were free of the curse." Einar's voice was loud in the silent room even though Amelia was certain he had barely whispered.

Marcus shook his head, dropped his chin, and stared at the floor, despondence flowing from him and into her. A curse? Had something stopped his wings from appearing? Why was she even starting to believe all this?

She recalled the two slits in the back of his blue and silver armour and stared at his chest. Without thinking, she moved around him and touched one of the slits on his back plate, running her finger down the inside of it. It was wide enough to accommodate three of her fingers side by side, if not more. Her fingertip grazed Marcus's skin and he inhaled sharply and closed his eyes. She frowned at his armour and the fragment of his tattoo that she could see through the opening. Wasn't it a tattoo?

"Would you like me to take a look?" Taylor said and Marcus nodded.

Amelia reluctantly stepped back, giving Taylor room as she rounded Marcus, and then took another step away when Marcus started to unbuckle his chest armour. Jealousy coiled and hissed inside her as he removed the back plate and the breastplate, revealing his body, and set them down on the nearest dark antique armchair. Einar looked at her, cocking his head to one side, and she glanced away, a blush threatening to colour her cheeks. She didn't want a complete stranger to see how flustered she was by the sight of Taylor so close to Marcus. It hurt when Taylor moved closer still, her delicate fingertips following the beautiful sweeping and curling design of the grey-blue wings on his shoulder blades just as Amelia had wanted to that night in her apartment. They shimmered as though a wave of light had passed across them and settled again. Amelia narrowed her gaze on Taylor, no longer caring if Einar was watching her. Heat blazed to life inside her chest, anger that collided with the jealousy there and filled her mind with desires to tear Taylor away from Marcus in order to stop her from touching him.

Amelia was so focused on Taylor that she jumped when silver-blue wings erupted from Marcus's back and stretched across the room, coming close to her face. A breeze washed over her skin, tousling her shoulder-length dark hair and her pale blue dress.

She stared at Marcus's wings instead of Taylor, eyes darting over each feather, taking in every inch. They were beautiful. Her breath hitched in her throat and awe flowed through her. Was this how those kooky people felt when they witnessed angels appearing before them?

Was she one of them now?

A believer.

Marcus turned towards her as Taylor moved away, and Amelia didn't hear what they were saying to each other. She stared at him, stunned into silence by his beauty, moved by the sight of him. An angel.

Incredible.

He stood before her, bare chest rising and falling with each breath he took, toned upper arms bloodstained from his battle, and broad pale wings furling against his back. She had never witnessed something so intrinsically male and so enchanting. She couldn't find her voice to tell him how she felt, how she had always known that he was different, too handsome to be of this world and too good to be a mere mortal, and how she believed with all of her heart that no matter what dangers lay ahead of her that he would protect her.

Taylor moved into view again, running her hands down his wings from behind, and Marcus closed his eyes, as though he enjoyed the feel of her touch. Amelia looked away, darkness obliterating the light that had been in her heart, stealing away the warmth and leaving her icy cold. He had said it himself. She was a mission to him. That was all. That was why he had told her to stay away. He couldn't involve himself with a mortal.

Was Taylor an angel too?

Amelia laughed inside at how crushed she felt and tried to shrug off the pain caused by the thought that Marcus didn't like her. She barely knew him. It wasn't like her to get so emotionally tied up in someone she had only shared a kiss or two with.

But what kisses they had been.

Mind blowing.

She shoved the memory of them aside, bitterness coating her tongue as her heart ached and she tried to convince herself that she was alright. This was nothing to hurt over. It was better it ended now and she pulled herself together rather than continuing to fool herself into believing that those kisses had meant anything. She was nothing but a mission to Marcus.

God, that hurt her so much that she couldn't breathe, needed to leave the room so no one saw the tears in her eyes.

She took a step backwards towards the door, hoping to sneak out without anyone noticing. She wouldn't give them the satisfaction of seeing her cry. She would find somewhere quiet, pull her shit together and bury her feelings in her heart, and then come back and find out what the hell was happening. Another step backwards and she was close enough to the door that she could make a dash for it.

"Someone certainly wanted to seal your powers," Taylor said and the dark haired woman's eyes lit on Amelia. "Because of her?"

"I do not know." Marcus moved away from Taylor.

Amelia refused to look at him, her focus on the door at her back and escaping. He came to stand toe-to-toe with her, caught her cheek in his palm and raised her head, and she couldn't avoid looking at him. He frowned into her eyes and she felt as though he was searching for something or trying to see inside her heart.

She closed it off to him by shutting her eyes.

He blew out a sigh and then stroked her cheek.

Amelia hated the warmth that caress caused and how her body betrayed her, flushing with desire as it had done when they had kissed.

"Amelia," he husked and she fluttered her eyes opened and looked back into his. There was hurt in them again, darkening his strange silver-blue irises, and she felt as though they were reflecting all of her feelings. His dark eyebrows pinched together in a frown and he swept his thumb over her cheek, erasing the moisture gathered below her eye. He sighed again and a deep desire to cup his cheek in return filled her. She wanted to take away the pain in his eyes, and wanted him to take away the hurt in her heart in exchange. "I must report what happened. Will you be alright here without me? I won't be long. Promise."

Amelia wasn't sure what she would be if he left her alone with two people she didn't know. She wasn't in the mood for company at all. Her head and heart were at war over him and she couldn't deal with it at the same time as trying to come to terms with what was happening and all the crazy stuff that she had seen and heard tonight. She wanted to sit on one of the dark sofas in the cluttered room and stare into the distance until everything had soaked in and she had made sense of it.

And she wanted Marcus to stay with her while that happened.

She wanted to feel his arms around her again and have him tell her that everything would be okay, and that she was wrong about him and he did feel something for her. She wanted him to kiss her again, because then she would know that what had happened between them last night hadn't been a lie and she wasn't the only one who felt something.

The look in his eyes said it couldn't be though. He had emphasised 'must'. While it warmed her to know that he didn't want to leave her, the knowledge that he was going to left her cold at the same time.

"What's happening?" She couldn't let him go without knowing. She wasn't sure what she was asking about. What was happening between them or what was happening in the world and why did it involve her?

He closed his eyes, sighed, and then met hers again.

"I only know that it is my destiny to protect you." He caressed her cheek, his fingers travelling down it to her jaw, and then lowered his hand to his side. "I will try to find out more from my superior. The men tonight were meant to stop me. I sent one of them for questioning. Perhaps Heaven will know by now what they wanted with you."

He smiled and there was so much sorrow in it that she wanted to take hold of his hand to comfort him.

A bright shaft of light like the one that had encased the demon on the rooftop shot down over him and her heart skipped a beat before smashing hard against her ribs. She reached for him, afraid that the light would hurt him. He closed his eyes, tilted his head towards the ceiling, and then disappeared. The beam faded, leaving her vision dull.

"What the hell was that?" She stepped forwards into the spot where Marcus had been and looked up as Marcus had. "Is he hurt?"

Einar shook his head when her eyes lit on him. "It is merely the most expedient method of travel to Heaven. I take it Marcus used something similar on one of the demonic angels?"

Amelia nodded absently, her focus split between listening to Einar and trying to figure out what had happened to Marcus. Had he really gone to Heaven? It seemed incredible that it actually existed. All of it was incredible and hard to believe, but she could no longer deny it was real. Angels. Heaven. God and the Devil. Hell. All of it was real.

Her head felt as though it was going to explode.

"Heaven will question the Hell's angel and Marcus may discover why they are targeting you. He might be gone a while though."

She didn't like the sound of that. Her gaze swept across the room to Einar where he stood near a low coffee table cluttered with weapons. Her pulse throbbed in her temples, fear threatening to rear its ugly head again as she looked from the weapons to Taylor and back to Einar. Marcus had said she would be safe with them. She hoped he was right.

"Why don't you make yourself comfortable?" Taylor's soft and soothing tone did nothing to allay Amelia's growing fears.

Only Marcus's safe return could do that.

She looked down at her right hand.

She hadn't managed to touch him. She had wanted to. She didn't like to see the sadness in his eyes. Whenever he looked like that, she wanted to hold him and tell him that it was all going to work out and that they would make it through this.

His armour was gone from the armchair. Amelia walked over to it, sat down, and curled up, holding her knees to her chest and staring at the wooden floor.

A moment later, she lifted her head and looked across the room at Einar and then Taylor.

"So where are your wings?"

CHAPTER 8

Taylor laughed. It wasn't an awkward giggle or shy chuckle. It was a full-blown laugh.

"I don't have wings. Silly. I'm a demon."

Amelia leaned back in her chair and eyed the woman closely. She didn't look like those demons she had seen on the rooftop, but then they had looked human originally too.

"She isn't like them," Einar said as though he had read her mind and her attention shifted to him. "As for me, I was an angel."

"Was?"

It was Taylor's turn to move forwards. She stood close to Einar and took hold of his hand. He briefly met her gaze, offering her a dazzling smile.

"My Romeo doesn't have any wings right now. We're in a bit of a pickle since Heaven frowns rather heavily on demons and angels having a relationship."

"You're fallen?" Now Amelia had heard it all. Einar was a fallen angel. What else awaited her out there? The angel of death? Gabriel from the bible? The Devil himself?

"In a way." Einar patted Taylor's hand and she nodded as though receiving a silent message.

"I'll make some tea. You could probably do with a cuppa. I'll find you something warmer to wear too. This old house can get chilly even in summer." With that, Taylor left the room.

Amelia waited for the sound of her footsteps on the stairs to disappear before returning her attention to Einar, who was busy clearing weapons off the furniture and stacking them on the large oak table near the fireplace.

"Where has Marcus gone?"

Einar stopped tidying, paused for a moment, and then crossed the room and sat on the sofa beside her armchair. He took a deep breath, sighed, and then rubbed his long tawny hair, a thoughtful shine to his brown eyes.

He pointed at the ceiling.

"Heaven?"

When he nodded, Amelia looked up, picturing the night sky beyond the roof of the townhouse. Heaven really did exist, and a fallen angel had confirmed it for her. If she'd had a shrink and had told them about the past few hours of her life, they would have thought she was crazy. Part of her still thought she was insane.

"I don't mean to sound rude, but I don't believe in God or Heaven or anything supernatural... really... so this is all a little hard to grasp."

Einar smiled. "Not even when you're staring it in the face?"

An image of Marcus dressed in armour with his pale wings stretched out shot into her mind.

Not a parlour trick.

"Have you been to Heaven?" Amelia already knew the answer to that question but hearing Einar say it would go a long way towards helping her shed the last of her disbelief.

He nodded. "Many times. I have even been in the presence of our master."

Amelia swallowed. Was he talking about God? That was too much too fast. She held back the questions that sprung to the tip of her tongue and narrowed her focus to her immediate situation, pushing away thoughts of the universe, higher powers and the fact that humans had been right to believe someone was watching over them.

She stared at her knees. Someone was definitely watching over her. Marcus had been there for her whole life. He had seen everything she had done. Her cheeks flushed with fire. God, she hoped he really hadn't seen everything. No wonder he hadn't wanted to get involved with her.

"I understand that it must be difficult to take it all in," Einar said in an intentionally soothing tone of voice and touched her hand. "Marcus was under strict orders not to reveal himself to you or I'm sure he would have mentioned something before things got this far."

"What do you mean, got this far?" The look on Einar's face suggested he was talking about their relationship rather than Marcus's mission to protect her.

"Marcus has watched over you since your birth. He has always been there for you."

Amelia frowned. He was ignoring her question.

"So where was he when I was going through Hell with my mum's death and all those bastards… why didn't he protect me then?" Tears rose into her eyes but she sniffed them back, unwilling to crumble under the weight of hurt and the fear that filled her whenever she thought about her mother.

It had killed her to wake one morning three years ago to a phone call from her father telling her that her mother had been murdered during a robbery at their home. Since then, she had felt as though her life had been slowly circling a plughole, ready to slip down it into oblivion at a moment's notice. Recently, she had been thinking more and more about her mother, and the terrible things that happened in the world, and that she was never going to find her feet in life and be truly happy. Things had gone downhill almost three weeks ago when someone had broken into one of the ground floor apartments in her building. Everything she had felt when her mother had died had come back full force. The fear. The pain. She no longer felt safe in her own apartment and feared that if she slept in her room, someone would break in and she wouldn't be able to escape. If she woke and the television was off, she panicked. She was petrified of dying.

If Marcus had been watching over her when her mother had died, why hadn't he done something to take her pain away or protect her from it by stopping it from ever happening? If he was an angel, why couldn't he take all the fear and the hurt away?

"We are not omniscient. We cannot see the future and know what will happen, or change the past. Marcus's mission was to protect you without influencing your life. He watched you from Heaven. When his superior deemed it necessary to watch over you from Earth, they sent Marcus here."

Hadn't they given Marcus a choice in the matter?

Maybe she had been wrong about him. He wasn't distant because he went from one bad experience to the next like she did or because he was an angel. He remained detached from everyone because he didn't want to be here.

He hadn't wanted to come to Earth. Where did that leave her?

Marcus had been different around her these past few days. He hadn't kept his distance as he did with others.

She looked down at her knees, wishing it was Marcus here telling her these things so she could ask him the questions burning in her heart. She touched her lips, the memory of their kiss seared on them, and frowned. Had it been real to him?

Einar's gaze bore into her mouth but she couldn't bring herself out of her thoughts about Marcus in order to look at him.

The kiss had been real to her.

"How close have you got to Marcus?" Einar's tone was low and cautious, as probing as his stare.

Amelia looked up at him through her lashes, her fingers still resting against her lips. It seemed it was all the answer Einar needed because he frowned and a flicker of surprise crossed his handsome features.

He sighed, hesitated, and then spoke in an even softer voice. "Marcus has never cared for mortals, or this world… and he has never… he would kill me for mentioning it."

He couldn't stop now. She wanted to know what it was that he shouldn't tell her. The guilty edge to his expression said that it was interesting.

"What is it you're not telling me? You wouldn't answer my earlier question and now you won't tell me something about him… I want to know. Please? If you know something that will set my head straight and stop it from exploding from trying to figure everything out, then tell me. You're an angel. That means you're supposed to be good and nice to people."

He smirked, as though he wasn't at all required to be nice to people and wanted to remind her of that. She had taken onboard what he had said about Marcus. Marcus didn't like people. Did he like her?

"I came through the ranks with Marcus. We were reborn at the same time and we have been friends ever since. Marcus has rarely ventured to Earth and in all the times he has, well… he has never… been… with a female as far as I know."

Amelia stared wide-eyed at him.

If that meant what she thought it did, then Marcus would definitely be angry with Einar for telling her.

"He's never?" Taylor's voice coming from the doorway caused Amelia and Einar to look around. Taylor looked as shocked as Amelia felt. She walked into the room and set a tray of tea things down on the coffee table in front of the sofa where Einar sat and then frowned at him as though he had said something crazy. "From what I gather, you boys are chocked full of passion… how could he have never?"

Einar's cheeks coloured and he smiled awkwardly at Amelia. "She's right."

Chocked full of passion. Marcus had certainly kissed the breath from her and the way he had pinned her to the wall had filled her mind with a thousand wicked scenarios. A frown slowly worked its way onto her face as she thought about the past few days and how Marcus had flitted between warm and open with her, and closed off and icy.

"Marcus is the most loyal and honourable angel I've met, and he has served Heaven his whole life—"

Amelia cut Einar off. "He's never loved."

A shiver tumbled down her spine.

Marcus had avoided human contact and he had been awkward around her at times, especially after she had kissed him. Her eyes shot wide. Oh Lord. She had been all hideously forward with him, suggesting that he could satisfy her without a doubt, and then he had told her they had to take things slowly.

Her cheeks blazed.

It wasn't her fault. The man broadcasted sexy and passionate, and it hadn't once crossed her mind that he might have never had a partner.

"Well, bloody hell." Taylor slumped onto the sofa opposite the one Einar occupied. "This is a new one on me."

"Not a word, Taylor." Einar frowned at her and she pouted before nodding.

"Fine. I won't tease him about it. I think it's going to take all night for it to sink in." Her blue gaze slid to Amelia and she smiled wickedly. "I take it you haven't deflowered him?"

Amelia buried her face in her knees, cheeks scalding hot. "No."

Why was this happening to her?

"I didn't know," she said to her knees and then leaned back into the armchair, tipped her head back and stared at the ceiling. "He didn't seem inexperienced when he kissed me."

"Don't let it bother you. If he's anything like my Romeo in the passion stakes, you'll be in for a wild rodeo ride regardless of experience."

Out of the corner of her eye, Einar turned bright red.

"Something I said?" Taylor's tone had turned mischievous.

Einar exploded into a tirade about how inappropriate it was for her to talk about that sort of thing and Taylor countered it with the fact that he had just announced Marcus's probable virginity to them. Amelia listened to their argument, using it as a distraction from her thoughts, but Marcus crept back into them.

She didn't care if he was inexperienced or not. He had never been with a woman before, which meant that she had been his first kiss. Judging by his reaction, he had enjoyed it and had wanted more last night.

Not just last night.

There had been moments this evening where she had felt he might kiss her, and times when he had been gentle with her, tender almost, and made her feel as though he really cared for her.

The next time she saw him, she would ask him the question burning in her heart.

Was she more than a mission to him?

CHAPTER 9

Marcus beat his wings, stopping high in the cool air above the dark city of London far below him. He hovered there, flapping his wings at a leisurely tempo to keep him stationary, and scoured the myriad of twinkling streetlights. It was like looking at some strange new version of the stars at his back. This high up, he couldn't make out the buildings and cars were mere flashes of white or red in the blackness. Silence reigned, cocooning him and giving him respite from the pandemonium of the mortal realm. He could never understand how they could live at such a fast pace, flitting from one thing to the next, cramming their lives with meaningless tasks that filled their short hours on Earth. If he were mortal, he would take things slowly and indulge in every little thing, giving it the time it deserved so his life would have been a full and meaningful one.

If he were mortal.

As an angel, he didn't have to worry about a lack of time, although he wasn't immortal and could die. He hadn't felt aware of that in all his lifetime as much as he had the past few days with Amelia. Something about her made him aware of the difference in their life spans and how easily either of them could die. If Amelia died, her soul would pass through into his domain, and she would recall her life and the things they had shared.

If he died, he would be instantly reborn as he was now only without his memories, left with only a vague notion of his previous life.

He wouldn't remember her.

And he wanted to.

With a heavy beat of his wings, he shot down towards the city, cutting through the cold air that buffeted against him, and spread his wings at the last moment, barely stopping himself from crashing into the ground. The thrill that bolted through him brought him to life, sending his blood rushing in his veins and his heart thundering. He flapped his wings and gently touched down outside Einar's house and then looked up the height of the pale stone building to the lit windows near the top.

Was Amelia still awake?

He had been gone for hours. After entering Heaven and washing the blood off himself, he had reported to his superior and the other two angels. It had taken longer than usual this time. There had been questions about the demons that had attacked Amelia. His superior had reported that the one he had sent to Heaven had killed himself in transit. It must have taken a lot of the demon's power to break free of the light's hold and move enough to kill itself. Why had it done such a thing? What information had it been protecting?

When Marcus had mentioned that his wings had failed to appear, his superior had sent him to report to the medical staff and undergo an examination. The results were inconclusive and they had suggested again that it was a psychological problem now rather than the curse.

He didn't believe that for one second. Not this time. All his focus had been on flying and taking Amelia somewhere safe, far away from London. When his wings hadn't materialised, and he had plummeted onto the roof of the next building, he had changed his plans and decided to go to see Einar instead. Why would he subconsciously stop his wings from appearing when in doing so he placed Amelia in more danger? She would have been safer away from this city with only him. The demons after her would have found it difficult to track them. Now he had to rely on Einar to protect them too. He wasn't sure how long it would be before the demons found them but there had to be something he could do to buy himself more time. Could he take Amelia away now? His wings were working again after all.

He furled them against his back and ascended the pale stone steps to the porch of the townhouse. Einar was quicker to answer the door this time. He must have sensed Marcus's presence and heard the message he had sent to him while en route from Heaven. At least being fallen didn't strip Einar of his powers.

Marcus glanced down at the cut across his thigh. He had forgotten to mention it during his medical examination so it had gone unhealed and now it was starting to bother him again.

He stepped into the marble foyer of the house and silently followed Einar up the staircase, focusing to put his wings away at the same time. He frowned when he entered the dark red drawing room and Amelia wasn't there.

"Where is she?" Marcus noted that Taylor wasn't present either. Had the two women gone somewhere? Had something happened? A spark of panic set his heart racing again. If someone had come after her, Einar and Taylor would have protected her. There was no reason for him to fear but he couldn't stop himself. Whenever he thought about what had happened and how Amelia might have been hurt, an urge to see her flooded him and he couldn't ignore it.

"Asleep." Einar motioned for Marcus to follow him and sat down on one of the two dark antique sofas that faced each other across a rectangular wooden coffee table. "Sit."

Marcus did, choosing to seat himself on the sofa opposite Einar, and frowned. He had the strangest feeling that Einar was about to pull rank on certain matters and a desire to remind him that they were almost the same age eclipsed his need to see Amelia.

"Don't look at me like that." Einar casually leaned back into the corner of the sofa, his black t-shirt blending into the dark material covering it. "You seem terribly in a hurry to see Amelia… concerned about her?"

Marcus's face darkened. "Of course I am. It is my mission to protect her."

Einar smiled knowingly. "Just a mission?"

"What else would she be?"

"You might be fooling yourself, but you are far from fooling me, my old friend."

Marcus wasn't fooling himself at all, and he had wanted to ask Einar for advice, but not face-to-face. It was embarrassing. He couldn't detach himself from the situation as easily as he could have if they had been talking on the phone or messaging each other through telepathy.

He exhaled and slouched into the sofa, grimacing when his armour pressed against his back in a painful way.

"What am I supposed to do?" he whispered, more to himself than his friend.

Einar leaned forwards, his elbows resting on his jean-clad knees, and smiled. "You do whatever comes naturally. It is not rocket science, Marcus. It must feel as though it is right now, but if you follow your feelings, I promise you it will be worth it."

Marcus closed his eyes, unsure what it felt like at the moment. Something far more difficult to comprehend than mere science, that was for sure. Amelia wanted him and he wanted her with all of his heart, he just wasn't sure how to proceed without making a complete fool of himself. She was expecting something that he couldn't guarantee, and while his passion for her burned like an inferno within him, fuelling the desire he felt for her and the feelings that just the sight or smell of her evoked in him, he was afraid that he wouldn't live up to that expectation. If he screwed things up, would she want nothing to do with him?

A small recess of his heart wished that he had followed his fellow warriors lead in all the times they had been on Earth together, celebrating a moment of freedom at the end of laborious missions, and had spent time with some females so he would know how to please Amelia.

"Do not think such things, Marcus."

Marcus looked up, meeting Einar's deep brown eyes, and then looked away towards the dark fireplace at the other end of the room. He hadn't said anything out loud so Einar must have read his fear in his expression.

"Would it make you feel better if I told you that she likes you?"

It did, although Marcus didn't want to know how Einar knew. What had they talked about since he had left them to report in? He had a sneaking suspicion that he had become the topic of conversation and looked back at Einar, trying to see if he had mentioned anything that he shouldn't have. Einar smiled warmly at him.

"Amelia likes you. She looked ready to fight Taylor when she was inspecting your curse."

She had? His eyebrows rose and he couldn't remain casual any longer. He leaned forwards, mirroring Einar by resting his elbows on his bare knees, closing the distance between them.

"Jealousy is one emotion that is not difficult to detect in a woman. They tend to wear it on the outside for all to see when it surfaces within them. Amelia did not like Taylor touching you, and the anger and hurt in her face confirmed her feelings to me. She likes you, my friend, although I cannot understand why." Einar's smile became a grin. "You have probably done nothing but distance yourself from her."

Marcus shook his head at how well Einar knew him. He had struggled with his feelings for Amelia, conflicted by them and his duty, and had tried to maintain a suitable distance from her. It had been slipping little by little, with each moment they spent together, and now it felt as though he couldn't continue that way. He needed to be close to her and not only so he could protect her.

"What does Heaven know about what happened?" Einar said and Marcus was thankful for the change in topic.

"More than they are telling me, that's for sure." He clasped his hands together in front of him and frowned at them. "They reiterated that I had to be on my guard and that my final task is not yet done. I have to continue to protect Amelia from the demons."

"You believe they're withholding information from you. Understandable. I have completed several missions in my years where they have intentionally kept things they have seen from me. We must remember that it is not our duty to question why they do such things, but to obey the orders they give to us."

Marcus wasn't sure that he could obey some of the orders they had given him recently. Seduce Amelia? At least they had acknowledged that it was beyond the time for that now. Amelia knew what he was and knew that she was in danger. He had gained her trust without resorting to using her feelings against her, and he was glad of it because it meant that whatever happened between them now, it was because of his feelings for her and hers for him, not because he was under orders.

"Where is she?" he said again and Taylor walked into the room, tying her long black hair up into a ponytail.

"She's sleeping." Taylor walked over to Einar and slumped onto the couch beside him with a weary sigh. "She's been through a lot. You've got to give the girl credit for not collapsing or having a meltdown. It must be hard for a human to take in all our crazy shit and come out the other end a sane person. She's strong."

"I know." Marcus focused, wanting to sense where she was, but the only people he could pinpoint were Einar and Taylor. He turned a questioning frown on Einar. "What room is she in?"

"If the reason for your frown is a lack of Amelia on your senses, then fear not. She is safe." Einar rose from the sofa and held his hand out to Taylor. "Taylor has sent her to sleep. She will be off the radar of any creature, no matter how powerful, until she wakes."

Taylor stood with Einar's assistance and Marcus followed suit.

"A power?" Marcus looked to Taylor for confirmation. She nodded.

"I can create spaces in people's minds, a world where they can hide. It drops you off this realm and into another personal to you, leaving you literally out of this world." Taylor smiled at him. "I'll send you deep into sleep too so they can't find you either. When you're both out for the count, we'll go and see what information we can beat out of the local lowlifes for you."

Marcus nodded his thanks and followed her out of the room. When they entered a large pale green bedroom on the next floor up, he paused. A single lamp on the bedside table illuminated the room and Amelia where she lay under the dark covers of a double bed. The only bed.

Einar clapped a hand down on his shoulder. "She's out for the count. No need to worry."

Marcus brushed his hand away and frowned at him. He wasn't worried. He just hadn't expected that he would be sharing a bed when Taylor sent him to sleep. What if Amelia woke and he was lying next to her? What would she do then?

A gut-tugging jolt inside him said that she could do anything she pleased and he wouldn't care as long as he got to kiss her again, or maybe more. He craved the contact with her more than he hungered for anything else. He could forgo food and even flying if it meant he could touch her.

"Strip," Taylor said, matter of fact, snapping Marcus out of his thoughts.

"Is that necessary?" He looked at them both.

Einar glanced at Taylor and something unspoken passed between them and then he nodded. "Not down to nothing, but you would hardly be comfortable sleeping in your armour."

Marcus could see where this was going and would be having words if his suspicions were confirmed, but reasoned that armour was uncomfortable to sleep in and removed it, placing it down on a chair in the corner of the pale room. When he was down to his dark blue loincloth, he turned back to face Einar.

Who frowned at his legs, crossed the room, and held his hand out over the cut on his thigh. Marcus gritted his teeth against the pain as warm golden light shone down from Einar's palm, caressing his skin, and the wound there slowly closed, leaving nothing behind.

"Thanks," he said and then eyed the bed, and then Taylor and Einar.

There was mischief on their faces but he went to the bed, lay on top of the covers on his back next to Amelia and settled his head on the pillows. He could smell her. Her soft fragrance filled his head, soothing his tension away and relaxing him. It felt good being so close to her, so good that he wanted to reach under the covers and take hold of her hand. Instead, he placed his hands on his stomach and waited.

Taylor appeared above him and rested her hand on his forehead. A part of him expected it to turn out to be a strange sort of joke and that Amelia was just asleep because of the late hour and everything that she had been through today, but as he stared into Taylor's blue eyes, his head started to feel heavy and foggy.

"Go to sleep, Marcus," she whispered and he fought the rising desire to drift away, trying to focus on her and his mission. He should be out there searching for the demons with Taylor and Einar, not hiding away in some other world. His eyelids slipped shut and he didn't have the energy to lift them again.

A chasm opened below him and he fell into it, spiralling down into the dark towards a shimmering light far below. He tried to resist it but the heat washing over him was too comforting and relaxing, subduing him and making him feel heavy.

Taylor's voice rang softly through the darkness, warm with a hint of amusement.

"Sweet dreams, Romeo."

CHAPTER 10

It was the location that alerted Marcus to the fact that this wasn't his world.

A golden sunset filled the sky directly before him, the sun slowly sinking into the infinite ocean, its light rippling on the water and sparkling like diamonds. The soft sound of waves gently breaking against the pristine white sandy shore filled the silence along with the rustling of the swaying palm trees in the light refreshing breeze that came from the sea, carrying a salty tang and her fragrance.

Amelia.

She sat on a chipped white metal pole that created a railing along the seafront, separating the sun-bleached wooden boardwalk from the sand, her back to him and shoulder-length dark hair dancing as the breeze caught it.

The sound of the ocean and the warm breeze soothed away the anger he felt over Taylor and Einar's trick on him. They had sent him into Amelia's inner world rather than to his own. He would have a word with his old friend when he woke. This wasn't allowing things to progress naturally at all. This was matchmaking.

Marcus walked across the boardwalk to Amelia and leaned his elbows on the metal railing that ran at waist height to him. Amelia didn't look down at him. She continued to stare into the distance, her skin glowing in the warm light of sunset and her hair threaded with golden highlights. Marcus drank his fill of her beauty, taking his time to put her face to memory as it looked in this moment. A slight smile played on her lips, shining in her eyes, and he knew without asking that she was happy here.

It was definitely her world.

But it wasn't her happiness that gave it away.

He hated sand.

It got in his feathers.

He looked down at himself and shook his head when he saw that he was only wearing a pair of loose black swimming shorts. That wasn't going to happen either. Water was a pain to get out of his feathers, worse than sand, and for some reason his wings were out and he couldn't convince them to go away.

Were they out because Amelia wanted to see him this way? This was her world which meant that in part she was controlling it, and controlling him too.

When he turned to ask her about his wings and whether she wanted to see them, his gaze caught on the skimpy black bikini top she wore. He stared unabashed at the flimsy triangles of material barely covering her breasts, his stomach tightening and temperature rising, and then slowly lowered his eyes to her hips. A short black near-see-through strip of material covered her from waist to just past her backside, tied on her hip closest to him. The light fabric fluttered in the breeze, revealing her creamy slender thigh.

"It's peaceful here," she said, distant sounding. "Am I dreaming?"

Marcus forced his focus back up to her face. "I do not think so. We are both awake. Taylor can make a world in which we can hide but I am not sure how long it can last."

"I'm scared, Marcus," she whispered and her grey eyes finally came to meet his.

"Of me?" He wasn't sure why he said it. The gnawing feeling that she feared him now had lingered at the back of his mind since he had rescued her from the Hell's angels and revealed his true self to her, but he hadn't intended to say anything about it. Her look instantly softened, warming again, and she smiled.

"No. You're the only thing that doesn't frighten me." She went to touch him but he shifted to one side, enough that her attempt failed, and stared at the ocean.

How could she look on him so kindly and with such compassion? She had seen him fight those Hell's angels, had witnessed him kill without hesitation and had been covered in blood because of him. He had shown his darkest side to her and she still looked at him with warmth in her grey eyes. It astounded him and drove him to question her, to confess the things that he had done and the reason he had warned her away from him. Need burned deep in his heart, a desire to know if she really could feel something for a man like him.

"I am a guardian… but there are times when I have been a warrior…" Marcus couldn't bring himself to look at her. He clenched his fists and stared intently at the sunset, afraid of what he would see if he turned to face Amelia. Would she look upon him with such warmth after his confession? He didn't think so, and while he wanted to stop now before he ruined everything between them, the greater part of him needed her to know what sort of man he was and why he felt he didn't deserve the love of such a pure and beautiful woman. She might have managed to convince herself that he had only done what was right when he had killed those demons in front of her but she had feared him at the time. He knew that. He had frightened her. Now he had to do that again so she would know him, and he would see in her eyes and hear in her voice whether she could ever bring herself to love him. "A bringer of death. I am not a good man, Amelia. I have killed many without remorse… hundreds… if not thousands."

He uncurled his hands and stared at his palms. Hands made for killing in the name of Heaven. He had followed those orders without question, obeying his superiors, loyal to his duty and happy to carry it out. Not once in his life had he regretted the things he had done. Not until he had met her, and then he had wished it all away.

He had wanted to be a better man so she would love him.

He could see that now. For all his attempts to remain distant from her, he had fallen for her, but new to the experience, he had not realised his feelings until she had first touched him, thrilling him with little more than a brief caress and bringing him to life with emotions he had never known existed.

"If you've killed, then I believe you did so out of loyalty, just as Einar said about you. You killed to protect others, and to protect me. I can't offer you absolution, Marcus, but I can forgive you for killing others in order to protect me. You are a good man. I believe that."

Marcus looked up to find her watching him, her grey eyes not full of icy cold or hatred, but full of the warmth and tenderness that had been in her words. There was no fear in her, only a calm that he knew was real and it touched him, warming his chest and making him crave a stronger connection to her. She smiled, twisted towards him, still holding on to the railing she sat on with her left hand, and stroked the unruly strands of his hair from his face.

And he stared at her.

Awed and transfixed by the beautiful acceptance she showed towards him.

For her, he could be a good man. He could be the man that she deserved.

"Was that why you stopped me the other night when we kissed, or was it because you're an angel and it was wrong?" She lowered her hand from his face.

"No." His eyes followed her hand, leapt to her thigh, and then he lifted them to her face again.

There was such understanding in her eyes.

"Was it because you've never been with a woman?"

Marcus exhaled and stared out to sea. The sun had set and a full moon was rising in its place, beautiful as it hung over the darkening ocean.

"Einar told you?"

Amelia made a small noise and then touched his hands where they were clasped together in front of him. He looked up at her, wanting to explain and needing to ask her not to believe him any less of a man because of it, and she dipped her head towards him. She kissed him before he could utter a word, her lips soft against his, slowly shifting in mesmerising waves that drew him into responding. He leaned into the kiss, eager to taste her again and believe that this was another good sign. When she broke away, briefly resting her forehead against his before sitting up, she was smiling at him.

"I think it's beautiful that you waited so long," she whispered and his heart leapt in response, turning his insides with it. He stared up at her, torn between kissing her again and saying something that would bring another smile to her face.

"I never really thought about it. I never cared about mortals." Marcus straightened and then cupped her cheek, keeping her eyes on his. "But I care about you."

Amelia's smile was brilliant and he thought that she would kiss him, but she slipped down from the railing on the other side, landing softly in the sand.

A mixture of light from the strings of white lights that hung between the palm trees, illuminating the boardwalk, and the moon played on her, turning her skin pale and eyes dark. It had turned dark quickly and the moon was far higher in the inky sky now. How long had the kiss lasted? It had felt like barely a heartbeat had passed but it must have been close to an hour.

She crooked a finger at him.

"I think we should swim."

Marcus warily eyed the sand and then the water. "Unwise. I don't seem to be able to put my wings away."

She looked at them and his eyes widened when they shrank into his back.

"No excuses." She reached over the railing to him.

Marcus vaulted it and looked down at the warm sand beneath his bare feet. Amelia laughed and ran down to the sea, leaving footprints in the soft sand for him to follow. He hoped his wings didn't reappear. Just as he looked up, Amelia untied the slip of black material around her waist and tossed it aside.

A deep pulse of arousal beat through him at the sight of her in such a small scrap of fabric. Her bikini bottoms didn't cover her buttocks at all. A single dark line disappeared between them, leaving them on display. Hell. His groin responded in an instant, cock twitching against the loose swimming trunks. He had been intent on mentioning that he couldn't swim but the thought of playing with her in the shallows and seeing her wet all over had him striding towards the sea.

She smiled and crooked her finger again, and Marcus could only obey. He followed her into the shallows and then hesitated as a gentle wave came rolling in and the dark water reached his waist. The current wasn't strong but he didn't dare venture further out. Taylor hadn't mentioned what would happen if one of them got into trouble inside this world. Would his consciousness be trapped here if he drowned?

Amelia took hold of his wrist and tried to tug him into deeper water. He stood firm and she frowned.

"You can't swim, can you?"

"I don't know. I have never tried." He might be able to swim. Angels sometimes remembered how to do things that they had experienced in a previous lifetime. If he had known how to swim then, he could instinctively remember it now, but he wasn't willing to risk drowning in order to find out.

It didn't seem to bother Amelia. She splashed his bare chest and face, and he responded by sweeping his arm across the warm water, sending a wave rushing towards her. She ducked under the surface and the water settled around him, lapping at his waist. He turned on the spot, searching for Amelia. When she didn't surface after a few seconds, his pulse picked up and he waded further out, fearing that something had happened.

Something brushed his backside and he turned sharply, causing ripples to spread outwards from his chest. His senses blared in warning but he wasn't quick enough. Amelia launched out of the water, looped her arms around his neck and her legs around his hips. Her playful attack caused his heels to dig into the soft wet sand under his feet and he fell backwards, sending them both underwater.

It went straight into his mouth and stung his eyes.

He broke the surface a split-second later, coughing the vile water up, and Amelia re-emerged, her sheepish smile visible in the strong moonlight.

She swam towards him and then around him, and his anger faded away when she came to stand behind him and stroked his back.

"They're beautiful. Are they really a curse?" she whispered, her warm fingertips tracing the wings marked on his shoulder blades.

Marcus stilled, his focus so intently fixed on her that every light touch stirred his insides, fanning his desire for her. Her breath washed over his wet skin, teasing it and he closed his eyes, wanting to absorb how he felt when she was so close to him. Warm. Hungry. Mad for her.

"Apparently so," he said and she came around him. He caught her bare waist and drew her flush against him. She surprised him by taking hold of his shoulders, lifting herself up and wrapping her legs around his waist. He groaned and clutched her backside to support her, and then remembered the flimsy thing she was wearing on her lower half. He pressed his fingers into her bare bottom and groaned again, his body stirring and aching as he familiarised himself with her soft flesh.

"How did you get them?" Amelia leaned in and peppered his shoulder with kisses, gradually working her way along towards his collarbone and then his neck. He couldn't think straight to answer her when she was touching him like this. It seemed like torture to have to think at all. She placed a single wet kiss on his jaw and then leaned back and rested her hands on his chest. Her pupils were wide in the low light, darkening her eyes, and he stared into them. "Well?"

She really expected him to answer.

"I got drunk and when I came around, I was sleeping face down and couldn't call my wings. Heaven called me back to them and I discovered that someone had drawn this curse on me whilst I was unconscious."

Her hands ran up his chest to his shoulders and then she leaned towards him and caressed his shoulder blades, her breasts pressing against him.

"That's terrible."

He murmured his agreement and stared at her mouth.

"It explains why you didn't want to drink the wine. And you're really an angel?" Her eyes searched his.

Marcus nodded.

She glanced away and a sense of sorrow flowed through him. He frowned and ducked to one side, trying to see her face so he could understand the sudden change in her emotions. Her gaze met his and the edge of hurt in it compelled him to comfort her even though he wasn't sure what was wrong.

"What is it?" he whispered, his brow furrowing as he waited for her to speak.

"Einar said that you aren't omniscient… or some fancy word… that you couldn't have stopped my mother from dying… I wished that you could have."

He did too. Watching her grieve had been one of the most difficult trials he had ever endured.

"I wish I could have been there for you." He let the confession slip out quietly, unsure of whether it would only hurt her further to know that he had seen her suffering and had done nothing about it.

Amelia rested her head on his shoulder and sighed, her breath skittering over his collarbones. Marcus closed his eyes, leaned his cheek against her forehead, and held her close to him, comforting her in the way he had wanted to then. Waves lapped against them, rocking them back and forth. It had been a long time since he had felt such peace.

"I could sleep here, like this. It's so hard to sleep these days." Her words were a bare whisper and she sagged against him.

He remembered the couch in her apartment and the blanket. "You haven't been sleeping well?"

She shook her head. "Not since that break in."

Marcus frowned. He hadn't thought to piece the two together. Her mother had died during a break in and one had occurred in the apartment building they shared. It had frightened her and he hadn't noticed it. That was why her ex had shaken her up by trying to bang her door down. She had feared him breaking in and hurting her.

He wrapped his arms tighter around her and pressed her close to him, enveloping her slender form in his protective embrace. Desire to call his wings out and wrap those around her too, to cocoon her completely, ran deep in his veins but he held them at bay.

"I will never let anything happen to you, Amelia. I promised you that and I mean to keep my word." The hardness in his voice surprised him as much as the intensity of the emotions that beat in his heart at the thought of her coming under attack and being afraid.

He pressed a kiss to her forehead, rested his lips there for a few heartbeats of time, and then drew back. Amelia emerged from his embrace, her eyes sparkling with tears. He kissed away the ones that had fallen onto her cheeks. She raised her head into his kisses, until their lips were a hair's breadth apart.

"You really are an angel." Her lips brushed his as she spoke, stirring his passion.

When she went to speak again, he swooped on her lips, silencing her. Her words became a quiet moan that sent a shiver through him and he held her closer, one hand supporting her backside and the other splayed between her shoulder blades.

He didn't want to talk anymore.

He wanted to show her without words how she made him feel, how much he craved her taste and her touch, and that he needed her. He hadn't promised to keep her safe and protect her because he was an angel. He had made that vow because he was a man, and he cared about her.

Marcus ran his tongue along the seam of her mouth and she opened to him, her tongue coming out to play with his and tease it inside. He slanted his head and claimed her mouth, plundering it with his tongue and drawing another heated groan from her. She shifted against him, pressing closer until her warm body was flush against his, driving him mad with the need to caress every inch of her, to taste her and seek out her sensitive spots with his lips. The water lapped at his waist, knocking against him, and he turned with her and carried her back to the beach.

The moment he was clear of the water, he laid her down on the hard sand and covered her body with his. The heat of her overwhelmed him, pushing his desire to new heights, and he moaned into her mouth as she scored her nails over his scalp and then tangled her fingers in his hair, anchoring him to her. He wasn't going anywhere.

She tore a groan from his throat when she raised her hips into his, rubbing her warm flesh against his hard length, and he ground against her, desperate for more. Nerves surfaced, whispered doubts at the back of his mind, and he pushed them away. He would let things progress naturally. He would make love to her and bring her pleasure.

He kissed a path along her jaw, so hungry to taste her that he nipped occasionally with his blunt teeth. Each playful bite drew a deep moan from Amelia that set his blood burning hotter and hotter, until he couldn't stop himself from biting her shoulder, sinking his teeth into her soft pale skin, ravenous for her. She groaned and giggled, and he released her, panting hard when she raked her short nails down his back. The blaze that followed their trail made him shudder and moan, bucking his hips against hers. Devil.

Her legs tangled with his, her feet sliding up his calves, driving awareness of their position through him. His hips nestled between her thighs, her body burning against his where they met and pressed together. Or was that his body on fire? He thrust forwards, rubbing his aching length, desperate to feel her beneath him. It felt so damn good, she felt so damn good, and he couldn't get enough of her. He wanted to devour her, to slow down and lick and caress every inch of her but needed to feel her, to bury himself in her heat and be one with her before he exploded from the sensations overloading his mind and his body. The conflicting feelings collided inside him, driving him out of his head until he was alternating between kisses and nips on her arms and shoulders, between stealing her breath from her lips with his own and caressing her body. He wanted to touch her everywhere at once, and have her touch him.

Needed to feel her hands on his flesh.

Water lapped at his feet and then swept over him to his knees. The distraction was enough that Amelia caught him off guard when she grabbed his shoulders and rolled with him, flipping him onto his back and knocking the wind from him. He stared up at her, transfixed as she straddled his hips, the warm apex of her thighs pressed against the full length of his cock. He groaned and rolled his eyes closed when she leaned forwards, lightly running her hands over his stomach and up to his chest in swirling patterns that pushed him closer to the edge.

His fingers shook as he placed his hands on her thighs and ran them upwards towards her hips. Amelia moaned and he wanted to see her again and see the pleasure he brought her. She smiled down at him, her hair tangled and wet, sand sticking to her shoulders and arms, and then looked at her breasts, drawing his gaze there.

Marcus's lips parted as she took hold of his hands and leaned towards him. He went along with her as she brought his hands around behind her to the bow tying her bikini top in place and tugged at the ends of the black string. The two black triangles covering her breasts fell forwards and he stared at them, wishing they were out of the way and no longer obscuring his view. Amelia untied the strap around her neck and his breath shortened as the wet bikini top fell onto his stomach.

Hell.

He was aware that he didn't look particularly manly as he stared at her full breasts and their dusky pink peaks but he didn't care. It wasn't the first time he had seen a female nude, but it was Amelia. The sight of her like this, so open and vulnerable, bared for him, made his cock throb and his body tighten with the urge to be inside her.

She caught hold of his hands and brought them to her breasts as she sat back on his groin again, torturing him with her warmth. Marcus thumbed her puckered nipples, teasing them into harder peaks, and watched the myriad of feelings flicker across her face, small ripples of pleasure that brought him warmth and increased his hunger. Her pleasure was his as he studied her face and her reactions to everything that he did. She moaned and leaned back, forcing her breasts into his hands, and he squeezed them, causing her to bite her lip and utter his name in a low sexy voice.

He raised his hips into hers, grinding his hard length into her soft mound, and she tilted her head back, moaning her pleasure at the starlit heavens.

He needed more.

Without hesitation, he focused his powers on ridding himself of the remaining obstructions between them.

Nothing happened.

He had forgotten that this wasn't the real world and that it was Amelia in control here, not him. He thrilled at that and the fact that she was astride him, in command. He wanted to be the one in control but it was equally exciting, if not more so, to be submissive to her desire instead. There would be time for him to take control. They would have all the time in the world once his mission was complete and she was safe at last.

Marcus squeezed her breasts again and then slid one hand around her back, forcing her to come to him so he could taste her. She leaned over him, breasts swinging freely, and he craned his neck to watch her face as he pulled her left nipple into his mouth. She bit her lip, screwed her face up and moaned with such heated desire that his cock throbbed again. He tried to rub against her to relieve some of his ache to be inside her but couldn't reach her hips now that she was leaning over him, her body away from his. He endured the torture and focused on rolling his tongue around the sweet bud in his mouth, eliciting another groan from her.

"Marcus," she whispered and took his left hand away from her other breast and brought it down to her groin.

He was the one groaning this time as she slipped both of their hands into her bikini bottoms. His heart pounded as she released him and he eased his hand down over the soft thatch of curls and found her moist core. Hell. He swallowed, sucked harder on her nipple, and delved his fingers into her warm petals to find her aroused nub.

"Marcus," she moaned again and he swirled his fingers around, teasing her and using her breathy little moans as a guide. She arched towards him and moaned louder when he moved his hand, venturing further towards her slick centre.

Her hand came down, shifted her flimsy bottoms aside, and guided his. Marcus stilled, his task of teasing her breasts forgotten as she eased his middle finger deep into her hot body.

It took every ounce of his willpower not to climax right then.

She rose off him, bare breasts on show, a feast for his eyes, but he couldn't stop staring at her groin. Her hand held his in place, moving his finger into her hot channel, thrusting it deep before withdrawing it, and he couldn't take it when she started to rotate her hips barely inches above his. He wanted her to do that on him, for it to be his aching cock inside her not his finger. Her eyes opened and she stared down at him, her gaze locked with his in a way that mesmerised him until he lay calmly below her, drinking in her pleasure, and started to thrust his finger into her. She frowned when he withdrew his hand and then gasped when he inserted two fingers into her and pumped her slowly.

She was beautiful. The way she writhed on him, moaning and arching, her eyes flitting between holding his and closing as she frowned, stole his breath and sent his heart pounding. His whole body tensed at the sight of her and the thought of being inside her, where his fingers were. He wanted that more than anything but he wanted to bring her pleasure first and give her a moment of bliss under her instruction.

Amelia's eyes opened again and she threw her head back and jerked against his hand, his name falling from her lips with each breath she expelled. Her body throbbed around his fingers, milking them and stirring his desire into frenzied need.

"Amelia," he husked and her eyes slowly opened, fixing on him, her chest heaving as she struggled for breath. Her cheeks darkened and she glanced down, briefly teasing her lower lip with her teeth before stroking a line down his stomach towards his swimming trunks.

Marcus's eyelids fell to half mast and he struggled to keep them open as she ventured further and cupped his hard length, running her fingers over the blunt head through the wet material and teasing it. He needed to be inside her now, sheathed in her warmth, one with her.

She tugged the waist of his shorts and cool air washed over his groin, tickling his balls and length, as she lowered them around his thighs.

He looked down, following her fingers as she undid the ties on either side of her bikini bottoms and then cast them onto the sand. His heart stuttered and breath faltered but she chased away all reasonable thought when she ran her hand down his cock, revealing the crown, and then swirled her fingers around it.

He couldn't take that.

He jerked his hips up, desperate to beg her not to tease him but unable to find his voice to warn her that if she did, he wouldn't even last until he was inside her. As though she had seen his silent struggle, she took mercy on him and moved up his body until her knees were against his waist and her groin hovered above his.

"Marcus," she whispered and he looked at her, dazed with passion and burning with the need to touch her again, to kiss her. She smiled and reached over to stroke his face. "Don't try to hold back."

She couldn't know what she was asking. As he was, he was liable to hurt her in his need to have her. Unless his supernatural strength had no meaning here in her inner world. He had to be gentle with her just in case he did still have his strength. He couldn't risk hurting her.

The wicked edge to her smile said that she knew his inner fears. What else did she know about him? What powers over him did this world grant her? She could make his wings disappear with just a touch. Could she handle him and make this moment everything he had dreamed it would be?

He tilted his head back into the softer sand beneath it when she took hold of his cock and positioned him beneath her. The heat of her as the crown of his length nudged into her slick core was almost too much to bear and he gritted his teeth as she eased gently down onto it, drawing him slowly into her body. It was exquisite and he had to keep still, every muscle in his body tensed, to stop himself from climaxing. She wiggled on him, tearing a moan from his throat, and then pressed her hands into his chest and leaned over him.

He opened his eyes and stared into hers, breathing hard and searching for some control.

Amelia smiled softly and then moved, and his entire world came to pieces.

Marcus grasped her hips, eliciting a groan from her when he dug his fingers into them, and opened his mouth in a silent sigh as she rode him. He couldn't stop himself from thrusting into her, meeting her downward plunges onto his cock. She buried her nails into his chest so deeply that he was sure he would wake with marks to remember this moment by and rocked against him. It was maddening. Each time she lifted off him, cold air swept over his cock only to be chased away by the fiery heat of her as she took him back inside her tight sheath. He groaned and stared into her eyes, lost in them and the pleasure crossing her face. He thrust harder and deeper, hungry to feel her and bring her to climax again. Each deep plunge of his body into hers tore another moan from her and from him, until they were groaning together and the world disappeared around him.

"Marcus," she uttered and clenched him, her body tightening around his in a way that sent sparks skittering over his skin, and he shuddered to a halt inside her, needing a moment to regain control.

She didn't give him one. She kept riding him, thrusting down hard onto him, and leaned back. Her hands pushed against his stomach and she arched away from him, her head thrown back and her moans filling the night.

And Marcus was lost.

He moaned, clenched his teeth, and then surrendered control just as she had told him to. He clutched her hips and drove into her, seeking his release, coming undone more and more with each deep thrust of his cock into her body and each answering moan she gave. The harder he was with her, the louder she groaned, until she was holding his hands on her hips, bouncing on his length and pushing him over the edge.

Marcus slammed his hips into hers, held her firmly in place over him, and groaned as he came, his whole body throbbing with release and melting into the sand.

Amelia took hold of his hand, brought it down to her aroused nub, and made him stroke it. He teased her until she climaxed, and the feel of her body quaking around his drew a response from him that he hadn't anticipated.

His cock twitched and hunger washed through him fiercer than ever before.

CHAPTER 11

Amelia woke half expecting to find blue skies stretching above her and warm sand against her bare flesh. She stared at the smooth white ceiling until it sunk in that the delicious dream she'd just had was over now. Tilting her head to one side, a slow smile spread across her face when she saw Marcus lying beside her wearing nothing but the dark cloth thing he wore beneath his armoured skirt.

His black hair caressed his forehead in tangled waves, tempting her to reach across and sweep it back, but she didn't move. She drank in the sight of him lying with her, his face peaceful in slumber, and then raked her gazed down the length of his body.

She still wasn't sure what had happened or whether Marcus had really been there, but it had been blissful.

Unable to resist any longer, Amelia rolled onto her front beneath the covers, the thick duvet warm against her bare flesh, and combed her fingers through the overlong lengths of his hair.

A frown flickered on his brow and then his eyes slowly opened to reveal their icy irises and he turned his head towards her. The dark blue flecks in his eyes were shifting again and the more she caressed his cheek and the cut line of his jaw, the more his eyes changed, his irises brightening until they were as blue as they had been in the stairwell during their fight with the demons.

"Morning," he breathed, rolled onto his side, and drew her against him. His lips brushed hers in a tantalising kiss and he sighed.

"Pleasant dreams?" She drew back and he smiled.

"I thought we had established it wasn't a dream?" he said, sending a warm wave of relief surging through her. He lured her in for another long slow kiss that had heat pooling in her belly and her mind racing back over everything they had done on the beach.

If Einar hadn't told her that Marcus wasn't experienced with women, she never would have guessed it for herself. The man was insatiable and she could see why Taylor had been so surprised to hear that Marcus had never been with a woman before, and could agree with her that angels were definitely chocked full of passion.

It had been fun to take command of the situation at first, but Marcus had proven to her that it could be just as exciting to let him take the reins. She had never woken feeling so sated but so tired at the same time.

Amelia kissed him slowly, savouring the quietness of the moment and some time alone with him in the flesh. It was reassuring that what they had shared together in that other world was going to continue here in the real one. When he had left her to report to his superior, she had thought that he would be different again when he returned, as distant and detached as he had often been around her. The way he was kissing her now, holding her snug against his delicious body, made it feel as though that side of Marcus had never existed and that she was crazy for thinking he would want nothing to do with her. She no longer felt like only a mission to him. What Einar had told her about him and what Marcus had told her about himself, gave her a better understanding of him and why he had always been so cold around her and others in their building. He wasn't used to being around people and he didn't like it here on Earth, but she was going to do all in her power to change his mind about that at least. She would give him a reason to like being here and hopefully he would stay with her when everything was over.

He rolled onto his back, bringing her with him, and stopped kissing her. He frowned at the duvet wedged between them and tugged at it. Amelia raised herself so the blanket came free and then sighed when he pulled her back against him, his bare body warming hers. It was so easy to forget everything when he kissed her. He wasn't an angel and she wasn't in danger. It all seemed so distant and irrelevant.

She kissed him again, teasing him with sweeps of her lips that barely grazed his. He made a short noise of frustration, snaked his hand around the nape of her neck, and brought her mouth down on his. The kiss was fierce and hungry, everything that she had come to think of whenever her mind turned to him. There was so much passion and desire in him, but such tenderness too. He had held her close to him in that other world, lying on his back with her body half on his and his fingers playing in her damp hair. She had felt so tremendously at peace with him there and she had known the depth of his feelings for her. It transcended such a simple word as care. It even went beyond what she knew as love. And it was something that burned deep within her too.

Marcus's hands skimmed down her bare thighs and she tingled wherever he touched, sparks racing over her skin and burrowing deep into her belly where they blazed into desire.

She loosed a moan and deepened the kiss, so their tongues softly danced and their breath mingled.

She wouldn't say no to a real-world encore to last night.

He stiffened beneath her, hands grasping her upper arms, and pushed her backwards. She was going to ask what was wrong but the way he stared at the closed bedroom door held her tongue. She listened, straining to hear what he had, if anything at all.

Marcus lifted her off him and rose from the bed, his back to her. He stood there, stock still and never once taking his eyes off the door. Had he heard something? It was probably just Taylor and Einar.

The sense of danger drifted away at that thought and she swept her gaze up Marcus, lingering a moment on his backside and the material that loosely covered it before continuing to the dimples above his bottom and finally following the strong line of his back up to his shoulder blades.

Her gaze tracked the grey-blue swirls of the wings marked on his skin.

A curse.

Someone had wanted to seal his power and he wasn't sure why.

Did it have something to do with her, so they could take her from him? She didn't want to go. She wanted to stay with him.

She stepped down from the bed and slipped her hand into his. He looked down at her, held his finger to his lips, and then nodded towards the chair in the corner of the pale green room. His armour and her clothes covered it. She nodded, let go of his hand, and went to them. As she reached the chair, Marcus's armour disappeared. She turned to look over her shoulder at him in time to see it materialising on his body. Was it the same power he had used to create the handkerchief for her? It certainly beat the hell out of having to manually dress.

Amelia hurried into her underwear, her pale blue summer dress, and her shoes, and returned to him. He opened the bedroom door and peered out into the hall. They were on the top floor of the building and there was no noise coming from below. Had he heard something? Did angels have hearing beyond human?

He took hold of her hand and she followed him down the stairs, their footsteps quiet on the wooden treads. When they reached the next floor, he led her into the drawing room. Taylor and Einar were standing in the middle of the dark red room, both dressed head to toe in black, and she almost said that she had known it was just them and nothing to worry about, but then Einar spoke.

"Something is wrong."

Taylor looked worried too. She stared at the windows and the fading night beyond. It was earlier than Amelia had thought. The sun hadn't risen yet and the world outside was bathed in hues of grey, blending everything together in the strange pre-dawn light.

"What's happening?" Marcus said.

Einar shrugged. "I'm not sure."

"I am." Taylor frowned and then stalked past them, heading out of the door and down the stairs at a quick pace.

Both men looked at each other and then Einar hurried after Taylor. Marcus drew Amelia closer to him and they followed his friend down the rectangular staircase to the lobby. It was dark without the lights on but Taylor took care of that by yanking the front door open.

An angel stood in the middle of the empty road in front of the building, his long flame red hair falling down around his shoulders and his crimson wings tucked against his back. The long flight feathers grazed the greaves of his obsidian armour.

Was this an angel of death?

"Wait!" Einar said and Taylor was out of the door, storming down the steps towards the angel. Einar raced after her.

Marcus was more cautious. He slowly walked out onto the porch with Amelia and stopped there. She wasn't sure why either man was making a fuss. It was an angel. One of them.

The red-haired angel spread his wings and her eyes slowly widened as the colour began to drain from their tops, revealing black feathers beneath. She followed the crimson as it flowed down and then took a step back when she reached the bottom of his wings. The red dripped from them like blood, creating patches on the tarmac beneath him. Her eyes widened further as the black feathers began to slide off, falling in clumps into the pool of blood surrounding him, revealing leathery wings beneath. A grin slowly widened the angel's mouth, turning his handsome face cruel and dark.

His eyes burned vivid red, flashing brightly. The wicked edge to his smile reminded her of those creatures Marcus had fought but this man still looked human, or at least like some sort of vicious angel. He didn't have black skin or red teeth.

That soon changed.

Marcus dragged her close to him, his arm tight around her, as the man's skin darkened and he grew taller, his body filling out until his breadth was the same as Einar and Marcus standing shoulder to shoulder.

Taylor didn't stop at the sight of him.

She didn't even slow when two more angels with red wings and black armour appeared, ascending out of hellish cracks in the ground that burned orange and black like lava. The tarmac hardened again and they landed there, flanking the one who had turned into something sinister.

Taylor strode right up to the demonic angel at the front.

He towered over her, his red eyes locked on her in a predator's stare, cruel and evil, and utterly shocked as Taylor leapt and landed a firm resounding slap on his cheek.

"Bastard," Taylor shouted and went to hit the demon again, curling her fingers into a fist this time.

He held a hand up, halting her, and changed, transforming back into the rough handsome man that had first appeared but retaining his leathery bat-like wings. His irises darkened but there was still a trace of red to them. Marcus's grip on Amelia didn't loosen and she was glad of it.

"Taylor?" The man raised an eyebrow and ran a glance over her, and then looked past her. Amelia backed into Marcus when the man's red-ringed eyes briefly settled on her.

Einar stepped forwards and drew a long steel blade out of thin air.

The man's eyes shifted to him, unconcerned, and then back to Taylor. "You know them? You're with them?"

Taylor shrugged.

"She's with me," Einar said and the man looked at him again and frowned.

"A fallen angel?"

Taylor walked back to Einar and looped her arm around the thick length of his. "He wasn't always fallen."

The man smiled but it was grim. He seemed even less pleased to know that Einar had once been an angel of Heaven like Marcus. He laughed derisively. "It makes sense now at least."

"What does?" Taylor said and the man waved a hand at the two men behind him. They nodded and the ground around them bubbled, burning red and orange again, and they descended back into it. Back to Hell, Amelia presumed.

She was so busy staring at the tarmac as it cooled again that she jumped when Marcus moved with her towards the edge of the porch and placed his hand firmly on her arm, as though she needed to be held in place. She had no intention of going anywhere near this man if that was what he was worried about. She was fairly certain that he was one of those Hell's angels that Einar and Taylor had mentioned last night. She just wasn't sure how Taylor knew the man.

Marcus stared at the man, his expression one of confusion.

"Do you know him?" she said and he looked at her, his eyebrows high and eyes wide, as though she had startled him.

"No." The conviction in his tone and the way he shook his head said that he definitely didn't, but the uncertainty that crept back in as his gaze returned to the man left Amelia wondering if he did know the newcomer.

"I found out about you and Villandry and went to lay into him, and he starts spouting shit about not being with you anymore. So this is… unexpected… but V makes sense now." The man shrugged, lifting his black leathery wings with it, and sighed. He rubbed his cheek and frowned. "You could have offered me a better greeting though."

"I was with Villandry over a year ago." The frustration in Taylor's voice made it clear that she knew this man intimately. An ex? Was Taylor as bad as she was at picking out the good men amongst the bad? "Bugger me… have you always been this slow? Christ only knows how I put up with you for so long. I've been with Einar for months!"

The man growled, stepped up to Taylor, and towered over her. The skin around his eyes darkened and they burned bright red, fixed intently on the woman in front of him.

"Word doesn't exactly travel swiftly to the lower reaches of Hell!"

"Back off." Einar stepped between them, pressed his sword to the man's throat and forced him away from Taylor.

"What in Hell's good name are you doing here anyway, Veiron?" Taylor touched Einar's shoulder but he didn't relent. He remained between Taylor and the man she had called Veiron, his sword at the ready.

Veiron's crimson eyes shifted coldly to Amelia. "I have come to stop her from dying."

"What the hell?" Marcus stole the words right out of Amelia's mouth. "What do you mean, stop her from dying?"

Veiron regarded him and then looked back at her, his eyes boring into hers in a way that made her feel intensely vulnerable.

"I thought the meaning would be obvious." Veiron shrugged easily again. "I have seen it in Hell. She dies. You're there when it happens so you must have known about—"

"You knew?" Disgust rolled through Amelia, burning in her heart, and she broke free of Marcus's grip and turned to face him.

His silver-blue eyes met hers and she couldn't bring herself to look into them.

"How could you lie to me?" She stared at her feet and then ran into the house, needing space and air that she couldn't find whilst standing so close to Marcus.

"Tetchy little thing, isn't she?" Veiron said and she had half a mind to head back and imitate Taylor by hitting the demon as hard as she could. It wouldn't get her anywhere, but it would certainly make her feel better and she doubted he would hit her in return.

He wanted to stop her from dying.

Marcus was going to be there when she died.

What the hell was going on?

Amelia hesitated in the entrance hall when she realised that she was trapped and Marcus would catch up with her, if he came after her at all. Hers were the only footsteps ringing out on the chequered marble floor as she paced it and she could hear him arguing with Veiron about what the man had seen. The way he was speaking made her want to believe that she was wrong about him and that this news really had come as a shock to him too, but the hurt in her heart was too great to ignore.

Instead of heading upstairs where she definitely wouldn't be able to escape, she ran down a corridor next to the staircase. It led to a kitchen at the back of the house and a door to what looked like freedom to her. She tried the handle, silently praying it wouldn't be locked. The door opened and she burst out into a small courtyard garden. It was chilly in the shade but it didn't bother her as she paced the cream York stone patio, treading across the narrow space from one tall wooden fence to the other, trying to gather her scattered emotions and gain control over them again.

The silence was just starting to become soothing when another set of footsteps met hers.

"I didn't know," Marcus said but she refused to look at him.

Even if he hadn't known that she would die, he still knew something and she wanted to know what that something was. She needed to know whether she was better off with Veiron, a demon, than she was with an angel.

"You knew something was going to happen to me though." Amelia kept pacing back and forth across the small space, too agitated to remain still. The constant motion helped her think and stopped her from lashing out at Marcus. She could easily hit him right now. She could hit them both for how they had tied her in knots inside with only a few words and scared her more than the fight with the demonic angels on the rooftop had.

He was silent for a moment.

"Yes, but—"

"But nothing." Amelia swept her hand sharply downwards through the air and drew in a deep shuddering breath as she came to a halt facing one of the wooden fences.

She had been fine when this had all been about protecting her. No one had mentioned death or anything like that. Just a little danger. Marcus had said things in a way that had made her feel as though he just had to keep her safe for a while and it would all blow over. Now she had a demonic angel telling her that it was his mission to keep her alive and that Marcus was going to be there when she died.

She wasn't sure who she was supposed to believe. Why would a demonic angel want to protect her? Why would he know that Marcus was going to be there at her death?

Amelia met his gaze. Was he destined to fail in protecting her?

She turned away from him and dug her fingers into her hair, clutching her temples. She didn't want him to die. She didn't want to die. She wanted all of this crazy shit to go away and wanted her life back.

"Amelia," Marcus whispered and she listened to his footsteps as he crossed the courtyard, undoubtedly coming to her.

She tensed when he lightly placed his hands on her shoulders and closed her eyes. No matter how much she told herself not to take any comfort from him and to remain angry, his touch began to calm her and chase her fury away, until she wanted to lean back into him and feel his arms around her.

"It came as a shock to me too." His low tone stirred warmth inside her, smoothing out the rough edges of her feelings as much as his touch.

She knew that. He had been genuinely surprised to hear what Veiron had said and had sounded horrified when confronting him. She should have stuck around to hear what the man had to say on the matter but she hadn't been able to ignore her need to escape it all. The feeling had been building inside her since the alley attack and she had reached breaking point.

"Will you look at me?"

Amelia shook her head. She wasn't strong enough to do such a thing. If she did that, her resolve would crumble completely and she would fall into his arms in search of the comfort she so badly needed. She wanted to hear him say that Veiron was wrong and that she wasn't going to die, and he wasn't going to fail her. They would get through this.

"Look at me."

She went to shake her head again and the world spun and suddenly she was facing him. There was so much hurt and sorrow in his eyes that she had to clench her fists and pin them to her sides to stop herself from reaching up and touching his face to chase away his pain and reassure him.

He lowered himself so they were eye level with each other and then sighed and released her right shoulder. He swept the hair from her face, tucking it behind her ear in a way that made her feel like a child, and brushed his thumb over her cheek. She was certainly playing the role of petulant child so she couldn't be angry with him for treating her like one. Ashamed of herself, she straightened, took a deep breath and blew it out, expelling all of her anger and weakness with it.

"I swear to you, Amelia, I did not know. They did not tell me what they saw." The sincerity in his look and his tone drove belief deep into her soul. He wasn't lying to her. "I have tried and tried to make them tell me about what happens, but they wouldn't."

"But they did tell you about me and they sent you to protect me, didn't they?"

"Yes." He lowered his head and then met her gaze again. "But my duty is not why I am here with you now… and it is not why I was intimate with you."

Amelia wanted to ask when his feelings for her had changed and altered his mission with their appearance. The affection in his silver-blue eyes and the tenderness in his touch as he stroked her cheek to calm her told her everything she needed to know about him. What had once been little more than duty to him was now a personal mission and he was confused because of it. Einar had said that Marcus was fiercely devoted to his duty and Heaven, and that love had changed many angels' loyalties in the past. Was the loyalty inspired by his feelings for her now battling his loyalty to Heaven? The conflict in him and his eyes said that it was, and that he was as unsure of everything as she was.

She placed her hand over his, bringing it closer to her so he cupped her cheek, and leaned into his palm. It was warm against her face, solid and real, a comfort to her.

"Am I more than a mission to you, Marcus?" She slowly opened her eyes and found his, holding them so he could see that he meant something to her and would be honest in his answer.

He nodded and brought his other hand up so he held both of her cheeks. "So much more, Amelia."

He drew her into his arms and she frowned at the cold feel of his armour against her face.

"Can we get away for a while?" she said so quietly that she was certain he wouldn't hear her. "I need to escape this insanity and just be with you."

"I would like nothing more." Marcus hesitated and her hope faded. "I must speak with Veiron about what he has seen."

Amelia didn't want that to happen. She needed to leave, to find somewhere quiet where she could be alone with Marcus and pull herself together. Her courage was spent. The events of the past day combined with the knowledge that she was going to die had her head spinning and left her quaking. She couldn't face Veiron yet, not when she feared that what he had said would come true if she saw him again.

Running away wasn't the answer but it would give her the time she needed to find the strength to face everything that was happening and to face her fate.

"Is it set in stone?" she whispered and he looked confused. "The future… Marcus… is it set in stone?"

Marcus lowered his head and pressed a kiss to her hair. "No. If there is one thing I have learned in my years, and during this mission, it is that nothing is set in stone. The future can be changed, and the slightest thing can avert the greatest disaster."

That was a small comfort at least.

"I don't want to die." Amelia buried her head against his chest armour and wished it wasn't there creating a barrier between her and Marcus's warm skin. She needed to feel him.

He brought one hand up and splayed his fingers through her hair, holding her gently against him as he sighed.

"I promise you, Amelia, with all of my heart, I shall not let you die."

She smiled at the strength in those words and the gravelly edge to his voice that left her with no option but to believe in the promise he made and his conviction to keep it.

"Is he really a demon?" She looked past Marcus's arm to the open backdoor of the townhouse and through it to the entrance hall. She couldn't see the porch or the world on the other side of the building from this angle. "He looked like one of you."

Marcus stroked her hair, his movements slow and gentle, as rhythmic as his steady breathing. That steadiness flowed into her, calming her fears and settling her heart. "Veiron would have been like me once, many millennia ago, or perhaps even less. He was once an angel of Heaven."

"Is he what happens to angels when they fall?" Amelia thought about Einar and how kind he had been to her, and hoped that Marcus said that it wasn't because she didn't want Einar to become evil.

Evil.

Veiron had said that he wanted to protect her. That didn't seem like a very evil thing to do. The other demonic angels who had attacked her in the alley clearly hadn't wanted to protect her though. Perhaps even the demon world had those who were good and those who were bad.

"Veiron is what happens when an angel's soul is corrupted so much that the damage is irreversible. He has pledged himself to the Devil and forsaken my master." Marcus paused and held her closer, his hand stilling against the back of her head, holding her to his chest. "I had not realised before yesterday that they had a second appearance. I had only ever heard of them, seen them, as a man with the wings of a demon."

"Why do they use such a human form if they have that other one?"

Amelia had never believed in deities before and even with this happening to her it was hard to bring herself to believe in their existence. She had seen angels and demons though, and believed in them now. Perhaps if she saw God and the Devil, she would believe in them too. She only hoped that seeing them wouldn't mean she was dead.

"I am not sure. Perhaps they do so to taunt us with what they have become and the fear that we too may one day be like them. They always appear to my kind in the same manner as Veiron did today, their tainted feathers disappearing to reveal their demonic wings beneath."

Veiron had certainly seemed to take pleasure from the manner in which he had appeared to them. He had enjoyed shocking her.

"We should see what Veiron has to say." It wasn't what she wanted to do, she wanted to stay here in Marcus's arms and forget the past few minutes had ever happened, but it was the right thing to do and she was starting to find her courage again. She would face whatever life had in store for her and she would survive. She had finally found a good man, a beautiful angel, and she wasn't about to give up and throw in the towel. She was going to live through this and be with Marcus.

Marcus held her a moment longer and then lowered his hand to hers, clasped it tightly, and led the way back through the townhouse to the front porch.

Veiron was gone.

CHAPTER 12

"What happened?" Marcus hurried down the stone porch steps to Einar where he stood near the black wrought iron gate to the townhouse.

Einar looked from him to Taylor. She kept her back to them, still standing in the road close to the spot where Veiron had been.

"What happened?" Marcus tried again, growing tired of no one answering him. Veiron couldn't have left. When Marcus had no longer been able to resist going to Amelia, he had told the man to wait and he had agreed, stating that they needed to talk. "I need to know what he saw."

"He'll be halfway to Hell by now." Taylor turned to face them, an edge of guilt in her blue eyes. Had she driven Veiron away? Marcus didn't care if she had been involved with Veiron and things had ended sourly. Amelia was what mattered now and he had thought that Taylor would see that and would have kept Veiron here while he had gone to speak with her.

"I don't care." Marcus stepped towards her, anger rising within him, and stared her down. She cast her gaze downwards. "I want to know why he left!"

"Marcus." Einar caught Marcus's arm, his grip so firm that Marcus wouldn't easily be able to shake it. "Taylor will try to get a message to him, won't you, Taylor?"

Taylor nodded.

It was too late now to argue about what had happened, but it wasn't too late to find Veiron and he wasn't about to wait around while Taylor tried to contact the man. He could find a way to go to Hell and track him down. He needed to know what Veiron had seen. He couldn't let anything happen to Amelia. It was more than duty driving him now and he couldn't fail her when he had promised that he would do all in his power to protect her.

Marcus looked skyward. The lightening vault of Heaven was turning blue as the sunrise wore on and it looked as though it was going to be another hot sunny day. Not a cloud marred the sky.

He called on his wings and stretched them, preparing himself for flight. He couldn't easily enter Hell to find Veiron, but he could enter Heaven and face his superior. This time he wouldn't leave without discovering what they had seen and why he had to protect Amelia.

"Where are you going?" Amelia said from behind him, her soft voice lined with fear.

Marcus tucked his wings against his back and turned to face her. Just as he did so, her hand slipped into his, fingers pressing into his palm, and a desire to remain with her battled his need to leave.

What if he left her and something happened?

What if Veiron returned and took Amelia, claiming that he wanted to protect her?

Marcus couldn't bring himself to trust a Hell's angel. Three of them had already come after Amelia and they hadn't done so to protect her. For all he knew, Veiron could be lying so he would hand Amelia over to him, believing that she would be spared a terrible future if he did so. Veiron or another demon might be the one who killed her. He had only said that Marcus was there when she died. That didn't mean that Marcus or anyone from Heaven was responsible for her death.

He made a short noise of frustration and looked at Amelia, deep into her grey eyes. The fear in them spoke to his heart and he couldn't bring himself to leave her side, not until she wasn't looking as scared. Veiron hadn't said when the event would take place, but it couldn't be soon or he wouldn't have left without a fight for Amelia. There had to be time before her death and Marcus would use it to find out what was going to happen so he could avert it.

First he needed to ease Amelia's fears.

"Taylor… please try to contact Veiron or anyone who might know about this," he said without looking at her and then took hold of Amelia's hand and led her back into the townhouse and through it to the small garden.

The patch of sky between the backs of the tall buildings that formed a quadrangle around him was already turning deeper blue, calling to him with promises of warm sunlight on his feathers and a cool breeze to chase away the heat of day.

It was soothing being surrounded by quiet with Amelia and the longer he stood there clasping her hand tightly in his, the more he shared her need to escape everything for a while and just be alone with her. It wouldn't solve anything but it would give him time to answer Amelia's questions, and perhaps find answers to his own, and would ease the fear in his heart and hers.

Marcus leaned down and pressed a kiss to the top of her head. "Put something warm on and come back here."

He released her hand and nodded towards the door. Amelia walked over to it and then looked back at him, uncertainty written in the beautiful lines of her face. When he smiled, she went inside and through to the foyer. Taylor and Einar were arguing outside. He could hear them and was certain that the neighbours could too. They fell silent a few seconds after Amelia had left him and he heard their low-spoken conversation and Amelia's request for warmer clothing.

Marcus tilted his head back and looked at the sky. Everything that had happened this morning ran through his mind and he analysed it, searching for clues and inspiration. He would take Amelia away for a few hours but that was all he could spare. He needed to find a way to uncover what Veiron had seen or discover what Heaven had witnessed about Amelia's future.

Heavy footsteps alerted him to someone's presence but he didn't take his eyes off the sky. It wasn't Amelia.

"I know you're angry with her, but cut Taylor some slack. She went through a lot of pain because of Veiron. He hurt her and it was the first time she had seen him since he broke up with her." Einar's tone was soft, careful and each word felt measured, as though he had put a lot of thought into what he had said.

Marcus sighed.

He hadn't realised that Veiron had been the one to leave Taylor. The way they had reacted to each other and the fact that Veiron had gone looking for her when he had heard about her being with someone else had led Marcus to believe that she had been the one to break things off between them. If Veiron had hurt her, she had hidden it well, but not good enough that Einar hadn't noticed.

"Veiron left because Taylor said that she wouldn't let him take Amelia, and that she believed that you were able to protect her and change her fate. She told him that he wasn't needed and that we wouldn't entrust Amelia to him." There was an edge to Einar's tone now, a note that warned of his increasing anger over how Marcus had reacted to the fact that Veiron had left. Had Einar been able to see his doubt about Taylor's desire to protect Amelia?

It shamed him that he had. He didn't know Taylor but he shouldn't have believed her capable of doing something that would endanger Amelia. Just because she was half-demon, didn't mean that she would side with another demon over an angel. She was in love with one after all.

It was difficult for him to see past his prejudice towards her kind though. He had never worked with a demon before. They had always been his enemy in the past and now he was expected to view one as an ally. It was going to take time to adjust and come to trust her.

Marcus looked across the yellow stone patio at his friend. The hardness in his rich brown eyes dared Marcus to say another word against the half-demon he loved. He sighed again, exhaling long and slow, and let his shoulders drop. The tension in them faded. He couldn't hold on to his anger towards Taylor now that he knew Veiron had hurt her and knew that she had defended both Amelia and him. Her actions went some way towards gaining his trust but he still needed more. If she tracked down Veiron, she would have his trust completely.

"I'm sorry," Marcus said and held Einar's gaze, hoping that he could understand what had driven him to suspect Taylor wasn't wholly on their side. Einar had once been one of the leading hunters for Heaven and had regularly been sent to the mortal realm on missions to destroy demons who were dangerous to humans. He had to understand because he must have struggled to overcome his hatred towards demons in order to love Taylor.

Einar's look softened and he crossed the patio and placed a hand on Marcus's shoulder. "I know how you're feeling. We were all shocked… but this cannot be completely unexpected. If Heaven has seen her demise, then it is likely your mission to change something so it won't happen. Heaven has ordered you to protect her, haven't they?"

Marcus nodded, a glimmer of relief swelling inside his chest as he considered his mission. Einar was right. Heaven wanted him to protect Amelia and he wasn't going to fail her. They would find out what Veiron had seen in Hell, even if he had to find a way down there so he could confront the man himself.

His eyes widened.

Hell.

"Apollyon." Marcus's eyes darted to meet Einar's. "Veiron saw what happened to Amelia when he was in Hell. Apollyon used to guard the pool there that records history for Heaven, didn't he? What if that pool could be used to see the future?"

"Yes, but Apollyon gave up his duty a few years ago in order to be with Serenity." Einar didn't look sure now. "I doubt he would help."

"It's worth a try. I have to try, Einar… I only need him to gain me access to Hell. I can handle the rest myself. Do you know where he lives?"

Einar still looked uncertain but nodded. "He lives in Paris. I think it's best if I go with you. I have seen him recently, plus I only know the way to his home, not the address. It will take some time to arrange the travel details."

Marcus had forgotten that Einar couldn't fly. It would slow them down but he was thankful for Einar's support. He couldn't do this without him. There was strength in numbers and he needed to protect Amelia. Einar and Taylor could prove crucial in any fight that might arise if Veiron or more Hell's angels came after them. They could at least protect Amelia while he fought.

"Arrange travel for yourself and Taylor. I'll handle getting Amelia there and we will meet you at the tower."

"I'll let Taylor know the plan and we'll get on it." Einar looked out of the corner of his eye and Marcus followed his gaze.

Amelia stood in the doorway, her hands twisted in front of her.

The dark jeans and dark jumper she wore suited her, although both were a little tight and she'd had to turn up the bottom of the jeans. His destination for some quiet time with her changed. She would need clothes for their trip and so would he. The danger of returning somewhere so familiar was present in the back of his mind, but taking her home for a few hours before they departed for Paris would alleviate her tension and go some way towards making her feel safe with him again.

Marcus stretched his silvery wings and then beat them a few times, not enough to lift him off the ground but enough that he felt comfortable with them and his flight feathers realigned. He frowned at each of his wings in turn and ran a hand along their length, preening them.

"Something wrong?" Amelia said and he shook his head.

"Just wanted to be sure they weren't going to act up before we got going."

"Going where?" She stopped in front of him.

He answered her by scooping her into his arms, cradling her like a princess, and giving one single hard beat of his wings. She shrieked as they shot into the air and then gripped his neck for dear life when he beat his wings again and they were suddenly high above London.

CHAPTER 13

Amelia stared at the distant world below her and then at the horizon. The sun broke it, bathing the world in warm golden light, sending a shiver over her skin. Now the warmer clothing made sense but she still wasn't sure what Marcus had planned. Was he going to just hover here, slowly beating his wings to keep them still in the chill air?

She looked up at his face and found him watching her, his pale blue eyes warm in the sunlight and a faint smile on his lips. She wanted to kiss him when he looked at her like that, with affection brightening his eyes and turning him even more handsome than usual.

Marcus beat his wings again, harder this time, as though he was going to fly off somewhere and she tensed.

"Wait."

He stopped dead in the air and cast a quizzical look her way before adjusting her in his arms, tightening his grip on her ribs and her knees. "As interesting as London is from up here, I doubt you had this in mind and the flight path over the city can make it treacherous."

Amelia looked around again, taking everything in. She just wanted a few more seconds to bathe in the sunrise and soak up the fact that she was hovering in mid-air in the arms of a gorgeous angel.

When she had said about wanting to get away, she hadn't considered that he would fly her somewhere. She had thought they would walk a while or maybe get the Tube to a nearby park. Now the choices seemed infinite and she found the fear that had been gnawing away at her insides since Veiron's appearance starting to drift to the back of her mind.

Amelia met Marcus's icy blue gaze. "How far can you travel?"

"On an empty stomach?" He smiled and then turned thoughtful. "I could probably reach France."

Her eyebrows shot up. "That's quite a way… on an empty stomach?"

He nodded. "I need to eat if we are going to reach our destination and we need to pack some clothes, so I thought we could return home for a few hours before heading off."

"Heading off where?" Her eyebrows fell into a frown. He was being mysterious and she didn't really need any more mystery in her life right now.

"Paris."

Paris?

Amelia looked around her in all directions, trying to figure out which way Paris lay, and gave up when she couldn't get her bearings. They were going to Paris.

"Why?" she said.

"To meet a fellow angel and ask for his assistance. Apollyon can gain me access to Hell and I need to go there in order to find out what Veiron saw."

Amelia didn't like the idea of going to Hell. She backtracked and frowned again when she realised that Marcus was talking about himself and not them. He was going to go to Hell without her. This was her fight too, and as much as it was frightening the living daylights out of her, she wanted in on it all. She wouldn't let him go without her. When they met this Apollyon, she was going to insist on going with them. It was her future they were talking about and her life on the line. She had a right to go with them.

Marcus swooped lower, catching her off guard, and she curled up against him, tucking in close to his chest as he flew. The world drifted by below them, silent in the warm light of morning, and it fascinated her when she started to recognise landmarks and then places near their apartment building. Marcus's firm grip on her didn't stop her from fearing falling from his arms. She kept her hands locked around his neck, using her fear as an opportunity to remain close to him.

"Won't Einar worry about us?" she said over the noise of the wind.

Marcus shook his head. "He is arranging travel for himself and Taylor while she tries to get a message to Veiron. If you need to tell them anything, or perhaps request something, I can send Einar a message."

"How?" Amelia had the distinct impression he wasn't talking about phoning him.

A smile lit his eyes. "Telepathically. I can receive orders and messages in much the same way."

She stared at him, trying to telepathically order him to fly higher so people wouldn't spot them. A small plane drifted past them, whirring eerily through the warming air.

"It can't see us," he said, as though he had received her message, and then she realised she had grabbed his shoulders and tried to steer him away.

She settled her arms around his neck again. "Can anyone see us?"

"Not if I don't want them to." Marcus's frown hardened.

Amelia watched the buildings gradually coming closer and then looked at Marcus's wings. The sunlight turned them golden and even more beautiful than they had been in the shade. She couldn't quite believe that she was flying with him and she wasn't scared. When he had first revealed his wings, they had fascinated her and she had tried to imagine what it would be like to fly with him, and at the time she had decided that it would be frightening to be so high up without being strapped safely into a seat like she would be when on an airplane.

Would Einar and Taylor have to fly to France in a plane or take the train? Einar didn't have wings, so they had to be travelling in a human way. Marcus was going to fly her there. He had mentioned he could only fly so far without food. Did he use it like fuel?

She took her eyes off the world below and watched him instead. He was concentrating hard. Was he afraid that something would happen to his wings whilst they were airborne?

She wanted to ask him questions about himself and life as an angel but was afraid to break his concentration in case it was the only thing stopping his wings from disappearing.

"Something on your mind?" he said without looking at her.

"Does flying use a lot of energy?"

"Flying, hiding my wings, using my powers, all of it drains me when I am in the mortal realm."

"So you have a healthy appetite for food too then?"

His eyes shot to meet hers and a blush burned across his cheeks. It brought a smile to her face. There was no need for him to be embarrassed about the voraciousness of his sexual appetite. She liked it. They were equally matched in the passion stakes, just as she had suspected they would be.

His pupils widened, swallowing the silver-blue of his irises, and something told Amelia that if she kept on the subject of sex that he would be touching down a little quicker than anticipated and then touching her up.

She leaned in and pressed a kiss to his cheek.

"Devil," he muttered and she screamed as he plummeted towards the ground and then beat his wings, shooting along a street only a few metres above the cars.

He had a vicious way of repaying her for teasing him. She had thought his wings had disappeared and they were in trouble. While he could land soundly from a leap like he had made the other night, she doubted he could land so easily when dropping from the sky.

Marcus set down in the street outside their apartment building and lowered her to the ground. It took her a moment to find her feet again and Marcus held her waist while her legs slowly stopped trembling and drew her in for a kiss. She smiled against his mouth. It was handy having an angel for a lover. It definitely beat having to ride the Tube on what was threatening to be a scorching hot day.

Marcus eased away from her and sniffed. "Something smells good."

He looked around them and then stopped and his pupils narrowed. Amelia looked over her shoulder at the café across the street that had a board outside advertising bacon baps and other breakfast goods.

His stomach rumbled so loudly that she looked at it and her desire flared back into life as her eyes settled on the toned ridges of his bare stomach. If it wasn't for the more practical matters popping into her head, she would have run her hands over his muscles and forgotten their surroundings.

"I think we have a problem. Actually, two problems," she said and then sneakily reached out and ran her fingers over his stomach, unable to resist. His muscles rippled and hardened beneath her touch, deepening her ache for him. "You're not dressed appropriately and I have no money in my apartment or keys to get into it."

"Neither of which are a problem." He took her hand from his stomach and kissed the back of it. "To human eyes, I appear mortal, wearing a rather fetching white shirt and cream linen trousers."

"No wings?" Amelia said and he shook his head. It was a relief to know that her suspicions the night they had walked to Einar's home had been correct and that people couldn't see a man wearing armour as she could. "Why can I see you like this and they can't?"

He hesitated, a glimmer of awkwardness briefly flashing in his eyes.

"I do not want to deceive you," he said and she couldn't help smiling. "It is difficult to maintain such a glamour, but if you look at me directly, you can see through it to my true appearance. I want you to see me as I am."

She was glad of that and had felt as much when he had confessed his sins to her in that other world where Taylor had sent them. It was beautiful of him to desire to be so open with her, to want her to see the real him and not some false appearance.

Amelia twisted her hand free of his and brushed the backs of her fingers across his cheek, silently thanking him for being so honest with her.

Marcus smiled. "As for money, I can just compel people to give me whatever I want."

"Isn't that like stealing? I don't think I can condone that sort of behaviour."

He raised a dark eyebrow and opened his mouth, starting a new sentence several times, and then shrugging. "I am hungry."

"Too hungry to last to your apartment and get your walle—what happened to your clothes when you rescued me?"

"I disposed of them." He took hold of her hand. "By which I mean that I used my power to remove them and send them somewhere else."

The look he raked over her as they entered their building made her feel as though he was considering using that power on her right that moment.

A frown settled on her face. "Have you compelled me to give you what you want?"

He laughed. "No… never."

He dipped his head and kissed her again, and it threatened to turn into serious petting as his hands slid around her waist and cupped her backside. Amelia broke free and chided him with a frown.

"Food." She pointed to the white building through the glass doors behind her and the store there. "We get some money, we come back down, and then we eat. Keep your eye on the prize."

His gaze narrowed on her body. "I am."

Amelia flushed with prickly heat and couldn't hold his gaze when he looked at her. "Maybe I should just let you magic us some money or compel them… I have a feeling that if we set foot in your apartment, you're going to forget all about eating."

The lift pinged and the doors opened.

He grinned. "Not all about it… what I'm hungry for might change though. I might need to eat you instead."

Amelia's eyes widened when Mrs McCartney came out of the lift just as Marcus finished speaking. She eyed them both from beneath the brim of her large pink sun hat and Amelia's blush deepened, burning into her cheeks. The old woman smiled knowingly when Marcus greeted her and then slowly moved to the doors. Marcus left her side and opened them for the old woman, his eyes on Amelia the whole time.

She had created a monster.

A very sexy, passionate and irresistible monster.

Marcus grabbed her hand and bundled her into the lift. She moaned when he pressed her against the steel wall and kissed her so hard that she couldn't keep up with him. Her teeth clashed with his but he didn't laugh when she did. He slanted his mouth over hers and plundered hers with his tongue, leading her mind to dream up visions of exactly what she wanted him to do to her with that instrument of divine torture.

The lift doors opened and he scooped her up into his arms, carried her along the neat cream hallway, and stopped outside her door.

She didn't have keys.

Marcus looked at the door and, before she could mention her problem, it opened. Another power of his?

He kicked the door closed behind them and started kissing her again, stealing the world away until all she could focus on was how good it felt to have his mouth on hers, his lips playing gently against it and their tongues sliding over each other. She wanted more.

Amelia wriggled out of his grasp, landed solidly on the floor, and took hold of his breastplate. She frowned at it and then reached up and unbuckled the straps over his left shoulder. He drew in a deep shuddering breath when she tackled the strap on his left side next, her hands grazing his bare skin as she did so.

"Wait," he said and she thought he was going to stop her when she caught him frowning at her.

His wings shrank, gradually disappearing into his back, and he tugged the chest armour off over his head. Amelia hurried to remove the armour around his waist, eager to touch him again and have him touch her. She wanted to feel him for real this time, needed to lay her hands on his delicious body and know that what was happening between them was reality and not a shared fantasy.

"This is taking too long." Marcus stepped back and looked himself over and his armour disappeared, leaving him nude in the middle of her living room, his cock rising out of its nest of dark curls.

Oh. She really wanted to touch him now.

Amelia stepped forward to do just that but he held his hand up and her clothes disappeared too. A wave of heat washed over her and she swore that she had blushed head-to-toe over her sudden nudity. Marcus didn't seem to notice. He stalked towards her, caught her wrist and tugged her into his arms, so the full length of her bare body brushed against his. His hardening length pressed into her stomach, the heat of it heightening her desire and filling her with an urge to wrap her hand around it, drop to her knees, and ravish it until Marcus lost control as he had in that other world.

"You are so beautiful." He pressed kisses to her bare shoulder, working his way along the curve of her neck to her jaw, and she slid her hands up his arms, sweeping them over his strong muscles to his shoulders and then down his chest.

The firm muscles of his torso tore a groan of hunger from her and she looked down at her hands, her gaze intently following her fingers, the sight of them running over his body only increasing the pleasure she felt from touching him. She curled her fingers as she reached his nipples, raking her short nails over them and his chest, and Marcus exhaled sharply, a groan following in its wake. She didn't stop there. She dragged her nails down his stomach, scoring red lines on his pale flesh, and her groin throbbed at the thought of where she was heading.

Marcus stilled when she reached his navel and his stomach tensed, revealing the compact muscles of his abdomen to her hungry eyes.

Amelia broke free of his grip and eased her hand downwards, fingertips pushing into the dark curls surrounding his cock, and watched his face. His eyelids dropped, hiding his beautiful icy irises from her, and his sensual lips parted, tempting her into kissing him and claiming them. She held back and kept watching him instead, seeing the pleasure he felt as she wrapped her hand around his hard length and gave it a gentle squeeze. He sighed and frowned when she moved her hand down, and then inhaled sharply again as she slipped her thumb over the sensitive head, teasing it and smearing the pearl of moisture there into his skin.

"Amelia," Marcus groaned and his whole body tautened as she thrust her hand down his length and back up again. His cock hardened in her hand, as tense as the rest of him, straining for her touch and attention.

Amelia lowered herself to her knees and looked at his erection. Was he ready for this? They had covered the basics back in that other world, making love several times, but there had been minimal foreplay. She hadn't put her mouth on him then, and he hadn't done similar to her, but she wanted that now. She wanted to know every inch of him intimately. She wanted to taste him.

Marcus loosed another husky moan as she ran her tongue over the blunt head of his cock and then jerked his hips forwards when she took him into her mouth. His warm length filled her, his taste as delicious as the rest of him, and she moaned as she slowly sucked him, savouring the feel of him under her tongue. She swirled it around the head when she withdrew, eliciting a deep rumbling groan from him, and his hands came to rest on her shoulders. He clutched her tightly as she teased him, investigating every inch of his beautiful cock with her tongue, and then pushed her back when she sucked him into her mouth again.

She looked up at him.

The way his teeth cut into his lower lip and the intensity of his frown said to give him a moment before she tried anything.

Amelia bided her time by running her hands down his lithe muscular legs. He chuckled when she stroked the backs of his knees and she did it again, trying to draw another laugh out of him. His knees bent and then she was standing before him, his hands firmly clutching her upper arms, and his mouth descended on hers.

She moaned and tackled his tongue with her own, too drugged by the feel of it sliding against hers to care that he had stopped her fun. He lifted her again and continued to kiss her as he carried her into her pale purple bedroom and then lowered her onto her double bed.

Amelia lay there in the middle of the bed at an angle, her gaze on his face, watching him as he looked her over from head to toe. His pupils widened as he swept his eyes over her breasts and down her stomach and by the time he reached her groin, they were dark with hunger.

"I want to taste you," he said thickly, sending a rush of heat through her, and caught hold of her knees and pulled her towards the edge of the bed.

He glanced at the bedside lamp and Amelia was glad when he didn't turn it on. Her closed curtains were barely a shade darker purple than the walls and let enough light through. If he had turned on the lamp, she would have felt as though she was at the doctors. The hunger in his look didn't fade as he eased down onto his knees before her and she found herself propping herself up on her elbows so she could see the desire that she stirred in him.

Amelia rested her feet on the edge of the bed and spread her legs for him. His eyes darkened another degree and his lips parted again as he ran a lone finger down the length of her and then another joined it. He gently opened her to him and drew a deep breath, his gaze flicking to hers. She smiled to encourage him and wondered if he needed instruction, but he drove that thought out of her mind as he lowered his mouth and swirled his tongue around her pert clit.

A low groan was her response, drawn from her by the warmth of his tongue on her flesh and the way he slowly circled her, filling her with a hazy desire to writhe against him and make him roughen his handling of her. He spread her further, licked up the length of her and groaned.

"I want to eat you."

Her eyes widened over the intensity of those words spoken so lowly in the dimly lit room and the way they sent another scorching wave of heat washing through her.

Amelia collapsed back onto the bed and submitted to him as he bent his head and devoured her, his tongue pressing harder into her sensitive flesh and sending her out of her mind. She bucked against his face and unleashed her desire, moaning with each sweep of his tongue, and then arched off the bed when he slipped two fingers into her core. He held them there, not thrusting but driving her insane with the need to feel them pumping into her, torturing her with their presence.

Unable to resist the need growing out of control within her, Amelia pressed her feet to his shoulders and worked her hips, riding Marcus's fingers as he suckled and licked her.

He moaned and pushed his fingers deeper into her core, and the sting of pain only added to the pleasure. In that other world, there had been times when he had shown a darker side to his passion and strength that had caused tiny flickers of fantasy to pop into her mind. How strong was he, and how much of that strength would he use on her if she asked it of him?

The thought of him playing rough with her tipped her over the edge and she bucked her hips up and clutched at the bedcovers as she came with a rush of tingly heat that chased over her body, radiating outwards from where Marcus was moaning between her thighs.

He slipped his fingers out of her, sat back, and fixed her with a look that said she was going to get her wish.

With a wicked smile, Amelia rolled onto her front and crawled onto the bed. Marcus caught her ankle and tugged her back to him, rubbing his hard cock against her slick core, but she broke away from him again, luring him onto the bed. He didn't let her get far. He mounted the bed, caught her thigh with one hand and her stomach with his other, and dragged her back to him.

Amelia moaned when he pulled her against him, his knees between her legs with her astride them and her back pressed to his front. He held her there, kneeling in the middle of the bed with her, and rocked his hips, thrusting his cock into the valley between her buttocks. His heavy moans and hot breath teased her ear as he clutched her to him, fingers pressing in, and she wanted him right that moment, wanted to have him inside her in the position they were in now.

Marcus tried to hold her in place when she moved and then relented, as though he had realised her intention. She crouched astride him, reached down between her legs and took hold of his cock. It was tricky but she guided him to her entrance and slowly sunk down onto him, savouring the way he filled her. He moaned into her ear again and held her waist, and slowly lifted her up. Amelia settled on her knees, leaned back into him, and lost herself as he moved her up and down on his cock at a slow torturous pace.

They couldn't go fast in this position but each deep glide of his steely length into her core was satisfaction enough.

She leaned her head back into his shoulder when he brought his hands up to her shoulders, grasped them and dug his fingers so hard into her that she was sure he would bruise her. Awareness of his strength flowed through her, heightening her arousal until she couldn't contain her moan of pleasure. There was something powerful and possessive about the way he held her and moved inside her, something primal, and she had never felt so turned on and aware of the dominant nature of sex as she was now. Every plunge of his cock into her sent shivers pulsing through her body, made her come alive with the sensation that he was claiming her as his, possessing her. She moaned and he held her tighter, using his strength on her as he coupled hard thrusts with pulling her down onto his cock.

The flex of his muscles against her ripped another husky low moan from her throat and she relaxed into him, letting him have his way with her as he groaned hotly into her ear.

"Harder." That word leaving her lips surprised her and it must have surprised him too because he hesitated for a moment, his movements weakening, and then tightened his grip on her. He moved her on his cock, faster now, plunging deeper into her, and nibbled her shoulder. "Oh, more, Marcus."

It still wasn't enough for her.

It seemed it wasn't enough for him either.

He took hold of her ribs beneath her arms and then her breasts, squeezing and teasing them as he tried to move deeper and faster inside her, and then unleashed a sound that was close to a growl and pushed her forwards. He rose behind her, tipping her onto the bed with his cock still wedged in her body, and she pushed herself up onto her elbows. Her breasts swung as he took her, his fingers painful points on her hips, his cock thrusting deep and hard into her welcoming body, claiming and possessing her with strength that made her quiver. She moaned, lost in the way it felt to be at his mercy, to have his body within hers and be one with him.

"Amelia," he uttered breathily and with a hint of concern in his lust-laced voice.

"More." It was all she could get out. He wasn't hurting her. She loved every hard thrust of his body into hers, the feel of his cock gliding in and out, and his passion for her. She wanted to release that desire and let him take it all out on her because she knew if he did, it would be bliss, her own personal Heaven.

Marcus moaned with each deep rough plunge of his body into hers and she couldn't hold out any longer. With a cry of his name, sparks chased over her and she arched forwards with her climax. It washed through her, satiating her desire, and Marcus kept thrusting, grunting her name with each meeting of their hips. He reared and plunged himself hard into her body as he found release, his throbs discordant with hers, sending another glimmer of satisfaction through her.

He stayed there a while, hands locked on her hips, the pressure of his fingers gradually lessening, and then pulled her up to him, so her back was against his chest again. He kissed her shoulder, light warm ones that stirred her insides until she felt as though she was floating and teased a smile from her.

"It was even better in the flesh," she whispered and covered his hands with hers, slipping her fingers between them so he released her and held them.

Marcus kissed her shoulder again, murmuring his agreement against it.

How long did they have before they had to leave?

Marcus had said a few hours.

She smiled lazily, disentangled herself from him and turned to kiss him.

She was going to make the most of every minute.

CHAPTER 14

Marcus had found it difficult to drag himself away from London and Amelia's apartment. He could have spent forever there alternating between making love and just laying with her in his arms. Amelia had started to flag though and eventually he had dared to look at the clock and had realised with dismay that it was heading towards afternoon. After lunch at her place, they had packed some clothes into two small rucksacks and headed to the roof of the apartment.

The flight to Paris had passed without a hitch so far, although the sun was hot against his back and his armour was beginning to feel less than comfortable. Amelia had been interested in her surroundings until they had started to cross the English Channel, and then she had turned her focus to him instead. It had taken several assurances that he wasn't going to drop her into the middle of the ocean before she had dared to take a look at the vast sea below them. Once the coastline of France had come into view, she had started to relax again. It was difficult to carry her whilst she was wearing one backpack and holding the other in her lap and when they had reached land, he had dropped lower, to a height that still afforded Amelia a good view of the lush green countryside but was less dangerous for her.

Amelia's attention was all over the place now and she kept pointing things out to him, chatting about them in an animated fashion that relayed the excitement that he could feel flowing through her. He smiled at how full of life she was and how it felt to have her in his arms. Only a month ago, he would have seen having to carry a mortal as nothing short of punishment and a degrading task, but having her in his arms now felt like bliss. So much had changed in such a small amount of time. A month was barely a passing moment in his life but he had never felt as alive as he did right now, and he knew that it was Amelia's doing.

Paris rose out of the distant heat haze and Amelia's grey eyes darted to it.

"Is that it?" she said and he nodded.

As they drew closer, the Eiffel Tower loomed into view, spearing the infinite blue sky.

"We are heading there." Marcus nodded towards it and Amelia's eyes widened.

"To the tower?" A smile lit her face and sparkled in her eyes. "That's a bit romantic."

"We are meeting Einar and Taylor there later." Marcus assessed the elegant dark grey metal tower as they approached it and then its base when it came into view. Tourists swarmed the massive square beneath it, moving in droves either flowing towards the tower or away from it along paths that crossed the bridge over the Seine towards the rows of fountains that led up the slope into the city or into the park on the other side. He would have to keep Amelia close to him so he didn't lose her.

He glanced at her.

That wouldn't be a problem. He wasn't going to let her out of arm's reach. He was going to keep her hand firmly locked in his the whole time from now on and not only because he wanted to protect her. The craving he had for the feel of her skin against his could only be satisfied by constant contact with her. It made him feel that she truly was his, and that made him feel like the luckiest angel in existence.

"Take me up." The sheer excitement in her voice led him to obey her command.

Marcus beat his silvery wings and shot upwards, spiralling around the metal tower towards the top. Amelia giggled and held on to him, her hands warm on the back of his neck, and her fragrance filling his senses as the breeze washed over them both. When he reached the top of the tower, he hovered there a moment, giving Amelia a chance to take everything in. The city stretched around them, pale stone buildings shimmering in the heat, bustling with life and imbuing him with a sense of peace. He couldn't hear the people from this height. The wind stole the noise from the world, lending another layer to the tranquillity he felt.

It couldn't hold his attention though. His gaze roamed to Amelia, her beauty entrancing him. How could he ever deserve such a beautiful creature? He didn't right now, that was for sure, but he would do all in his power to become deserving of the woman holding on to him so tightly. He would become a good man for her, so she would love him and always be with him.

"It's beautiful." Amelia leaned her head against his chest and held him tighter. "You said we're meeting someone in Paris… another angel?"

"Apollyon." Marcus decided to leave out certain facts about the dark angel they were going to meet. It would only frighten Amelia if he mentioned that Apollyon had once guarded the Devil in Hell and that he would one day be responsible for destroying the world during the Apocalypse. "He lives somewhere in Paris now with his woman and has forsaken his duties, but he may still be able to gain me access to Hell."

"Hell," Amelia echoed and he sensed her excitement fade.

"Let's not talk about this now." Those words left his lips without him considering what he was saying. For the first time in his life, he wanted to forsake his duties too and just spend time with Amelia, getting to know her better. It was one thing watching someone from a distance and trying to understand them from things they said to others or things they did, but it was completely another to speak directly with them and learn about them from themselves, and part of him felt that they had a lot to learn about each other.

"What do you want to do?" There was a wicked edge to her look as her eyes met his and his heart beat harder at the thought of drawing her in for a slow passionate kiss.

She beat him to it, pulling herself up with the arm around his neck and bringing her lips to his. His pulse raced as they gently grazed his, tender and far softer than he had wanted the kiss to be. The lightness of it did strange things to his insides, warming and lifting them until they flipped and giddiness ran through him. Amelia gently traced her tongue along his lower lip and it tingled, sending a shiver over his skin, and he groaned. He wanted more, harder contact between them, but didn't at the same time. They had never kissed like this and he had never realised that such a bare meeting of lips could stir so much feeling within him. He was bursting with emotions, with happiness and desire, and most of all love.

Amelia drew back, her gaze meeting his and holding it, and he stared into her eyes, lost in the affection shining in them and the feelings still sweeping through him.

When she looked down, a hint of colour creeping onto her cheeks, Marcus blinked himself out of the trance she had put him under and descended slowly towards the park near the base of the Eiffel Tower.

He landed softly on the grass there and gently lowered Amelia onto her feet. She put his backpack down on the grass and shrugged out of hers, and then smoothed her dark jeans and removed the cream jumper she had chosen to wear, revealing a plain white t-shirt beneath. She tied the jumper around her waist, taking her time over it. A rosy hue still stained her cheeks and her eyes sparkled when she finally looked at him. His heart pounded over the shy smile she gave him on seeing he was watching her and he wanted to tell her how radiant she looked and not to be embarrassed because he had been looking at her. She was so beautiful that he couldn't take his eyes off her.

She intoxicated him.

Marcus had never felt so possessive and had never desired to protect something so much. It was impossible to ignore the feelings that she inspired in him now that he was becoming aware of their depth and how much he needed her. He constantly desired contact with her, wanted to touch her whenever he looked at her, and needed her smiles and her kisses. They were manna to him. They gave him strength enough to fight a thousand Hell's angels or the Devil himself.

He hungered to pull her into his arms and tell her everything he felt for her. She was becoming so much more than a mission to him. She was becoming his everything. He had never felt love before, at least not in this lifetime, and he wasn't sure how to interpret his growing feelings for her or how to express them. If he told her that he thought he was falling for her, would it drive her away or make her happy? Was she falling for him too?

Marcus caught her wrist, lured her to him, and kissed her instead, expressing without words just how he felt about her. Amelia was smiling when he broke away and looked into her eyes, the flush of colour on her cheeks darkening until they turned crimson.

"How about dinner while we wait?" Marcus said and picked up his backpack. If he didn't eat something, then he was going to eat her instead. He wanted her honey on his tongue again, needed to devour her, but they didn't have time for an encore, no matter how much he wanted one. Einar would be arriving soon.

Amelia nodded and looked around while she slipped the straps of her backpack over her shoulders again. "I need to put something cooler on. It's even hotter here than it was in London. I think there are bathrooms at the base of the tower."

Marcus nodded too. While he was fine with using a glamour to change his appearance to everyone else, he didn't want to use one on Amelia and she wouldn't be comfortable dining with him while he was dressed in his armour.

Although, she had been comfortable having lunch with him in the nude.

He took hold of her hand, carrying his rucksack in the other, and led her across the grass to the Eiffel Tower. It was manic in the square below the huge structure, the swarm of tourists trying his patience, but it didn't take him long to spot the bathrooms. Amelia let go of his hand and went into the female one, and he headed into the male. It was filthy but it would do as a changing place.

Marcus went into one of the stalls, set his backpack down on the closed toilet lid, and focused so his wings disappeared. When they were gone, he sent his armour away with the exception of his boots, and then unzipped the bag. He changed as quickly as possible in order to spend the least amount of time in such an unclean environment. He rapidly followed his black trunks with loose fitting jeans and a white linen shirt with the top few buttons undone to allow some cool air to circulate and sleeves rolled up to midway along his forearms. He replaced each boot in turn with his black leather shoes and zipped his bag closed, and then headed back out into the busy square to wait for Amelia in the shade.

She was right. It was even hotter in Paris than it had been in London, and while he hadn't noticed it as they were flying and he was wearing only his armour, he definitely felt it now. Even the shade was hot. He slipped his finger down the line of open buttons on his white shirt to settle in the V above his chest and tugged at it, shifting it back and forth to fan himself.

Amelia emerged from the bathroom and Marcus paused.

She took his breath away.

The small dark blue dress she wore clung to her torso, the neckline plunging deep enough to reveal cleavage, and then flared out from her hips into a short skirt that ended just before her knees. She had tied her shoulder-length dark hair up into a neat ponytail, revealing the full extent of her beauty to him, and had her backpack slung over one shoulder.

He wasn't sure what to say when she stopped in front of him and twirled, sending the skirt of her blue summer dress swirling outwards and revealing her thighs.

"You like?" she said with a breezy smile and mischief in her eyes. "I'm guessing that look means you like it."

"What look?" He feigned ignorance and tried his best to look as though he hadn't just been considering finding a quiet hotel instead of a restaurant. He wanted to eat her again, devouring every inch of her because she looked delicious and he was ravenous for her.

She giggled, sidled up to him, and ran her fingers down the patch of chest he exposed by holding the front of his shirt. When she tilted her head back and looked up at him, her shiny lips parting at the same time, he gave up his pretence and snaked his arm around her waist and kissed her. It didn't last nearly long enough.

Someone bumped them and Amelia sighed, pulled back and frowned at the people around them.

"Let's get out of here." She took hold of his hand.

He wasn't sure where they were going to eat. He had never been to Paris other than flying over it once or twice when on missions, and that had been a long time ago. It seemed Amelia had visited the city because she led him away from the tower and turned down the next street. Bistros and restaurants lined the quieter leafy avenue. Marcus tried to recall when she had visited Paris but the delicious smell coming from the first restaurant made it impossible for him to think. He almost groaned when Amelia scrunched up her nose at the menu outside and moved on to the next one.

After the third restaurant, Marcus couldn't take anymore. Amelia seemed intent on scrutinising the menus and the smells coming from each establishment had Marcus's stomach growling louder and louder. He had expended a lot of energy flying to Paris and he was starving now that he knew food was close at hand. He looked at the next café along and used his superior hearing to listen in on the conversations. Most of them were in French. Locals using the place had to be a good sign so he dragged Amelia to it, ignoring her protests about not having seen the menu. She quietened when she spotted a free table outside and sat at it, hiding from the sun by a combination of the large cream coloured umbrellas that stood between the tables and the tall trees that cast cool shadows along the street.

A waiter bustled over to them and spoke in French. Marcus had never mastered the language and the few things he did know how to say probably wouldn't be much use. Amelia dived in and said something, and then the waiter gave her two menus and moved to another table.

"You speak French?" Marcus shifted his chair closer to hers at the small round metal table. He couldn't remember her mastering a language.

"Only school level stuff. Honestly, I'm surprised I can remember it." She handed him a menu and frowned at her own.

Marcus glanced down. It seemed fairly ordinary fare although there were some questionable items included, or the French to English translations were wrong. Either way, he was going to avoid the snails and other strange offerings.

Steak caught his eye and his stomach growled. Meat would go a long way towards replenishing his energy.

Amelia ordered for them and the waiter returned a moment later, carrying a tray with two tall icy glasses on it, as well as a bottle of water. He set the items down and disappeared into the crowd of patrons. Marcus picked up his glass of cloudy yellow liquid and sniffed.

"Still lemonade," Amelia said and sipped hers. "It's heavenly on a hot day like today."

Marcus tried it and the zingy taste made his eyes pop wide. It instantly refreshed him and he found himself leaning back in his chair and savouring it. He tipped his head back, looked past the edge of the sun umbrella and up at the sky through the branches of the trees. It wouldn't be long until Einar reached them. As much as he just wanted to spend some quiet time with Amelia, his mission had to come first.

Their food arrived and Amelia fell into an easy conversation with him as they ate, questioning him in a coded manner about his life as an angel and talking about her life as a mortal, and the dreams she had for her future. It seemed so alien to him and so very human to be sitting at a restaurant in a new city with a woman who was stealing his heart.

"What's wrong?" Amelia said and Marcus realised that he had stopped eating and was looking at her.

"I was thinking how strange it is for me to be here… like this."

"Like this?"

"Talking… eating with you… not thinking about my duty."

Amelia laughed and touched his hand, and then smiled deep into his eyes, her grey ones bright with amusement.

He was smitten. It wasn't just physical desire he felt for her. It went deeper. So deep that he was beginning to question whether he would be able to leave her when his mission came to an end.

Could he?

Marcus frowned and tilted his head back again.

"What is it now?" Amelia said.

"Einar has arrived. He is wondering where we are."

"That's still freaky." Amelia smiled and set her fork down, and signalled the waiter.

There was a hint of nerves in her eyes now. He felt it too. The past few hours with her had been a dream and now they had to face reality again. He had to return his focus to his mission and protecting her. His duty waited.

Duty.

It was all he had known since his rebirth and his heart had been dedicated to it but now he wasn't sure what he was doing.

When his mission was over, could he return to his duty and to Heaven?

It was all he had wanted for so long. It had kept him going throughout his time trapped in Heaven, wingless, and after that when he had been assigned to watch over Amelia. Now he was no longer certain about what he wanted. No. He was certain but he was finding it difficult to believe that he felt such a way.

He wanted to stay with Amelia.

Even if that meant turning his back on Heaven.

CHAPTER 15

Einar stopped in front of a dark door on the top floor of the Parisian townhouse and knocked. Taylor hung back on the short strip of hallway outside the apartment, a wheeled black travel case beside her, leaving Marcus and Amelia standing on the step below. Both Taylor and Einar had complained about the heat when they had met them at the base of the Eiffel Tower, and Marcus had felt inclined to mention that their usual tight black combat clothing probably wasn't the best choice considering the weather. His gaze shifted to the travel case. Did it contain clothes or was it packed with weapons? It wouldn't surprise him if Taylor had somehow managed to conceal a large number of knives in the innocent looking piece of luggage. The only thing that would surprise him was if she had actually come here unarmed. He couldn't remember a time when he had seen her without a weapon on hand.

She looked over her shoulder at him, causing her long black hair to sway in its ponytail, and eyed him suspiciously. It seemed half-demons could sense when an angel was watching them closely. Marcus smiled and her hard look softened and then a smile of her own curved her lips when her blue gaze shifted to Amelia.

"Anything strange happen on the way here?" she said.

"Other than the fact I was flying in the arms of an angel?" Amelia smiled brightly and then shook her head. "Nothing out of the ordinary except that."

"Good to hear. The local demons in London haven't encountered any Hell's angels, so those three you fought must have been the only ones in the vicinity. That means we couldn't get any intel on what they wanted, I'm afraid." Taylor's attention shifted back to Marcus.

He nodded. Taylor held his gaze, a silent challenge in her eyes, a dare to mention that those three Hell's angels hadn't been the only ones in London. Veiron had been there too. The faint trace of hurt that shone in her blue irises alongside that dare stopped him from saying anything. Einar was right. Whatever had happened between Taylor and Veiron, it had hurt her, and bringing him up again would only renew that pain.

The door opened to reveal a petite blonde woman wearing a pale dress similar to Amelia's deep blue one. Marcus wasn't familiar with her but she smiled at them all in turn.

"We were not expecting you," she said, her English thick with a French accent.

Was this the woman that Apollyon had sacrificed everything for? Einar had explained that the woman was a witch. Marcus had never met one of her kind. Power flowed from her, a force that held an underlying note of darkness.

"Apollyon is out. We needed food for our guests." Her smile brightened. "I will have to send him out for more now."

"You already have guests?" Einar said and she nodded.

Marcus focused and picked up the quiet conversation taking place inside the apartment. He would recognise the male voice anywhere.

"Rookie." Marcus grinned and the petite blonde looked confused and turned to Einar for an explanation.

"He means Lukas." Einar smiled warmly. "I hadn't seen him since his rebirth until only recently."

"You are lucky. I had to re-train him in combat with spears. He was terrible." Marcus laughed at the memory of having to teach the angel that had once taught him. That was the downside to being reborn on death. Not only did you forget your past life, but you forgot everything you had learned too. The slate was wiped clean. Languages, knowledge, fighting techniques. All of it was gone and it was rare to instinctively remember anything. Most angels only recalled how to do one or two things and it often took centuries for those to come back to them.

Marcus had come through the ranks with Einar under Lukas's instruction. It had been strange to be his junior one day and his superior the next.

"Come in," the woman said and Einar passed her. Taylor followed him into the apartment. The woman's gaze met his. "I am Serenity."

Marcus stepped up onto the small hallway. "I'm Marcus and this is Amelia. We need to see Apollyon as soon as he returns."

She sighed. "He will not be pleased to see you… if you ask… no… if you have come to ask him to bring you to that place."

Something in the weary edge to her hazel eyes said that she wasn't pleased to see him either. Marcus knew requesting access to Hell was asking a lot of Apollyon and that his old friend wanted to be rid of all of his duties that bound him to that place and Heaven, but all of Marcus's hope rested on him saying that he could take him there so he could find out what Veiron and Heaven had seen.

"I must." Marcus held his hand out to Amelia. "Her life depends on it."

Serenity's eyes shifted to Amelia and softened. "In that case, you may enter and wait for him. Do not expect a good response."

She stepped aside and fixed him with a hard look as he passed and he got a clearer sense of her power. She was strong, her magic emanating from her in tangible waves and mingling with the anger evident in the set of her jaw. It warned him not to argue with her. It seemed Apollyon wasn't the only one who was upset whenever someone asked him to travel to Hell.

Marcus could understand her reluctance and her feelings. Apollyon would have to accompany him in order for him to gain access to Hell, and it was a dangerous place for angels, even those as powerful as Apollyon. The pool that recorded the history of the mortal realm from Hell was close to the bottomless pit where the Devil resided. The Devil had a strong voice and had swayed hundreds of angels with his promises.

"This is a beautiful apartment," Amelia said from behind him.

"It is Apollyon's big taste and my décor." Serenity giggled, seemingly more at ease with Amelia than she was with him. "We have lived here since we met."

"I think Marcus must be the only angel who isn't rich." Amelia laughed and glanced his way, her bright eyes enchanting him. "Everyone else seems to have amazing apartments and he's stuck in a one-bed next door to me."

Marcus walked over to her and touched her arm. "I am only there because you are there."

Amelia's laughter faded. "I hadn't thought of that. I guess I'm the poor one." She turned back to Serenity and then looked across the pale living room to Einar and Lukas where they were talking. "Do you think Marcus would have an amazing place like this if he lived on Earth?"

The look on both men's faces dropped away to reveal their shock and their hesitation drew a frown from Marcus.

"Marcus living in this world?" Lukas broke the tense silence and smiled at him, his green eyes shining with amusement. He was quiet for a few seconds and then shook his head. "Nope… I can't picture that at all."

Marcus turned his frown on the man. He was tempted to cross the room, take hold of him by the mess of sandy hair that crowned his pretty face and drag him into a headlock. It was the truth and he hadn't expected either angel to say that they could see him living in the mortal realm, but a tiny part of him had wanted to hear them say something more positive to Amelia.

She stood silent beside him, her eyes cast down at the pale wooden floor. Lukas leaned his bottom against the back of the beige couch and concern slowly replaced the amusement in his eyes. The redheaded woman sitting on the arm of the couch scowled at Lukas and he looked over his shoulder at her as though he had sensed her anger. Even Einar looked unimpressed and Taylor was crossing the room to Amelia.

"Let's get some air." Taylor took hold of Amelia's hand, turned her back on him and led her from the room.

"I will go too," Serenity said and cast a frown Lukas's way before following Taylor and Amelia out of the room.

Marcus glanced through the open door into the beech wood kitchen beyond. The redhead frowned at Lukas for a few seconds longer and then followed the rest of the women.

"Annelie…" Lukas said as the woman stalked away from him without looking back, his deep voice quiet in the bright room. When she had reached the kitchen, Lukas slouched and then shrugged. "Guess I put my foot in it… sorry."

"Try thinking before you speak next time." Marcus dumped his backpack down on the wooden floor, exhaled a sigh, and rubbed his jaw.

"It's not my fault that it's almost impossible to imagine you living in this world." Lukas stood and Marcus just stared him down. They might be the same height, but Lukas wasn't about to intimidate him. When it came to a fight, Marcus could easily best him, and the way he was feeling right now, he might even start it.

"Do you think she was testing the water?" Marcus ignored Lukas and looked to Einar for help.

Einar nodded. "I think she wanted to see where she stood."

"Great." Marcus glared at Lukas again. "I thought you would know better. I presume that is your female who was looking as though she was going to murder you in your sleep."

Lukas glanced towards the door, the shock back on his face as though he hadn't noticed the bitter disappointment in Annelie's eyes before she had left, and then folded his arms across his chest, pulling his pale blue shirt tight across his muscles. He leaned back against the couch and crossed his legs at the ankle, drawing Marcus's glare down their long cream linen-clad length to his feet. They were bare. Lukas was certainly comfortable in Apollyon's apartment. How often had they seen each other? That seemed strange to him. The last time Lukas had seen Apollyon before his rebirth they had parted on a monumental argument that had shaken the ground and turned the sky black. Lukas would have forgotten the argument but Apollyon wouldn't have. Had he even told Lukas about it?

"I admit I was tactless and should have thought about what the girl was really asking, but there's no need to fly off the handle about it… all of you," Lukas groused and turned a frown on both him and Einar.

"Tactless. Certainly a good word for you, Rookie." Marcus clenched his fists, drew a deep breath, and then blew it out. "I need to speak with her."

Einar's hand clamped down on his shoulder. "I think you should give her a moment. The women will take care of it."

Would they? The temptation to go to Amelia and explain was strong but he held himself back. If Einar believed that the women would handle the situation and bring things between him and Amelia back on track, then he would trust them with that mission. He frowned at the wooden floor. She wanted to be with him. She wanted him to stay on Earth. He had hated this place so much in the past, had carried that feeling into battle with him so many times, but now his feelings were changing thanks to one woman. A pure soul. A beautiful creature in a world filled with cruelty, despair, death and destruction. If she let him, he would give her all she deserved. He would give her a place like this in whatever city she desired to live in as long as she would remain with him.

"Is he in love?" Lukas whispered in Einar's direction.

"It certainly seems so."

Did it? Marcus closed his eyes and turned his focus inwards, trying to decipher his feelings and put a name to them. He was attracted to Amelia, she was constantly on his mind, and he couldn't stop thinking about doing things that would make her smile or feel safe or would make her want to kiss him. He cared about her and wanted to see her survive the event that lay ahead of her.

And he was considering staying in the mortal realm.

Marcus looked at Lukas and then at Einar. Both men had chosen to come to Earth in order to be with their women. Even Apollyon had forsaken his duties in order to be with his witch. Was his desire to remain with Amelia on Earth and follow in his fellow warriors' footsteps a sign that he was in love with her?

He loved her.

The door behind him opened and then closed.

"Well, this is certainly a surprise," Apollyon drawled and Marcus turned to face him.

The darkness in Apollyon's clear blue eyes matched the anger that Marcus could sense in him. Serenity had been right. Apollyon didn't want to see him and he hadn't even mentioned anything about needing to go to Hell yet.

"To what do I owe the pleasure?" Apollyon lowered the plastic bags of groceries he held to the floor. "I haven't seen you in a long time… Marcus."

It had been centuries since they had last met but before that they had often seen each other, especially when Marcus had lent a hand as a temporary angel of death.

As far as he could recall, he had done nothing to gain such a cold greeting from his friend.

"I need your assistance with something." Marcus stepped forward.

At that same moment, the four women came in from the kitchen. Serenity hurried towards Apollyon and he smiled at her. Apollyon's blue eyes rose to take in the other women and darkness crossed his face and his irises brightened. Serenity stopped dead. A wave of anger crashed through the room and Marcus could only stare at Apollyon as his black wings tore through his crisp white dress shirt and he let out an ungodly growl. His clothing shredded, revealing his black armour, the gold edging and the rampant lions on his vambraces gleaming in the bright expansive room.

He clutched at the sides of his head, burying his fingers into his long black hair and tugging strands free of his ponytail.

"Apollyon… what is wrong, mon ange?" Serenity went to move but stopped again when he raised his head, his vivid blue eyes locking on her. A pained look crossed his face and then he growled again.

"Must leave… send me far away… far… now! All in danger." Apollyon pressed his fingers into the sides of his head and hunched over. "Now, Serenity!"

The world shifted around Marcus, swirling and distorting in a way that made him feel as though his insides were doing the same, and when it came back again, they were standing in the middle of a corn field with Paris far in the distance.

Apollyon looked up, sheer horror on his face. "No… what did you do… I said to send me."

Marcus moved towards Amelia when Apollyon looked at her, his pupils narrowing and then widening, flickering between the two. Apollyon shook his head, closed his eyes, and then looked at Serenity, imploring her.

"Run… get away from me." The desperation in his tone sent a bolt of fear through Marcus.

He caught hold of Amelia's hand, sent his clothes away and called his armour. He grabbed one of the blades from his waist and clutched it tightly, watching Apollyon for a sign he might attack. Einar must have sensed something too because he motioned for Taylor to come to him. Lukas moved to stand in front of Annelie, shielding the redhead with his body.

"Apollyon?" Serenity's voice trembled. "What is wrong?"

Apollyon snarled, whimpered and then looked at her, his eyes full of pleading. "Take them and go… please? I cannot… I cannot fight it."

Serenity took a step backwards, away from him, her pale dress blending into the corn that reached to her hips. She looked over her shoulder at Marcus and the others. Marcus wasn't sure what was happening and it seemed the rest didn't either. Apollyon had been fine when he had first arrived in the apartment. It was only once the women had come through that he had changed.

Marcus's eyes widened.

It was when he had set eyes on Amelia.

There was only one explanation Marcus could come up with and it chilled him to the bone.

Heaven wanted her dead and was ordering Apollyon to do it.

"Take them," Apollyon whispered. "I will hold off as long as I can."

"I can't." Serenity shook her head. "I used all my power to bring us here."

"No." Apollyon stared at her, horror filling his bright blue eyes. Tears laced his dark lashes, trembling on the brink of falling, and his struggle was visible for all to see. His battle against whatever order was being sent to him was tearing him apart along with the fear of hurting those he cared about. "No… why… why did you have to come? Why?"

The tears in Apollyon's eyes fell when he looked at Marcus, dashing down his cheeks. He had never seen such pain in his friend or witnessed such torment. It was so strong that Marcus could feel a sliver of it mingling with his own fear.

"I should never have set eyes on her… I do not want this."

The truth in those words and the agony that crossed Apollyon's face as he struggled with himself drew a dark curse from Marcus. He couldn't imagine the depth of what his friend was feeling or what it would be like to do something against his wishes, to have Heaven seize command of his body, but he knew one thing. It was killing Apollyon and it wouldn't be long before he lost what little control he had over himself.

Marcus guided Amelia behind him and shielded her with his wings.

"Stop this," Serenity said in a commanding tone and Apollyon looked at her, his jetty eyebrows furrowed, and shook his head. "I order you to stop this."

"No use." Apollyon held his hand out in front of him and a curved golden blade appeared in his grasp. "It won't work… our contract cannot override something I was born to do. This is my eternal duty."

Marcus stared at him. Apollyon was unlike other angels in one respect. He had an eternal duty that could never be erased. Even if Apollyon fell from grace like Einar, he would be called upon to use his powers during an apocalyptic event, either to trigger or halt it. It was the reason he had been born.

"Run," Apollyon ground the word out and then stared at Marcus. "I cannot hold it back… this fury… she must take it."

A thousand tiny needles pricked down Marcus's spine. He didn't know why Heaven had ordered Apollyon to kill Amelia and he didn't care. There was no way that he was going to let anything happen to her. Even if her survival meant the end of the world as they knew it, even if her existence beyond this point caused a catastrophe, he wasn't going to let her die. He couldn't allow it. Not even if it was Heaven's decree.

"No!" Marcus stepped forwards, keeping hold of Amelia's hand. It trembled in his. Her fear flowed into him and he wanted to take it away and tell her that nothing was going to happen to her, but he couldn't lie. All he could do was protect her.

"She must! It is her destiny." Apollyon struggled and then brought his other hand forwards and a second curved golden blade appeared in it. He spread his black wings and the sky above them darkened, heavy clouds blocking out the sun. The air around Marcus cooled, turning frigid, and he hesitated.

Destiny wasn't set in stone for anyone. He wasn't going to step aside and let her die. The slightest thing could change her fate and he was willing to do all in his power to ensure that change happened.

Even if it came down to sacrificing himself in her place.

Einar and Lukas moved away, leading the three other women off to a distance. He wanted them to take Amelia too and leave him to fight Apollyon but it wouldn't do any good. The battle and pain in Apollyon's blue eyes told Marcus that much. Apollyon was no longer in control of himself and if Amelia went to the others, there was a chance he would attack and hurt them all. Apollyon was already suffering enough. If he harmed Serenity, it would kill him. Marcus couldn't let that happen, but he couldn't let him kill Amelia either.

"You must allow this to happen for the sake of mankind."

Marcus shook his head. "I cannot do that. I won't let you hurt her."

"Then you must take this wrath upon yourself." Apollyon raised both of his curved blades and the black clouds gathered above them swirled and opened to reveal a circle of blue sky.

The wind increased, sending the golden corn swaying and ruffling both Marcus's and Apollyon's feathers as they stood facing each other barely twenty metres apart.

"Try to take it easy on me," Marcus said with a half-smile and pushed Amelia behind him. He braced one foot out in front of him, drew his other blade, and brought his arms together in front of his face so his vambraces were shielding his head. The two ends of the grips on his weapons moulded together on contact and then extended until he held an engraved blue and silver staff tipped with two curved silver blades. "Fight it if you can."

"I will try. Forgive me." Apollyon threw his head back and yelled at the sky.

"No!" Amelia shrieked.

White light shot down in a twisting beam from the hole in the sky, hit Apollyon's crossed golden blades, and rocketed towards Marcus. Marcus didn't have a chance to brace before it hit him. The first blast of power burned over him, bouncing off his vambraces and cutting into two shafts of light as it hit his spear. It was far stronger than he had anticipated. He hunched forwards, leaning into the light, and closed his eyes and gritted his teeth. He wasn't strong enough to survive such a direct assault and something told him that it was only going to get worse. If Apollyon increased the power of his attack, it wouldn't be long before Marcus didn't have the energy to deflect it.

He had fought great powers before but they were nothing compared with the furnace blasting him now, pushing him backwards towards Amelia. Marcus took a laboured step forwards and growled, his teeth clamped together so hard they hurt. He pushed forwards, sheer desperation driving him. He had to protect Amelia.

Another wave crashed over him, stronger this time, and his knees threatened to give out. Tears filled his eyes and streamed across his temples and into his hair as he endured it. It tore at him, heating his body as it whipped against him, lacerating his armour. He focused his power and fought it even as his hope of saving her faded. The longer he withstood it and shielded Amelia, the more time Apollyon had to fight for control over himself. He was counting on his friend.

The beam increased in power and his right arm slipped under the intensity of it. It struck his right shoulder, knocking it backwards and unbalancing him. He immediately brought his right armguard up again, battling through the burning light to get it back in front of his face.

Marcus gritted his teeth, planted his feet firmly on the burning ground, and called all of his strength, using his power to deflect the destructive force battering him. His right arm blazed so hot that it was numb and fiery needles pierced his shoulder where the light had caught his flesh.

There was no hope for him now. He knew that. All he could do was shield Amelia until the last of his strength left him and he could no longer withstand Apollyon's attack, and then it would tear through him and through her.

He had never wished for strength as much as he did now. With more power, he might have been able to defeat Apollyon and save her. He wished he could do that for her sake. He had changed nothing by taking her fate upon himself.

He had failed her.

She at least deserved him to die for her because of that.

He would die for her.

The layers of blue on his vambraces wore away under the force of the golden light. Flakes of the enamel flew past his face, catching his cheeks and ears, leaving thin trails of blood in their wake. The steel blades of his spear melted and dripped to the ground, hissing as the flames there engulfed them. The strength of the light increased again, pushing against him, and as he braced himself, he felt his armour fracturing and burning away.

His focus moved to Amelia where she huddled behind him, her fear and pain as real in his veins as his own, and he wished that he could see her one last time. He wished that he could look upon her beautiful face and tell her that he was sorry.

He wished he could tell her that he loved her.

In his attempt to save her, he had brought her to meet her fate, and there was nothing he could do to stop it now. He wasn't strong enough to defeat Apollyon, not even when he wanted it with all of his heart so he could keep his promise and protect her.

Another blast of light shattered his vambraces and tore at his feathers, ripping them away. He bore the pain, pleading for it to end and for Amelia to be safe. He had to stand firm and last a little longer. He had to for her sake.

In the midst of the deafening roar and searing pain, Marcus found calm, a feeling of emptiness and a sense that he was no longer alive. Was this death? He had never been aware of it before.

Apollyon stood before him, darkness embodied with his black armour and wings and vicious blades, and light surrounded him, so bright that he couldn't see anything else. He looked into Apollyon's eyes and saw the anguish there, and the tears streaking his cheeks as he directed the might of his power at Marcus. Marcus couldn't hate him for what he had done. They were all pawns for their master, slaves to his voice. The light faded enough that he could see Serenity and the others as they tried to stop Apollyon. There was such pain in his fellow warrior's eyes and Marcus was sorry that he had made him do this.

He sensed Amelia behind him.

He didn't want to die.

The power ripped through his arms, cutting him to the bone, and slashed at his legs.

He didn't want to leave her even when he knew that he must in order to attempt to protect her and the world.

His life was eternal. This wasn't death. It was only a new beginning.

He grimaced when a stronger wave of power struck him, tearing into his wings and his chest. The remains of his spear crumbled under the intense heat. The last of his strength slipped away.

He battled his pain and focused everything he had left on enduring Apollyon's attack for Amelia. For his love. There was no hope for him but he still had hope for her. He would die here, now, and though that filled him with immense sorrow because he would never see Amelia's smile again or touch her soft face, he could at least say that he had died for a purpose—protecting her to the end—and that he had died knowing what love was.

His heart burned in agony with the knowledge that he would be reborn but would never remember her. He wanted to see her again, wanted to find her in his new lifetime. It was impossible. He was destined to live again knowing that a part of him was missing only never knowing why. He could only hope that his death meant Amelia's survival.

The silence around him ceased and the roar of death filled his ears. He lowered his arms and stood tall to face it, raising his chin. It was over. His power was gone now, his body too weak to continue the fight, and he couldn't hold out any longer.

Nothing could save him now.

His eyes widened as a shape broke the light and tears stung them as it came into focus.

Amelia stood with her back to him, her arms outstretched, shielding him from the wrath of Apollyon's power with her fragile body.

"Amelia!" Marcus reached for her, pulled her into his arms, and turned his back on Apollyon, falling to his knees at the same time.

He held her close to him as he battled to remain conscious, tears blurring his vision. He tried to blink them away but more came. He needed to see her again. Just one last time before he died. It was all he wanted. His final wish.

The heat of power against his back abated but it wasn't soon enough. Marcus collapsed against her frail form and drifted into the darkness.

He knew what the end of Apollyon's attack meant.

He had failed her.

Amelia was gone.

CHAPTER 16

Pain beat deep in Marcus's chest and throbbed through his bones. He couldn't recall a time when his rebirth had hurt. His first memories last time he had died were full of warmth and light, not agony and darkness. How had he remembered that?

Marcus slowly opened his eyes. The bright light he expected wasn't there. A dull golden glow filled his blurred vision. Shapes shifted across the fuzzy canvas, growing darker and then lighter, and he tried to focus on them. The only sound that came to him was a high pitched ringing. He frowned, drew in a shaky breath, and blinked several times. His entire arm burned when he lifted it and rubbed his eyes with his knuckles, trying to clear his vision. It helped a little.

A darker shape appeared in front of him, coming in from his right. No, not in front of him. Above him, he realised as something prickly dug into his bare back, bottom and legs.

He narrowed his eyes and the shape grew clearer. He recognised them.

Taylor.

He wasn't dead.

"Keep still." Her voice was distant in his ears, watery sounding. She placed her hands on his bare shoulders when he tried to sit up, pushing him down into the sharp spikes sticking into his back. He grimaced and then stared at her, trying to get his head back into order and remember what had happened. He had been sure that he was going to die.

Other voices started to drift through the ringing in his ears as it dulled and he tilted his head to one side. Across scorched black ground he saw Einar knelt beside someone, his hands shining brightly as he swept them over her body, light beaming down on her. Marcus looked at his hand and then his arm. He could remember his flesh burning away under the duress of Apollyon's power. It was perfect again now. Not a scratch or a bruise to show for his battle.

His eyes slowly widened as more came back to him and he looked back at Einar.

Amelia.

Serenity knelt on the other side of Amelia's body to Einar, her eyes closed and words Marcus couldn't hear falling from her lips.

Marcus shoved Taylor aside when she tried to stop him again and pushed himself up. He made it onto his knees and then retched, coughing up blood onto the charred stubs of corn.

"You shouldn't move." Taylor tried to take hold of his arm.

He shirked her grip and continued, bringing his right knee up first and setting his foot down, and then slowly following it with his left. It took all of his strength to push himself up into a standing position and all of his willpower to remain there once he managed it. The sharp broken stems of corn pierced his bare feet but he didn't care. His head spun and the urge to vomit rose up again. He swallowed it down and stared blankly at Amelia's body as Einar and Serenity worked furiously to save her. Was it too late?

Taylor spoke to him again, her words lost on him. He couldn't rest. Not now.

He laboured onwards, the warm air washing over his bare body, the gentle whisper of it and the effort of moving causing every inch of him to ache and throb.

Apollyon paced a short distance away with Lukas and his redheaded woman speaking to him. He didn't look as though he was listening. The agitated way he moved backed up the anger Marcus could feel burning within him. The sky above them was black, the clouds heavy and forbidding, and not even the light of sunrise could warm them. They were as dark as the man controlling them, turbulent to reflect his distress. Heaven would pay for what they had made Apollyon do, Marcus was sure of that, but it wasn't any consolation.

Marcus took a heavy step forwards and followed it with another, keeping his momentum going as he stumbled across the blackened ground to Amelia. Pain blazed in every muscle and bone, paralysing him and stealing what little strength he had. Serenity looked up as he reached them and caught him as he fell to his knees, hitting the ground hard. She muttered something soft in French against his shoulder as he collapsed into her. The overwhelming urge to sleep crashed over him but he fought it, pushing away from it and Serenity. His gaze dropped to rest on Amelia. Her face was still but he couldn't see any peace there. Cuts littered it and patches of skin had burned away, leaving angry red welts on her pale face and her body. Her dress was ruined, the remains of the blue fabric doing nothing to hide her body from everyone's eyes.

Tears burned his as he leaned over, running a shaky hand across her cheek and silently begging her to come back to him. He had found love for the first time and it couldn't be over now, not before he had told her how he felt about her and had asked her whether she would ever consider being his.

"There's nothing I can do," Einar whispered and Marcus looked up at him, sending his tears tumbling down his cheeks.

"Please," Marcus ground out and drew a deep breath, struggling to hold back his tears and stop himself from breaking down. "You have to save her."

"I'm trying… nothing I do is working. Not even Serenity's magic can revive her." Einar's eyebrows furrowed and Marcus cursed him for showing him pity. It wasn't over. He wouldn't let her go so easily. There had to be something that he could do.

Apollyon looked across at Amelia, briefly met Marcus's gaze, and then turned his back on them.

Marcus shared his anger. What Heaven had forced Apollyon to do was unforgivable. They had wanted Amelia to die. Why hadn't they told him that? Why had they ordered him to watch over her until now if they were only going to let her die? There had to be a reason. If they had wanted her dead, they could have changed events to make that happen or sent one of the angels of death for her. Why had they made him work so hard to protect her?

None of it made any sense.

Serenity left his side.

Was she giving up on Amelia too?

Marcus sucked in a deep breath, wiped away his tears with the heels of his hands, and clenched his fists. He refused to give up on her.

He pulled Amelia into his arms, cradling her to his bare chest and ignoring the pain that tore through him whenever he moved. It didn't matter that his body was still healing and was still incredibly weak from enduring Apollyon's attack. All that mattered was Amelia. He pressed a kiss to the top of her head. She still smelt the same. Hot tears rose but he shut his eyes, not letting them fall, and held her close, rocking with her. The pain in his heart eclipsed that in his body, pounding so strongly that he couldn't bear it. It tore a sob from him that he couldn't contain, not even when he wanted to be strong for her. She couldn't be gone. He had done everything he could to save her. He was supposed to protect her. Heaven had said nothing about her dying.

Veiron had though.

He had known that this was going to happen.

If Taylor hadn't driven him away, he might have got the answers he had wanted and might have discovered that Apollyon was responsible for carrying out the death sentence on Amelia. He slowly lifted his head and glared at Taylor, rage burning in his heart, overwhelming the pain and sorrow there.

"Don't you dare blame this on her." Einar's tone was as black as the clouds above them and Marcus turned his glare on him, his blood on fire with the need for revenge.

His anger abated when he saw the pain in Einar's brown eyes and the weariness, and then sensed how weak he was. Einar had used all of his strength healing him and trying to save Amelia. Serenity's magic was weak on his senses too, and the combined pain of those around him made him feel as though he was suffocating. Einar was right. Taylor didn't deserve his fury, just as Amelia hadn't deserved Apollyon's.

Heaven was to blame.

They had seen this event and they had known about it since the start of time. Apollyon couldn't overrule any order which had been given to him on his creation. Amelia's death sentence would have to have been given to him then and that was why Serenity hadn't been able to stop him.

Marcus growled out his frustration from between clenched teeth and lightning slammed into the fields around them, filling the morning with deafening crashes of thunder and blinding flashes of light. He clutched Amelia to him and pressed his lips to her forehead, and wished with all of his heart that Einar hadn't been able to save him either.

Marcus frowned when she shifted in his arms. He must have imagined it. She moved again and he drew back, looking down at her, and his eyes slowly widened as she lifted out of his arms.

Everyone stopped, turning towards Amelia as she floated up into the air as though suspended by her waist, her arms and legs hanging limply below her, and silence fell over the corn field.

Long sheer white material flowed around her, covering her breasts first and then wrapping around her ribs and her waist before finally encasing her hips. It fanned outwards from there, forming a long skirt and gradually turning indigo near her feet.

Marcus stared at her back when something glittered there as she hovered above him.

Pure silver feathers sprouted from her pale skin, knitting together to create the backbone of what looked like wings. Feathers grew out of them, filling the shape, each row larger than the last, until she had wings similar to his, only brighter and so pure they caught the light and dazzled him.

Her bare feet dipped downwards and she righted in the air, until she stood above them, the wind buffeting her dress so it danced around her legs.

The lacerations and burns on her skin faded, leaving pale unmarked flesh behind, and then her hair grew out, stretching far down to the small of her back. Silver spread from the roots, cascading down the full length of her hair until it had completely changed colour.

Marcus couldn't take his eyes off her or believe what he was seeing. It seemed his fellow warriors couldn't either because Einar was suddenly beside him with a sword in his hand. Marcus rose to his feet and focused with great effort. It was slow to come and the deep pain it caused him to use so much energy brought him close to passing out but his blue armour gradually materialised. It covered his chest and back, encased his forearms and shins, and a sense of calm washed through him as he felt the weight of his weapons at his waist.

Amelia didn't move.

She hovered there with her eyes closed.

If she even was Amelia now.

"What is this?" Lukas voiced his question so perfectly that Marcus wondered if he had sent it to him telepathically.

There was no such thing as a female angel.

The rest of the group gathered behind him and his heart pounded as he waited, unsure of what was going to happen.

Amelia's eyes slowly opened and she stared back at them.

Marcus stepped forwards and reached out to her. "Amelia?"

Her only reaction was to look at him and coolly say, "I do not know that name."

All of Marcus's hopes shattered again and anger blazed through him, turning his blood to flame. He turned, locked eyes with Apollyon, and drew his blade with his left hand.

"This is your fault," he snarled and flicked his hand outwards, extending the handle of the blade into a staff. "You did this."

Apollyon didn't react when Marcus charged at him, spear raised and body screaming in agony with each step. His hands trembled, arms weakening as pain tore through him, stripping away what little strength he had regained.

"Desist!" The sharp female voice stopped him in his tracks.

Marcus looked over his shoulder at Amelia. She descended gracefully and silver shoes appeared on her feet before she touched down on the scorched ground.

"Why do you fight?" she said, her voice distant and cold, nothing like the Amelia he had known and loved.

The Amelia he had lost.

Marcus lowered his spear so the blade rested on the dirt and relaxed his shoulders. His head spun, the world distorting with it, and he clenched his jaw against the weakness sweeping through him, battling to remain upright. He couldn't retain his grip on the staff of his spear. His fingers opened, lax against it, and he barely kept hold of it. His pulse raced, driven by both his lust for vengeance and the pain beating fiercely in his heart.

"Because you do not know me," he whispered and her silver-grey eyes briefly softened before turning cold again.

"I know you all." She regarded them in turn. The spark of hope that had flared back into life within him died again when she continued, "The guardian, the warrior, the mediator, and the destroyer."

Apollyon scowled at her and Marcus could feel his anger growing again, the strength of it now matching his own.

"There are always four of you. I recall that much." She looked at her surroundings and then back at him.

"She might remember more in time," Lukas said softly as though she wasn't standing there. His words didn't draw a reaction from her. She continued to watch him with her eerie silver eyes. "It might be temporary."

Marcus didn't dare hope that it was. Amelia had died and had been reborn in a way similar to that which angels experienced, but he couldn't bring himself to believe that she was one, or that she would remember anything about him. Whatever she was now, she was no longer Amelia.

Wind beat against him and then Amelia landed beside him, close enough that he could smell her. He ached inside at the familiar fragrance. This was a torture he couldn't endure. He wanted to scream and lash out at someone or something, wanted to tear Heaven itself down in order to release the pent up fury locked deep in his heart. He couldn't live like this, seeing her and smelling her, but knowing that it wasn't his Amelia who stood before him now. She was gone.

He turned to face her and she surprised him by reaching up and gently laying her hand on his cheek. A hint of concern warmed her eyes and her touch soothed him in a strange way, as though life was pouring back into his tired body from the palm of her small hand. His heart beat harder when she looked deep into his eyes and spoke again.

"My knight." She ran her fingers into his messy black hair. "My guardian angel."

"Do you know me?" Pain cracked his voice and he didn't think he could bear it if she said that she didn't, not when she was beginning to look as though she did.

She smiled and it warmed his heart to see it. He had fought for that smile. He had come close to dying for it. But now it didn't seem real. It wasn't the smile he had wanted to see one last time. It was given to him by the same lips but not the same heart.

"I would know my knight anywhere."

"Do you remember me?"

A frown creased her brow.

"No… but I know you." She lowered her hand away from his face and touched the spot over her heart. "I know you in here… beyond conscious memory… I remember you but not in that way."

She knew him beyond conscious memory. Did that mean that Lukas was right and there was a chance she might regain her memories given time? Whenever he had been reborn with a sense of knowing something, but not understanding why, he had eventually remembered it, although it was always centuries after his rebirth when that finally happened.

He could wait centuries for her to remember him. He would wait forever if it took that long.

Amelia knew him in her heart. That eased some of the pain inside his and gave him the strength to continue as her guardian. His duty wasn't done yet. Whatever this mission was, it wasn't over. He could feel it. Heaven hadn't released him from it and hadn't called him as they would have if it was finished, and that meant he had to stay by her side and continue to protect her.

He only hoped that he wasn't going to have to protect her from Heaven itself.

He wanted blood for what they had taken from him, and it was hard to remain here when he wanted to return home to Heaven and force an explanation from his superior, but such a rash reaction would only place Amelia in danger. Not only Amelia. There was no way he could defeat his superior should the angel choose to fight him. He wasn't strong enough.

As much as he hated it, as much as he needed to find out why Heaven had killed the woman he loved and why they had made him guard her so closely if they only wanted her dead, he had to bide his time. Heaven would call him to them eventually. They needed to issue new orders to him now and would require a report on what had happened. He just had to be patient and he would have his answers.

"We should leave this place," Einar said and Amelia looked at him, the cold returning to her eyes, and dropped her hand to her side. "I don't know what's going on… but someone is going to realise something has happened here and they'll come looking."

"We should report to Heaven and see what they have to say about this event." Lukas stepped forwards and Marcus noticed for the first time that his casual clothing was gone, replaced by his white and gold armour, and his white wings were out.

"Maybe we should take a moment to assess the situation before trusting anyone," Taylor said, gaining a dark look from Lukas.

Marcus could understand Lukas's loyalty to Heaven but he couldn't side with his old friend this time. He would go to Heaven, but it wouldn't be before they called him or he knew more about what was happening. He needed to go in there prepared, not blind with rage as he was now.

"Heaven made Apollyon kill Amelia, and it was willing to destroy me too." Marcus moved away from her, leaving her at the periphery as he moved into the group. She didn't follow him but he could feel her eyes on him, closely tracking his every move. "Veiron was right. Heaven knew that this was happening. They wanted her dead."

"You can't know that," Lukas interjected and turned his glare on Marcus.

Apollyon heaved a sigh and everyone looked at him. He stood with his eyes downcast and his black wings tucked against his back. Serenity stood beside him, her hand on his, slowly stroking it.

"I do not care much for what Heaven made me do… or the fact that they forced me to do it against my will," Apollyon whispered in a low voice. "But you are a fool, Lukas, if you believe that running to them is the right answer."

"What would you know?" Lukas strode up to him, stopping only once their chests were almost against each other, and tilted his head back to stare into Apollyon's blue eyes. "It is right that we go to Heaven and report what happened. They will know what to do."

"Lukas is right. Heaven will help us," Annelie said and didn't wilt when Apollyon turned his stare on her. She defiantly flicked her red hair out of her face and held his gaze. "They'll know what we need to do."

"You are both fools then. Did Heaven care about helping Amelia? They wanted her dead… they made me kill her and they didn't care that I almost killed Marcus in the process!" Darkness descended as Apollyon scowled at them both, stealing the light from the world, and his fists trembled at his sides.

Serenity murmured soft words in French to him and continued to stroke his arm, her motion rhythmic and slow, designed to soothe a man on the verge of unleashing Hell on someone. Marcus wasn't sure that such a small action could quell the rage in Apollyon's heart but it was certainly keeping him from attacking Lukas. The old Apollyon that Marcus knew would have been at Lukas's throat by now. They had fought each other over less in the past.

Einar intervened, pressing his hands against both men's breastplates and trying to force them apart.

"Desist!" Amelia said and everyone looked at her again. "I will not allow anyone to leave. I will destroy any who try."

Marcus frowned. Destroy? She looked strong for a moment as she stood tall, her silver wings outstretched and bright in the darkness, and then wavered. Marcus rushed to her, shutting out the pain caused by moving so quickly, and caught her before she hit the ground. Her wings disappeared and he looked down at her. Without them, she looked much as she used to and he could easily fool himself into thinking that Amelia was alive again. The silver hair made it impossible though. It shone like starlight, otherworldly in its luminescence.

"I am with Apollyon and Taylor," Marcus whispered and then raised his head. "What about the rest of you?"

"There is something off about what happened," Einar said. "We should bide our time and play things coolly before deciding which side to trust. Veiron had wanted to stop Amelia from dying. There had to be a reason for that."

"She turned into an angel." Annelie pointed at Amelia where she lay in Marcus's arms. "Would that be reason enough? Is there something magical about female angels?"

"There are no female angels." Lukas gently placed his hand on Annelie's shoulder and she frowned up into his green eyes.

"What is she then?"

"I don't know," Marcus answered her and looked down at the woman lying unconscious in his arms. "I want to believe that she is an angel though… and that was why Heaven had us do this to her… in order to awaken her. Some mortal souls join the ranks of angels on death. Perhaps she is one of them, and is special because she is female. Perhaps that is why they wanted her dead… so she would transcend her mortality and become like us."

Serenity looked at Apollyon. "Why would it take your power to awaken her?"

"Because I am death… or I was. I was the original angel of death. The legion that does it now came long after my creation." Apollyon's blue gaze fell on Amelia. "I am not sure what she is, but her death by my hands is one of the reasons for my existence, which means that Heaven knew about her before I was brought into this world as one of the first angels. There is a chance that the power Heaven gave to me was necessary to awaken her in this form, and that death by any other hands would have sent her mortal soul to Heaven instead."

It made sense. If Amelia's death was part of Apollyon's eternal duty, one of the reasons for his creation, then there was a chance that only he had been given the power to trigger her change into the angelic creature she had become.

Apollyon straightened, tilting his shoulders back, and cast his dark eyes over them all. "We are returning to Paris for now. We will discuss this matter further there."

Marcus nodded and waited to see if anyone would argue against Apollyon. Lukas didn't seem to have the courage and Annelie was looking less certain now. Marcus smiled his appreciation when Einar came and took Amelia from him, allowing him to stand, and then handed her back to him. Marcus cradled her in his arms and looked down at her, drowning in the maelstrom of his feelings.

He wasn't sure who to trust anymore, but he needed answers and fast. If Amelia's death hadn't been his final task, then what was it? The urge to go to Heaven and question his superior was hard to ignore, no matter how many times he told himself that it was better he waited until they had more information or until Heaven called him to them.

It beat inside him, strong and fierce, compelling him to do as his heart dictated and demand payment in blood for what had happened to Amelia.

He wished that he could obey it and unleash his fury on Heaven but he couldn't.

It wasn't Apollyon's decision that they would all return to Paris stopping him or the pain that still beat through him as his body slowly healed.

It was his wings.

They wouldn't come out.

CHAPTER 17

Marcus paced the small pale uncluttered bedroom in Apollyon's apartment. The day was wearing on and Amelia hadn't stirred. Upon their return to Paris, Marcus had placed her on top of the light blue bedclothes on the white wooden bed in the airy room and had stayed with her, leaving the others to discuss events in the other room. Serenity had checked on him twice so far, both times asking if he needed anything and if Amelia had come around. Everyone else had stayed away, although Einar and Apollyon had checked in on him telepathically, sometimes asking him questions about his mission and other things.

Both angels were concerned about the transformation that Amelia had undergone.

Lukas hadn't said much since they had returned. Marcus could hear everyone in the other room and Lukas's voice was absent from most of the conversations. Marcus could understand Lukas's need to question Heaven about it, and even now wished that he could go there and find out from his superior just what was happening and what his final task entailed. It was the right decision to be here though and to bide their time before trusting anyone again. As difficult as it was for him, he had to endure it. He wanted to trust Heaven and believe that their plan for Amelia was worth her death, but it became increasingly difficult with each moment he spent watching over her.

He had changed out of his armour on returning to Paris and had found himself going through Amelia's bag before he had got the better of himself. He had touched her things, held the jumper she had worn during their flight here to his nose so he could catch her lingering scent on it, and had come close to breaking down under the strain of it all. Pain continued to beat in his heart, running through his veins like acid that ate away at him, and he knew it would lessen if he left her presence, but he couldn't bring himself to do it. He needed to stay with her and guard her while she was vulnerable.

He looked at her when she stirred long enough to roll onto her front, her legs tangling in the layers of soft white and blue fabric she wore and her silver hair splayed out across the pillows.

Amelia.

It killed him that she didn't remember him or that name. She was Amelia to him, the woman he loved and needed more than anything. In the short time they had been together, she had become more vital to him than air, had given him love and awakened him to feelings he could no longer ignore. He ached so deeply for her, still craved the feel of her soft skin beneath her fingers and the warmth of her smiles. He hungered for the heat of her lips on his, the taste of her in his mouth and the smell of her on his skin, and the sound of her voice whispered in his ear. The more he looked at her, the more he could see past the changes and fool himself into seeing his Amelia.

He stopped near the side of the bed, lowered his hand, and gently ran his left index finger down her spine. He half expected her to wake and smile at him as she had back at her apartment after they had last made love, to reach for him and slide her hand around the nape of his neck and lure him down for a long unhurried kiss. Her skin was velvet beneath his fingertip, warm and soft, soothing yet tearing at him at the same time. It was miserable torture. He replayed her smile over and over again, wishing with every drop of his blood that when she woke she would remember him and this nightmare would end.

"Stop punishing yourself." Lukas's quiet voice stole into his fantasy and he frowned at Amelia, keeping his back to him. "Come and talk with the others."

Marcus hadn't expected Lukas to be the first of his fellow warriors to physically check on him. It made sense in a way. Out of all of them, Lukas was the most sensitive when it came to this sort of thing. It was probably why he had been reborn as a mediator these past two lifetimes, an angel made for talking people down off ledges and making people see sense. Marcus didn't think that Lukas could easily ease his suffering or take it away. It hurt too much. All he knew was pain.

"I am fine," he whispered and glanced past Lukas through the open door that led into the bright living room. Annelie was watching him with pity in her dark eyes. Everyone else seemed to be avoiding looking at him.

That room bore more punishment than his current location.

He smiled tightly at Lukas. "I will take first watch."

He walked past Lukas into the living room, turned away from the others as they looked at him, and headed straight through the kitchen to the small rooftop balcony that overlooked a leafy park. The warm light of evening heightened the verdant colour of everything and he sighed as he leaned against the iron railings.

He could still feel everyone's eyes on him and could hear them as they talked, discussing him in low voices.

Marcus watched the world below, eyes tracking couples as they walked through the park, or families as they played together. Even this was torture. The sun slowly sunk towards the horizon until it disappeared from view behind the trees and buildings, and the sky began to darken. Marcus remained there, standing sentinel with his senses on high alert in case something happened.

The conversation died down inside the apartment and gradually the streetlights came on, illuminating the road below that ran alongside the darkening park. Someone entered the kitchen, Serenity judging by the sense of power, and hesitated a moment at the door behind him before leaving again. He heard cupboards open and close, and what sounded like crockery being piled and cutlery gathered.

His stomach growled at the thought of food but he ignored it and remained where he was, part of him afraid of facing the others. He didn't want their pity and couldn't bear the way they looked at him as though he would break under the slightest breeze. He was stronger than that, or he would be if they gave him time. These feelings were new to him but he would master them.

The moon rose and his gaze followed it, watching as it changed from deep orange through to white. Stars began to appear but only the brightest ones. The yellow haze from the streetlights drowned out the rest. He would have given anything in that moment to fly away until he was high in the sky, far from Earth, between it and Heaven, and could see the stars properly. He couldn't leave though, and it wasn't his wings stopping him this time. He had to remain here and watch over Amelia. Even if she didn't remember him right now, there was a chance that she would regain her memories. He couldn't be weak and run away from her. She needed his protection now more than ever.

His resolve to face everything crumbled when he sensed someone step out onto the balcony behind him, their footsteps silent on the terracotta tiles, and then they stepped into view.

Amelia stood beside him, a vision in her sheer white flowing dress that barely concealed her body and her silver hair shining in the moonlight. Her eyes were still a shade too close to silver, brighter and more otherworldly than his Amelia's had ever been. He quickly cast his gaze downwards to the hem of her dress where it turned blue and her bare feet, staring at them in order to avoid having to look into her eyes and torture himself with the differences between this woman and his lost love.

A breeze blew the hem of her dress against her legs, revealing the cherub tattoo on her ankle. Marcus frowned at it, pain spearing his chest as he remembered the first time he had noticed it. She had been in the hall outside her apartment, wearing that plum coloured slip that had left little to his imagination and had sparked the awakening of his suppressed feelings for her. He could still remember the warmth of her hand on his as she had iced his knuckles, and the heat of her gaze on his bare back. Everything between them had started that night. It had been their beginning, and now they had reached their end, and he would give everything to go back to that moment and do things differently so she didn't have to die.

So she didn't have to leave him alone in the world with only an eternity of suffering and loneliness ahead of him.

He tore his eyes away, skipped over her and stared at the moon.

The bright orb held his eyes but not his attention. That wandered back to Amelia where she stood beside him and he ached inside. He wished that everything would end so he no longer felt the pain burning in his chest. The past day had been a nightmare and he hated what had happened and hated that Einar had saved him. He would rather be dead than face this torment. He couldn't bear it. He tried so hard to cope with everything and to be strong, to find his resolve to continue his mission and protect the woman now standing beside him, and when she wasn't present, he could find it and some sense of peace. The moment he set eyes on her again, it shattered, leaving him weak, and his heart cried out for Amelia to return to him.

He drew in a slow deep breath and then forced himself to look at her.

Amelia.

His heart still called her that even when he knew she was no longer that soul.

What was she now?

Not an angel, that was certain.

Was she still Amelia?

The temptation to raise his left hand and gently brush the backs of his fingers across her cheek was overwhelming. If he did, he wouldn't get the reaction he expected. She wouldn't lean into his caress or look at him with love in her eyes as she used to. She would remind him that she didn't know him and his heart couldn't bear to hear it again.

He shut down his emotions, forcing them away until he was cold inside, as empty as the silver eyes watching him.

"What do you want?"

CHAPTER 18

A deep sense of pain in her heart woke her and it wouldn't be ignored. She stared down at her chest, confused by the feeling burning inside her, trying to understand it. She knew nothing of emotions. Not positive or negative. What sort of feeling was this? It drove her to leave the bed although she wasn't sure why and then led her from the room. She regarded the mixture of mortals and angels gathered in the next room with cold eyes, unaffected by their presence. They watched her and when they looked as though they might speak, she turned away, following the pain in her heart into another room.

She looked ahead of her and raised her eyebrows when she saw that her knight was alone and the pain in her chest began to lessen. Was it his doing? She didn't understand it at all. How could laying eyes on him alleviate the strange hurt inside her?

The air was cool outside on the small balcony and she walked forwards, desiring to see what it was that held her knight's attention so intently. The moon. It hung above them in an inky sky, surrounded by bright pinpricks of stars. She stared at it, bathing in its strong light, and then looked at her knight.

He avoided her, choosing to look at her feet instead of her face, and she recalled the pain that had been in his eyes and his heart when they had met in that field.

He had called her Amelia.

She wished that she recalled that name but it was foreign to her, as mysterious as he was and the others too. While she knew what they were, she didn't know who they were, and she had no desire to either. They were instruments to her, three angels who would eventually do her bidding or would die.

Three?

Four angels.

She looked at her knight when her heart hurt again and the pain eased. Why couldn't she think of him as one of the rest? Why did she want to set him apart from them?

"What do you want?" he said in a deep voice and she wasn't sure how to respond to such a demanding question. She wasn't sure yet what she wanted or what she needed to do. It would come to her in time. She was sure of that much at least. "You should remain indoors where it is safe."

She looked back into the apartment and through it to the living room where the others waited. There was truth in his observation. He was a single angel and there were three in the other room, one of which was superior in strength, power and experience. Logically speaking, she was safest there, surrounded by three angels.

But logic didn't seem to matter much in this instance. Something overruled it.

"There is nowhere safer than near you." It was an answer she derived from the fact that her pain had eased when she had laid eyes on him and that it was almost gone now that she was close to him.

She was certain that was what the feeling was about. She wasn't safe without her knight and he hadn't been in the room when she had awoken. It had shocked her and she had felt the need to find him.

He turned to regard her with startled eyes. "Why?"

His silver-blue eyes were warmer for a moment and then turned hollow again.

Amelia touched his hand and felt his pain. "You are sad."

"I am," he said without inflection, cold and emotionless.

"Because I do not recall you?"

He exhaled slowly and looked at the moon again. "Something like that."

She felt different inside again, no longer cold or empty, and struggled with the new feelings as she looked at his profile, her gaze tracing it. The more she looked at him, the stronger the feeling became, spreading through her until she could no longer bring herself to see him as nothing more than a creature that was beneath her, one who should sacrifice himself to protect her. A sense that she knew him flowed through her in the wake of the first feeling and she tried to grasp it but couldn't.

The sight of him in pain moved her to go to him and comfort him. She stepped around him, a trickle of fear running along her nerves, confusing her further, and cupped his cheek, her eyes meeting his.

"Did I do something to upset you?" she whispered and his eyes widened. "Is it the mortal soul that shared this body with me?"

His face darkened and he pushed her hand away from him, scowling at her. "I don't want to talk about this with you."

Amelia frowned back at him. She wanted to put him in his place for speaking so disrespectfully to her but she couldn't bring herself to go through with it. She had never witnessed such suffering. It filled her with a sense that she should feel something for him or do something to help him.

"There must be something I can do to ease your pain," she said and he looked at her again, eyes soulful and full of hope.

"Do you remember me?"

Amelia thought about it as she stared into his eyes, searching her fragmented memories for knowledge of him and his kinsmen. A flicker of something beat in her chest again as it had done in the field when he had posed that question to her before.

"I know you… in here." She touched her chest and then her head. "But not in here. I wish that I knew more about you than just this sensation within me. You are familiar to me." She curled her fingers up and then touched her chest again, focusing there. "Dear to me… or perhaps I was dear to you. I wish I remembered you."

"Why?" His voice cracked and the pain in her chest increased as his eyes searched hers.

Amelia touched his face again and he closed his eyes and leaned into her palm. She sensed the moment his pain eased because the ache in her heart eased too. Whatever connected them, it was strong and fierce, a bond that couldn't even be undone by death.

"This is not Amelia touching me now," he whispered to himself and frowned, his eyes still closed. The sense of sorrow and hurt in him increased. "Whatever this divine being before me is, it is not the woman I was falling for."

"I wish that I remembered you because then your pain would cease. I want to ease your suffering."

He opened his eyes and looked so deep into her eyes that she felt as though he was trying to see the answer to his question before he posed it. "The others believe that in time you will remember things… will you?"

The pain that beat in her heart now was so intense that it stole her breath and hot liquid rose into her eyes, threatening to spill onto her cheeks. The feelings awakening inside her both confused and surprised her. Whatever this angel had felt for the mortal soul within her body, it had been strong. She had meant a lot to him.

She didn't understand the emotions involved, struggled to grasp their meaning, and had thought that angels didn't bear such mortal feelings.

They had changed since her last life. She didn't recall exactly what they were like before, only that they were cruel beings fit only for destruction.

Marcus was anything but cruel. There was such warmth in him and affection, and she honestly felt safest around him, as though they still shared a bond.

He looked at her, his icy eyes full of turbulent emotions that she could feel through the point where she was touching him. He lowered his head, causing his overlong black hair to fall forwards and caress his forehead, and a desire to brush it back again so she could see his face momentarily burst into life inside of her.

She raised his head so he looked at her again, leaned in and tiptoed, bringing her mouth up to his. He knocked her hand away and stepped back before her lips could touch his.

"Don't!" he snapped and the anger that radiated from him and flowed into her gave her a sense of the true depth of his power and how dangerous he was. She had underestimated him. The dark angel wasn't the most powerful after all. There was something about Marcus, a hidden strength that she hadn't noticed before. Did he even know that he had it? "It doesn't work that way… you can't just do something like that."

He stepped back again and she didn't like the gap that opened between them or how it felt as though it was a vast crevasse rather than a mere few feet. He glared at her, eyes void of warmth now and full of unending darkness.

"I can't take it," he growled the words and his power rose again, his fury burning through her and warning her away. "I can't… not if you don't remember everything that has happened between us." He clenched his fists and they shook at his sides. "You don't remember anything?"

His anger faltered and hope flickered in his eyes again.

She shook her head. "Perhaps I will in time. Perhaps the feeling in my heart… the sense that you were dear to me… will revive the memories I have lost and restore them. Would you like that?"

She trembled as she waited to hear his answer, suddenly unsure of herself and of anything. What had he done to her? Angels were nothing but instruments. They were disposable. They were not creatures that she sought to placate and soothe.

They were beings she had little care for. She had little care for anything. How had this angel changed that about her?

Part of her was afraid. The emotion was as alien as the rest of the ones she had experienced since waking this evening and made her feel vulnerable and weak. For the first time, she was aware of the power an angel held, and it scared her. While she could take him in a fight, she couldn't defeat him in this war of feelings. They stripped her of her defences and left her bare, exposed to him and at his mercy, and she couldn't grasp why they were flooding her. She hadn't asked for them, and couldn't recall ever feeling anything for one of his kind before. In the past, she had never cared what they had thought of her, but now she stood hanging on every breath he drew, waiting to hear the answer to her question.

He lowered his gaze so he was staring down into the street below them with his face turned away from her and whispered, "I would like that more than anything, because being with you when you are no longer Amelia is killing me… and I wish that Apollyon had finished me off."

He closed his eyes, turned, and walked back into the apartment, leaving her alone on the balcony staring at his retreating back.

He wished for death?

That shocked her and left her cold.

Her knight wanted to die because of her.

She looked down at her hands and then at her body, and then gazed at her reflection in the full length window beside the doors.

Who had she been?

She had to remember because if she didn't, she would lose her knight, and she didn't think that she could bear that.

A flash of images danced over her reflection.

Moonlight. Palm trees. Dark waves lapping at a white shore.

And then her knight. Marcus.

Carrying her through the water to the shore, his eyes locked with hers and so full of passion that she was hot all over, burning for him.

It wasn't passion heating her now though.

It was a single feeling that crashed over her like a wave and swept her away, leaving her dazed.

Love.

She had fallen in love with Marcus that night.

CHAPTER 19

Marcus woke to the sound of an argument. Rather than hearing two familiar voices locked in noisy combat, he only recognised one—Apollyon. The object of his wrath was a young male voice but one filled with anger that almost matched Apollyon's. Marcus couldn't sense the power of the other angel. Apollyon's eclipsed it, pressing down on the apartment so heavily that Marcus was surprised it hadn't woken him before the shouting had.

He rose to his knees on his uncomfortable makeshift bed on the floor next to Amelia's bed, his muscles stiff and sore from healing, and checked to see if she was still asleep. Her eyes were closed and she didn't seem awake, although how she could sleep through such a racket was beyond him. He sleepily rubbed his hair and then caught the topic of the argument. It purged the tiredness from his body in an instant. He stood and called his armour to him as he strode to the door, and opened it. Apollyon stood in the middle of the spacious living room with his back to him, his black armour and wings making him as dark as ever and a sharp contrast to the paleness of his surroundings.

Marcus didn't recognise the other angel. He wore armour similar to Apollyon's, black with gold edging, but seemed younger and not only in appearance. How old was this angel? Too young to be let out into the world if he was foolish enough to argue with Apollyon about something.

The confidence that shone in the youth's blue eyes surprised Marcus. It didn't waver as he and Apollyon stared each other out.

"I can't leave without her," the blond man said at last, casting a look in Marcus's direction. "A mission is a mission."

"Leave," Apollyon snarled and the room darkened for a moment, the sense of anger pervading it intensifying and then ebbing away.

Marcus looked across the room towards the kitchen door. Einar, Taylor, Lukas, Annelie and Serenity all stood there in a group. Einar and Taylor were wearing what looked like the clothes they had chosen to sleep in, both in dark shorts and loose t-shirts, and Serenity was wearing a short pink dress. Lukas was dressed in his armour. He had come to relieve Marcus and take over the watch this morning. Marcus glanced at the brass circular sun-like clock hanging on the wall near the group. Only a couple of hours ago. When had the newcomer arrived?

Judging by the fact that the bedding was still down in the living room, arranged with one set in the L of the beige couches, and the other set where Apollyon now stood on the other side of the couch that had its back to the front door, their guest had arrived when most people had still been sleeping.

"I keep saying I can't." The blond folded his arms across his chest. He was slimmer than all of them, scrawny in comparison to most angels that Marcus knew. It was strange to see such a weak looking man facing off against Apollyon. Marcus hadn't been able to defeat him. This boy wouldn't stand a chance. He wouldn't even survive the initial blast of Apollyon's power.

"I won't let you take her," Apollyon said and turned his head slightly to one side, enough that he could glance over his shoulder at Marcus. "I won't. I have done enough to cause others pain. I will not allow this to happen too."

"Sorry, old man… I wasn't giving you a choice."

Apollyon laughed. "I seem to be getting that a lot recently. It doesn't change anything. You can try to take her, Lysander, and you will die trying."

Serenity went to move forwards to Apollyon but Einar caught her arm, holding her back. Her brow furrowed, her hazel eyes locked on the man she loved, and Marcus could feel a glimmer of her pain in her power. She feared that he would fight again. It must have been difficult for her to see Apollyon trying to kill him and killing Amelia and not be able to do anything to stop it. It must have been difficult for them all.

Marcus looked at Apollyon's back and his broad black wings. Especially his old friend.

"Listen, kid—" Apollyon started.

"I told you never to call me that." Lysander cut him off and the room darkened again and Marcus sensed the barest thread of Lysander's power through the mask of Apollyon's. He could take him out if necessary but, judging by the way Apollyon was acting, it wouldn't be. Apollyon would deal with this man for him. Lysander tipped his chin up. "I was under your wing for six centuries and I'm not a child anymore. I never was."

Apollyon made a dismissive motion with his hand.

"What right do you have to order me around anyway? You're retired. Out of the game, remember?" Lysander said and Serenity looked nervous. What had she seen crossing Apollyon's face? Einar and Lukas looked concerned too.

"If I am 'out of the game' as you put it, then what was yesterday all about?" Apollyon took a step towards Lysander and the young blond man stepped back, keeping the distance between them steady. It seemed he had some sense after all. Apollyon was strong enough to take such a weak angel down with one blow and he had been looking for someone to level his anger at since the event that had brought them to this point.

"What do you mean?" The confusion in Lysander's blue eyes caused Marcus to frown.

Heaven must have done some serious cover-up work to hide Apollyon's battle from the angels of death, or any angels in fact. Apollyon's power was so destructive and so intrinsically linked to Heaven and their master that most of them should have been aware of its use the other day. Had Heaven somehow shielded the power so other angels didn't realise what had happened? Why would they do such a thing? The part of him that had been loyal to Heaven and his duty all these centuries said not to question them and to obey their orders, but it was becoming impossible to trust them. They had wanted Amelia dead and had succeeded, and now they had sent an angel of death to retrieve her.

Apollyon heaved a sigh. "Go home, Lysander, and tell them you were never here."

"They know I'm here… and now I want to know why. They tell me to come to your apartment and that I would find a soul here that required transport to

Heaven… and then you tell me that you can't let me take her… and everyone here seems to know something I don't. I want to know what that is."

Marcus could sympathise with Lysander. He was feeling the same way and had been for a long time now. His demand was redundant though. No one here knew what was happening either.

"No, you don't. Just get out of my apartment and go home. This isn't your fight, kid. Leave." Apollyon waved towards the door.

"I'm not leaving until you tell me—"

"I killed her," Apollyon interjected and stalked towards Lysander, grabbed him by the throat and beat his wings. He slammed Lysander into the wall beside the front door, causing Serenity to gasp and reach out to him, and tightened his grip around the young angel's neck. "Do you understand that? Is that clear enough for you? They forced me to kill her and I cannot let you take her away… not again… not from Marcus. I took her from him once… and I have to make it up to him now."

"They made you?" Lysander said, his eyes wide as he stared into Apollyon's.

"Mon ange," Serenity whispered and held her hand out to him, a pleading look on her face.

Apollyon sucked in a deep breath, glanced over his shoulder at Serenity, and then released his grip on Lysander. The young angel dropped to his feet and sagged against the wall, rubbing his throat.

Apollyon smiled sourly. "I was a fool. There is no leaving. Never. It killed me to do that and to do something against a friend's wishes, which is why I must make it up to him now… and why I cannot let you take Amelia."

Marcus started when Amelia brushed against him in the doorway, her silver eyes full of sleep and confusion. They brightened as she took everything in and then narrowed when she saw Lysander. Marcus moved in front of her, blocking Lysander's path. He doubted that Apollyon would back down without a fight, and that should be enough to drive Lysander away, but he wasn't going to take any chances. He wouldn't allow Lysander to take Amelia from him. She had been through enough.

Apollyon moved back another step. "Do not make this into a fight, kid. You would not win."

Lysander sensibly remained pressed against the wall but made no move to reach for the door.

"I can't go without her. I'm sorry, I really am, but they know that I'm here. They're watching me." Lysander looked up and then back at Apollyon, and then past him to Marcus. "It doesn't matter what you all want. I can't go without her. If you won't hand her over, then I will have to fight you, and I won't be alone."

A shriek from the group gathered near the kitchen door snapped Marcus's attention to them. Annelie rushed into Lukas's arms and he pulled her close, his gold and white spear at the ready, as three more angels of death came into the room, pushing past the group and crowding around Apollyon. Serenity moved to one side, coming closer to Marcus, and colourful threads of magic wove around her fingers and up her arms. Her power grew, swamping Lysander's, and almost reaching the level of Apollyon's.

Marcus drew one of his blades with his left hand and kept Amelia behind him with the other.

"It doesn't matter how many angels you bring to this fight or whether my actions go against Heaven's decree, I will not let you take Amelia from me." Marcus flicked his hand out to extend the handle of the blade into a staff. The silver engravings flashed under the lights and Lysander looked past Apollyon to him.

Apollyon held his hands out in front of him. Twin curved golden blades appeared in his grasp and he brought them both down to his sides, cutting swiftly through the air.

Einar materialised two silver swords and handed one to Taylor. She shifted into a fighting stance.

Amelia lightly touched Marcus's left hand, warming him to the bone with the soft caress, and nudged it downwards, as though telling him to lower his weapon. He wouldn't.

Her fingers trailed over the back of his hand and she moved out from behind him. Marcus grabbed her wrist to stop her and she turned to face him, her expression detached and cold, a reflection of how he had looked so many times in his month on Earth. She placed her hand over his and removed it from her arm, and then walked out into the space between the couches.

Everyone watched her in silence.

"I will go with you," she said and he swore that he heard fear in her voice.

Marcus shifted his spear to his right hand and held his left one out to her, the pain spreading outwards from his heart threatening to consume him. He silently begged her to take it and come back to him. She didn't have to go with Lysander and these angels.

"I will go," she said with more conviction.

"No," Marcus ground the word out and she looked at him with wide eyes. "I can't… won't let you go."

He reached to her again and for a moment she looked as though she would take his hand but then she turned away and lowered her head.

"Too much blood has already been spilt because of me," she whispered and Lysander edged around the outside of the room, as far away from Apollyon as possible, and came up beside her.

"No." Marcus shook his head. This wasn't happening. He hadn't meant to make her feel as though she had to leave. It had been a moment of weakness that had made him say those things to her last night. He wasn't ready for her to go. Not yet. Not ever.

He kept his hand outstretched to her, imploring her to take it and come back to him.

Lysander took hold of her arm.

Light began to fill the room.

The other angels disappeared, leaving Amelia and Lysander behind.

As a beam shone down on her, she raised her chin and her eyes met his, and he saw them as they had been when she was human, a beautiful stormy grey. She smiled faintly.

"I'm sorry, Marcus… for everything."

She was gone before he could react, the light fading and revealing only blankets where she had been. He stared at the spot for long seconds, frowning and trying to comprehend what had just happened.

It couldn't be. She couldn't have.

He pushed past everyone, shoved the French doors open so hard that they rattled, and ran out onto the balcony. He clutched the black iron railing and stared at the sky.

"Amelia!" Marcus flung his head back and yelled at the heavens, distraught and enraged, the bitter taste of fury coating his throat and tongue. The sky blackened and the wind picked up, whipping into a howling rage around him, tearing leaves off the trees in the park.

He dug his fingertips into the railing, bending the metal into his palms.

"You remembered me… why… why leave?"

Lightning crashed down into the park, filling the air with the scent of earth, and he ground his teeth together, fighting to regain command of his emotions as they threatened to send him out of control. Liquid fire blazed in his veins, burning him from the inside out, consuming him. He bit back his desire to scream out his fury and glared at the darkening tempestuous sky.

He needed to go after her. His wings erupted from his back and then disappeared. He tried to call them again but they wouldn't come. He growled in frustration as an order came through into his head and he realised that his lack of wings wasn't due to his curse this time. His orders were clear. Heaven was closed to him pending further investigation into the events that had occurred over the past forty-eight hours and his part in them. He was to remain out of the realm of Heaven until they called him to them, and then he would be able to see Amelia again. Until then, she would be safe with them.

Marcus's knees gave out and he hit the tiles, cracking them, his fingers still clutching the buckled railing. He hung his head forwards and broke down, sobs racking him as he struggled against his feelings and his desire to tear Heaven apart in his search for Amelia. He couldn't let her go so easily and he refused to believe that they meant her no harm. As soon as he could, he was going to Heaven to find her and bring her back. She remembered him.

He had never felt so alive and relieved, yet so dead and cold too.

A heavy hand on his right shoulder caused him to drag in a sharp breath and hold it in an attempt to stop his tears. It was Apollyon's power flowing into him through that touch. He couldn't let Apollyon see him like this, so weak and pathetic.

Apollyon crouched beside him and Marcus let go of the railing. His fingertips were bleeding. He stared at them and then at the bent balustrade.

"I will pay for a new one," he whispered and Apollyon sighed but didn't say anything. "She remembered me… why did she go?"

"Because she felt it was the right thing to do." Apollyon patted his shoulder. "She did not want you to fight and saw a chance to stop that from happening."

"Why?"

"Perhaps she remembered more than just your name." Apollyon sat beside him on the cold tiles and leaned his back against the low white wall that ran at a ninety degree angle to the iron railing, joining it to the wall beside the French doors. "You must have said something that triggered the return of some of her memories."

"I doubt that… I told her to stay away from me… and that I wanted to die."

"Death is certainly convenient in its own strange way. You wanted to forget her. Perhaps that is why she remembered you." Apollyon smiled but it didn't reach his blue eyes. He swept a hand over his long black hair, pushing it back into his ponytail, and then loosed a long sigh.

He touched Marcus's shoulder again, regaining his attention that had started to wander back to Amelia and where Lysander had taken her. "We will not allow anything to happen to her. She declared us her knights, remember?"

Marcus nodded and then looked skyward. "Heaven has sent me orders to stay away. They are investigating my actions and will not allow me to see Amelia until they call me. Why would they do such a thing?"

Apollyon's power shifted, darkening again. "Who knows… but I do know one thing… they have a reason for everything they have made us do and we must find out what that reason is. Come inside and we'll discuss it with the others."

Apollyon stood and offered Marcus his hand. Marcus took it and hauled himself onto his feet, and then rubbed the heel of his hands across his eyes to clear away his tears so the others didn't see them. Serenity and Annelie cast a fearful glance his way when he entered the living room. He hadn't meant to lose control of his power and scare them. It had been impossible to contain it all and he had done his best to keep his wrath away from them so he wouldn't hurt anyone.

Taylor didn't look at all bothered. She was talking to Einar and Lukas about something and just smiled at him when he stopped next to Serenity and Apollyon.

"What do we do now?" Lukas no longer looked as though he was going to keep insisting they file a report with Heaven about what had happened. He looked as though he was ready to fight them instead. He still wore his white and gold armour, his white wings furled against his back, and there was a hard edge to his green eyes.

"There's a Hell's angel named Veiron who said that he witnessed it all. We need to find him," Marcus said and Taylor stepped forwards.

"I can do that… I know some of his old haunts in the underworld. We'll find him and find out what's happening, Marcus." She offered him another warm smile full of reassurance.

Apollyon frowned. "We need to go to Hell then. There is a chance that the pool there might show details of the event too and what is yet to happen in your mission. Lukas, I need you to remain here and look after Annelie and Serenity for me again."

Lukas looked irritated and then started to nod, but Serenity shook her head, causing her long fair hair to sway against her slender shoulders.

"I can take care of Annelie alone. You need Lukas with you," she said, her French accent laced with determination. Marcus looked away, unable to bear the affection in her gaze as she stared into Apollyon's eyes, silently conveying her desire for him to be safe.

"If Taylor is going down there with you, then I'm coming too," Einar said and Apollyon sized him up.

"I suppose I can carry you if one of the others carries Taylor." Apollyon didn't look pleased at the prospect.

Lukas smiled. "It's like old times."

Apollyon's look soured further. "Only he looks heavier than you were."

Both Einar and Lukas frowned at him.

Marcus looked back through the kitchen to the world outside. It was settled. As soon as they were ready, they would depart for Hell. He would uncover the truth about Amelia and why Heaven had wanted her dead, and then he would go after her.

He curled his fingers into fists.

Amelia.

She had remembered something about herself, about himself, and she had gone with Lysander in order to protect him and his friends.

She had to hang on and wait for him.

He would find her.

He wouldn't fail her again.

CHAPTER 20

The bright light receded but rather than the ground being puffy white clouds and a golden sun shining down on her, Amelia found herself surrounded by a large entrance hall. The pale marble caused everything to blend into each other, until she could barely distinguish the elaborate twin staircase that swept upwards following the curved walls that it hugged. In front of her, a wide arch filled the space below the balcony at the top of the staircase. Beyond it was a long corridor in equally eye-numbing white marble.

As she stood there with the angel called Lysander gripping her arm, everything began to dull to a more reasonable level, as though her eyes were finally adjusting to the obscene brightness of it all. It had only taken a few seconds of exposure to the light to give her a headache.

Another memory of Marcus popped into her head and replayed, revealing a moment with him that caused a blush to burn her cheeks.

Perhaps it was the returning memories that were giving her the headache. Since remembering their moment together in that other world where Taylor had sent them to keep them hidden, she had recalled at least six other memories of being with him. There had been a fight against two Hell's angels on a rooftop overlooking a city, a meeting with another Hell's angel who had been far more handsome than his predecessors and had seemed familiar to Taylor, a time when she had been high above the world in Marcus's arms, their flight around the Eiffel Tower, the memory that had just come back to her, and then there was the one that had woken her today.

It had felt like a nightmare at first and had left her heart beating painfully fast against her chest.

Marcus had been before her with his silver-blue wings bloodied and torn, and his armour decimated. There had been pain in him and in her heart, a feeling that had ripped her apart from the inside out and still lingered deep in her chest. She hadn't been able to bear seeing him suffering for her at the hands of a man he had called friend. She hadn't wanted him to die because of her but she had hesitated, afraid of taking that pain and that death upon herself instead. When the power that had been blasting against him, aimed for her, had started to shred his flesh, she had reacted on instinct and had found the courage to take responsibility and face her destiny.

She had leapt in front of him, desperate to shield him so he wouldn't die. She had sacrificed herself.

Her death had jolted her awake and she had panicked when Marcus hadn't been there with her and there had been raised voices in the other room.

She had sat in the middle of the bed, clutching the covers to her chest and struggling with the two sides of her soul. The one that Marcus had loved had returned, bringing with it a flood of emotions that had threatened to render her unconscious. It had been difficult to battle them and find a sense of balance again, to assimilate them and the memories into herself. There were times when she still felt like two people in one body.

It wasn't just memories of her life as Amelia that were returning. She had seen things in her slumber that she knew were flickers of her previous life. She had been through this before. The scenario was becoming familiar and a sense of foreboding was growing inside her.

She couldn't shake the feeling that there was a reason she believed angels were only fit for destruction and were cruel beings.

"This way," Lysander said, jolting her back to reality.

She had almost forgotten where she was. How could she have? She had come to the place that had ordered her death at Apollyon's hands and she wasn't sure what she was going to do now. Leaving with Lysander had spared Marcus but it had hurt him, and part of her wanted to go back and change the past. If she could do it again, she would have left without letting him know that she had remembered him. She would have spared him that pain too.

He had suffered enough because of her. It was time that she took her fate on her own shoulders and bore the weight of it. It was time that she faced Heaven and found out why they had killed her.

The growing sliver of fear in her heart questioned her every move and sent doubts into her head, threatening to steal what little strength and courage she had found.

The longer she spent in the white fortress surrounding her, the stronger the sense of foreboding became, until she couldn't shake the feeling that she had been here before.

Several times.

Amelia walked forwards with Lysander and looked around, taking in the hallways that led off the long columned corridor and disappeared into the distance, their ends so far away that they were impossible to see. Opened doors led off those corridors, some of them revealing another hallway. The place was like a maze. She couldn't keep track when Lysander turned down one hallway and then onto another, and then took her up several flights of white marble steps. They were cold beneath her bare feet.

She glanced across at her guard. He seemed so out of place in this stark white environment. The brightness of it caused his black armour to seem even darker than it was, and the gold detailing shone so fiercely that it hurt her eyes. He looked at her out of the corner of his eye, his blue ones meeting hers only long enough for her to realise that she wasn't the only one with doubts about why she was here, and then faced forwards again.

Amelia looked there too.

They were coming to another junction in the featureless labyrinth of corridors. There were no windows. What did the outside of this fortress look like and where were all the other angels? She hadn't seen anyone other than the man escorting her. Even the angels who had appeared when he had threatened to fight Apollyon and Marcus were nowhere to be seen.

She shivered as a blast of cold air chased over her and then paused as she stepped out into another corridor.

A double row of arches lined the wall opposite her, one set stacked on top of the other, revealing a large pale courtyard. Tall white trees rose up in the middle of it to tower beyond the reach of her vision. The whole image seemed false to her. Trees had green leaves, not silver-white ones that glittered and shone in the golden sunlight flooding the courtyard. The brilliant white trunks of the trees and the grass surrounding their roots twinkled like diamonds as the light filtered through the branches and caught them. It was beautiful, yet the sight of it filled her with sadness and left her with a sense of finality. Why? Lysander tugged on her arm and she continued to walk with him, her gaze fixed on the arches. There were other angels on the opposite side of the courtyard, walking along the corridor on the same level as her. They wore blue armour like Marcus's. Would they know him if she broke free of Lysander's grip and crossed the courtyard to them to ask? There were probably thousands of his kind, and the three angels he was closest to were all of a different class to him.

A mediator, a hunter, a destroyer, and a guardian.

Why did she know them? It wasn't only her memories as Amelia that contained them. She had known them in her past life too, was aware they were always there at the start but never there at the end. Did they die? At the end, there was only ever a guardian.

Marcus.

A memory glimmered in the corner of her mind, just out of reach, and she struggled with it, wanting to bring it into focus so she could know its contents. A flash of colour and brightness that faded into red as deep as blood filled her vision and she stopped and closed her eyes against it. She couldn't close her heart to the pain that rushed through her though. It blazed in her chest, burned in her veins, and sent her trembling.

She knew Marcus.

Not in this life.

But in her last one.

Why?

Had she met all of them before, in her previous life?

Lysander tugged on her arm and led her down another corridor and she lost sight of the other angels. She looked back, hoping to catch a glimpse of others, but no one was there. Time lost meaning as she walked with him. She wasn't sure where they were heading but her feet were freezing now and her legs were tiring, trembling beneath her.

Amelia searched her mind, trying to see why she felt she knew these corridors and that courtyard, and why she knew Marcus and the others. Her head felt fuzzy and heavy, and every time she tried to focus, her thoughts became tangled. Perhaps she didn't know them or this place at all. Perhaps she was mixing things up in her mind. It was hard to assimilate two sets of memories and make sense of them.

She looked ahead at the end of the corridor and a bright room beyond. Her heart started to pound. Her palms sweated. She slowed her steps as a sense of awareness swept through her and Lysander pulled on her arm again. Her footsteps faltered. Fear crawled through her veins.

She knew this place.

Her gaze tracked up the tall thick white columns that rose into the bright heavens above her, disappearing there. Sunlight streamed down onto her, warming her skin, but it was the flush of panic that heated her through.

This place was familiar.

It pained her.

Why?

She walked forwards, heading towards the wide aisle between the gargantuan columns that speared the dazzling sky.

Her heart missed a beat and she hesitated again, a sudden wave of fear pinning her feet to the floor. A deep sharp ache throbbed in her chest and a desire to turn back filled her trembling body.

"Come along," Lysander said and Amelia shook her head.

He tugged on her arm but she didn't move.

She couldn't.

Whatever memories she had of this place, they were full of pain, as though all of her experiences here had been bad.

She had made a mistake.

A terrible one.

She backed away from Lysander, casting a fearful glance around her. She shouldn't have come here. She should have stayed with Marcus or asked him to come with her. Lysander might have allowed that. She wanted to go back to Marcus.

"Is something wrong?" Lysander looked genuinely concerned, his blue eyes bright with it.

"Where are you taking me?" she whispered and swallowed hard, gaze darting around the columns and fear that she wasn't alone here with him creeping down her spine.

Others were watching.

She could feel it.

"I want to know where we're going and what's going to happen to me." She backed away again when he stepped towards her and shot a glance at the door they had entered through. If she was quick, she might reach it before Lysander could catch her. What then? She couldn't remember the way back to the entrance and even if she could, she didn't know how to get back to Earth. Could she fly back there?

Her shoulder blades itched and the first feathers broke the surface of her skin, growing out of her in a way that turned her stomach. Lysander took another step towards her and her silver wings burst out of her in response. She cried out in pain and clutched her shoulders. Sharp throbbing waves spread over her skin from her shoulder blades but quickly faded.

"There is no need to panic," Lysander said in a soothing tone and her gaze darted back to him. He held his hands up, palms facing her, and paused in the same way Marcus had when Einar had been talking to him telepathically. Receiving orders from those watching her? He smiled. "We only need to keep you here for a short while."

"Why? Until when?" The door was starting to look like a good option. There was something about this place that made her skin crawl and urged her to escape, that called to her instinct to take flight and get the hell away from it. Why couldn't she remember what had happened to her here?

"Until Marcus comes."

She stilled and her fear lessened at the sound of that name and the thought that she would see Marcus again.

"Marcus is coming?" she said, her brow furrowing, and steadied her breathing so her panic began to subside. Maybe she was overreacting and being here without Marcus was causing her fear rather than any memory she might have of the place.

Lysander nodded. "He will be. We shall get you comfortable and then they will call Marcus to you."

Amelia glanced at the door again. The thought that Marcus was coming soothed away some of her fear but not all of it. The unsettled feeling she had whenever she saw the columns stretching into the distance before her wasn't going away, and neither was the sense that this was a bad place. No matter what she told herself, no matter what she wanted, she couldn't deny that she had been here before, just as she couldn't deny that she had known Marcus in her past life.

Lysander held his hand out to her.

Amelia hesitated and then stepped forwards.

There was no turning back now. She had come here of her own free will, out of desire to discover what was happening to her and to spare Marcus more pain.

Only, Marcus was coming.

She hadn't spared him at all.

Amelia told herself that it was only fear of those watching her and her surroundings that was unsettling her and forced herself to believe it so she could continue on the path she had chosen to walk. She would go with Lysander and await Marcus's arrival. Once he was here, she would feel safe again, stronger, and they would face Heaven together and uncover the truth behind her existence.

She could trust Marcus. He would protect her from any danger that lurked in Heaven. He would uphold that promise she had remembered him making.

Her nerves didn't fade as she walked along the aisle with Lysander. They steadily grew worse as the sense of danger inside her increased. She kept telling herself that Marcus would come for her soon and she would feel foolish for being so scared when he did. He would find it silly of her not to trust the people who he worked for when she trusted him so much.

What was silly about not trusting the people who had ordered her death and forced one of their own to kill her?

Amelia closed her eyes, pulled in another deep breath to calm her nerves, and ignored that question and the memories that threatened to surface in her mind.

Heaven had killed her and had almost killed Marcus too.

Her hands shook so she clenched her fingers into tight fists to steady them.

She couldn't lie to herself.

But she could face her fear.

Amelia tilted her chin up, straightened her spine, and tucked her wings against her back. She walked with her head held high. Her heart beat hard in her chest and blood rushed in her ears. Marcus would be here soon. She just had to hold it together until then and she would be safe.

Lysander turned right at the end of the long aisle and she followed him down another corridor lined with columns on her right and a wall on her left.

Bright golden light shone out of the doorways at intervals in the white wall, warming her as it touched her as she passed.

She glanced inside one of the rooms and froze as cold swept through her from below.

Amelia stared at the raised white marble altar in the middle of the large bright room and her eyes widened when it was suddenly overflowing with blood, the crimson stark against the clean marble. Her heart stammered and she couldn't breathe when an angel appeared in front of it, his back to her, silver-blue wings spread so they covered her view of his arms.

He lowered his hand to his side and her gaze fell with it. The sight of it chilled her down to the marrow and she felt as though her heart would stop. Blood ran down the length of the curved silver blade, dripping from the gleaming tip to the grooved white marble floor under his feet. She panted hard, panic pushing her to the limit, and forced her gaze back up to his head.

He turned his head to one side but moved at the same time and his large wings concealed his face from her.

He was so familiar.

A shiver tripped down her spine and spread over her arms and thighs, reaching right down to her fingertips and toes.

Lysander tugged on her arm and the vision faded, leaving a clean white room behind. She stared at the altar, unable to shake the terror that had gripped her.

She was in danger.

Lysander yanked her arm and she stumbled forwards and into him. He grabbed her other arm and she tried to break free, fear driving her to escape. She stamped on Lysander's toes, kicked him in the shin with the flat of her foot, and then kneed him hard in the groin. He released her and she turned and ran for the vast columned room. She only made it a few steps before he grabbed her from behind, restraining her arms. With a low growl of frustration, she beat her silver wings, battering him in an attempt to force him to let go of her. His grip tightened until she cried out and he twisted her right arm hard behind her back.

An older looking sandy-haired angel wearing blue armour like Marcus's appeared at the end of the corridor near the cathedral-like room she had run towards. Two bright curved silver blades hung from his waist. His cold eyes fixed on her.

Amelia's gaze darted to the altar in the room to her right, fear rushing through her veins. Her head spun.

They were going to kill her again.

She struggled with all her might, kicking and writhing and beating her wings as the older angel approached her, his steps measured and slow, driving fear deep into her heart. Lysander tightened his grip on her arms and she cried out again when her right shoulder almost popped out of its socket. Intense pain swept through her and she sagged forwards for a moment, and then rallied and threw her head back, smacking it into Lysander's nose. He stumbled backwards with her and she broke free of him. Before she could beat her wings, he had caught her right wrist and twisted it, forcing her to bend forwards to stop her arm from snapping. Her knees gave out and she hit the white marble floor hard, the impact reverberating up her spine.

Lysander wrapped one arm around both of her wings near her shoulder blades, effectively pinning them, and grabbed a fistful of her silver hair with his free hand. He yanked her head back and she looked up into the cold eyes of the guardian angel.

He towered over her, his immense power washing through her, keeping her on the ground as much as Lysander was.

She stared at him. He might be powerful, but his strength was nothing compared with what she had felt in Marcus the other night. Her heart reached out to him. Her only hope. Her guardian angel.

The older angel smiled slowly and drew one of his curved silver blades.

Amelia screamed.

"Marcus!"

CHAPTER 21

Lightning split the sky above Paris and Marcus looked up at the raging clouds. Was it his doing? There was so much darkness in the world and in his heart right now, fury that threatened to seize control of him and lead him into unleashing his burning desire for destruction. The feeling pounded in him like a drum, a beat which his heart followed, growing darker by the second as he watched the thunderstorm.

He screamed at the sky and a bright purple fork of lightning slammed down into the heart of the city, shaking the earth and sending car alarms blaring. It wasn't enough. The darkness within him needed to be sated and he was growing weary of resisting the urge to unfurl his wings and fly after Amelia. He wanted to see her again and he would do anything to achieve that. He would disobey his orders and go to Heaven. There were ways in, methods that he could use.

He needed to see Amelia.

What would she think of him if she saw him like this and knew the black feelings he held within his heart? If she knew the limits of his desire to reach her and the lengths he would go to in order to achieve it, she would no longer believe him a good man.

He wasn't.

The image she had of him was a lie.

He would kill all in his way in his quest to find her again. He couldn't be the good man that she wanted him to be, not when he was feeling like this. The lust for violence was too strong to ignore.

He hadn't been able to contain it during the discussion with the others and had left when the women had started to look afraid again, seeking the balcony so he could be alone with his black thoughts.

Lightning crashed down again, further away this time, illuminating the landscape surrounding Paris. The clouds were so black that they blocked out the day and had caused the streetlights to come on. Rain poured, saturating him, slicking his black hair to his head, but he didn't care. He relished the cold feel of it against his skin, sapping his warmth, and stood staring out at the city, his heart burning in his chest, ablaze with the desire for vengeance.

Lysander had taken Amelia from him. Heaven had taken her from him.

He wanted her back.

The streets were empty below him. The park was void of life. The sensible residents of Paris had remained indoors. That knowledge only weakened his grip on his power. With so many hiding away in the buildings, he could unleash Hell on Earth with only minimal casualties. If anyone was foolish enough to be outside when a thunderstorm of this magnitude was hanging over the city, then they deserved what they got.

Marcus frowned and clenched his fists. Amelia would hate him for thinking such a thing. She had offered him forgiveness and it hadn't changed him. He wished that it had. He wanted to be a good man for her, one that she could love, but it was impossible when he was in so much pain.

"They don't deserve your wrath," Einar said from behind him and Marcus looked over his shoulder.

Einar's tawny long hair was already soaked through, unruly curls of it tufting out behind his ears. His deep brown eyes held Marcus's silver-blue ones, and a sense of peace grew inside him, chasing away some of the darkness in his heart.

"You are even starting to scare Taylor… although she does her best not to let it show." Einar moved forwards and leaned his elbows against the buckled black railings.

The rain continued to pour down, sticking Einar's black t-shirt to his chest. Water trickled in rivulets down Marcus's skin beneath his blue breastplate and soaked into his loincloth, making him uncomfortable.

He closed his eyes and drew long deep breaths to calm himself and claw back control over his power. The thunder eased and the rain lightened to drizzle that chilled his skin. Long minutes passed before the lightning ceased completely and he found some balance. They would depart for Hell soon and he would be able to find out more about Amelia's destiny and why Heaven had made Apollyon kill her. The memory of that moment threatened to push him out of control again, sending pain deep into his heart until he felt as though he was dying again.

Amelia.

He wanted to see her. He wanted to make her smile and make her feel safe.

She had been so scared.

He realised that now.

When she had gone with Lysander and Marcus had seen that her eyes were normal again, that she was becoming the woman he loved, he had been too confused to take in the feelings in her grey gaze. It was only now that he had replayed that moment countless times that he could see that she had been afraid of leaving him, but she had done so anyway, had gone through with it so he and his fellow angels wouldn't have to fight again.

She had wanted to spare him pain but he was suffering more now than he would have been if a battle had ensued.

He needed to see her.

Orders meant nothing to him anymore. He wanted to believe in Heaven, just as Lukas did, but their actions had stripped him of his faith and had left him broken. He no longer trusted them. After centuries as their obedient soldier, as a dutiful son of Heaven, he was finally following his own orders. It was difficult for him to adjust and disobey his master but he had to. They had driven him to this.

The rain let up and the clouds began to lighten, drifting away and breaking apart to reveal patches of blue sky.

Marcus drew a deep breath and made his decision.

He couldn't wait to see what Hell revealed.

He needed to go to Amelia.

He went to unfurl his wings but they wouldn't come. This time, they didn't appear at all, not even for the briefest time. He focused on them and a familiar prickling sensation formed where they should have been. The curse. It had bothered him before too, prior to Heaven ordering him to remain on Earth.

Why?

He needed his wings.

Marcus looked across at Einar. "Help me with something."

Einar nodded and then his brown eyes widened when Marcus removed his breastplate and the back plate of his armour. He looked over his shoulders, trying to see the curse marks, but they were too far down.

"My wings won't come," Marcus said and turned his back to Einar. "What do they look like?"

Einar stepped up to him and ran his fingers over the elaborate marks on his back. "They are shifting like sunlight on water. What are you thinking about?"

Marcus tried to see them again. He had seen the marks in a mirror before when the curse had been active and the colours had shifted then, rippling with lighter and darker hues of blue.

"I was going to disobey my orders to remain outside Heaven and go after Amelia." Marcus looked at Einar to gauge his reaction.

Einar's expression turned pensive. "And when did you have a problem with them before that?"

"When Amelia died… I wanted to go to Heaven and question my superior." Marcus looked up at the broken clouds and the shafts of sunlight streaming down onto Paris. "Before that, it was when Amelia came under attack and I saved her, just before I came to see you."

"When you escaped the Hell's angels?"

Marcus frowned in the direction of the marks. "Do you think the curse is their doing? A way of hindering me so they can catch Amelia?"

Einar stared at Marcus's shoulders for a moment and then shrugged. "I don't know. Why would they want to hinder you now? Amelia has died. Veiron had wanted to stop that from happening and failed."

Marcus stared down into the street below. He needed to find Veiron and ask him about Amelia, and also about his curse. Taylor thought that it was demonic but the further he ventured into this mission, the more doubts he had. Could it be the work of the Hell's angels?

His gaze rose to the sky again.

As much as he desired to go to Heaven and to Amelia, he needed to uncover the truth about her destiny and his mission first, and something told him that Veiron could help with that. Heaven's message had stated that he would be called to them and Amelia soon. He had to trust that meant that she was safe with them for now. Once they called him, he would see her again and he would save her from whatever fate had in store for her.

"It's time." Apollyon stepped out onto the small balcony, dressed in his black and gold armour with his wings tucked against his back. "We should go now."

"There's a problem," Einar said and Apollyon's dark blue gaze darted to him. "Marcus's wings."

Marcus's silvery wings unfurled from his back, hitting Einar and almost knocking him over the railing. Marcus stared at them, unable to believe that they were there now when a moment ago they hadn't responded to his call. What the hell was happening to him?

He needed to find Veiron and fast. Einar's questions had planted more in his head and he wanted answers.

They played on his mind as he followed Einar and Apollyon into the apartment, calling his breastplate and back plate to him at the same time. The blue and silver armour materialised over his torso and he focused on his wings, furling them against his back. They felt stable now but for how long?

He couldn't shake the feeling that the curse was reacting to him just as the medical staff had said, but it wasn't triggered by his emotions. The trigger was the decisions he made, the things he wanted to do. It was rigged to respond to some thoughts but not others. There were countless times when he had wanted to use his wings for a purpose and they had been fine, and only a handful when they hadn't come when he had called. Each of those times, his need for them had been related to Amelia. That only confused him further. He placed his left hand on the grip of the blade hanging from his waist and tightened his fingers around it. Resolve flowed through him. There had to be a way to remove the curse, something that they hadn't tried, and he was determined to find it and free himself.

Taylor clicked her fingers in front of his face. "Earth to Marcus."

His eyes widened and he blankly looked at her.

"You're my escort for the evening." She smiled at him and finished tying her long black hair up into a neat ponytail. She was head to toe in black again and sporting some nasty looking knives in a holster that fitted snugly over her black t-shirt. He counted four on either side of her ribs, each with small rings on the end so she could quickly tug them free and throw them, and a larger knife was strapped to her leg. His gaze dropped to her combat boots and he wondered where else she was concealing blades. She put her leather jacket on, hiding the short blade that was against her back, and her smile widened, brightening her blue eyes.

He wasn't sure who would be escorting whom. With an arsenal like that strapped to her body, she could probably take down most enemies without any problems or any need for assistance.

"I still don't like the idea of you flying with another man," Einar said and Taylor turned her smile on him. It warmed and widened.

"Marcus will be a gentleman, I'm sure, and it's your fault for losing your wings." Her smile turned mischievous.

"You are right, it is my fault… perhaps I shouldn't have decided to sacrifice them so we could be together. I will just send a message to Heaven saying that I've changed my mind."

Taylor's smile dropped away and she stared at him. "You wouldn't dare… you're mine, Romeo, and you'd better remember that."

"Look who's talking. You speak to Marcus like you're propositioning him and then—" Einar didn't get a chance to finish. Taylor ran at him, threw her arms around his neck and almost knocked him off his feet.

Einar grinned and wrapped his arms around her, holding her against him, and lowered his mouth to kiss her. She wriggled free.

"Dammit, Einar, you're all wet!" Her scowl stopped him mid-attempt to grab her again and she caught his wrist instead and led him to their bags on the beige couches.

"It was raining," Einar groused and then, in a swift move, broke free of her grasp, grabbed her wrist, and pulled her against him. She didn't struggle this time as Einar bent her over, his hands grasping her waist, and kissed her. Taylor buried her fingers into his mousy brown hair, twisted them in his short ponytail at the nape of his neck, and tugged the leather thong out.

Einar looked unimpressed as he released her, setting her back on her feet, and fixed his hair back in place.

Marcus smiled when she tossed a t-shirt at Einar, hitting him in the face with it, and then started to unload even more short swords and knives, tucking them into her jacket. Einar must have used his powers to conceal all that weaponry from human eyes at the airport. It was possible for him to alter the appearance of the luggage's contents.

He looked away from them and his gaze lighted on Apollyon and Serenity. The moment Apollyon bent down, wrapped his arms around the petite blonde and lifted her for a kiss, Marcus looked away from them too. Luck wasn't with him, but Lukas was getting a serious good luck kiss from Annelie, her slender fingers wrapped in his messy sandy hair whilst his hand splayed through her red locks, holding her against his mouth.

Marcus turned around and stared at the balcony, unable to bear the sight of the three couples. It was torture. He wanted Amelia in his arms again, her sweet lips against his and her body nestled close. They had only been together a short time, but the moments they had shared with each other had been blissful and had changed his life. He couldn't live without her anymore. The world was dull and grey when she wasn't with him and he couldn't think straight. He needed her and he was starting to waver again, the desire to find her battling his need to go to Hell with the others and discover more about what was happening.

Amelia was safe with Heaven. They had told him that and he forced himself to believe it. They had never lied to him before. They had only neglected to tell him things. He couldn't hold that against them. When his mission had begun, he had been told to watch over Amelia and that he would be given more information in time. They had kept their word, telling him that there would be a point in time when he had to protect her until. Had that point in time been her death at Apollyon's hands? If it was, then Marcus had fulfilled that part of his mission, but his duty wasn't done yet. Heaven had made it sound as though there was more to come. What if Amelia's death wasn't the end but only the beginning of something? She had been reborn as a being similar to an angel. There had to be a reason for it.

If he went flying off to Heaven now, intent on killing everyone who stood in his way and saving Amelia from a fate he knew nothing about, he could end up destroying her real destiny. The slightest change of events could lead to something catastrophic. Heaven had a reason for what they had done and they had a reason for needing him to stay away until they called him. He would find out what they were and then he would make a decision—to follow their orders or follow his own desire.

It was hard to bring himself to trust them when he needed to see her again and see that she was safe.

The longer he waited for Apollyon to announce their departure, the stronger his desire to go to Heaven instead of Hell became. He needed to leave now and go down into the bowels of the underworld. Only that would stop him from surrendering to his desire to see Amelia. All would be well if he could rein in that feeling until they reached Hell. Taylor would find Veiron and Apollyon would scour the pool that recorded the events of the mortal realm, and they would use that knowledge to discover the truth about Amelia's destiny. Armed with that knowledge, he would be able to save her without further endangering her life.

Until then, he had to hold himself together.

Hell was a dangerous place for an angel.

If he went in there with his feelings in disarray, his heart would be easily swayed.

The Devil had a strong voice.

And Marcus had never felt so weak.

CHAPTER 22

Marcus kept half of his focus fixed on his silvery-blue wings as the grey asphalt road below him began to crack and open, revealing infinite darkness. Was this really the way to Hell? Apollyon hovered just metres in front of him, his hand outstretched and his eyes closed. Hot air blasted out of the crevasse, tousling his dark feathers and long black hair. It ruffled Marcus and Lukas too, sending their hair swaying. Taylor moved closer to Marcus, curled close to his breastplate in his arms. Her array of blades made her difficult to carry without cutting himself but something told him that she wouldn't surrender them. He could feel her heart racing. She was putting on a brave face and she wasn't the only one. Marcus couldn't recall a time he had felt this nervous.

Lukas held Einar, gripping him under his arms so Einar dangled below him. Taylor had laughed at the sight of her lover held so ridiculously at first but had fallen silent once Apollyon had started the ritual that opened the path to Hell.

None of them had said a word since the first crack had appeared. Now, Marcus could see a tiny orange forked line. Either it was going to open wider, or it was a long way down into the Earth. Marcus had never been to Hell but he knew that Lukas had, and when he had asked him about it, Lukas had told him to be on his guard against the voice of the Devil. Did it really present such a temptation?

Apollyon turned to face them. "Mind the walls on the way down. Sometimes they shift. The old git doesn't like us going down there. I hear he has become worse since I left my post. Several angels have already been corrupted by his offers."

Marcus presumed he meant the Devil. Apollyon and the Devil had a special relationship. Every so many centuries, Apollyon fought the Devil in order to keep him locked away in the bottomless pit. There had been instances when the Devil had won, killing Apollyon, and had roamed the mortal realm, causing pestilence and amusing himself with destroying human lives until Apollyon was reborn and defeated him.

It took a strong heart and even stronger belief to resist the temptation that the Devil offered to angels who entered his realm. Apollyon had withstood it for millennia. Marcus marvelled at that as the dark angel took Einar from Lukas and started his descent into Hell. Lukas had withstood it during his short visit there. If the rookie of the group could hold out against the Devil, then Marcus was sure that he could too. He could be strong for Amelia. For her sake, he would endure it all and resist the Devil's offers, no matter what they were.

Doubts began to creep in as he flew downwards, gliding most of the time. Taylor held on to his armour, her fingers tightly clutching his blue and silver breastplate. She whispered things to herself that sounded like protective charms. Was she afraid of the Devil too? He had thought that she would be immune to his voice. Part of her was demon. Wasn't that protection enough from the Devil's sway?

He looked down at Apollyon and Einar, and then across at Lukas who flew beside him. Lukas pointed downwards and Marcus saw that the tiny orange fault line was growing into a glowing fiery streak below them. They were getting closer. The smell of sulphur tainted the air, choking him, growing denser with each metre closer he got to Hell. The temperature rose as he descended and hot air blasted against him, threatening to send him rising upwards. He beat his wings to force himself to continue downwards and adjusted his grip on Taylor as his palms started to sweat.

"I shouldn't have brought this jacket with me. I didn't realise it would be so balmy," Taylor said with false lightness in her voice and he looked at her. The fear in her eyes echoed how he felt in his heart.

"Have you been to Hell before?" he said with concern as she rubbed the back of her hand across her forehead, clearing the beads of sweat away.

"Once or twice, but never to this place. Most of us keep away. He doesn't like to be disturbed."

Marcus looked down. The bright glowing light had abated to reveal a wide expanse of rough stony ground and he could see the edge of the plateau. It dropped away into a fiery pit hundreds of feet below.

Apollyon was the first to land, setting Einar down before releasing him. He beat his black wings a few more times and then folded them against his back. The temperature increased again as Marcus passed the end of the black walls that they had been travelling past since leaving the mortal realm and entered a huge cavern. It stretched as far as the eye could see, covered in black shards of rock and belching pits of fire.

He lowered Taylor to the uneven ground and then landed and tucked his wings back. His gaze roamed to the edge of the plateau. The bottomless pit. He could feel the demons down there and the power they commanded, stronger than most angels, and it chilled him. Lukas landed beside him and covered his mouth and nose with his hand, a frown on his face.

"It smells far worse than I recalled."

Marcus could barely breathe through the acrid stench of brimstone. It burned his lungs and made his eyes water. He couldn't even begin to imagine how Apollyon had endured living here for so long.

"It is worse near the pit." Apollyon motioned for them to follow him towards an outcrop of rough black rock away from the edge of the plateau.

Lukas followed him. Marcus lingered where he was, keeping Taylor company as she stared at the fiery glow of the pit. Einar joined them and placed his arm around Taylor's shoulders.

"Are you sure you don't want me to come with you?" Einar said and held her close, rubbing her back.

Marcus could sense his unease and shared his concern. Even though Taylor was half demon, she was half mortal too, and that meant she wasn't as strong as the beasts that lurked in Hell. And she was scared.

"I'll be fine, Romeo." Her smile faltered and she ran her fingers down Einar's chest and then looked up into his eyes. "It's better if I go alone… if you come along, there'll be trouble. I'll keep my head down, check out a few of Veiron's haunts, and get a message out to him if I can't find his stupid arse. I'll be back before you know it."

Einar stroked her cheek and held her gaze. "Just be careful."

She nodded and leaned into his touch, closing her eyes as she placed her hand over his, holding it against her face. "I will. I love you, you big oaf."

"Love you too." He kissed her softly and then she stepped backwards out of his arms, her other hand lingering in his.

Einar materialised a sword in his free hand and held it out to her. Her blue eyes widened.

"But it's your favourite."

He shrugged easily, his broad shoulders barely moving an inch, and smiled at her. "There's a blessing on it strong enough to make most demons think twice. Take it with you."

Taylor took it, swung it a few times, and then walked back to Einar, tiptoed and kissed his cheek. "It's the sweetest thing you've ever given me. You're so romantic."

Marcus frowned. Giving a woman a sword was romantic? It didn't seem romantic to him. He was sure that most women would think a man was insane if they gave her a sword as a present. Then again, most women weren't about to embark on a dangerous mission through the lower reaches of Hell in search of a demonic angel who was also their ex-lover.

Taylor waved at them both and then headed off into the gloom.

When she was out of sight, Einar turned back to him. "She loves it when I give her weapons."

"Why? I mean, she is certainly in love with her knives and guns, but what's romantic about a sword?"

Einar patted his shoulder. "It shows her that I love her and I care about her."

"Surely it is more romantic to accompany her?"

"I get your point, but Taylor would see me going with her after she has plainly told me not to as me undermining her strength. Not romantic. Taylor's strong and she's right, she can handle herself and it's safer if she goes alone. The inhabitants of this realm won't bother her if she's alone. If I'm with her, they'll see her as the enemy, even though I'm technically a fallen angel."

Marcus could understand it when he put it like that, but he still couldn't see Einar's gesture as romantic. He reasoned that Einar was a hunter and so was Taylor. They were built to work alone, tracking and capturing or killing their prey. He was a guardian and it was probably that nature in him that was telling him that it was more romantic to offer to protect someone and go with them than it was to let them go alone with a blessed sword for company.

Einar pointed in the direction that Apollyon and Lukas had gone. Marcus nodded and started to follow him, and then stopped when dark words curled up from the pit behind him, flowing around him.

He looked back over his shoulder at the edge of the plateau and the burning void beyond it, trying not to listen to what the Devil had to say but unable to move away. Hot fingers of air drifted around him, stroking over his arms and his chest, and then his back. They crept under the back of his armour and then it felt as though they were burrowing into his skin, setting him on fire.

The marks on his back blazed white-hot and Marcus hit the dirt, jagged rocks cutting into his bare knees. He curled forwards into a ball and clutched the sides of his head as tremendous pain ripped through him and every inch of him burned.

He yelled out his agony and it echoed around the cavern, mocking him along with the Devil's voice.

Marcus screwed his eyes shut and tried to close his mind to the words drifting around him and close his heart to the pain. He couldn't shut either out.

His wings faltered and disappeared and the burning intensified, until it scorched his skin, dredging up memories of how his flesh had begun to peel away during his battle with Apollyon. The Devil's voice grew louder and clearer, turning increasingly like Amelia's, and Marcus couldn't bear it. He dug his nails into his scalp and whimpered, his back on fire as fingers of air as hot as flames danced over his skin.

The Devil.

He wasn't strong enough to endure his voice let alone his caress. It would be the end of him.

He couldn't take it.

"Marcus!" Einar's voice broke through the heavy haze of agony in his mind and he clung to it, fiercely holding on and using it to push away from the stronger voice of the Devil.

"Leave him alone." The command in Apollyon's tone caused the rough ground to tremble and black words rolled out of the pit again. "Ignore him, Marcus. You are stronger than this."

"Can't." Marcus could barely breathe as fresh pain engulfed him, tearing at his shoulders, and arched backwards and screamed at the ceiling of the cavern.

"Bastard," Apollyon spat and growled something dark in the old language that caused the ground to shake again.

"Marcus, listen to me," Einar said and he tried to, wanted to focus on him and ignore the voice in his mind, but he couldn't. Whenever he came close to shutting it out, it came again, stronger and even more like Amelia.

He yelled when his wings burst free, ripping out of his back so fast that it caused him more pain and tore his armour away. He breathed hard, battling the hurt and the Devil's tempting words, struggling to overcome both.

Amelia's voice whispered in his mind and he couldn't block it out.

Nasty little curse.

Marcus sucked in sharp gulps of acrid air and swallowed them down, fighting the pain. If he could lock that down he would be able to move all of his focus to shunning the Devil.

Not like them to take things this far.

He stopped breathing and stilled when the pain began to subside. It wasn't his doing. Not like who to take things this far?

His focus shifted to the pit and he stared at it with blurry eyes, able to sense the Devil watching him but unable to see his form. Hot fingers of wind curled around his feathers and he lost focus, hazy with the feel of them touching him. Einar spoke to him, his voice so distant in Marcus's ears that he didn't hear what he said.

Amelia's voice came to him again.

Inhibiting their own.

Marcus's eyes widened. He wouldn't believe it. The Devil was lying to him, using his doubts to sway him over to his side. It wasn't true.

Not true?

You do not remember?

The world in front of him faded into darkness and another replaced it, growing piece by piece from the ground upwards until the interior of a dimly lit wooden building surrounded him. People dressed in dirty meagre clothing bustled around him, crowding low wooden tables and filling the room with loud laughter and rowdy conversation. The scent of faeces and alcohol assaulted his senses. Mead. Marcus stared down at the flagon in his hand and couldn't stop himself from lifting it to his lips.

He laughed with the men around him, his fellow warriors, thrilled by what they were doing and the stories of battles they shared.

The memories came flooding back. He had drunk with his kin, breaking the law and seizing a moment of freedom that he had paid dearly for. They had all broken the rules that night and had drunk until they were unable to walk as far as their lodgings and had ended up spending the night in a nearby barn.

Only now that he was watching the moment all over again, he realised that the events of that night were different to how he had remembered it, and it wasn't a lie fabricated by the Devil to sway him. He recalled it clearly now. He could recollect everything that had happened and his suspicions that his fellow angels had been deceiving him. They had only pretended to drink. At the time, he had convinced himself that they had no reason to deceive him when it had been their idea to bend the rules and indulge in something wicked for once in their lives.

The vision in front of Marcus unravelled and Hell came back, and he curled up on the black basalt. The sharp edges of the rocks beneath him scraped at his sides but he didn't care. His brethren had deceived him. Why?

Amelia's voice came to him again, light and beautiful in his mind.

Because they did this to you.

No. He wouldn't believe that. He didn't want to, not even as he remembered coming around in the barn in the dead of night and discovering them doing something to his back. At the time, they had told him that they were up because they had heard something and had come to check on him. He had been in pain.

Marcus's shoulder blades burned again and his wings disappeared. The marks there heated up until he couldn't take the fiery inferno and screamed. The ground trembled and the pain faded again, and so did the voice in his mind. He felt the Devil's grip on him slip and opened his eyes.

Apollyon stood with his back to him at the edge of the plateau, his black wings spread and his curved golden blades in his hands. Dark words rolled off his tongue, shaking the ground, and the Devil cursed back at him. Apollyon was drawing his attention, giving Marcus a chance to regain control of himself and find the strength to shut out the Devil's voice.

He was weak from the pain, numb down to his core from the knowledge of what his kind had done to him, but he wouldn't submit to the Devil. He pushed himself onto his knees and then strong hands gripped his arms and helped him onto his feet. He stumbled with them away from the edge of the pit, leaving Apollyon there to taunt the Devil, and again wishing that he was as strong as his friend.

Einar and Lukas guided him around the corner of the outcrop of rocks and then set him against it. Marcus leaned there, breathing hard and not caring that the air was like acid. He needed to breathe and focus on it and steadying his heart in order to find the strength to ignore the Devil.

His heartbeat began to level out and the pain ebbed away, leaving him trembling.

"What happened?" Apollyon said and Marcus opened his eyes and looked across at him. He stood on the other side of Lukas, closer to the pit than the rest of them, his expression as black as the curses he had hurled at the Devil.

Marcus reached over his shoulder and touched his bare back, feeling the lingering heat on his skin.

"Cursed," he spat the word out and anger rolled through him, stronger than anything he had ever felt before.

The ground trembled beneath his feet and he pushed away from the rocks and walked past Apollyon, wearily dragging his feet. He stared at the bright fire of the pit and felt the Devil watching him still, although he made no attempt to speak to Marcus this time. Was he satisfied with his work? He had driven Marcus beyond despair into something wholly darker and more dangerous.

"They cursed me." Marcus closed his eyes and grasped the meaning behind those three words. Everything he had trusted and believed in had betrayed him and it cut him to the bone. His fists trembled at his sides. They had done this to him. Why?

"The demons?" Lukas's tone was low and cautious, as though he had sensed Marcus's rising anger and was afraid that he would unleash it on him.

"No." Marcus tilted his head right back and stared at the black ceiling of the cavern, looking beyond it to the mortal realm and then Heaven beyond that. "Not the demons."

Veiron's voice echoed around the black cavern.

"The angels."

CHAPTER 23

Marcus's silver-blue gaze slowly shifted to Veiron.

He walked across the blackened field of rock towards them, a vision of darkness in his obsidian armour and with his leathery dragon-like wings furled against his back, their clawed tips gleaming in the fiery light.

"What do you mean?" Einar said and held Lukas back when he materialised his gold and white spear in his hand. "This is Veiron… the one who foresaw Amelia's death."

Lukas and Apollyon looked Veiron over and neither seemed impressed. Marcus didn't like it either, but they needed Veiron's help and he was starting to think that this man was more trustworthy than any in angel in Heaven. Veiron had said plainly what would happen to Amelia. He hadn't lied to them as far as Marcus could tell, but then he couldn't call himself a good judge of character anymore. He had been so easily deceived by those he had placed his trust in.

"It is an angelic curse," Marcus said and all eyes were on him.

Apollyon didn't seem shocked and neither did Einar. After the conversations that Marcus had shared with them, their response didn't come as much of a surprise to him. All three of them had their doubts about Heaven and now those doubts had been proven sound.

Lukas looked between Marcus and Veiron, his green eyes full of disbelief. Marcus had heard Lukas's story from Einar, about how another angel had used Lukas and pinned the murder of hundreds of humans on him, and the punishment he had endured because of it. It must have been difficult for Lukas to bring himself to trust Heaven again and now they had shaken his faith in it once more.

Marcus could feel a sliver of his pain and confusion, and they were feelings that he shared. His own belief lay in tatters and everything he had fought for was gone, tainted by lies and deceit, and he felt as though he had lost a part of himself because of it. Or more than a part. He felt like a different person now. The once dutiful and loyal soldier who had been happy obeying his orders and had believed in everything he had been told was gone. Naïve. Foolish. How had he been so blind to everything that had been happening around him? How had he been so stupid as to cling to belief and never question the things he was told to do? Even when he had demanded answers, he had lacked conviction, easily swayed by his superior into giving up his quest for the truth behind his mission, trusting that they knew what they were doing and the path they had chosen for him was the right one.

"Poor little soul," Veiron said in a sweet voice and Marcus curled his fingers into tight fists and glared at him. "Only a powerful demon can lift that curse or possibly the angel that gave you it, but something tells me that you didn't come down here to beg the Devil to remove it now, did you? You didn't know."

Marcus clenched his jaw and steeled himself, battling his rising desire to grab Veiron by the throat and shake some answers out of him. No good would come of it. The Hell's angel had left when Taylor had turned nasty towards him and he couldn't risk driving the man away now. As much as he hated it, he would endure the demon's mocking for Amelia's sake.

"What possible reason could they have for cursing you?" Veiron ran his gaze over him. There was an edge to it that made Marcus feel as though Veiron already knew the answer to that question. "You must have done something very bad… or perhaps it was something they didn't like."

Marcus thought back to the night he had gotten drunk with his so-called friends and had awoken with the curse. He had spoken to them about something after their last mission, something that had been dear to him at the time.

He had talked about requesting a change in his duties and position so he could become a soldier of Heaven, one of the many who protected it against intruders and went to battle in times of war. That was his dream. They had cursed him that night and he had ended up having to watch over mortals instead, bound in Heaven with no ability to fly, useless without his wings.

If the curse hadn't happened, he would have asked for that change in duties and headed into a role that had nothing to do with mortals or guarding them, an area of servitude where he would have had no reason to meet Amelia.

Did this curse have something to do with her?

His wings had returned when he had been assigned to watch over her and the curse had remained ineffective until he had met her. The more he thought about it, the more he realised that the times when the curse had hindered his wings, stopping them from appearing, were all related to her.

Something else dawned on him and he didn't like it one bit.

When he had defeated the Hell's angels and had leapt with Amelia, expecting his wings to come when he called them, he had been thinking about leaving with her, taking her somewhere far away where it would be difficult to find them. The moment his wings hadn't appeared, his plan had changed. He had decided to go to Einar instead.

When Amelia had died and awoken as something angelic, she had mentioned that she knew them all.

A shiver rushed down his back.

The curse had changed his plans and led him to Einar. Einar in turn had led him to Apollyon and Lukas. Heaven had used the curse to bring all four of them together so Apollyon's duty would come into effect and he would have no choice but to follow his orders and kill Amelia.

Marcus stared into Veiron's red eyes, struggling to comprehend what he was thinking.

"I used to do work like that fancy curse you bear." Veiron sighed wearily. "Now you can understand why I switched sides. I was already doing a demon's work."

"I need to know what's going on, Veiron, and I need to know how to get rid of this curse." Marcus took a step towards him and ignored the black voice that curled out of the pit, offering him assistance with it.

"Have you seen Taylor?" Einar said and Marcus couldn't believe that he had forgotten about her. He had been so caught up in his own problems that he hadn't thought about the fact that she was wandering around Hell searching for the very man standing in front of him.

"No, why?" Veiron frowned at him. "I figure she's playing house back in London, Wingless."

"She isn't. She came down here with us and went to find you. You haven't seen her?"

Veiron's look darkened and his red eyes brightened until they glowed like embers in the low light. "What do you mean, she's down here? How could you be so irresponsible?"

Marcus intervened when Einar started towards Veiron and placed himself between them. "I am sure she will be back soon, Einar… we are here to find out what's going to happen to Amelia now that she has died, so—"

"She isn't dead yet." Veiron's words dropped on him like lead weights, each one dragging his insides down a little further, and he turned slowly to face the demonic angel.

"What the hell do you mean?" he whispered and took another step in his direction. "I saw her die and I saw her reborn as an angel."

"An angel?" Veiron laughed. "She isn't what you could call an angel and she isn't dead yet. I've seen her death, remember? Do you think I would be standing here hindering you with idle conversation if it had already happened?"

"Hindering me? Not dead?" Marcus spat out another dark curse and the Devil laughed this time, his voice booming out of the pit and mocking him. His army was almost within reach of Heaven. Veiron's kind was going to attack it to retrieve Amelia. Why?

Marcus growled in frustration, ran at Veiron, and tackled him to the ground. The rough basalt scratched at his knees as he straddled Veiron and then scraped his back when the demonic angel used his leathery dark wings to knock him away. Before Marcus could get back onto his feet, Veiron was kneeling astride him, his hands pressing down hard into his shoulders, pinning him to the sharp ground.

"Tell me what the hell you're talking about!" Marcus struggled, trying to get free, causing the rocks to cut into his back. The scent of blood joined that of brimstone in the choking hot air.

Apollyon tore Veiron off him and held him off the ground by his neck from behind. Veiron beat his wings and Apollyon snarled and grabbed one, twisting it behind Veiron's back and tearing a growl of pain from the demonic angel. Veiron's teeth sharpened and turned the colour of blood and his eyes glowed brighter, burning as fiercely as the pit.

"Enough." Apollyon cast him aside, sending him tumbling across the black charred ground.

Veiron was still a moment, laying on his side, and then slowly pushed himself back onto his feet. Marcus took Einar's hand and hauled himself onto his feet too. He scowled at Veiron who returned it a hundredfold.

The Hell's angel kept his distance this time, warily eyeing him and the three angels flanking him.

"Why isn't Amelia an angel?" Marcus had wanted to believe that she was because then Heaven would have no reason to harm her, at least he had thought that at the time they had taken her. Now, he wasn't so sure. They had done something terrible to him, cursing him in order to keep him in check and to control his actions. What was their objective? Were they going to kill Amelia?

Panic lanced his heart but he refused to surrender to the need to fly out of Hell and go to her. He needed to know what he was dealing with. He needed a plan if he was going to save Amelia, and that meant staying where he was until Veiron told him the truth about her, no matter how much it hurt him to remain.

"There are no female angels. I thought this was something everyone knew?" Veiron looked at each of them in turn and then settled his red gaze on Marcus.

"We knew."

"She may look angelic, but appearances can be deceiving can't they?" Veiron smiled and stretched his wings out, and black feathers began to grow on them, hiding the leathery membrane. When the feathers were all in place, they turned crimson. He stared into the distance beyond Marcus, his expression turning thoughtful. "She once had wings like ours… they were beautiful and dripped with blood that was fatal to us. A female angel. The original creation. Our forebear. God believed that women would be perfect angels, gentle and caring, mothering and protective. God gave her everything, endowing her with power the likes of which no angel has ever been blessed with since. He realised his mistake too late. Instead of helping mankind in its earliest form, she drove them to sin and to the point of destruction. God destroyed her, but angels are eternal. He could not undo his mistake."

"So she is an angel like us."

Veiron shook his head. "She had been tampered with during her creation. While her body had been born in Heaven, her soul had been born in Hell. The power that flows in her blood has rendered her a pawn in their eternal game."

Veiron's focus came back to him.

"She's a pawn, Marcus, just like you and me, only she's a divine instrument. A weapon."

"A weapon?" Marcus's heart started at a pace, beating hard against his ribs, and the desire to leave Hell now and go to her flowed through his veins and burned in his soul so strongly that he couldn't ignore it this time. He tried to call his wings but they wouldn't come. The marks on his back blazed and he flinched at the intense heat, grinding his teeth together in an attempt to endure it without the others noticing.

"Marcus?" Einar touched his shoulder. He looked at him and saw that he was staring at his back. Marcus gave up his fight to hide his pain and growled. It was useless. The changing colour of the marks would give away what he was thinking and that his curse was active, and they would know his pain. "Stop it."

Marcus shifted his focus back to Veiron and away from his desire to leave Hell and go after Amelia.

"She can't be a weapon," he whispered, his heart aching at the thought of Heaven using her to that end. He didn't care where she had been spawned or what she was. She was Amelia to him. The woman he loved.

"I'm afraid she is. She became a weapon the moment both sides realised the potential of her blood. She was the first, born of both God and the Devil, a union of infinite strength and power. Her blood is sacred. Within it she holds phenomenal power, more than both had thought possible."

"What power?" Marcus said and Veiron smiled as the Devil's voice rose from the pit.

Marcus couldn't understand what he had said but Apollyon clearly could because he moved forwards, his gaze locked on the pit, a flicker of shock in his blue eyes.

"What?" Marcus caught his arm and Apollyon looked back at him, his black wings partially obscuring his face.

"It's a seal."

"A seal?" Marcus looked back at Veiron and the demonic angel nodded. "Her blood can seal this realm?"

"Not just this realm." Veiron pointed upwards. "It has sealed your own in the past. If her blood is spilt in one realm, it will seal the other until that blood loses its power. Eventually, she is reborn and the race to find her begins again."

"They're going to kill her." Marcus turned his back on Veiron and cursed when his wings wouldn't emerge. Veiron was right. Amelia wasn't dead yet. She had only been awakened. The event surrounding her death was still to come. That was why his mission hadn't ended with Amelia's death at Apollyon's hands.

"Not them," Veiron said. "You."

Marcus froze to his core. His heart beat loudly in the silence echoing in his mind. His hands shook. He stared blankly ahead into the black field full of belching pits of magma, trying to take in that single innocent sounding word that held such pain and foreboding.

"You, Marcus," Veiron repeated, his voice lowering and filling with darkness. "I said that you were there at her death."

"No… I am not going to kill her. I love her! I am going to save her." Marcus spun on his heel to face him. "I won't kill her."

"Strong words considering that you killed her last time." There was conviction in Veiron's red eyes, belief in the words that he was saying, and Marcus covered his ears.

"No. You lie. I have never met her before. I don't know what you are talking about but I am not going to kill her!" Marcus scowled at him and then turned to his fellow angels. "Apollyon… tell me he is lying. You were alive when I was reborn."

Apollyon stared at the broken ground, his eyes gradually brightening until they were vivid blue and Marcus could feel his anger.

"I have no memory of killing her or of anything that followed, but… now that I am thinking about it, I have a feeling that something had happened then… only I cannot remember it."

Marcus fell to his knees. This wasn't happening.

"You were reborn in a time of peace?" Veiron said and Marcus hung his head forwards and nodded, his hands resting between his knees.

He had been reborn at a time when the world had been serene and beautiful, and Einar had been reborn then too.

"A time of peace always follows her death if Heaven spills her blood."

"I didn't do it."

"Your proof is right there. See it for yourself." Veiron pointed to the small pool in the distance near a rugged semi-circular outcrop of black rocks. It shimmered brightly, changing colour as it reflected the events occurring on Earth.

Marcus hesitated. The pool would reveal the truth but he wasn't sure whether he wanted to see it. It had hurt him when he had realised that Heaven had betrayed him. He wouldn't be able to cope with the pain if he discovered that Veiron was right and he had killed Amelia in his previous life.

"It is a terrible fate we endure, Marcus," Veiron said on a sigh. "Each time I am reborn, I succumb to the Devil and do his bidding in this game. I grow weary of it and the memories that return as the game goes on. You are not the only person who has killed her."

How many times had he killed her though? He wanted to ask that question but he feared it. It was bad enough knowing that he had killed her once.

"I had never thought they would take things this far though."

Marcus wasn't listening anymore. He stared at the pool, building up the courage to accept his fate and what he might have done in his past. If he had killed her last time, had betrayed her, that didn't mean he had to repeat history and follow his destiny and do it all over again. He didn't want to see the terrible things he might have done to her, but he dragged himself to his feet and crossed the uneven ground to the pool, shunning Einar and Apollyon as they attempted to stop him.

He collapsed to his knees at the edge of the small oval pool and held his trembling left hand out over it, focusing on the point of his rebirth two thousand years ago and then taking the images back beyond that. He focused on himself and his existence at that time, and stopped when he saw Heaven stained with blood.

Marcus looked away, unable to bear the sight of himself in the pool. He covered his mouth with his hand and stared at the ground, shaking his head and cold to the bone. He had killed her.

His gaze crept back to the frozen image in the pool and he couldn't take his eyes off his spear where it pierced her blood-soaked chest.

He had killed her.

"Come away," Apollyon said in a soothing low voice and gathered him close, forcing him to look away from the image. It branded itself on his mind and his heart, seared there for eternity.

He had betrayed her.

What if she remembered that?

"You see the sort of game we are involved in, Marcus?" Veiron's tone was cold and dark, and he looked as angry as Marcus felt. More black words rolled out of the pit and Veiron looked over his shoulder and barked a curse back at the Devil. "We are all pawns. They play with us… toy with our memories… twist our fate so we do as they desire of us."

Marcus moved out of Apollyon's arms and nodded. He did see the extent of it all now. They had changed Apollyon's memories of that time, and had cursed Marcus so he would never falter on the path they had chosen for him, driving him ever onwards towards this moment. They used them all cruelly, Amelia most of all. It wasn't her fault that she had been born this way. It was their fault and they used her as a weapon when they should have been finding a way to undo what they had done, or to let her live in peace and die a natural death.

He wouldn't let it go on.

He was going to save Amelia even if he had to fight both Heaven and Hell to achieve it.

"You saw her death by my hands… when will it happen?" Marcus glared at Veiron and tried to call his wings. He wasn't surprised when they didn't emerge and the curse marks blazed against his back.

"The planetary alignment comes into effect soon. Her blood must be spilt before the planets move out of alignment in seven days time."

"Seven days." If he could keep her safe for that length of time, would that mean she would be free of this destiny? The look in Veiron's eyes said that he wasn't sure of the particulars around her sacrifice. There was little point in him asking the Devil. He couldn't trust either Heaven or Hell with this.

"Can you lift this curse?" Marcus said and Veiron hesitated. "What is it?"

"I said that they had gone too far this time and that's why I don't want to play this game of theirs anymore. It's one thing having to remember everything I've done in service of the Devil whenever I join his ranks, it's another for them to use me against you. I placed that curse on you and was there when they erased your memories."

Marcus's eyes widened and he tried to recall seeing Veiron in the memories that had come back to him. He couldn't remember him but Veiron had felt familiar to him back when they had met outside Einar's home in London.

"I was like you once," Veiron whispered and the feathers on his wings started to drain of colour and fall again, revealing the dark membrane beneath. "A guardian… we always start out together, you know, reborn into the ranks of the guardians at the same time. And then I fall. They've never made me curse you before though or gone so far with altering your memories… but perhaps you were in danger of changing your destiny. I can help you with that curse. I'm tired of you winning all the time. She isn't the only one who dies when that happens."

Marcus stared at him. What hideous game were they playing with them all? He had been reborn in a time of peace. He had died shortly after killing her, and from what Veiron was saying, so had he.

Their purpose had been fulfilled. Heaven and Hell had wiped the slate clean and started the game over again.

He cursed and the Devil sent one back at him. Veiron shifted further away from the edge of the plateau when parts of it crumbled into the fiery abyss, sending up showers of vivid orange sparks in an intense wave of heat.

"I think I shall get into trouble for this." Veiron smiled, revealing sharp red teeth. "He doesn't like to be disobeyed, and neither does your master."

"Have we ever worked together against them before?" Marcus looked towards the pit and then up at the ceiling of the cavern.

Veiron moved around him and touched the marks on his back. They burned again. "Never… it has to be worth a shot. I really don't feel like dying again, not when life was just starting to become good. Just keep your head on straight when you see her again and remember why you're there. If you can do that, there's a chance you can beat this."

Marcus nodded. He would. He would remember that he loved her with all of his heart and that he had come to take her away from that place and make her feel safe again so she would smile at him as she had before.

So they could be together.

The pain in his shoulders faded and his wings burst free.

"You're going to have to be quick. Heaven will know what I've done and they'll do all in their power to stop you long enough for the planets to align so they can spill her blood and activate the seal." Veiron drew the sword from the sheath at his waist and looked across at Einar. "We won't have much time if Marcus fails. I'm not leaving without Taylor and I'm figuring you feel the same."

Einar nodded and unsheathed his own sword. He met Marcus's gaze and smiled. "I'm relying on you… don't you dare get me stuck down here."

Marcus smiled back at him and Einar turned away before he could say anything, running into the dark distance with Veiron leading the way. Marcus looked back at Apollyon and Lukas and his confidence faltered. What if his love for Amelia wasn't enough to stop him from following the destiny Heaven had planned for him? Apollyon hadn't been able to fight his destiny to kill Amelia. If they took control of him, he wouldn't be strong enough to break free of their command and save her.

He didn't want to betray her again and kill her. He loved her so much. If he ended up killing her, it would be the death of him too. He couldn't live knowing what he had done.

"It can be different this time." Apollyon spread his black wings and flapped them, beating hot air against Marcus's legs.

The confidence in Apollyon's blue eyes bolstered his own and he took a deep breath and unfurled his silvery-blue wings. He flapped them and silently begged them not to disappear on him now. If the Devil's army was attacking Heaven, it could be the chance he had been waiting for. Heaven's attention would be firmly on the battle. They might not notice that he was free of his curse and was on his way there.

A voice at the back of his mind said that there might be another reason they weren't revoking his wings. They wanted him to come to them now that the planets were falling into alignment so he could spill Amelia's blood in Heaven.

Marcus drew another long steadying breath and called his armour so it covered his chest and back. That wasn't going to happen. He would save her, not kill her.

"You can make it right. History does not have to repeat itself. Believe in your feelings for her and the future you desire, and you will be strong enough to fight," Apollyon said and a crack appeared in the black ceiling of the enormous cavern.

Lukas lifted off beside him. "I'll go on ahead and return to Annelie and Serenity to let them know what's happening."

Apollyon nodded and Marcus looked at him.

"You are not going with him?" Marcus said as Apollyon beat his broad black wings and his feet left the ground but he made no move to follow Lukas.

Apollyon shook his head this time and smiled. The darkness in it unnerved Marcus.

"I have a score to settle."

Apollyon shot upwards and the ceiling above them split open, revealing a jagged streak of blue. Marcus beat his wings and followed him, heading for the mortal realm and glad to be leaving Hell behind. He wouldn't fail Einar or Veiron, or Amelia. With Apollyon at his side, he was sure that he would find the strength to end this once and for all.

He would save her.

CHAPTER 24

Marcus beat his silvery-blue wings, speeding up through the layers of air that turned from warm to cold as the world dropped away below him. Apollyon flew a few metres off to his right, his noble profile turned upwards, fixed on their destination. The clouds parted and Marcus's pale blue eyes widened when he saw what lay ahead of them.

It was pandemonium.

The gate of Heaven was under siege by hundreds of Veiron's kind, their black forms swarming against the huge pale walls of the fortress that floated above the clouds.

In amongst them were angels, battling ferociously against the foe that threatened not only to breach the wall and enter Heaven, but to take that which Heaven had stolen from Marcus.

They were here for Amelia.

"This could prove useful." Apollyon looked across at him and drew one of the curved golden blades hanging at his waist. He nodded towards the gathered armies.

Marcus didn't slow his approach. He unsheathed the blade hanging on his right side, clutching the silver and blue engraved grip tightly in his left hand, and narrowed his eyes on their target.

Apollyon was right.

Heaven's focus was on the demonic intruders waging war ahead of them. It was a chance to get into Heaven unnoticed. All they had to do was get past the battle and slip inside. The first wave of soldiers drew closer and the sound of the fight rang in the air, a symphony of metal on metal chiming out, and the scent of blood reached him.

That was going to be easier said than done.

"You should turn back," Marcus said and Apollyon offered him a grim look in return. Marcus had tried several times to convince Apollyon to return to the mortal realm so he wouldn't get into any more trouble with Heaven, but the former angel of death wasn't listening. He was intent on having vengeance for what Heaven had made him do.

The larger part of Marcus was grateful for his assistance during this battle, but there was still a sliver that felt guilty and wished he would return. He had already dragged his friends into this mess and didn't want them all to suffer punishment from Heaven for helping him go against their orders.

"Try to keep up." Apollyon beat his black wings and shot into the fray. A bright light exploded a moment later, sending both angels and demons alike flying in all directions.

Marcus's heart bolted into action, thundering as adrenaline pounded through him and he geared up for battle.

Another explosion sent a demonic angel hurtling his way. Marcus flicked his left hand out, extending the short handle of his silver blade into a long staff, took hold of it in both hands and swept it up in a fast sharp arc. He caught the demonic angel in between his obsidian breastplate and loincloth, hitting him hard in the black-skinned stomach, and propelled him upwards into the air.

Marcus beat his wings and shot through the next wave of the battle, twisting in and out and spinning to zip through the gaps between the soldiers that swarmed in the cool air.

He spied Apollyon ahead, raining dark fury down on those blocking his path. The light burned a path through them and those quick enough made their escape, leaving a wide gap for Marcus to fly through and take the lead. Apollyon followed him, drawing his other blade, and Marcus did the same. He kept the blade in his right hand short, using it to defend himself as the demonic angels turned their attention to him now.

The edge of a hot blast of white light slammed into him, sending him tumbling upwards through the air, flipping over and over until he felt sick. Marcus spread his wings, stopping himself high above the fray, and glared at Heaven. The heavy artillery blasted into the battle below him, scoring wide tracts of air in it. If it had hit him directly, it would have killed him.

"I think we have been noticed." Apollyon stopped beside him in the air, beating his broad black wings to keep himself stationary.

Marcus scoured the battle below and then the dazzling white walls that surrounded Heaven. The angels lining it at intervals were some of the most powerful in Heaven, rivalling Apollyon's strength. It was going to be difficult to break through them to reach the interior of the fortress but it wasn't impossible.

He watched the few demonic angels that had reached the wall as they tried to fly over it. The force-field created by the angels on the other side was too powerful to penetrate physically. It would take great strength to tear through it and defeat one of the angels responsible for creating it, forming a hole in the dome-like shield.

Apollyon ran his dark blue gaze over the battle, the walls, and then the white fortress ahead of them that spiralled high into the air, tall towers shining golden at their tips as they caught the sunlight.

"Are you feeling up to this?" Apollyon glanced at Marcus. He nodded. His friend didn't need to worry. Marcus was intent on entering the fortress and saving Amelia, and he was going to use every ounce of his power to achieve that. It wasn't as much as Apollyon commanded, but it would be enough to get him through the fight ahead. "Then follow me. You will have one chance. As soon as one of them falls, they will shift formation to counteract the breach."

Marcus nodded again, wondering what Apollyon had planned, and followed him. He tucked his wings back and dove when Apollyon did, cutting through the colder air. His eyes watered from the constant stream of wind over his face but he kept them open and fixed on Apollyon. They reached the battle again and Apollyon blasted another hole in it and then wove through the thickest part of the fight, where the most soldiers were gathered.

A bright white beam shot through the soldiers again and Marcus flapped his wings and rolled to one side to avoid it, zipping around demons and angels, his focus fixed on Apollyon. He was gaining speed and leaving Marcus behind. Marcus tried harder, alternating between cutting at any who got in his way and sweeping his right blade in an arc and sending a wave of power towards them to knock them out of his path.

Demonic angels snarled at him as he passed, too slow to hit him with their attacks. Another beam of light shot towards him and he dove downwards through their ranks, using them as a shield and coming out beneath the main bulk of the fight. A section of the angels that were fighting them broke away and followed him. He flew faster to evade them but they gained on him as he searched for Apollyon. Nothing would stand between him and reaching Amelia before it was too late, not even his own kind. He turned sharply onto his back, swept his blade in their direction, releasing another shockwave, and then dived off to his right.

Where had Apollyon gone?

Marcus turned onto his back again, flying beneath the battlefield, scouring it for Apollyon. The divisions of angels involved were mixed, not only guardians but mediators with their white wings and hunters with their tawny eagle-like ones. There were no angels of death present other than Apollyon, but Marcus couldn't spot him anywhere.

His tail caught up with him and Marcus turned on a pinpoint and shot upwards through the battle, knocking as many of the angels and demons out of the way by grabbing their legs and dragging them downwards to cover him from the angels following him.

He shot to one side when someone slammed into him and cried out as he hit other soldiers, his wings twisting painfully as he barrelled through them. A broad chest stopped him and he looked up, his eyes widening as they took in the mountainous black form before him. A heavy fist swung towards him with an ungodly snarl and Marcus ducked. It struck the angel behind him and Marcus came around behind the monstrous creature, trying to evade another attack and escape. He wasn't here to fight the demons. His battle lay with the angels.

The demonic angel turned and grabbed him by his left wing, tugging him back into the fight. Marcus growled and turned, bringing his right blade around at the same time. He slashed down the demon's thick armour and then twisted his wrist and kept cutting downwards, slicing into his stomach. The demonic angel snarled and hit him with a hard left hook, sending Marcus flying into a group of guardian angels.

Not good.

They took one look at Marcus, paused with a blank expression on their faces that warned Marcus they were receiving orders, and then attacked. Marcus ducked and dodged most of their punches and the jabs that they made with their own spears, but one of the young men landed a solid uppercut on his jaw, snapping his head backwards. Marcus rose with the punch, ending up a few feet higher than the rest of them. He beat his tired wings to gain more height, forced the end of the spear in his left hand against the base of the blade in his right so they merged into a double-ended spear, and darted his gaze over them all, assessing their positions below him. This was not a technique he had ever thought he would use on his own kind, but they were in his way and time was running out for Amelia.

Marcus spread his wings, took a deep breath so his mind cleared, and reached into the depth of his power. He twirled the spear faster and faster in a circle above his head, barely missing his wings, and then yelled as he sent it hurtling and spinning into the group below them. A bright explosion of light blinded him and screams rang out over the din of battle. Marcus held his hand out, calling his double-ended spear back to him. It snapped into his left hand and he shot upwards, not waiting to see the horrific extent of his attack.

The sun blinded him as he neared the fringe of the battle and he hacked his way through to the open air, heading upwards. A small shadow formed on the sun and his eyes widened again.

Apollyon.

He was far above the battle, the bodies of those foolish enough to follow him falling from the sky and dropping past Marcus before they disappeared.

What was he going to do?

Marcus looked at the wall. He was far closer to it than he had realised. A bright spot behind the shield warned that another devastating beam of light was coming. The shield around the area glimmered in the sunlight and then faded. It was opening to allow the attack through.

Before the angel on the other side could unleash his power, a tremendous burst of golden light blasted down onto that section of wall from high above, tearing through it and sending a shockwave of dust and light out in all directions. Apollyon. It was the same power that Apollyon had used on him during his mission to kill Amelia, only this time it was infinitely stronger. Marcus's heart exploded into action and he shot upwards, his eyes on the wave of power decimating everything in its path and coming straight at him, and barely avoided it. The heat scorched the soles of his boots and warmed his legs.

A black spot fell from the sky and Marcus could only watch as Apollyon plummeted through the air, his black wings in tatters and streaming feathers in his wake.

"Apollyon!" Marcus went to dive towards him but stopped when he received the message.

Go. Save her.

Marcus shot towards the breach in the white wall of Heaven but wasn't about to leave his friend unaided. Apollyon had given every morsel of his power to create this chance for Marcus and it had left him close to death. He wouldn't be able to stop his descent with his broken wings.

Marcus focused on Lukas, surrendering some of his strength in an attempt to reach him from such a great distance, and sent a message to him. Apollyon needed assistance.

A weak reply came back, barely clear enough for him to understand it, but he caught enough to know that Lukas had received his order and was en route.

He hoped that he would make it in time and that Serenity had regained her strength, because Apollyon needed them both now more than ever. He had given everything for Marcus and he wasn't going to fail him. He was strong enough to do this. He would save Amelia.

Marcus rocketed through the gap in the wall, not slowing when he reached the white gardens on the other side. He twisted and dived through the waiting horde of blue-armoured angels, sending them flying with both his power and his speed. He wouldn't relent. Not until Amelia was safe in his arms again.

He blasted through the doors to Heaven's fortress and beat his wings, shooting into the bright corridors, following his instincts to Amelia. He wasn't familiar with this area of the fortress but something deep within him said that this was the way. He ground to a halt when he reached narrower white marble corridors and couldn't use his wings anymore.

Marcus brought his spear out in front of him, focused so the staff shortened in his hand, and then broke the two blades apart again. A spear was no use in such narrow hallways. He pounded on foot through the maze of corridors, diving into doorways whenever he spotted angels ahead. His mission wasn't to fight all who stood in his way. It was faster to avoid as many as possible and conserve his energy.

That wasn't going to be possible when he came close to Amelia though. She would be under heavy protection. He was going to have to fight his way through them and then he was going to have to fight his way out of Heaven.

He ran down another corridor and came out in a hallway with a two-tiered row of arches down one side that revealed a courtyard and beautiful white trees. Closer. Marcus looked around him, trying to figure out which direction he needed to go in next. He paused when he sensed someone approaching and then heard their footsteps echoing. Too much of an echo to be the hallway. He looked to his left, towards another long corridor. Whatever lay that way, it was so bright that he couldn't make anything out.

Marcus headed down the corridor, following it until he reached an arched doorway. He stopped when the light faded enough to reveal a huge rectangular room with white marble pillars that stretched so high into the heavens that he couldn't see their ends.

He brought his gaze down and fixed it on the angel he had heard.

Lysander.

"Where is she?" Marcus strode forwards, furled his wings against his back, and readied himself. He slid one blade back into its sheath at his waist and flexed the fingers of his left hand around the other.

Anger rolled through him, fiercer than before, driving him onwards.

His footsteps were loud in the cathedral-like room, echoing for what seemed like forever, and he didn't slow his approach when Lysander raised his hand. Marcus unfurled his broad silver-blue wings, beat them and shot straight at Lysander. He caught the angel of death around his throat, closing his grip on him until he choked, and flew with him, slamming him into the far wall at the other end of the room. The marble splintered under the impact and Lysander grunted.

"Tell me!" Marcus tightened his grip, throttling Lysander, his icy blue eyes holding the young angel's gaze, and then started to unleash some of his power.

Lysander's eyes widened and he looked down towards Marcus's hand. If Lysander didn't start speaking soon, he was going to use his power to cut the man's head off. A black part of his heart wanted Lysander to remain quiet. The urge for violence, the dark desire to tear Lysander apart as payment for his role in all of this was too great to ignore. It blazed within him, fire in his veins, controlling his actions.

He slowly tightened his fingers around Lysander's throat and unleashed a little more of his power. A twisted sort of satisfaction flowed into him as the panicked edge to the young angel's eyes grew into outright fear. It would expend energy that he couldn't afford to waste but Marcus was tempted to release him and force him to fight so he could assuage his hunger for revenge.

Marcus narrowed his gaze and Lysander choked out a noise that sounded positive. He reined in his need to release the full wrath of his power on Lysander. It took long seconds for his fury to abate enough that he could convince himself to loosen his grip, but eventually he eased his fingers away from the young angel's throat and let him slide down the wall to his feet.

"They'll kill me for telling you," Lysander croaked and the fear in his eyes this time wasn't inspired by Marcus.

Had they threatened the young angel to force him to obey their orders? The things he knew about Heaven now and how far they would go to achieve their goals, he wouldn't put it past them.

"I will kill you if you don't tell me. Make your choice."

Lysander's gaze slid to one side and Marcus looked there to his right. Another corridor and the sight of this one filled him with dread.

He knew it.

With a roar, he turned and threw Lysander, sending him hurtling down to the other end of the room, close to the courtyard, far enough away that the young angel wouldn't be able to catch him before he reached the hallway.

Marcus dived to his right, running down the corridor at full pelt, his blade at the ready. He slowed to a jog when he saw the other end of the hallway in the distance. No one was there. Could he have been wrong? He was sure he would find Amelia here, had felt this was the right place, but there were no guards.

Why wouldn't they guard her?

Marcus skidded to a halt and backtracked when he passed a bright white room. He paused on the threshold, breathing hard, and relief bloomed in his heart when he saw Amelia lying on a raised white marble slab with her eyes closed, her face peaceful in spite of her condition. Heavy chains secured her ankles and held her wrists above her head, tangling with her long silver hair. He quickly scanned over her. No trace of blood.

His heartbeat started to level but he resisted his desire to rush over to her, instead taking calm measured strides into the room, cautious to the last. There were no guards and it played on his mind. They had left Amelia here with only weak little Lysander to protect her. It didn't make any sense.

They had left her so he could walk right up to her.

His foot slipped into something and he frowned down at the pale marble floor and the grooves on it. They emanated from the altar where Amelia lay, forming an intricate pattern that created a circle around her. There were grooves in the altar too, deep cuts at intervals along the edges and down the sides.

For her blood to run into.

Marcus tightened his grip on his silver blade and stepped forwards.

The moment he set foot inside the circle, white-blue light shone up from it and he fell to his knees. His blade clattered to the floor beside him and he curled up, clutching the sides of his head as pain ripped through his skull and then down his back, burning through him until he was on the verge of passing out.

No.

Marcus screwed his eyes shut and fought the words in his head, refusing to listen to them and acknowledge the order that was being sent to him.

He shouldn't have come.

He had been a fool to think he was strong enough to refuse his duty.

There was no need to guard Amelia from him when they had wanted him here, in this room with her, within this mark. The power of it flowed through him and tears stung his eyes as he tried to resist the command racing through his blood, pushing him to stand and take up his spear.

He wouldn't.

He hadn't come here to kill Amelia.

He had come here to save her.

Apollyon had risked his life for him, to give him this chance, and his friends believed in him. Amelia had believed in him. She had trusted him and he had to prove himself worthy of that trust now. He could be the man she believed him to be. He could be a good man. He could be worthy of her love.

Another wave of power tore through him, stronger this time, and forced him to his feet. He shook his head and fought it, pain beating in his heart at the thought of betraying Amelia. Heaven had used him, deceived him, and it had shattered his world and broken his heart, tearing at his soul. He couldn't do that to her too. He loved her too much to sacrifice her.

Marcus focused on that feeling and looked at her, using the sight of her to reinforce the strength he gained whenever he thought about her and his love for her. He fought the command to take up his spear from the ground and pierce her heart with it, grasping the side of his head and twisting his black hair into his fingers. He wouldn't do it. They couldn't make him.

The command that came this time was so strong that he couldn't disobey. His limbs moved of their own accord, beyond his control now, and he held his left hand out. His silver blade rose into it and the moment he closed his fingers around the grip, the staff extended.

He didn't want this.

But neither had Apollyon, and his friend hadn't been able to stop himself either.

It was inevitable.

It broke his heart.

Amelia's eyes fluttered open and calmly came to rest on him, all the sorrow in his heart reflected in their silvery irises.

"Have you come to kill me again?" she whispered and Marcus closed his eyes, unable to bear the sight of the hurt in hers. It stabbed deep into his heart until he felt as though he was bleeding inside.

Doomed to failure.

"You will die with me," she said in a quiet voice and then inhaled shakily. "You have the past three times you have killed me. I have taken you with me into the darkness."

Those words cleaved at his heart until he couldn't take any more. Tears slipped from the corners of his eyes and he looked at her, had to see in her eyes that she had remembered the terrible things that he had done to her and that she didn't hate him. There were tears on her cheeks too, diamond drops that sparkled in the bright light engulfing the room.

It was fitting that he died with her. Did he go out of choice, because he loved her and couldn't bear what he had done, or because he paid the price for spilling her deadly blood?

His heart said it was the former. These realms were nothing without her at his side. He could never live knowing what he had done to her. He deserved to die.

The command came again and he struggled against it, gritting his teeth and holding his left wrist, desperate to stop it from moving. It shifted against his will and he battled it, trying to hold it back. He was stronger than this. He couldn't kill her.

He fought the order, wrestling with his arm and trying to regain control, and cursed Heaven for what they were making him do. His left hand moved and the grip of his right began to loosen. He spat out a curse aimed at himself this time. Fury burned through him, hatred of Heaven filling him with a dark need to tear the realm asunder and destroy it. This wasn't how his mission was supposed to end. This wasn't right. He couldn't do this. He couldn't hurt her. He loved her so much, with all of his heart. It was hers now. He was hers now.

His heart, his soul, his body. All of him. She was his master, the one who ruled him and the one for whom he would do anything.

Marcus's right hand shifted to grip the staff of his spear and he raised it, unable to stop it from moving. Amelia stared at him with wide fearful eyes and they were grey again, not silvery as they were when she was angelic. Tears stung his eyes and he growled through clenched teeth as he turned his spear so the blade was aimed at her chest. He couldn't stop himself.

His gaze met hers and a shiver coursed down his back and spread over his limbs.

Amelia.

She smiled at him through her tears.

The smile he had ached to see these past few days.

"I love you, Marcus."

CHAPTER 25

Amelia flinched away and braced for impact when Marcus brought his spear down. The sound of metal rang out, echoing in her ears until she couldn't hear and reverberating through her body until her fingertips tingled. She waited for the pain to come, her heart breaking over what Heaven had put Marcus through, and wished that it hadn't turned out this way. She loved him so deeply, with all of her, and seeing him suffering because of her had been unbearable, but it was over now.

Wasn't it?

She cracked an eye open and then screwed them shut when Marcus brought his spear down again with such force that her legs echoed with the vibrations of his powerful blow and her feet tingled.

The chiming brought with it memories she wished that she had never remembered, images of all the times they had done this. She could remember dying in his arms so many times and how he would kiss her goodbye, taking her blood into his body as she drew her final breath and destroying himself in the process. She didn't want that to happen again. She wanted to live with him, wanted to love him and be with him and escape this endless torture.

His warm fingers closed around her right hand, the cold chains fell away from her, and then she was in his arms.

"We need to get out of here," he said close to her ear and disbelief crashed over her, swiftly followed by relief so sweet that tears filled her eyes.

She struggled against her desire, afraid that this was all some cruel trick and that things were going to end in bloodshed and pain any moment now, that Heaven was only toying with her by making her believe that she was safe, and then surrendered to it and threw her arms around Marcus's neck, burrowing her face into his throat.

Marcus's right arm slid around her back, holding her to him, and she wept against his skin, catching his scent each time she sucked in a sharp breath in an attempt to regain control and not look like a complete weakling. She had been so afraid, had battled those feelings and fought to keep them locked deep in her heart so none would see them, but now they flooded her, carrying her away and stripping her of her strength.

Marcus murmured softly against her hair, whispered words full of warmth and affection and reassurance, and pressed a kiss to it.

He held her a moment longer and then said something that put an end to her tears and reminded her they weren't out of danger yet.

"Can you fly?"

Amelia thought about it. Since coming to Heaven, her consciousness and that of the other side of her had been slowly merging into one and she felt human again now. She wasn't sure if she could manage to fly because she wasn't sure if she remembered how. She had forgotten that she had wings at all.

"No time." Marcus took hold of her hand, shoved one of his curved silver blades into it, and then slipped his right hand into her left one. He held it tightly as they ran and Amelia struggled to keep up. Her legs tangled in the long flowing white and blue dress and it was hard to lift it out of the way when she was carrying a heavy blade. The thing weighed more than she could handle and she was afraid that she wasn't going to be much use in a fight.

She would be.

She couldn't let Marcus do all the fighting. Two swords were better than one, even if she had never swung a blade before. She could help him. They were in this together.

Amelia pulled Marcus to a halt. He started to say something as he turned to face her but stopped when she used her blade to cut through the irritating skirt of her dress. It was a little higher up her thigh than she had aimed for. By the time she had finished tearing the material away, it barely covered her backside and Marcus was staring wide-eyed at her legs.

His pupils dilated, darkening his silver-blue eyes, and she wanted to kiss him when he looked like that, so full of passion and desire for her. She wanted to kiss him for being here with her and coming to her rescue. He had fought his order and had overcome it for her, but she wasn't going to let her guard down around him. She wasn't sure if he was free of the compulsion to kill her or whether he was still fighting it.

She nodded and they started running again, side by side, back through the maze of pale corridors.

"What's the plan?" she puffed, fighting to keep up with him.

"Out of here, and then upwards."

"Out the front door?" That didn't sound like a good idea to her. She really wasn't much of a fighter and she didn't want Marcus to get hurt trying to protect her, or to have a chance to lose concentration.

He glanced across at her. The beads of sweat dotting his brow and the pain in his eyes weren't due to exertion from running.

He was still fighting his orders and it was hurting him.

The sight of him in so much pain, suffering so much, stirred darkness within her, anger she had never felt before. Fury. She wanted to destroy Heaven for what it had made him do and for what it had done to her. She had never raised a hand to anyone but all that was about to change. Heaven would feel her wrath. It would pay.

They broke out into the open white-grassed area in front of the building and Amelia's fury spiked at the sight of a row of guardian angels blocking their path, their blue and silver armour shining brightly in the golden sunlight.

Marcus moved in front of her, his single blade at the ready, and she sensed his fatigue through where he touched her. It was taking all of his strength to fight his orders. He didn't have the energy left to fight these angels too.

He released her hand and extended his blade into a spear.

Amelia had had enough.

She wouldn't let him suffer because of her. Heaven shouldn't make them suffer.

It should suffer.

Her silver wings unfurled from her back and, without hesitation or an ounce of fear, she beat them, lifting slowly off the ground, anger fuelling her. She dropped Marcus's blade and opened herself to the feelings colliding inside her, letting the fury flow through her unrestrained. It swept outwards from her heart until it reached the tips of her limbs and then came back in on itself.

She wouldn't let them hurt Marcus.

The rage inside her bounced back and forth, growing stronger each time it passed itself and with each beat of her wings that lifted her higher into the air. She glared at the scores of angels below her.

Beneath her.

Amelia unleashed her feelings in a cry of sheer fury and swept her hand out, cutting through the air with it. Her eyes widened when an invisible wave of power ripped through the angels in the same path she had cut with her hand, sending them flying in all directions. They tumbled across the white grass, spun high into the air, or smashed into the white walls of Heaven's fortress, creating impact craters.

A smile curved her lips, drawn by the sense of strength flowing through her.

The angels that had escaped her attack looked up at her, drew their silver blades, and spread their wings.

Time to test the limits of her power. She wasn't sure how it worked and she wasn't going to question it. Instinct had controlled her actions just now and she was sure it would be the same this time. She would know how to use her power if she let it flow through her and didn't think about it too much, just as she knew how to use her wings.

She beat her wings to take her higher and half of the angels took flight and followed her, leaving the eerie white grounds of the fortress. When she was level with the highest tower, she turned and looked down at the dizzying drop below her. Angels filled the space between her and the ground where Marcus still stood, fighting those who had remained with him.

Tears blurred her vision as she watched him, the bitter taste of fury coating her tongue. It shouldn't have been like this. Marcus shouldn't have to fight his own kind. It hurt him to do so. She had felt his pain and his struggle when he had been holding her hand.

The feel of that pain still beat in her heart, fuelling her anger with Heaven and controlling her actions. Heaven shouldn't have treated him this way. Marcus's duty had been everything to him, his whole world. He had been so loyal to his master, had trusted Heaven and his superiors, and had believed in them. They had taken that loyalty and used it against him, forcing him to do things against his will even when it hurt him. No one should be used and betrayed like that.

Especially not someone as wonderful and kind as Marcus.

Amelia flung her wings back to stop herself, brought her hands out in front of her and focused on the space between her palms. She brought them closer together as her power flowed into them. Dazzling blue and white sparks skittered over her skin and leapt along her arms.

The sparks jumped from one palm to the other, snapping against her flesh and crackling as they thickened and intensified.

She frowned as the energy leapt and twisted, forming a small orb in the gap between her hands. It glowed bright blue, throwing off beams of light as it spun faster and faster.

Amelia slowly pulled her hands apart again and drew a deep breath, channelling all of her anger and feelings into the sphere of white-blue energy growing between her palms.

When the orb reached a foot across, she focused and brought her hands around behind it, shifted herself upwards with a gentle beat of her wings, and looked down at the angels swarming towards her.

Heaven would pay.

The bluish sphere of light turned to shimmering silver and shot towards the angels coming at her, growing as it headed for them. They tried to evade it but it was growing too swiftly, spreading outwards until it engulfed all of them. It didn't stop there. It brightened until it blinded her and started growing towards her too, rapidly expanding in size until it was over fifty metres across. Amelia held her hand out towards it, afraid that it was going to suck her into it too.

Blue light danced across its surface as it halted just inches from her palm, and then it collapsed in on itself so quickly that she was pulled down through the air with it. She jerked to a halt and snapped back a few feet. A dazzling flash of light pierced her eyes and then it winked out of existence. Her vision slowly came back.

Her head spun.

Her wings faltered.

Perhaps she should have tested the limits of her power before going all out.

Amelia fell backwards, expecting to drop from the sky, but she hung there instead, suspended by her waist with her wings streaming out below her.

"Not so much next time. Leave some for yourself," Marcus said with strain in his voice and Amelia felt his arms around her as the world slowly came back into focus.

He flew downwards with her and her eyes widened when she saw what she had done.

She hadn't only taken out the angels.

The orb of power had cut through the ground too and the thick white stone wall, and even the shimmering blue shield over the entire area.

She might have killed Marcus.

He pulled her closer to him as they descended through the huge hole she had created in the grounds and then tucked his wings against his back once they were on the other side. They shot downwards together.

Marcus flew hard and the wind numbed her face, feet and fingers. Droplets of moisture coated her skin as they dropped through the clouds, freezing against her flesh and soaking her flimsy dress. The clouds thinned and then cleared, revealing the world below them. They were almost home.

"Tell me again," Marcus whispered into her ear and she looked up at him. There was so much pain in his eyes and such tiredness that she reached up and touched his cheek. His skin was hot against her palm. He had risked everything for her and was still fighting himself.

"I love you so much."

He smiled but there was such sorrow and hurt in it. "Catch me."

She didn't understand.

He stopped with her, held her against him with one arm and took hold of her hand. His smile faded and he pressed a kiss to the back of her hand and then stared into her eyes. His irises burned bright blue and he grimaced, screwed his eyes shut, and then looked back into hers. His hand shook against hers, the trembling relaying his fight to her. Heaven was trying to seize control of him again.

Marcus brushed his lips across hers, so softly that her insides flipped, and then drew back and smiled at her.

"I renounce my master and my duty… I love you, Amelia."

He closed his eyes and then they were dropping fast. Marcus turned with her and her eyes shot wide when she saw his wings were gone and so was his armour and weapons. He slipped from her grasp and dropped further from her. Amelia's heart slammed against her chest and she reached for him, tears stinging her eyes and blurring her vision. He shot through the patchy clouds ahead of her and she came through it with him, out into warmer air high above the Earth.

The distance to the indistinct green and blue world below turned her stomach.

It dropped along with her heart when she saw that Marcus was even further below her now.

Amelia sucked in a sharp breath and focused. Catch him. He had renounced everything for her and had fallen. She had to catch him. He had placed his faith in her and she wouldn't fail him, not as Heaven had.

She tucked her wings against her back and rocketed towards him, cutting through the air so fast that it froze her damp skin. Closing. The ground was coming at them fast now and she recognised the area they were over. Europe. Home. It seemed surreal to see it like this. She beat her wings and gritted her teeth, using everything she had to go faster and close the distance between them.

Warmer air buffeted her, sending her silver hair flying across her face and tugging at her clothes.

Marcus continued to fall below her, his legs and arms bent towards her, his back taking the brunt of the wind as he plummeted to the ground.

Amelia growled and focused everything she had, everything she didn't understand herself, into one last attempt to reach him. She beat her wings and then tucked them right against her back and shot towards Marcus.

And straight past him.

Damn.

She opened her wings enough that she shot upwards, back past him, and then dropped again. She stretched her hands out to him and caught hold of his, and then inched her grip on him to his wrists, tightly grasping them so he couldn't escape her.

"Marcus!" she yelled over the wind but he didn't stir.

The ground was closing in fast now.

They shot past a passenger plane and she hoped that she was invisible to human eyes just like an angel could be and that the people onboard hadn't just seen an angel falling holding a naked man.

Amelia struggled and pulled Marcus closer to her, fighting to get her arms around him. He murmured something and relief briefly touched her heart but then the world below started taking on shape and colour, and she could distinguish cities and towns. Not good.

With a low growl of effort, she yanked Marcus up to her, wrapped her arms around him and then spread her wings. They shot up again but she was still coming in too fast and her grip on Marcus was tenuous at best. He was heavy in her arms, slipping through her grasp and dragging her down.

Amelia desperately beat her wings and tried to slow her descent. The cities took on more shape and she recognised one.

Paris.

Marcus murmured something that sounded a lot like 'pull up' and she tried to but he was so heavy and she wasn't accustomed to flying. She wasn't sure how to pull up. He leaned into her, forcing her shoulders back, and her feet came down.

Trees.

She was heading straight for them.

This was not going to be a good first landing.

Amelia shrieked when she hit them, her feet catching the highest branches, and then screamed when she was flipped head over heels. She spun through the air and came crashing down into a green field on the other side of the clump of trees. Marcus hit the dirt first and she followed him, tumbling and bouncing along, her wings twisting underneath her and snapping into painful positions. She stopped rolling but the world didn't stop pitching.

She lay there a few seconds, staring at the dirt, grass in her mouth and pain blazing through every inch of her, and then closed her eyes.

"No rest."

Those two words forced her eyes open and she looked across the grass to Marcus where he lay sprawled on his back, naked and covered in green stains and dirt.

"What happened?" She pushed herself onto her knees and crawled across the knobbly ground to him.

"Must go." He nodded upwards.

Amelia looked there and she didn't like what she saw.

Angels.

They were tiny dots in the sky but they were coming at them fast.

She didn't have the power left in her to take them down. Even if she did, she couldn't unleash it on Earth. It had caused so much devastation in Heaven. She didn't want to imagine how many it would kill if she used that same attack down here.

Amelia struggled to her feet, pulled Marcus onto his, and slung his arm around her shoulder.

"Hold on," she said and ran with him, trying to gain speed so she could lift off.

She beat her silver wings and rose into the air with Marcus, holding him close to her, but could only manage to fly a few feet off the ground. How the hell did he fly with her so effortlessly? He was a dead weight in her arms and she was tiring.

Paris loomed ahead of them, the Eiffel Tower her beacon of hope. If they could reach civilisation, surely the angels wouldn't attack her. They wouldn't harm the mortals. Would they?

A dark spot appeared on the horizon.

Another angel?

She kept flying. If it was, then she would deal with it, but she couldn't slow down now. She had to get Marcus to safety. She wasn't sure what damage he had done to himself by renouncing everything but she had certainly broken him with that landing. He was bleeding and hurt, and he felt weak to her.

Was he mortal now?

Did that mean he could die?

She prayed that their crash wouldn't kill him and redoubled her effort, determined to get to Serenity so the witch could heal him.

The dark dot grew into a man that she recognised.

Veiron.

Had he come to finish her off?

She braced herself for his attack as they neared and then frowned when he nodded at her and shot past her, heading for the angels. A loud explosion rent the peaceful summer morning a moment later. She looked over her shoulder at him. He was fighting the horde of angels, holding them back for her. Was he on their side now?

Amelia flew onwards, heading over the city. Marcus came around again and tugged on her shoulders, steering her right.

"Others," he whispered and she nodded.

She knew where to go only she didn't know the way. She was relying on Marcus to remain conscious long enough to guide her to Serenity and Apollyon's home.

A brighter spot appeared on the horizon above the grey slate roofs of the city and came into focus.

"Lukas!" She couldn't contain her relief. While she barely knew the angel, she knew that he could lead her to Apollyon's home and that he wouldn't harm her.

He halted in mid-air and she almost collided with him. Clearly she needed to practice stopping as well as landing.

"What happened?" Lukas said with a look over Marcus and then took him from her.

"Renounced." It was the only word she could get out between breaths. She felt faint again and wasn't sure how much longer she could keep flying.

"Hurry. We shall leave the angels to Veiron. He will keep them busy long enough for us to reach safety without them seeing where we went." Lukas turned and flew back in the direction he had come from.

Amelia followed him. Another explosion shook the air and she looked back towards where Veiron was battling the angels. He was on their side. She found that hard to believe but she wasn't going to complain. Veiron was lighting up the sky with his attacks and she could feel their strength regardless of the great distance between them. He was a powerful ally and she needed all she could get right now.

She had escaped Heaven but she hadn't won yet.

Amelia touched down on the tiled balcony of Apollyon's rooftop apartment and followed Lukas inside. She frowned when something washed over her and looked back at the French doors. Purple light shimmered there. A barrier?

"You are alive!" Serenity's high squeak, still laced with her thick French accent at such a pitch, brought a smile to Amelia's face.

Amelia went to step towards her but her wings shrank and disappeared into her back and the last of her strength left her.

Einar caught her around the waist and she tried to thank him but couldn't find her voice. She looked across at Marcus in Lukas's arms and reached for him.

"Take them into the room," Serenity said and then looked at Lukas. "I will need you back here right away."

Lukas nodded and carried Marcus into the room where Amelia had slept before. He laid Marcus down on the white wooden double bed there and covered him with a pale blue blanket. Einar helped her onto the bed beside him and she leaned back into the pillows. They were warm against her chilled skin and comforting.

"Angels are coming," she whispered and Einar nodded.

"It's under control. Rest now. I will see to Marcus first." Einar smiled at her and then rounded the foot of the bed to the other side.

Amelia tracked him with her gaze and then watched him as he pulled the covers away from Marcus and held his hands out above him. Pale light filtered down from his palms, washing over Marcus's bruised and dirtied skin.

"Will he be alright?" Amelia tilted her head to one side and took in Marcus's profile.

"He'll be fine."

Those words brought comfort to her heart and seemed to give her leave to surrender her fight against the tiredness running through her aching body. She slipped her hand under the covers and into Marcus's, locking their fingers together.

"Let's send you to sleep, shall we?" Taylor's voice cut into the darkness of her closed eyes and Amelia sighed out her breath and sunk into the pillows as a warm hand came to rest on her forehead.

Sleep sounded good.

She wanted to sleep forever in Marcus's strong arms.

Safe at last.

CHAPTER 26

Marcus's head felt heavy and his limbs weak, drained of strength and limp at his sides where he lay shrouded in darkness. His soul was in agony, torn at and beaten, and it was a struggle to breathe through the pain. He hadn't considered the consequences of his actions. He had thought only of ending his duty and saving Amelia.

She was a divine being, made of God and the Devil, and he had heard the strength of her voice when he had cut her loose from the chains that had bound her. It had reached deep inside him, filling him with the images of countless deaths they had shared and with her fear of dying again. She had wanted to live with him. She had wanted this to end and for them to finally be together.

He had wanted that too.

It had taken only a handful of words from her to give him the strength to fight Heaven's rule over him and then only a small amount of his power to change the course of his spear so it struck the chains, smashing them instead.

But Heaven hadn't relented.

It had pushed him throughout their escape into the open gardens surrounding the white fortress and then when they had been flying back to the mortal realm, and he had known that they would never give up. They would continue to push and send that same command to him until he was too weak to fight back and would succumb again.

His strength and power had left him just moments before he had made his decision, and he had realised that he would no longer be able to fight the command that Heaven was hammering into his skull. It had driven him to do the only thing he could in the hope that it would work and it would save her.

He had sacrificed everything for her.

His wings had disappeared in an instant.

His armour and weapons taken from him.

Yet he didn't feel mortal.

He had none of the weakness he had felt during the times when Heaven had limited his power.

Was this being fallen?

Einar would know but Marcus didn't have the energy to open his eyes and seek the former angel out.

A cool breeze washed over him, sweeping upwards from his toes.

"Marcus." Her voice was soft, as though the wind had carried it to him, restoring his strength with its sound, and he slowly opened his eyes and looked for her.

She descended from the inky moonlit sky above him, her arms outstretched and a smile curving her sweet rosy lips. Her silver hair caught the moonlight and shone brightly as it fluttered out behind her. Her wings beat the air but they were changing, some of the long silver feathers falling away to reveal leathery membrane. She looked at them with concern and then her gaze met his again, shier this time.

"Marcus." Amelia drifted down and halted barely a metre above him. He closed his eyes at the first touch of her hand on his face, and then leaned into her caress.

"Amelia," he whispered and sighed as her touch sent warmth flowing through him. Wherever it ran, his strength returned. The pain in his soul began to lessen when her hand came to rest above his heart and she landed beside him, kneeling between his right arm and his side. "I am so tired."

He opened his eyes and sought hers. The smile was still there, heating his chest through and stealing his heart. It was hers anyway. He had forsaken everything for her, so they could be together, free of the game Heaven and Hell had played with them. He only hoped their time together lasted more than a few moments. He wanted it to go on forever.

"Rest then, my love." She leaned over and pressed a kiss to his lips and the ache in his soul disappeared. "My guardian angel."

Marcus closed his eyes and mourned the loss of her mouth on his when she drew back. She draped herself over him, curling up with her head on his bare chest, and placed her hand over his heart.

The ground shook and she tensed.

"What is happening?" He stared at the black expanse of sky above them. Stars twinkled at him and the full moon was so bright that it was dazzling. This wasn't the real world.

"We're safe here, I think," Amelia whispered and traced patterns on his chest, following the lines of his muscles and then circling his right nipple. "Taylor has sent us to sleep again."

"We are in Paris?" Relief beat in his heart when she nodded against his chest. He couldn't recall much after choosing to fall. The immediate drain on him had rendered him unconscious and then he had come around to find them close to crashing. They had crashed. He looked down at Amelia. She lay with her head on his left pectoral and her eyes closed. There was a cut across her left cheek and he gently touched it. "You are hurt."

"Only a little," she said and opened her eyes, meeting his. They were dark in the low light but didn't seem silver. Was she back to his Amelia again now? He still wasn't sure how it worked but there seemed to be two sides to her, the angel and the mortal. Right now, she looked like a mixture of both, as though those two sides had merged into this one beautiful being lying with her head on his chest. "Are you alright? You look so tired."

He nodded to stop her from worrying.

"We should go back, shouldn't we? Everyone is fighting because of us." The worry didn't leave her eyes.

Marcus shook his head this time and realised that he was laying on something soft and warm that moved with him. He scrunched up his free hand where it rested at his side. Sand. Taylor had sent them to Amelia's inner world again.

"The fight will not last," he said with a soft smile aimed at soothing her. "This world keeps us hidden from Heaven and Hell."

"They won't stop until they have me. I can stop this. I don't want anyone else to be hurt because of me." Amelia pushed herself up until her breasts pressed against his stomach and she was looking down at him.

"I cannot let you do that… and they won't either." Marcus brushed the backs of his fingers across her cheek, sweeping the long strands of her silver hair from her face. "They fought for you, Amelia. I fought for you."

"You fell for me." She looked away and tears filled her eyes. "That's what you did, wasn't it? You gave it all up for me and I don't deserve it… I don't deserve someone like you."

He smiled now. "You do… you deserve someone better than me."

Amelia looked at him again out of the corner of her eye, uncertainty shining in them.

Marcus swept his hand back to stroke the soft silver feathers at the top of her wings and she turned her face away, casting her eyes downwards, as though ashamed.

"I don't know how you can look at me now. I wish I didn't look this way."

He frowned at those words and the feelings behind them. So much hurt.

"Why?" Marcus caught her cheek again, trying to make her look at him. She refused, keeping her face firmly turned away from his.

Her wings shrank into her back and disappeared.

"How can you feel anything for me when you know what I am… when I dragged you into all of this… when I look like a demon?"

A demon? She looked like an angel to him.

"You are beautiful, Amelia," he whispered and she frowned, sending tears running over her cheeks. They shone in the moonlight as brightly as her silver hair. He ran his fingers over the long silken lengths. "I love everything about you. Your hair is like moonlight… and your wings are beautiful… you don't need to hide them from me. You are still the woman I fell for."

A tiny smile touched her lips. "You really did fall for me."

He cupped her cheek and lightly swept the pad of his thumb across it, erasing her tears. "I really did."

"I hope you won't regret it one day."

"I will never regret anything when it comes to you. You mean so much to me and that will never change, no matter how long we are together for. I will always love you, Amelia."

She looked at him at last, fear still lingering in her grey eyes, and he sighed at the sight of it. What could he say to make her realise that he did love everything about her?

Marcus slipped his hand under her chin and turned her head so she was facing him again, looking into his eyes.

"Will you let me see your wings again? I hate the thought of you hiding them from me."

Hesitation flitted across her face and then her wings slowly emerged.

The stars blinked and flickered above her, a halo of shimmering pinpricks that matched her hair. The silvery feathers that had remained on the top half of her wings shone too, pure and bright, just like her heart and her soul. Beautiful. Breathtaking.

Marcus held her cheek and smiled into her eyes. "You deserve so much more in life than pain and suffering, and I wanted to give that to you. I wanted to be a man worthy of your love… and I… wish that I was… I don't know if I am, or ever will be, but I want to be a good man for you. I love you, Amelia. All of you."

She smiled brilliantly and leaned down and kissed him, her mouth playing slowly and gently over his, breathing life back into his weary body.

Marcus wrapped his arms around her and held her close to him, savouring the feel of her body against his and how good it felt to have her in his arms again. He had fallen for her but he wasn't sure whether that was stopping Heaven from calling to him now or whether it had something to do with where Taylor had sent them.

Amelia was in command in this world. She had total control over him here.

Apollyon had told him that Heaven wasn't easy to leave and neither was his duty. When they left this world, would Heaven call him again or come for him? Would they try to make him kill Amelia?

"You're worried," Amelia said and placed a soft kiss against the corner of his mouth. "I can feel it."

It wasn't just because this was her world. It was because she was like him in some ways now and could sense a sliver of people's emotions when she was close to them.

"I was wondering how long Taylor can keep us hidden."

"Not forever, that's for sure. When we go out there, the angels will be waiting, if they haven't found us and taken our bodies already." There was such a solemn edge to her tone and Marcus hated to hear it and to feel that she had given up already. He could give her courage at least and a reason to hold on to hope.

"We only need to remain hidden until the end of the planetary alignment."

Her silvery eyebrows rose. "The one I told you about?"

Marcus recalled now that she had tried to speak to him at the café in London about a programme she had watched on the subject. At the time, he had been so lost in her beauty and in battling his growing feelings for her that he hadn't been able to focus on their conversation. He nodded.

"Seven days. If we can remain here or out of their grasp for seven days, then your blood will no longer be of use to them."

"What does it do?" She looked down at her hands where they rested on his chest. "What is it they wanted me for?"

They hadn't told her? She had her memories back, which meant that if she didn't know now why Heaven had captured her and had wanted to spill her blood then she had never known. She had died each time without ever knowing what they had wanted from her.

Marcus gathered her closer to him when the ground trembled again and tried to bring her focus back to him rather than on the attack taking place where their bodies were. He had faith in his friends that they would all survive this. Heaven wasn't foolish enough to start an all out war on Earth. It went against its principles and creed, against its purpose.

It was difficult to bring his own focus away from the attack when the desire to return to the real world and join the fight beat deep in his heart. He wasn't convinced that Heaven would leave them alone once the planetary alignment ended and he still hungered for revenge for his sake and Amelia's. He wanted to settle everything once and for all, to return to Heaven and somehow ensure they would never come after Amelia again.

How could he fight them now though? He had no wings to reach Heaven and no power to use once he got there. It was impossible.

Amelia moved in his arms, her heart beating against his chest. He stroked her cheek to soothe her fears and pushed away his impotent desire for vengeance, focusing on her instead.

"Your blood could activate a seal that would close Heaven if it was spilt in the right place in Hell, and Hell if it was spilt in the right place in Heaven… but only if the blood touched the marks at the right time, and it would only last until the moment the last of your blood dried out and left the seal." He grazed the backs of his fingers along the soft line of her jaw and kept her attention on him, his eyes locked with hers. "If we can keep you safe until that time has passed, then they would have no reason to come after you anymore."

Unless they wanted to kill her so she would start the cycle of rebirth again. Marcus would never allow that to happen. They would keep moving, remaining out of sight and free of both Heaven's and Hell's angels. He would protect her forever if he had to.

That was, if forever was still within his grasp.

"They will always be after me, won't they?" she whispered and he couldn't lie to her.

"I will protect you, Amelia. I promised you that, remember?"

Her smile said that she did. He slowly caressed her cheek, absorbing the softness of her skin and her warmth. The sea rolled over his bare feet and up his shins, and it dawned on him that he was nude and had been from the moment he had shunned Heaven.

Amelia didn't seem to notice. She lay on him wearing a beautiful smile and her ruined dress, her wings grazing his thighs and the sand by her feet.

"I do not know what will happen when we leave this place." He ran his right hand over her bare thigh down to her knee. "Heaven might still have the power to command me."

A frown flitted across her face and then melted away. "Serenity commanded Apollyon when he wanted to kill me… if I do the same, would it work?"

He wasn't sure. She had reached him once and given him the strength to fight Heaven's orders, and she had power beyond the grasp of most. There was a chance that if she formed a contract with him, that it would overrule any orders that Heaven might send him, even those attached to his eternal duty.

"It might. If you call to me and bind us by contract, it might work."

"Contract?"

"Serenity called to Apollyon, requesting something of him, and he agreed to it. That's how they can be together and how Serenity can command him. If you do the same, then there is a chance that it will forge a bond between us… or perhaps something stronger."

"Stronger?"

She had power beyond an angel's reckoning. Was it possible that she could call him to her and bind them as master and servant? Marcus's heart raced at the prospect. It was worth a shot.

"You could call me over to your side. You are powerful, Amelia. You could do more than place a contract between us. You could bring me over, as the Devil can to an angel."

"You mean… make you like me?" The tremble in her voice betrayed her nerves.

Marcus nodded. "It is what I want, Amelia. I wish to be like you… I wish for the strength to protect you. You can give that to me."

She pushed away from him and rose to her knees and then onto her feet, a vision with her half-angel, half-demonic wings and her long silver hair shining in the moonlight.

Amelia held her hand out to him. He slipped his into it and she surprised him by hauling him easily onto his feet and then casting a shy glance at his groin.

"I think I should start with your appearance. You're a little distracting at the moment." She frowned at his body and Marcus looked down as his feet tingled and warmed. The cuts and scratches on them disappeared, followed by those on his legs and then his torso and arms, and finally the heat touched his face. Amelia smiled at him. "Much better."

"What are you doing?" he said, trying to grasp whether this was real or just a flight of fancy possible in this inner world of Amelia's.

"Making you mine." Her cheeks coloured and then she straightened up and looked deep into his eyes, her grey ones full of confidence and strength that was so familiar to him.

That was his Amelia. Never afraid. Always facing things head on. She had strength like no other mortal or immortal. She had seized his heart for herself when it had long been in Heaven's grasp, had snatched him from them and changed him so much.

This had to be possible.

He wanted it to be.

"Your knight?" he said and she nodded.

"My knight… should wear armour."

Marcus marvelled down at himself when familiar boots appeared on his feet, followed by greaves to cover his shins. Only they were different to the ones he was used to. Rather than being blue with raised silver edging, they were bright silver with royal blue edging and bore a raised form of a rampant winged horse on each greave. He was still staring at them when he felt the matching vambraces form over his forearms. A rearing winged horse decorated each of them too. A royal blue loincloth covered him and then beautiful pointed rectangles of pure silver inlaid with blue patterns appeared, attaching themselves to a belt around his waist. His breastplate followed it and Marcus wasn't surprised to see a winged horse on each pectoral of the silver armour.

What did surprise him was what happened when Amelia looked at his shoulders.

Wings burst from his back.

He looked over his shoulders at them, expecting them to look like hers. They didn't. They were the same wings he'd had as an angel.

Marcus turned back to her.

"Do you like them?" she said with a smile.

"No."

Her smile faded and hurt surfaced in her eyes. He stepped towards her, took hold of her hand and looked down into her eyes.

"I mean… give me wings like yours, Amelia… so all will know that we are one and so that you will never feel as though your wings are something that will come between us. They are beautiful, and I want mine to be like them too."

Tears sparkled on her lashes and she nodded.

Marcus stepped back and power washed over him when she looked at his shoulders. He waited for it to ebb away and then looked at his wings. They were as beautiful as hers were, pure silver feathers catching the moonlight and giving way to reveal a dark leathery membrane and clawed tips.

Amelia looked nervous and then held her hands out in front of her and two curved silver blades similar to those he had once owned appeared on her palms. She looked down at them.

"I can't give you back what you sacrificed to be with me. Part of me knows that… on some level… somehow. I'm not sure what I am yet or what I'm going to do, but I know I want you at my side throughout the journey that lies ahead of me. I don't want to go on without you, Marcus." She closed her eyes and tears streaked down her cheeks and fell onto the blades. They shimmered brightly and then dulled again. "I believe you are worthy of me. You are the only knight I need… the only man I need. I love you with all of my heart and I want to stay with you this time… I don't want us to suffer anymore."

He smiled, eased down to his knee in front of her, and held his hands above his head with his palms turned upwards.

She placed the twin blades into them and he looked up at her, meeting her gaze, and then lowered his head again and offered his blades back to her.

He closed his eyes when she touched them and he felt the power flow from her through them and into him.

"Marcus, I am offering you the eternal duty of protecting me, of becoming my guardian and my knight, and in exchange I offer my heart."

Marcus's hands trembled and he drew in a long steadying breath as he heard those words deep in his heart, echoing there and calling to him. He had only ever known the call of his master's voice. Amelia's was softer than it but no less powerful. It warmed him as much as her touch did and soothed him more than it ever could.

He raised his eyes to meet hers and the nerves in them tugged at the corners of his lips. He suppressed his desire to smile at how unsure she was. It had been a good speech, although all she had truly needed to do was say his name and let her heart tell him the rest. It said so much more than her words had. Her heart had called to his, filling him with her feelings and her love, and it was that which he sought in exchange for his vow of obedience.

He wanted her heart as forever his.

"I accept, my master." Marcus lowered his head again and then rose to his feet, coming to stand barely a few inches in front of her. He looked down into her eyes and smiled at last, letting her see and feel what this meant to him. "I love you."

A smile burst onto her lips and she tiptoed, threw her arms around his shoulders, and kissed him.

Marcus dropped his two blades onto the sand, slipped his arms around her waist and drew her in for a long heated kiss, making the most of this moment with her. Her tongue swept over his lips, teasing him, and he delved his into her mouth so it tangled with hers. She tasted as sweet as he remembered and he had been dying to do this again with her, had thought it would never happen after she had awoken as an angel. It seemed almost too good to be real and he didn't want to let her go in case it turned out to be only a dream and not Taylor's doing after all.

The ground shook again and Amelia gasped and hid against his chest when the tremor lasted longer this time.

Marcus looked around him and frowned. The scenery had changed. In place of the sea and the shoreline, a bright green sunlit valley filled his vision. The hill they stood on sloped downwards into it and he heard a river far below, and caught glimpses of it through the trees that lined its bank in the valley bottom. The hills rolled around them, stretching far into the distance.

"Is this your world?" Amelia said and Marcus frowned.

"I do not think so."

"It's mine." A familiar deep voice boomed down the hill and Marcus turned with Amelia, looking up the lush green slope to the owner of it.

Einar stood above them wearing the deep-earthen-coloured armour of a hunter angel with tawny wings tucked against his back. He looked over his shoulder at the wings and smiled.

"Taylor likes to let me fly here once in a while."

Marcus smiled to reassure his friend. He didn't have to explain. He had lived for five centuries without his wings and knew how painful it could be. Einar looked him over with raised eyebrows.

"I have a message," he said at last and his brown gaze shifted to Amelia. "Taylor is tiring but Serenity has moved you to another location. Apollyon has gone to plead your case—"

"Apollyon?" Marcus interjected. The last time he had seen his dark friend, he had been falling from the sky having expended all of his power. "What does he plan to do?"

"He has gone to make a bargain." Einar sat down on the grass and stretched. It didn't hide the weariness in his eyes from Marcus. Einar had been fighting for them too. "He has gone to reason that if Amelia is kept alive and under its protection, then Heaven has no reason to fear Hell capturing her and killing her to restart what Veiron referred to as their game."

"Why would they listen to him?"

"Because if they don't, he will release the Devil from the bottomless pit and also assist Amelia in ravaging Heaven."

Amelia's eyebrows shot up. "I don't particularly want to destroy the place… I mean… it does have its purpose, and I do hate them for what they've done to me and Marcus, but—"

"Apollyon knows that, but Heaven does not," Einar cut back in. "While it cannot easily track you when you're in here, it can detect changes that occur within its ranks."

Marcus frowned.

"That's nice armour and wings you have there, old friend," Einar said with a smile. "You certainly gave Serenity a fright when she was watching over you and all those changes happened."

"They happened there too?" Marcus stepped forwards, took hold of Amelia's hand, and led her up the hill to Einar, who nodded and his smile widened.

"She ran for Apollyon's room, dragged him out from under me when I was still trying to heal him, and brought him to you. Apollyon instantly decided to go to Heaven." Einar stretched his wings and the weary edge to his eyes increased. Marcus could sense his fatigue. It was written in every blade of grass and leaf in this world, flowing through him. "The angels ceased their attack when they saw him, agreed to take him in, and then we moved you so the Hell's angels would not be able to find you while he was in Heaven."

"I've put you all through so much trouble," Amelia said on a sigh and Marcus squeezed her hand to comfort her.

"Apollyon likes trouble. He will probably thank you for it later." Marcus smiled for her and she managed one in return.

A warm breeze sent several pale blue butterflies dancing between Marcus and Einar, and then a voice boomed out of the heavens.

"Get your arses back here, Romeo and co."

The world around them darkened and Marcus frowned as incredible tiredness crashed over him and he ached right down to his bones. He opened his eyes to find himself staring at a thatched ceiling made of what looked like twigs. Warm air lingered around him, humming with the sound of insects, and the smell of the sea carried on it.

Where had Serenity moved them to?

He looked to his left when something moved there and smiled when he saw Amelia lying next to him, a similarly confused look on her face. Her wings were gone but he knew that it wouldn't always be that way. Whenever she needed them, she would only have to call them, just like him. He would always be there for her, ready to do whatever she asked of him, protecting her to the end.

She looked over at him and a smile curved her lips, reaching her grey eyes.

"How are you feeling?" she said and rubbed her face. "Feels as though we were asleep forever."

It had felt like only a few hours to him.

Marcus reached over, caught her wrist, and pulled her against him. She giggled when he kissed her and he relished how it felt to do this in reality. They would always be together now. He wouldn't allow anyone to separate them again and he wouldn't let anything happen to Amelia. He would keep his promise. He would be a good man for her. Starting right now.

He stood, pulled her to her feet, and beat his wings to get used to them.

Amelia's smile faltered. "You're going back there, aren't you?"

He nodded. The look in her eyes and the feelings flowing into him from her conveyed that she didn't want that to happen but he knew that she wouldn't stop him.

"I have to," he said and smiled for her. Power flowed through him, stronger than he had ever felt, and he drew a deep breath, savouring the feeling. "I feel invincible… is this your doing?"

Amelia shook her head, surprising him. "No. I haven't given you any of my own power. I wouldn't know how. You were always this strong, Marcus, you just never believed that you were. Belief is a powerful thing."

Marcus felt the truth in those words in his heart. When he had been in that room in Heaven on the verge of obeying his orders, it had been Amelia's confession of love and his belief in the depth of that feeling, and in the depth of his love for her, that had given him the strength to fight back.

He believed in their love and in her, and he knew that she would never betray him, and that she believed in him too. She had faith in his strength and his promise to protect her. Armed with that faith, he felt invincible.

He felt he could take on Heaven and win.

Amelia stepped up to him, rested her hand against his cheek, and smiled into his eyes, affection shining in the warm grey depths of hers. "You found a reason to believe in your power and a reason to fight, and that's why you feel stronger now. And that's why you have to come back to me, you understand? Promise me that you'll come back."

Marcus placed his hand over hers, holding it against his face, and bent his head. He brushed his lips across hers, savouring their softness and how sweetly she responded to the kiss, and then drew back.

"That is an order I can easily obey," he whispered and she smiled, her beauty catching his breath and stealing it away. "I will never leave you, Amelia."

He took a step back, lowered her hand from his face, and led her from the hut. Turquoise blue sea stretched into the distance beyond a crisp white sandy shore fringed with swaying palm trees. An island. What better place to hide them than somewhere remote and small?

Amelia would be safe here until he returned.

Marcus looked along the shore to the next hut.

"Lukas," he said and the sandy-haired man looked his way and then left Serenity and Annelie.

"Glad to see you back with us." Lukas clapped a hand down on Marcus's shoulder.

"Can you do me a favour?" Marcus looked up at the endless blue sky. "I need to get into Heaven but I have a feeling they won't exactly welcome me with open arms now, and I need to get into the fortress and to Apollyon as soon as possible."

He brought his gaze back down to Lukas. Serenity and Annelie had joined him, their expressions as curious as his friend's was.

"I can send you in, but you will come out in the detention block," Lukas said.

Marcus nodded. "That is fine. I can deal with things from there."

Lukas didn't look convinced.

Amelia slipped her hand into his and he gave it a gentle squeeze to reassure her.

"You're going back?" Einar said as he joined them with Taylor in tow. It was good to see her safely out of Hell.

"I must."

Einar nodded, understanding shining in his deep brown eyes. "I would do the same."

Marcus glanced down at Amelia, brushed his thumb over her cheek in a light caress, and then released her hand. He took a few steps backwards, placing some distance between himself and everyone else, and blew out his breath to steady his nerves. He was strong enough to do this. He looked into Amelia's eyes and the belief in them boosted his strength, filling his heart with resolve and empowering him.

"Ready when you are, Lukas."

Bright white light blinded him.

CHAPTER 27

The light engulfing Marcus stung his eyes and burned against his skin. That wasn't a good sign. It swirled around him and he sensed himself rising although he couldn't see his surroundings. Every time a ribbon of light purer than the others brushed across his flesh it felt like a razor scraped over his skin, dragging numbness in its wake.

His haste to reach Heaven might end up costing him at this rate. He hadn't considered the changes he had undergone and the implications they would have. Normally when he travelled within the light to Heaven, it was warm and tingly, not cold and sharp.

Marcus tilted his head backwards and gazed into the infinite brilliant white above him.

When he reached the detention block, would he be able to escape?

When an angel used the light in the manner that Lukas had, the captive was sent straight into a cell.

Those cells were designed to dampen the power of demons, rendering them weak and leaving them with only enough strength to remain conscious and answer the questions of their captors. If the changes that had occurred when Amelia had bound them as master and servant had shifted him away from the biology of an angel and into demon territory, then he was going to be in trouble when the light receded. He would have barely enough strength to fight the weakest of angels and win, and the guards patrolling the detention block were stronger than most in Heaven.

His stomach twisted, turned and then the light began to dull. It flickered to reveal glimpses of his new surroundings and then faded completely.

Marcus drew in several deep breaths to steady his stomach and flexed his fingers, trying to sense whether he still had his powers without using them. He couldn't draw attention to himself. Not until he was sure that he could escape.

Grimy white walls enclosed him in a solid hexagon. Not a window or door broke the smooth surfaces, but Marcus knew better than to trust his eyes. On the other side of one of the walls would be a door, hidden from him where he stood inside the cell.

What cluster was he in?

There were thousands of interlocking circular clusters of the hexagonal cells, punctuated by round open spaces in the centre of them and linked by hallways. Together they formed an intricate hexagon that stretched as far as the eye could see. Hopefully, Lukas had sent him to one of the outer rings. He didn't like his odds of making it through the entire complex unnoticed if he was on one of the inner rings of cells.

Marcus walked forwards, pressed the flat of his palm against the dirty wall, and closed his eyes, trying to sense what was on the other side.

A flicker of something there brought a smile to his face and warm relief to his heart.

Not a demon then.

Whatever he had become on forming the pact between himself and Amelia, he wasn't wholly demonic. If a trace of his angelic side lingered, he would be able to walk right out the door once he located it.

The wall his palm rested against backed onto another cell. Occupied by the feel of it. The blockers were in place, creating a buzz on his senses.

Marcus walked on, trailing his hand along the wall, his focus wholly on it and sensing what was on the other side. The next wall was void of feeling, and the next produced the same sensation. The fourth wall sent a wash of tingles over his palm. Occupied again, but the blockers were different this time and he suspected he knew why. The captive wasn't one hundred percent demonic. Special precautions had been taken with that cell.

The next wall was blank again, and the final wall. He paused and pushed his hand forwards and was met with resistance. He pressed his hand harder into the cold wall, and smiled grimly when his arm disappeared up to his elbow, the material that formed the door to the cell thick like molasses against his skin.

Marcus followed his hand into the wall, battling against the barrier, and pulled in a deep breath before his head entered. The substance sucked at his flesh and pressed into his body, almost forcing the air from his lungs. He waded through it, tired from having to push so hard, and his hands broke through the surface on the other side and into warm air.

Partly demonic, he surmised as he finally reached the circular courtyard. An angel would have been able to walk out of the cell as though there wasn't a door at all.

A twinge stabbed his chest at the thought that there was no turning back for him now. He had given himself to Amelia, and he was glad that he had and didn't regret it, but it was going to take him time to come to terms with the fact that he was no longer truly an angel.

He unfurled his wings and looked at their hybrid form. Neither demon nor angel. Something in between. Something new, like Amelia. If she could cope with what she had become, could bravely accept that she was different now and embrace that side of herself, then so could he. He had asked her for these wings and she had blessed him with them, and he would never forget that.

Amelia had given him purpose. She had given him a reason to fight.

And fight he would.

He would fight so she didn't have to. He would fight so no one would dare come after her or seek to harm her ever again. He would fight so they could be together.

Marcus scanned his surroundings. Black and deep blue doorways punctuated the bright white semi-circle of cells behind him. Black meant occupied. The doors on either side of the cell he had exited were as dark as sin, but there was a red hue to the one to the right. The one with a special blocker in place.

He needed to buy himself time to get out of the detention block and into the main fortress, and pandemonium would give him just that.

Without a second thought, Marcus swept his hand towards the crimson tinted door on his right. It responded to his power and faded to reveal the cell on the other side.

A man stood there.

His red-ringed eyes shifted to Marcus, narrowed, and turned vivid scarlet. Marcus felt the man's anger reflected within him. He should have known that his superior had lied to him about the demonic angel killing itself in transit. Escaping the light was impossible. His superior had told Marcus the man was dead so he wouldn't ask questions about him and his motive for attacking Amelia. He had done it to keep him in the dark so he would continue to obey his orders.

"I am not here to fight you." Marcus spread his wings so the Hell's angel saw them. "Our fight has long passed. Amelia has awoken and I will not allow any to harm her again. If you wish to fight me, then do so, but know I will kill you."

The man looked him over, gaze lingering on his wings, and then stalked out of the cell.

"Go, escape with the others when I release them… I only ask you cause a little devastation on your way out." Marcus held his gaze until the man grinned to reveal sharp red teeth and nodded.

His skin blackened and he doubled in breadth and grew in stature. Dragon-like wings unfurled from his back and he growled before unleashing a roar.

There was a moment of silence and then alarms blared.

The Hell's angel grunted, beat his wings, and took flight, ascending into the open air above the cells.

Marcus swept his hand out towards the other black door and it opened. Heavy footsteps rang down the corridors on both sides of him. This was taking too long. He needed to get all the doors open at once.

He glanced up. Angels were already battling above him, trying to subdue the Hell's angel. If he flew, they might spot him, but he needed altitude if he was going to set all the captives free.

With a single beat of his wings, Marcus lifted into the air. They felt different, strange and new, and it took him a few moments to grow used to flying with them. By the time he was accustomed to them, he was over forty foot above the cells. They created a spiralling pattern of circles below him and he could see the ranks of angels as they marched in formation through the complex.

Marcus focused his power, flapped his wings to remain stationary, and then unleashed it with a wave of his hand. One by one, the black doors disappeared and their inmate escaped. The angels below broke rank to deal with the demons as they wreaked havoc. He smiled grimly, turned in the air, and dove back down so he was flying only a few feet above the flat tops of the cells. He flung his hand out before him, opening every cell between him and the detention block exit ahead.

Demons spilled out into the corridors and tried to grab him as he flew past. He twisted and turned in the air to evade them and then landed heavily in one of the corridors of the outer ring of cells and broke into a run.

The moment he was clear of the last row of cells, he dived down a side corridor and focused. With the angels occupied by trying to recapture the demons, he would be able to pass as a regular angel but only if his wings were away. His armour was different to anyone else's but only in colouring. If luck were with him, the angels rushing into the detention block to help contain the demons would be in too much of a hurry to notice.

The angels that waited ahead in the fortress would be a different matter, and he still didn't know where Apollyon had gone.

Marcus waited for the next wave of angels to pass him and then bolted out of his hiding spot and made a break for the exit. He pounded the steps and kept his head down as another group of angels came towards him. None of them even looked at him. They were too busy listening to the orders of their commander as he led the charge. Marcus's heart pounded and he fought to steady it and to contain the turbulent emotions racing through his blood. Now wasn't the time for fear or doubts. Now was the time to fight.

He could feel the fear of battle later, once he was back in Amelia's arms and she was finally safe.

He turned down one corridor after another, heading upwards whenever he could, and finally broke out into the open white grounds of Heaven.

His eyes widened.

He didn't need to search for Apollyon after all.

The dark angel was standing barely two hundred metres away, surrounded by a mixture of mediators and guardians, and the occasional hunter and angel of death.

In amongst them was a face that Marcus had been itching to see since Apollyon had taken Amelia's life.

His superior.

Marcus's wings burst free of his back and he sprinted towards the older sandy-haired angel, driven by fury and the pain of seeing Amelia die. He drew both of his curved silver blades, kicked off the ground, and flew at him.

His superior turned towards him. So did several other high ranking angels.

When his superior raised his hand to signal the others to stand down and narrowed his gaze on Marcus, he expected to feel the pressing weight of his power driving him into the ground. He didn't. Rather than the oppressive sense of weakness that he usually felt when his superior lost his temper and tried to put Marcus in his place, he felt only a small amount of pressure.

Marcus brought the ends of the grips of his two blades together and they melded and then extended into his double-ended spear. He roared and cut through the air with it, scattering the angels surrounding his superior in all directions, and then levelled his glare on him.

Anger pounded through his body and thrummed in his blood, a drug that addled his mind and called him to surrender to his desire for violence. He battled it, told himself that fighting this man would get him nowhere, but the lure was too sweet to resist. He growled out his frustration, twirled his spear in his hands, and swept it through the air again, sending another shockwave crashing into the ground. It rent the earth bare metres to the left of his superior, gouging a great gash in the pristine white land.

Blue-white sparks of power crackled across the backs of Marcus's hands and along the shaft of his spear.

He wanted more.

"Marcus." Apollyon's voice cut through the red haze of rage in his mind, bringing clarity with it.

Marcus looked down at the scored ground, the angels as they struggled to their feet, and finally his superior.

The man kneeled below him, pallid and clutching his stomach. Sweat dotted his brow and exertion tightened the lines of his face.

Marcus didn't understand.

His gaze tracked down to Apollyon. The dark angel stood off to his right, his face pale and expression grim. His limbs visibly trembled, as though he was battling to remain standing. Was he still weak from using his powers to gain Marcus access to Heaven? Apollyon's blue eyes brightened and he grunted and fell to one knee, his right hand pressing hard into the white grass beneath him. His laboured breaths and the pain in his face as he raised it towards Marcus were familiar enough that he realised what was happening.

His eyes widened again and he looked around him at the other angels. They weren't struggling to their feet at all. They were fighting his power. His gaze leapt to his hands, to the brilliant sparks of power as they leapt along the engraved silver and blue staff of his spear. He couldn't believe it. He stared at it for long minutes, trying to comprehend his own strength. He had rendered the strongest of angels powerless without even realising it.

"Marcus?" Apollyon sounded hoarse and Marcus shot him an apologetic look and closed his eyes, focusing on his power.

It took him a few attempts to bring it back under complete control and to let his anger flow out of him so he no longer craved the delicious tang of blood tainting the air and the feel of it sliding over his skin.

"What are you doing here?" Apollyon again, but this time he sounded incredulous rather than pained.

Marcus opened his eyes and regarded the angels gathered before him as they slowly got to their feet. He held the gaze of each high ranking angel until they looked away, and eventually settled his eyes on his superior. The man instantly looked down at his feet.

"I have come to deliver a warning," Marcus said and descended. He touched down close to the deep scar in the white grounds and glanced into it. There were places along the ragged line where his power had cut through to the other side, revealing chinks of light. He swallowed. He hadn't even unleashed that much of his power in the strike. Just how strong was he now?

He pushed away his fear of his newfound power and embraced it, letting it flow through his body and imbue strength in his heart. He was strong enough to protect her now and that was all that mattered. He would protect her.

"I desire nothing more than to destroy this wretched place, to bathe the white lands of Heaven in crimson as revenge for what it has done to me and my master, but she would not want that and I have vowed to be a good man for her sake." Marcus lowered his spear and let the staff shorten.

He broke it apart into two blades and held them down at his sides to show he was no danger to the angels present. He would not sheathe them though. They were a deterrent, there on display so no one would get any ideas. They had witnessed what he was capable of and would be foolish not to believe that he would resort to the destruction he had spoken of if they tried anything.

"My demands are simple. None will come after us. Not Heaven nor Hell's legions. None will seek to harm Amelia. You bear witness to my appearance and my power. Amelia has the voice to command an army, to raise warriors who will aid her, to take from your ranks and give them new strength. If you leave us in peace, then we shall offer you the same respect. If you do not, then we shall destroy all who stand against us."

The angels gathered before him glanced at each other and then looked back at him, no response leaving their lips and no sign of acceptance shining in their eyes. Their expressions remained schooled. It was the reply he had expected.

He hadn't come here for an answer.

He had only come to deliver the warning.

He nodded and turned to Apollyon.

"I cannot involve you in this, old friend." Marcus sheathed one of his blades and placed his hand on Apollyon's black-armoured shoulder. "You have done enough. Return to Paris with the others. Though we shall never see each other again, I will not forget you and all you have done for me and for Amelia. I wish you good fortune."

Apollyon nodded. "And I you."

The dark angel beat his black wings and shot into the air. Marcus waited until he was lost to the distance and then turned back to the angels.

He regarded them all and slowly released a fraction of his power, keeping it under control this time, steadily applying the pressure on the angels until one by one their faces contorted with the strain of resisting him and they crumbled to their knees.

He took a step back, held his superiors gaze, and then took flight.

In time, he would know Heaven's answer, whether it was through peace or through war.

They would be ready.

He would see to it.

CHAPTER 28

Marcus descended slowly through the layers of air, savouring the way they turned from icy cold to warm and then to hot as he approached the island. It had taken him a while to find it deep in the Pacific Ocean. At first, he hadn't been sure where to look and had cursed himself for not asking one of the others where the island was so he could find his way back, but then he had felt a glimmer of something inside himself.

He had focused on that feeling as it beat in his heart and felt her calling to him. One heart to another. The strength of the feeling had increased as he had followed it, letting it guide his course during his descent from Heaven. Now it was so fierce that it warmed him through, drawing a smile from him as it became so clear that he could discern her emotions within it.

She worried about him.

He shook his head when he realised why.

Rather than heeding his advice, Apollyon had chosen to return to the island and had remained there with Amelia and the others.

He had wanted to keep his friends out of whatever danger lay in his and Amelia's future, but if they chose to help him, then he wasn't going to turn them away. His desire to protect Amelia demanded that he accept their assistance. They had all been invaluable over the past few weeks and he couldn't thank them enough for everything they had done for him, and for Amelia.

The island grew out of the heat haze, the halo of crisp white sand gleaming around the dense green core, and deep blue ocean gave way to clear turquoise shallows.

Marcus approached the tropical paradise from the far side, flying over the quiet beach and tall palm trees that fringed the shore, and then the lush centre. His heartbeat quickened with anticipation of seeing Amelia again and having her in his arms once more. He wanted nothing more than to feel her nestled close against him, her warm soft hands pressed into his chest, and her beautiful grey eyes locked with his. He wanted to stroke her face and lose himself in her, and the love they shared, even if it was only for a short while.

Heaven would heed his warning, but for how long?

It didn't matter when they came. He would be ready for them.

The sweeping inlet on the other side of the island came into view and he spotted the thatched huts through the thinning palms. A smile broke out on his lips and his heart leapt when he saw Amelia standing on the shore, her back to him. Was she watching for him?

He was sure that she could feel him in her heart just as he could feel her.

He beat his wings and came down a few metres behind her, gliding to land silently on the soft white sand. She didn't stir. Marcus smiled mischievously and padded towards her. He felt eyes on him but ignored the owners of them, not wanting to risk Amelia noticing him by signalling his friends to be quiet.

Marcus brought his hands out before him, dropped his gaze to rest on the remains of her white dress as it fluttered against her thighs in the warm breeze and then settled it on her luscious hips. Target acquired.

She yelped the moment his hands caught her hips and he twisted her in his arms, narrowly avoiding the fist that flew at his face.

Her scowl quickly gave way to a smile so warm and full of affection that it pierced his soul and he couldn't resist his desire any longer. He pulled her into his arms, holding her close to his chest, and smiled when she made a stiff motion with her right hand and his breastplate disappeared. It seemed she was already growing used to some of her powers.

The feel of her softness against the hardness of his torso, her warm palms pressing into his pectorals and her heart beating against his, instilled peace in him. He exhaled slowly and then drew in a breath, catching her fragrance. It deepened the tranquillity flowing through him and he closed his eyes, bent his head, and pressed his lips against her silver hair.

"I was so worried about you," she whispered and stroked his chest, her fingertips tracing swirling patterns that burned into his skin and threatened to turn his mood from peaceful to hungry for her.

"I know." He pressed another long kiss to her hair and she drew back, her hands sliding down to settle on his waist. The warmth of them and the fire they stirred in his veins was too much to bear so he caught her hands and tangled them together with his between their bodies. Her grey eyes sought an answer to a silent question. "I felt your fear."

He brought their joined hands to his chest and smoothed her palms over it. She stared at them and the call from her heart to his came again, stronger than it had ever been. Her eyes rose to meet his, her rosy lips parting as she tilted her head back.

"I feel so connected to you." Her fingertips caressed his chest, maddening him with the desire for more. He thought about removing her hands again but his need to feel her skin-to-skin with him was too great. He craved the contact too fiercely to break away.

"And I you," he whispered and dipped his head.

Amelia lifted her chin and he accepted the invitation to kiss her, bringing his mouth gently down over hers. She leaned into him, tiptoed, and swept her tongue along the seam of his lips. He groaned and danced his lips over hers, caressed her tongue with his own, and fought his need to drag her closer to him and devour her. The brush of her hands over his bare chest and the sweet moan that left her lips broke his restraint.

Marcus fisted his left hand into her hair, tangling his fingers in the long silver threads, and dragged her against him. She moaned again, heated and hungry, and he bent into her, pressing the full length of his body into hers. The action only elicited another delicious whisper of pleasure from her and only served to torture him further, but it felt too good to shift away from her and end his torment. He plundered her mouth with his tongue, drinking in her taste and losing himself in her. Time drifted away, carrying the world with it, and endless minutes passed as he explored her lips with his own. Each sweep of them against hers and each meeting of their tongues drove the world a little further away. She arched into him, pressing her breasts against his chest, and he felt the pounding of her heart, felt her need rise to match his, and felt powerless to deny his hunger.

All too soon, Amelia stepped back, her breathing as ragged in his ears as his own was and her cheeks flushed crimson.

He frowned.

Embarrassed?

She cast her grey gaze to her right and he remembered that they weren't alone.

Marcus turned slowly to face the others.

Four of them were staring at him and Amelia.

The other two?

Taylor had Einar in an embrace that Marcus ached to re-enact with Amelia. Taylor's legs were around Einar's waist, her arms around his neck, and Einar's hands gripped Taylor's backside, squeezing firmly as he kissed her. Marcus glanced at Amelia, catching a flash of her in the small black bikini she had worn in that other world when he had held her like that, standing in the water with her wrapped around him. He looked past her to the tempting turquoise waters. He wanted to do that again.

Apollyon strode across the white sand, his blue eyes raking over Marcus's silver armour and then his wings. "That is a new look for you. It suits you well and I am glad love has turned you foolish enough to embrace such an appearance, and your new master."

"Because Heaven saw it?"

"Because they saw it, and I used it to illustrate my point."

"Was my showing up there part of your plan?" Marcus said and when Apollyon only smiled, he knew that his friend had expected him to find his way back into Heaven and to showcase his power and Amelia's ability to turn angels to her cause.

"Amelia's blood is of no use to them now that the planets are no longer in alignment, and my threat to allow the Devil to win our next match when coupled with your display of power will go a long way towards convincing them that it is better Amelia is allowed to live rather than die."

Serenity came up beside Apollyon, wearing a short pale dress that matched her fair hair that she had twirled into a knot at the back of her head.

"Will they come after her?" she said, concern in her hazel eyes.

Apollyon's grim look matched how Marcus felt about the answer to that question.

"I doubt they would do so right away. They have their hands full with the damage done to Heaven and the demons I allowed to escape… but I fear they will come after her one day," Marcus said and clenched his fists, resolve flowing through him. "I will be ready when they do."

Lukas and Annelie joined them, both of them dressed in swimwear, and Taylor finally released Einar. He set her down, smiled sheepishly at Marcus, and then led her over to him.

Amelia slipped her arm around Marcus's and held it with both hands. Her side pressed against his and he looked down into her eyes, absorbing the love that shone in them.

"We will be ready when they do," she said with determination.

Marcus looked at the others and they all nodded, even Lukas. He didn't know how to thank them, so he nodded, silently accepting their support. It was more than he could have asked for.

He would do everything in his power to protect Amelia, and with the help of his friends, he was sure they could keep her safe. She was his now. His to protect, to cherish and care for. His to love.

And he loved her with all of his heart.

Marcus looked down at Amelia, gathered her into his arms and kissed her again. Apollyon made a disgusted noise and Marcus sensed everyone move away, leaving them alone. He slipped his hand into hers and walked with her along the beach, heading away from their friends to a quiet spot where rocks reached out into the endless clear sparkling water.

The sun was hot on his skin, warming him down to his bones and chasing away his tension. Amelia slipped her arm around his again and when he looked at her, she smiled brilliantly and with so much love that he couldn't help himself. He stopped, pulled her into his arms, and slowly explored her soft lips, drawing a quiet moan from her.

She slid her hands over his chest and he frowned when he felt a breeze against his forearms and shins. He drew back to look down at himself. His armour was gone, replaced by a loose pair of black swimming trunks. He glanced at Amelia and his gaze stuck on her when he saw the black bikini barely covering her body and the small black sarong around her waist. She was definitely growing accustomed to abusing her new powers.

Her shy smile gained a wicked edge that he liked and she stepped into him, so her soft body pressed against his again, and tilted her head back, inviting him in for another long drawn out kiss.

Her heart beat steadily against his chest. His heart. She had given it in exchange for his.

"I love you," he whispered against her mouth, marvelling at the power of those three small words as she smiled at him, affection shining in her grey eyes. Those words had saved them both, had reached deep into his heart and given him strength he never knew he had, and he knew they would always empower him whenever she spoke them. He waited, hesitant and with a trace of nerves running through him. He needed to hear her say them again and feel the effect they had on him.

"I love you too." She brushed her fingers across his jaw, sweeping them up his face and then into his black hair.

Marcus stared into her eyes, warm water lapping at his feet and the sun relaxing him. It was over for now, but not for ever. One day, Heaven or Hell would come after them, and they had to prepare for that day.

Amelia slipped her hand into his. "I like it here… I'd like to stay for a bit. I know so little about you… and now I feel as though I know so little about myself.

I have so much to learn. You trained Lukas once… could you train me? Can you teach me how to fight, and how to fly, and could we stay here a while and just be together, away from the world while I find my feet and learn about you?"

He nodded. She didn't need to ask. Whatever she commanded, he would carry out. He would do anything for her, even endure irritating sand and water, and he intended to teach her everything he knew. Together they would learn about her powers and the depth of his, and they would hone them until not even God or the Devil himself could defeat them.

"I want to learn about you too." He cupped her cheek, looking deep into her eyes. "There is so much about you I don't know."

"You've watched me all my life—"

"I might have watched over you," he interjected, "but I never really knew you until the night we spoke properly for the first time. I am still learning about you, and it is something we can do together. We will always be together now… I swear it… I will never leave your side."

"Mmm, I do love the sound of that." She tiptoed and rewarded him with a kiss that was far too brief and only served to reignite the embers of his desire rather than satisfy his need for her.

Her smile turned mischievous.

His wings shrank into his back without him ordering them to do so.

Marcus looked down at her hand when she started walking towards the water and then into her eyes. "I cannot swim, remember?"

Her smile didn't falter. "Then someone should teach you. I'll teach you how to swim if you teach me how to fly and how to use my powers."

He wasn't sure about allowing her to teach him how to swim.

It didn't seem very manly to have such lessons from a woman and he wanted her to always see him that way. The look in her eyes said she wasn't going to relent and it brought a smile to his face. That was his Amelia. Never one to back down. She was going to teach him whether he liked it or not and something told him that she wasn't above ordering him to obey if he tried to refuse.

His mind raced back to the night they had last been in the water together and where things had gone after that, and he stalked towards her, forcing her backwards until she was waist deep. Her eyes widened, cheeks colouring as her pupils dilated, and she held her hands up. Marcus grabbed her, dragged her through the warm water and up against him, and kissed her.

She moaned into his mouth, her hands pressing into his shoulders, and wrapped her legs around his waist.

This, he could get used to.

If all of his swimming lessons were going to be like this, he would willingly subject himself to them, and he would stay here with her for as long as it took for him to learn. Which, right now, was feeling like years rather than days. He could be a slow learner when he wanted to be.

Marcus gently kissed her, taking his time as he held her against him, the water lapping at their bodies and gently rocking them. He couldn't believe everything that had happened to him over the past few weeks, and how much his world had altered.

How much he had changed.

He had always thought that it wasn't possible for him to change, that he would forever be loyal to Heaven and would never want anything to do with mortals, but Amelia had proven him wrong. She had altered his loyalty, stealing his heart for herself, and shaken his world to its foundations, rebuilding it with each kiss and stolen glance, and now he could only think of her. She was his world. His angel. She had given him back everything that Heaven had taken from him, and so much more besides. She had made him into a good man, and he finally felt as though he was worthy of her.

He loved her.

And he would always be with her, wherever she went, whatever she did. He would be there to protect her.

Always.

Her knight.

Her guardian angel.

The End

PREVIOUS BOOKS IN THE HER ANGEL SERIES

Her Dark Angel

An angel without a mission, Apollyon lives trapped in Hell guarding the bottomless pit. Surrounded by endless darkness, he longs to fly free on Earth once more but his master hasn't called him in centuries. When the call finally comes, it's to serve a new master, a beautiful woman he has often watched over, a woman who has always captivated him.

Serenity is shocked when a gorgeous black-winged angel shows up in her city of Paris claiming that she called him when she was only casting a simple vengeance spell. He's no other than the angel of death! When Apollyon offers to obey her and help her have revenge on her cheating ex-boyfriend, she can't resist the temptation, but can she resist him? Can an angel as dark as Apollyon ever fall for a mortal woman like her?

Dark, passionate and erotic, Her Dark Angel is a tale of intense desire and deepest forbidden love guaranteed to get your heart racing.

Her Fallen Angel

Annelie fell for Lukas the moment he walked into her pub three years ago. He's stunning, his vivid green eyes lending to his otherworldly beauty, but he's seriously out of her league. When he tells her that she's beautiful and confesses that he wants her, she can't resist him and his passionate kiss. She unleashes her desire and seizes the moment and Lukas with both hands. But Lukas has a secret, one that will test Annelie's love for him and threaten to tear them apart.

He's an angel.

Annelie can't believe it when Lukas says that their feelings for each other aren't a sin, but she can believe his pain when he tells her the reason he's on Earth. He is fallen, cast out of Heaven as punishment for a crime he didn't commit. Lukas isn't about to give up and accept his fate though. He's determined to prove both his innocence and his love for Annelie, and to show her that the intense passion they share is real.

When Lukas and Apollyon discover who framed him, will he be able to stop them from going after Serenity and Annelie? Will he be able to protect the woman he loves and fly away with her into their forever after?

Her Warrior Angel

Einar is one of Heaven's best hunters and he's on a mission to uncover why an angel was working with demons. When he finds the first demon fighting a beautiful woman named Taylor, he intervenes and saves her life. Taylor has spent her whole life protecting London from the lowest demons and she's not about to let an angel waltz into her city and take over her job, and she's certainly not about to fall in love with him, even if he is gorgeous. The reason why she can't is simple—she's half demon.

There is no love in this world more forbidden than that between an angel and a demon.

Sense tells Taylor to get out before she gets her heart broken, but she winds up convincing Einar to partner with her instead. Einar is certain that working with Taylor is a bad idea, and not only because he can't focus when he's around her, but he can't let her go. The mission leads them deep into the city's underworld, where old flames burn Taylor while new flames of passion and fear of the consequences consume them, and the threat of Einar's demons hangs over them both.

Can a love so forbidden ever have a happy ending or are they destined to break each other's hearts?

ABOUT THE AUTHOR

Felicity Heaton is a romance author writing as both Felicity Heaton and F E Heaton. She is passionate about penning paranormal tales full of vampires, witches, werewolves, angels and shape-shifters, and has been interested in all things preternatural and fantastical since she was just a child. Her other passion is science-fiction and she likes nothing more than to immerse herself in a whole new universe and the amazing species therein. She used to while away days at school and college dreaming of vampires, werewolves and witches, or being lost in space, and used to while away evenings watching movies about them or reading gothic horror stories, science-fiction and romances.

Having tried her hand at various romance genres, it was only natural for her to turn her focus back to the paranormal, fantasy and science-fiction worlds she enjoys so much. She loves to write seductive, sexy and strong vampires, werewolves, witches, angels and alien species. The worlds she often dreams up for them are vicious, dark and dangerous, reflecting aspects of the heroines and heroes, but her characters also love deeply, laugh, cry and feel every emotion as keenly as anyone does. She makes no excuses for the darkness surrounding them, especially the paranormal creatures, and says that this is their world. She's just honoured to write down their adventures.

To see her other novels, visit: **http://www.felicityheaton.co.uk**

If you have enjoyed this story, please take a moment to contact the author at **author@felicityheaton.co.uk** or to post a review of the book online

Follow the author on:
Her blog – http://www.indieparanormalromancebooks.com
Twitter – http://twitter.com/felicityheaton
Facebook – http://www.facebook.com/feheaton

FIND OUT MORE ABOUT THE HER ANGEL SERIES AT:
http://www.felicityheaton.co.uk

Printed in Great Britain
by Amazon.co.uk, Ltd.,
Marston Gate.